FAR FROM THE
MADDING CROWD
Thomas Hardy

Introduction by George Dickerson

SBS SCHOLASTIC BOOK SERVICES
New York • London • Richmond Hill, Ontario

Special contents copyright © 1968 by Scholastic Magazines, Inc. All rights reserved. This edition is published by Scholastic Book Services, a division of Scholastic Magazines, Inc.

2nd printing .... March 1968

Printed in the U.S.A.

INTRODUCTION

A Word to the Reader

The countryside by the sea in southern England where Thomas Hardy was born was seemingly placid. One might not expect to find the passion and violence that lay just below the surface of the inhabitants' daily lives. But Hardy was well aware that conflicts of emotion and weaknesses of character could create madness, hatred, and murder—even among these well-mannered Victorian farmers.

In *Far from the Madding Crowd*, Hardy first explored the people and their passions that were to make him well known as a writer. He carefully describes their daily struggles in such a way that his characters seem immediately alive and their personal defects painfully obvious. For instance, the simple act of taking out a mirror in the open countryside is enough to introduce the vanity of Bathsheba Everdene. And it is her vanity that causes much of the destruction around her.

Removed in time and manners from our own fast-changing world, the passions and conflicts of Hardy's characters are just as moving and real today as they were in Victorian times. And recently a major motion picture, remarkably true to the original novel, has been made from *Far from the Madding Crowd*.

The Characters

Bathsheba Everdene (played by Julie Christie in the film) is a strong-willed, beautiful young woman. Early in the book she becomes responsible for a large farming estate, and tries to manage it herself. This strength is admirable, particularly in a young girl of twenty. But while she is both generous and fair to her farmhands and the townspeople, she is also vain and naïve. A simple trick of sending a valentine to a neighboring farmer causes disaster. She did not mean it, but he falls deeply in love with her. Meanwhile, she ignores her own shepherd, who loves her passionately and proudly. And then she throws away her life because of the glamorous attentions of a young cavalryman.

Gabriel Oak (played by Alan Bates) is the man most in tune with nature. Patient and steadfast in his love for Bathsheba, he is simple in his ways, but he is also capable of deep thinking. He begins as a young but experienced shepherd on his own farm, but the destruction of his sheep ruins him. By accident he comes to work for Bathsheba, with whom he has already fallen in love. On several occasions, through his devotion and sense of duty, he is able to save her farm and the surrounding community from disaster. In many ways, he appears to be Hardy's presentation of the ideal man. Yet, he has an honest bluntness mixed with pride that makes him human.

William Boldwood (Peter Finch) is the gentleman farmer who owns the estate next to Bathsheba's. Because of her valentine, he falls desperately in love and loses all sense of reason. A man who has had little to do with women for most of his 40 years, he suddenly finds that he cannot live without Bathsheba as his wife. Through his passion he changes from an austere, respected farmer to a helpless and depraved criminal.

Frank Troy (Terence Stamp) is the dashing young cavalryman whom Bathsheba falls in love with and marries. Hardy describes him as a man who lives for the moment and who believes primarily in the satisfaction of his immediate sensual pleasures. He is a drinker and a gambler. His indifference toward the harm he might be doing others, particularly the young women of Wessex, eventually leads to his own destruction.

While the minor characters, Liddy, Coggan, Poorgrass, Tall, and so forth might be seen as only extras used to fill up the story, they are also what might be called Hardy's Greek chorus. Their speeches and feelings echo the tragedy that is going on around them. For it affects them deeply, since their very lives depend so intimately upon the management of the farms of Bathsheba and Boldwood. Their combined voices are all the comment needed on the troubles of the main characters.

The Meaning

Far from the Madding Crowd is more than a book simply about the courtship of Bathsheba by three men, although this is the central story. While he writes about small details, Hardy is exploring large themes that might be stated abstractly—romance *vs.* duty, reason *vs.* the impulses of the heart, man *vs.* nature. His book not only reflects and comments on the nature of men and women, but it also explores how a society as a whole is affected by the actions of its members, for better or worse. When man acts against nature, when reason and the emotions are not balanced, Hardy seems to be saying, then only disaster can follow.

About Hardy

Thomas Hardy was born June 2, 1840 on Egdon Heath, which he wrote about in *The Return of the Native*. *Far from the Madding Crowd* was his fourth novel, but it was the first to bring him financial success and literary fame. It enabled him to turn from architecture, with which he had supported himself, and devote himself to writing. After publishing seven novels, he wrote only poetry. He died in 1928, a master novelist and poet.

GEORGE DICKERSON

Contents

PREFACE

IN REPRINTING this story for a new edition I am reminded that it was in the chapters of "Far from
the Madding Crowd," as they appeared month by
month in a popular magazine, that I first ventured
to adopt the word "Wessex" from the pages of early
English history, and give it a fictitious significance
as the existing name of the district once included in
that extinct kingdom. The series of novels I projected being mainly of the kind called local, they
seemed to require a territorial definition of some
sort to lend unity to their scene. Finding that the
area of a single county did not afford a canvas large
enough for this purpose, and that there were objections to an invented name, I disinterred the old
one. The region designated was known but vaguely,
and I was often asked even by educated people
where it lay. However, the press and the public
were kind enough to welcome the fanciful plan,
and willingly joined me in the anachronism of
imagining a Wessex population living under
Queen Victoria—a modern Wessex of railways, the
penny post, mowing and reaping machines, union
workhouses, lucifer matches, laborers who could
read and write, and National school children. But
I believe I am correct in stating that, until the existence of this contemporaneous Wessex in place of
the usual counties was announced in the present

story, in 1874, it had never been heard of in fiction
and current speech, if at all, and that the expression, "a Wessex peasant," or "a Wessex custom,"
would theretofore have been taken to refer to nothing later in date than the Norman Conquest.

I did not anticipate that this application of the
word to modern story would extend outside the
chapters of these particular chronicles. But it was
soon taken up elsewhere, the first to adopt it being
the now defunct *Examiner,* which, in the impression bearing date July 15, 1876, entitled one of its
articles "The Wessex Laborer," the article turning out to be no dissertation on farming during the
Heptarchy, but on the modern peasant of the south-
west counties.

Since then the appellation which I had thought
to reserve to the horizons and landscapes of a partly
real, partly dream-country, has become more and
more popular as a practical provincial definition;
and the dream-country has, by degrees, solidified
into a utilitarian region which people can go to,
take a house in, and write to the papers from. But I
ask all good and idealistic readers to forget this, and
to refuse steadfastly to believe that there are any
inhabitants of a Victorian Wessex outside these
volumes in which their lives and conversations are
detailed.

Moreover, the village called Weatherbury,
wherein the scenes of the present story of the series
are for the most part laid, would perhaps be hardly
discernible by the explorer, without help, in any
existing place nowadays; though at the time, comparatively recent, at which the tale was written, a
sufficient reality to meet the descriptions, both of
backgrounds and personages, might have been
traced easily enough. The church remains, by great
good fortune, unrestored and intact[1] and a few of

---

[1] This is no longer the case (1912).

the old houses; but the ancient malthouse, which was formerly so characteristic of the parish, has been pulled down these twenty years; also most of the thatched and dormered cottages that were once lifeholds. The heroine's fine old Jacobean house would be found in the story to have taken a witch's ride of a mile or more from its actual position; though with that difference its features are described as they still show themselves to the sun and moonlight. The game of prisoner's-base, which not so long ago seemed to enjoy a perennial vitality in front of the worn-out stocks, may, so far as I can say, be entirely unknown to the rising generation of schoolboys there. The practice of divination by Bible and key, the regarding of valentines as things of serious import, the shearing supper, the long smock-frocks, and the harvest-home, have, too, nearly disappeared in the wake of the old houses; and with them has gone, it is said, much of that love of fuddling to which the village at one time was notoriously prone. The change at the root of this has been the recent supplanting of the class of stationary cottagers, who carried on the local traditions and humors, by a population of more or less migratory laborers, which has led to a break of continuity in local history, more fatal than any other thing to the preservation of legend, folklore, close intersocial relations, and eccentric individualities. For these the indispensable conditions of existence are attachment to the soil of one particular spot by generation after generation.

1895-1902.   T. H.

1. Description of Farmer Oak — An Incident

WHEN FARMER OAK SMILED, the corners of his mouth spread till they were within an unimportant distance of his ears, his eyes were reduced to chinks, and diverging wrinkles appeared round them, extending upon his countenance like the rays in a rudimentary sketch of the rising sun.

His Christian name was Gabriel, and on working days he was a young man of sound judgment, easy motions, proper dress, and general good character. On Sundays he was a man of misty views, rather given to postponing, and hampered by his best clothes and umbrella: upon the whole, one who felt himself to occupy morally that vast middle space of Laodicean neutrality which lay between the Communion people of the parish and the drunken section—that is, he went to church, but yawned privately by the time the congregation reached the Nicene Creed, and thought of what there would be for dinner when he meant to be listening to the sermon. Or, to state his character as it stood in the scale of public opinion, when his friends and critics were in tantrums, he was considered rather a bad man; when they were pleased, he was rather a good man; when they were neither, he was a man whose moral color was a kind of pepper-and-salt mixture.

Since he lived six times as many working days as Sundays, Oak's appearance in his old clothes was most peculiarly his own—the mental picture formed by his neighbors in imagining him being always dressed in that way. He wore a low-crowned felt hat, spread out at the base by tight jamming upon the head for security in high winds, and a coat like Dr. Johnson's; his lower extremities being encased in ordinary leather leggings and boots emphatically large, affording to each foot a roomy apartment so constructed that any wearer might stand in a river all day long and know nothing of damp—their maker being a conscientious man who endeavored to compensate for any weakness in his cut by unstinted dimension and solidity.

Mr. Oak carried about him, by way of watch, what may be called a small silver clock; in other words, it was a watch as to shape and intention, and a small clock as to size. This instrument, being several years older than Oak's grandfather, had the peculiarity of going either too fast or not at all. The smaller of its hands, too, occasionally slipped round on the pivot, and thus, though the minutes were told with precision, nobody could be quite certain of the hour they belonged to. The stopping peculiarity of his watch Oak remedied by thumps and shakes, and he escaped any evil consequences from the other two defects by constant comparisons with and observations of the sun and stars, and by pressing his face close to the glass of his neighbors' windows, till he could discern the hour marked by the green-faced timekeepers within. It may be mentioned that Oak's fob being difficult of access, by reason of its somewhat high situation in the waistband of his trousers (which also lay at a remote height under his waistcoat), the watch was as a necessity pulled out by throwing the body to one side, compressing the mouth and face to a mere mass of ruddy flesh on account of the exertion, and drawing up the watch by its chain, like a bucket from a well.

But some thoughtful persons, who had seen him walking across one of his fields on a certain December morning—sunny and exceedingly mild—might have regarded Gabriel Oak in other aspects than these. In his face one might notice that many of the hues and curves of youth had tarried on to manhood: there even remained in his remoter crannies some relics of the boy. His height and breadth would have been sufficient to make his presence imposing, had they been exhibited with due consideration. But there is a way some men have, rural and urban alike, for which the mind is more responsible than flesh and sinew: it is a way of curtailing their dimensions by their manner of showing them. And from a quiet modesty that would have become a vestal, which seemed continually to impress upon him that he had no great claim on the world's room, Oak walked unassumingly, and with a faintly perceptible bend, yet distinct from a bowing of the shoulders. This may be said to be a defect in an individual if he depends for his valuation more upon his appearance than upon his capacity to wear well, which Oak did not.

He had just reached the time of life at which "young" is ceasing to be the prefix of "man" in speaking of one. He was at the brightest period of masculine growth, for his intellect and his emotions were clearly separated: he had passed the time during which the influence of youth indiscriminately mingles them in the character of impulse, and he had not yet arrived at the stage wherein they become united again, in the character of prejudice, by the influence of a wife and family. In short, he was twenty-eight, and a bachelor.

The field he was in this morning sloped to a ridge called Norcombe Hill. Through a spur of this hill ran the highway between Emminster and Chalk-Newton. Casually glancing over the hedge, Oak saw coming down the incline before him an ornamental spring wagon, painted yellow and gaily marked, drawn by two horses, a wagoner walking alongside bearing a whip perpendicularly. The wagon was laden with household goods and window plants, and on the apex of the whole sat a woman, young and attractive. Gabriel had not beheld the sight for more than half a minute, when the vehicle was brought to a standstill just beneath his eyes.

"The tailboard of the wagon is gone, Miss," said the wagoner.

"Then I heard it fall," said the girl, in a soft, though not particularly low voice. "I heard a noise I could not account for when we were coming up the hill."

"I'll run back."

"Do," she answered.

The sensible horses stood perfectly still, and the wagoner's steps sank fainter and fainter in the distance.

The girl on the summit of the load sat motionless, surrounded by tables and chairs with their legs upward, backed by an oak settle, and ornamented in front by pots of geraniums, myrtles, and cactuses, together with a caged canary—all probably from the windows of the house just vacated. There was also a cat in a willow basket, from the partly

opened lid of which she gazed with half-closed eyes,
and affectionately surveyed the small birds around.

The handsome girl waited for some time idly in
her place, and the only sound heard in the stillness
was the hopping of the canary up and down the
perches of its prison. Then she looked attentively
downward. It was not at the bird, nor at the cat; it
was at an oblong package tied in paper, and lying
between them. She turned her head to learn if the
wagoner were coming. He was not yet in sight; and
her eyes crept back to the package, her thoughts
seeming to run upon what was inside it. At length
she drew the article into her lap, and untied the
paper covering; a small swing looking glass was dis-
closed, in which she proceeded to survey herself attentively. She parted her lips and smiled.

It was a fine morning, and the sun lighted up to
a scarlet glow the crimson jacket she wore, and
painted a soft luster upon her bright face and dark
hair. The myrtles, geraniums, and cactuses packed
around her were fresh and green, and at such
a leafless season they invested the whole concern of
horses, wagon, furniture, and girl with a peculiar
vernal charm. What possessed her to indulge in
such a performance in the sight of the sparrows,
blackbirds, and unperceived farmer who were
alone its spectators—whether the smile began as a
factitious one, to test her capacity in that art—nobody knows; it ended certainly in a real smile. She
blushed at herself, and seeing her reflection blush,
blushed the more.

The change from the customary spot and necessary occasion of such an act—from the dressing
hour in a bedroom to a time of traveling out of
doors—lent to the idle deed a novelty it did not intrinsically possess. The picture was a delicate one.
Woman's prescriptive infirmity had stalked into the
sunlight, which had clothed it in the freshness

of an originality. A cynical inference was irresistible
by Gabriel Oak as he regarded the scene, generous
though he fain would have been. There was no
necessity whatever for her looking in the glass. She
did not adjust her hat, or pat her hair, or press a
dimple into shape, or do one thing to signify that
any such intention had been her motive in taking
up the glass. She simply observed herself as a fair
product of Nature in the feminine kind, her
thoughts seeming to glide into far-off though likely
dramas in which men would play a part—vistas of
probable triumphs—the smiles being of a phase
suggesting that hearts were imagined as lost and
won. Still, this was but conjecture, and the whole
series of actions was so idly put forth as to make it
rash to assert that intention had any part in them
at all.

The wagoner's steps were heard returning. She
put the glass in the paper, and the whole again
into its place.

When the wagon had passed on, Gabriel withdrew from his point of espial and, descending into
the road, followed the vehicle to the turnpike gate
some way beyond the bottom of the hill, where the
object of his contemplation now halted for the pay-
ment of toll. About twenty steps still remained between him and the gate, when he heard a dispute.
It was a difference concerning twopence between
the persons with the wagon and the man at the
toll bar.

"Mis'ess's niece is upon the top of the things, and
she says that's enough that I've offered ye, you great
miser, and she won't pay any more." These were
the wagoner's words.

"Very well; then mis'ess's niece can't pass," said
the turnpike keeper, closing the gate.

Oak looked from one to the other of the dispu-
tants, and fell into a reverie. There was something

in the tone of twopence remarkably insignificant.
Threepence had a definite value as money—it
was an appreciable infringement on a day's wages,
and, as such, a higgling matter; but twopence—
"Here," he said, stepping forward and handing
twopence to the gatekeeper, "let the young woman
pass." He looked up at her then; she heard his
words, and looked down.

Gabriel's features adhered throughout their
form so exactly to the middle line between the
beauty of St. John and the ugliness of Judas
Iscariot, as represented in a window of the church
he attended, that not a single lineament could be
selected and called worthy either of distinction or
notoriety. The red-jacketed and dark-haired
maiden seemed to think so too, for she carelessly
glanced over him, and told her man to drive on.
She might have looked her thanks to Gabriel on a
minute scale, but she did not speak them; more
probably she felt none, for in gaining her a passage he had lost her her point, and we know how
women take a favor of that kind.

The gatekeeper surveyed the retreating vehicle.
"That's a handsome maid," he said to Oak.

"But she has her faults," said Gabriel.

"True, farmer."

"And the greatest of them is—well, what it is always."

"Beating people down? aye, 'tis so."

"Oh, no."

"What, then?"

Gabriel, perhaps a little piqued by the comely
traveler's indifference, glanced back to where he
had witnessed her performance over the hedge, and
said, "Vanity."

2. Night — The Flock — An Interior — Another Interior

IT WAS NEARLY MIDNIGHT on the eve of St. Thomas, the shortest day in the year. A desolating wind wandered from the north over the hill whereon Oak had watched the yellow wagon and its occupant in the sunshine of a few days earlier.

Norcombe Hill—not far from lonely Toller-Down—was one of the spots which suggest to a passerby that he is in the presence of a shape approaching the indestructible as nearly as any to be found on earth. It was a featureless convexity of chalk and soil—an ordinary specimen of those smoothly outlined protuberances of the globe which may remain undisturbed on some great day of confusion, when far grander heights and dizzy granite precipices topple down.

The hill was covered on its northern side by an ancient and decaying plantation of beeches, whose upper verge formed a line over the crest, fringing its arched curve against the sky, like a mane. Tonight these trees sheltered the southern slope from the keenest blasts, which smote the wood and floundered through it with a sound as of grumbling, or gushed over its crowning boughs in a weakened moan. The dry leaves in the ditch simmered and boiled in the same breezes, a tongue of air occasionally ferreting out a few, and sending them spinning across the grass. A group or two of the latest in date amongst the dead multitude had remained till this very midwinter time on the twigs which bore them, and in falling rattled against the trunks with smart taps.

Between this half-wooded, half-naked hill, and the vague still horizon that its summit indistinctly commanded, was a mysterious sheet of fathomless shade —the sounds from which suggested that what it concealed bore some reduced resemblance to features here. The thin grasses, more or less coating the hill, were touched by the wind in breezes of differing powers, and almost of differing natures— one rubbing the blades heavily, another raking them piercingly, another brushing them like a soft broom. The instinctive act of humankind was to stand and listen, and learn how the trees on the right and the trees on the left wailed or chanted to each other in the regular antiphonies of a cathedral choir; how hedges and other shapes to leeward then caught the note, lowering it to the tenderest sob; and how the hurrying gust then plunged into the south, to be heard no more.

The sky was clear—remarkably clear—and the twinkling of all the stars seemed to be but throbs of one body, timed by a common pulse. The North Star was directly in the wind's eye, and since evening the Bear had swung round it outwardly to the east, till he was now at a right angle with the meridian. A difference of color in the stars—oftener read of than seen in England—was really perceptible here. The sovereign brilliancy of Sirius pierced the eye with a steely glitter, the star called Capella was yellow, Aldebaran and Betelgueux shone with a fiery red.

To persons standing alone on a hill during a clear midnight such as this, the roll of the world eastward is almost a palpable movement. The sensation may be caused by the panoramic glide of the stars past earthly objects, which is perceptible in a few minutes of stillness, or by the better outlook upon space that a hill affords, or by the wind, or by the solitude; but whatever be its origin the impression of riding along is vivid and abiding. The poetry of motion is a phrase much in use, and to enjoy the epic form of that gratification it is necessary to stand on a hill at a small hour of the night, and, having first expanded with a sense of difference from the mass of civilized mankind, who are dreamwrapt and disregardful of all such proceedings at this time, long and quietly watch your stately progress through the stars. After such a nocturnal reconnoiter it is hard to get back to earth and to believe that the consciousness of such majestic speeding is derived from a tiny human frame.

Suddenly an unexpected series of sounds began to be heard in this place up against the sky. They had a clearness which was to be found nowhere in the wind, and a sequence which was to be found nowhere in nature. They were the notes of Farmer Oak's flute.

The tune was not floating unhindered into the open air: it seemed muffled in some way, and was altogether too curtailed in power to spread high or wide. It came from the direction of a small dark object under the plantation hedge—a shepherd's hut—now presenting an outline to which an uninitiated person might have been puzzled to attach either meaning or use.

The image as a whole was that of a small Noah's Ark on a small Ararat, allowing the traditionary outlines and general form of the Ark which are followed by toymakers—and by these means are established in men's imaginations among their firmest, because earliest impressions—to pass as an approximate pattern. The hut stood on little wheels, which raised its floor about a foot from the ground. Such shepherds' huts are dragged into the fields when the lambing season comes on, to shelter the shepherd in his enforced nightly attendance.

It was only latterly that people had begun to call

Gabriel, "Farmer" Oak. During the twelvemonth preceding this time he had been enabled by sustained efforts of industry and chronic good spirits to lease the small sheep farm of which Norcombe Hill was a portion, and stock it with two hundred sheep. Previously he had been a bailiff for a short time, and earlier still a shepherd only, having from his childhood assisted his father in tending the flocks of large proprietors, till old Gabriel sank to rest.

This venture, unaided and alone, into the paths of farming as master and not as man, with an advance of sheep not yet paid for, was a critical juncture with Gabriel Oak, and he recognized his position clearly. The first movement in his new progress was the lambing of his ewes, and sheep having been his specialty from his youth, he wisely refrained from deputing the task of tending them at this season to a hireling or a novice.

The wind continued to beat about the corners of the hut, but the flute playing ceased. A rectangular space of light appeared in the side of the hut, and in the opening the outline of Farmer Oak's figure. He carried a lantern in his hand, and closing the door behind him came forward and busied himself about this nook of the field for nearly twenty minutes, the lantern light appearing and disappearing here and there, and brightening him or darkening him as he stood before or behind it.

Oak's motions, though they had a quiet energy, were slow, and their deliberateness accorded well with his occupation. Fitness being the basis of beauty, nobody could have denied that his steady swings and turns in and about the flock had elements of grace. Yet, although if occasion demanded he could do or think a thing with as mercurial a dash as can the men of towns who are more to the manner born, his special power, morally, physically, and mentally, was static, owing little or nothing to momentum as a rule.

A close examination of the ground hereabout, even by the wan starlight only, revealed how a portion of what would have been casually called a wild slope had been appropriated by Farmer Oak for his great purpose this winter. Detached hurdles thatched with straw were stuck into the ground at various scattered points, amid and under which the whitish forms of his meek ewes moved and rustled. The ring of the sheep bell, which had been silent during his absence, recommenced, in tones that had more mellowness than clearness, owing to an increasing growth of surrounding wool. This continued till Oak withdrew again from the flock. He returned to the hut, bringing in his arms a new-born lamb, consisting of four legs large enough for a full-grown sheep, united by a seemingly inconsiderable membrane about half the substance of the legs collectively, which constituted the animal's entire body just at present.

The little speck of life he placed on a wisp of hay before the small stove, where a can of milk was simmering. Oak extinguished the lantern by blowing into it and then pinching the snuff, the cot being lighted by a candle suspended by a twisted wire. A rather hard couch, formed of a few corn sacks thrown carelessly down, covered half the floor of this little habitation, and here the young man stretched himself along, loosened his woolen cravat, and closed his eyes. In about the time a person unaccustomed to bodily labor would have decided upon which side to lie, Farmer Oak was asleep.

The inside of the hut, as it now presented itself, was cosy and alluring, and the scarlet handful of fire in addition to the candle, reflecting its own genial color upon whatever it could reach, flung associations of enjoyment even over utensils and tools. In the corner stood the sheep crook, and along a shelf at one side were ranged bottles and canisters of the simple preparations pertaining to ovine surgery and physic; spirits of wine, turpentine, tar, magnesia, ginger, and castor oil being the chief. On a triangular shelf across the corner stood bread, bacon, cheese, and a cup for ale or cider, which was supplied from a flagon beneath. Beside the provisions lay the flute, whose notes had lately been called forth by the lonely watcher to beguile a tedious hour. The house was ventilated by two round holes, like the lights of a ship's cabin, with wood slides.

The lamb, revived by the warmth, began to bleat, and the sound entered Gabriel's ears and brain with an instant meaning, as expected sounds will. Passing from the profoundest sleep to the most alert wakefulness with the same ease that had accompanied the reverse operation, he looked at his watch, found that the hour hand had shifted again, put on his hat, took the lamb in his arms, and carried it into the darkness. After placing the little creature with its mother he stood and carefully examined the sky, to ascertain the time of night from the altitudes of the stars.

The Dog Star and Aldebaran, pointing to the restless Pleiades, were halfway up the Southern sky, and between them hung Orion, which gorgeous constellation never burnt more vividly than now, as it soared forth above the rim of the landscape. Castor and Pollux with their quiet shine were almost on the meridian: the barren and gloomy Square of Pegasus was creeping round to the northwest; far away through the plantation Vega sparkled like a lamp suspended amid the leafless trees, and Cassiopeia's chair stood daintily poised on the uppermost boughs.

"One o'clock," said Gabriel.

Being a man not without a frequent consciousness that there was some charm in this life he led,

he stood still after looking at the sky as a useful instrument, and regarded it in an appreciative spirit,
as a work of art superlatively beautiful. For a moment he seemed impressed with the speaking loneliness of the scene, or rather with the complete abstraction from all its compass of the sights and
sounds of man. Human shapes, interferences, troubles, and joys were all as if they were not, and there
seemed to be on the shaded hemisphere of the
globe no sentient being save himself; he could
fancy them all gone round to the sunny side.

Occupied thus, with eyes stretched afar, Oak
gradually perceived that what he had previously
taken to be a star low down behind the outskirts of
the plantation was in reality no such thing. It was
an artificial light, almost close at hand.

To find themselves utterly alone at night where
company is desirable and expected makes some people fearful; but a case more trying by far to
the nerves is to discover some mysterious compan-
ionship when intuition, sensation, memory, analogy, testimony, probability, induction—every kind
of evidence in the logician's list—have united to
persuade consciousness that it is quite in isolation.

Farmer Oak went toward the plantation and
pushed through its lower boughs to the windy side.
A dim mass under the slope reminded him that a
shed occupied a place here, the site being a cutting
into the slope of the hill, so that at its back part the
roof was almost level with the ground. In front it
was formed of boards nailed to posts and covered
with tar as a preservative. Through crevices in the
roof and side spread streaks and dots of light, a
combination of which made the radiance that had
attracted him. Oak stepped up behind, where,
leaning down upon the roof and putting his eye
close to a hole, he could see into the interior clearly.

The place contained two women and two cows.
By the side of the latter a steaming branmash

stood in a bucket. One of the women was past middle age. Her companion was apparently young and graceful; he could form no decided opinion upon her looks, her position being almost beneath his eye, so that he saw her in a bird's-eye view, as Milton's Satan first saw Paradise. She wore no bonnet or hat, but had enveloped herself in a large cloak, which was carelessly flung over her head as a covering.

"There, now we'll go home," said the elder of the two, resting her knuckles upon her hips, and looking at their goings-on as a whole. "I do hope Daisy will fetch round again now. I have never been more frightened in my life, but I don't mind breaking my rest if she recovers."

The young woman, whose eyelids were apparently inclined to fall together on the smallest provocation of silence, yawned without parting her lips to any inconvenient extent, whereupon Gabriel caught the infection and slightly yawned in sympathy.

"I wish we were rich enough to pay a man to do these things," she said.

"As we are not, we must do them ourselves," said the other, "for you must help me if you stay."

"Well, my hat is gone, however," continued the younger. "It went over the hedge, I think. The idea of such a slight wind catching it."

The cow standing erect was of the Devon breed, and was encased in a tight warm hide of rich Indian red, as absolutely uniform from eyes to tail as if the animal had been dipped in a dye of that color, her long back being mathematically level. The other was spotted, gray and white. Beside her Oak now noticed a little calf about a day old, looking idiotically at the two women, which showed that it had not long been accustomed to the phenomenon of eyesight, and often turning to the lantern, which it apparently mistook for the moon, inherited instinct having as yet had little time for correction by experience. Between the sheep and the cows Lucina had been busy on Norcombe Hill lately.

"I think we had better send for some oatmeal," said the elder woman, "there's no more bran."

"Yes, aunt; and I'll ride over for it as soon as it is light."

"But there's no sidesaddle."

"I can ride on the other: trust me."

Oak, upon hearing these remarks, became more curious to observe her features, but this prospect being denied him by the hooding effect of the cloak, and by his aerial position, he felt himself drawing upon his fancy for their details. In making even horizontal and clear inspections we color and mold according to the wants within us whatever our eyes bring in. Had Gabriel been able from the first to get a distinct view of her countenance, his estimate of it as very handsome or slightly so would have been as his soul required a divinity at the moment or was ready supplied with one. Having for some time known the want of a satisfactory form to fill an increasing void within him, his position moreover affording the widest scope for his fancy, he painted her a beauty.

By one of those whimsical coincidences in which Nature, like a busy mother, seems to spare a moment from her unremitting labors to turn and make her children smile, the girl now dropped the cloak, and forth tumbled ropes of black hair over a red jacket. Oak knew her instantly as the heroine of the yellow wagon, myrtles, and looking glass: prosily, as the woman who owed him twopence.

They placed the calf beside its mother again, took up the lantern, and went out, the light sinking down the hill till it was no more than a nebula. Gabriel Oak returned to his flock.

3. A Girl on Horseback — Conversation

THE SLUGGISH DAY began to break. Even its position terrestrially is one of the elements of a new interest, and for no particular reason save that the incident of the night had occurred there Oak went again into the plantation. Lingering and musing here he heard the steps of a horse at the foot of the hill, and soon there appeared in view an auburn pony with a girl on its back, ascending by the path leading past the cattleshed. She was the young woman of the night before. Gabriel instantly thought of the hat she had mentioned as having lost in the wind; possibly she had come to look for it. He hastily scanned the ditch, and after walking about ten yards along it found the hat among the leaves. Gabriel took it in his hand and returned to his hut. Here he ensconced himself and peeped through the loophole in the direction of the rider's approach.

She came up and looked around—then on the other side of the hedge. Gabriel was about to advance and restore the missing article, when an unexpected performance induced him to suspend the action for the present. The path, after passing the cowshed, bisected the plantation. It was not a bridle path—merely a pedestrian's track, and the boughs spread horizontally at a height not greater than seven feet above the ground, which made it impossible to ride erect beneath them. The girl, who wore no riding habit, looked around for a moment, as if to assure herself that all humanity was out of view, then dexterously dropped backward flat upon the pony's back, her head over its tail, her feet against its shoulders, and her eyes to the sky. The rapidity of her glide into this position was that of a kingfisher—its noiselessness that of a hawk. Gabriel's eyes had scarcely been able to follow her. The tall lank pony seemed used to such doings, and ambled along unconcerned. Thus she passed under the level boughs.

The performer seemed quite at home anywhere between a horse's head and its tail, and the necessity for this abnormal attitude having ceased with the passage of the plantation, she began to adopt another, even more obviously convenient than the first. She had no sidesaddle, and it was very apparent that a firm seat upon the smooth leather beneath her was unattainable sideways. Springing to her accustomed perpendicular like a bowed sapling, and satisfying herself that nobody was in sight, she seated herself in the manner demanded by the saddle, though hardly expected of the woman, and trotted off in the direction of Tewnell Mill.

Oak was amused, perhaps a little astonished, and hanging up the hat in his hut went again among his ewes. An hour passed, the girl returned, properly seated now, with a bag of bran in front of her. On nearing the cattleshed she was met by a boy bringing a milking pail, who held the reins of the pony whilst she slid off. The boy led away the horse, leaving the pail with the young woman.

Soon soft spirts alternating with loud spirts came in regular succession from within the shed, the obvious sounds of a person milking a cow. Gabriel took the lost hat in his hand, and waited beside the path she would follow in leaving the hill.

She came, the pail in one hand, hanging against her knee. The left arm was extended as a balance,

enough of it being shown bare to make Oak wish
that the event had happened in the summer, when
the whole would have been revealed. There was a
bright air and manner about her now, by which
she seemed to imply that the desirability of her
existence could not be questioned; and this rather
saucy assumption failed in being offensive because
a beholder felt it to be, upon the whole, true.
Like exceptional emphasis in the tone of a genius,
that which would have made mediocrity ridiculous
was an addition to recognized power. It was with
some surprise that she saw Gabriel's face rising
like the moon behind the hedge.

The adjustment of the farmer's hazy conceptions
of her charms to the portrait of herself she now
presented him with was less a diminution than a
difference. The starting point selected by the judgment was her height. She seemed tall, but the pail
was a small one, and the hedge diminutive; hence,
making allowance for error by comparison with
these, she could have been not above the height to
be chosen by women as best. All features of consequence were severe and regular. It may have been
observed by persons who go about the shires with
eyes for beauty that in English women a classically
formed face is seldom found to be united with a
figure of the same pattern, the highly finished features being generally too large for the remainder
of the frame; that a graceful and proportionate
figure of eight heads usually goes off into random
facial curves. Without throwing a Nymphean tissue
over a milkmaid, let it be said that here criticism
checked itself as out of place, and looked at her proportions with a long consciousness of pleasure.
From the contours of her figure in its upper part
she must have had a beautiful neck and shoulders;
but since her infancy nobody had seen them.
Had she been put into a low dress she would have
run and thrust her head into a bush. Yet she was

not a shy girl by any means; it was merely her instinct to draw the line dividing the seen from the unseen higher than they do it in towns.

That the girl's thoughts hovered about her face and form as soon as she caught Oak's eyes conning the same page was natural, and almost certain. The self-consciousness shown would have been vanity if a little more pronounced, dignity if a little less. Rays of male vision seem to have a tickling effect upon virgin faces in rural districts; she brushed hers with her hand, as if Gabriel had been irritating its pink surface by actual touch, and the free air of her previous movements was reduced at the same time to a chastened phase of itself. Yet it was the man who blushed, the maid not at all.

"I found a hat," said Oak.

"It is mine," said she, and, from a sense of proportion, kept down to a small smile an inclination to laugh distinctly. "It flew away last night."

"One o'clock this morning?"

"Well—it was." She was surprised. "How did you know?" she said.

"I was here."

"You are Farmer Oak, are you not?"

"That or thereabouts. I'm lately come to this place."

"A large farm?" she inquired, casting her eyes round, and swinging back her hair, which was black in the shaded hollows of its mass; but it being now an hour past sunrise the rays touched its prominent curves with a color of their own.

"No; not large. About a hundred." (In speaking of farms the word "acres" is omitted by the natives, by analogy to such old expressions as "a stag of ten.")

"I wanted my hat this morning," she went on. "I had to ride to Tewnell Mill."

"Yes, you had."

"How do you know?"

"I saw you."

"Where?" she inquired, a misgiving bringing every muscle of her lineaments and frame to a standstill.

"Here—going through the plantation, and all down the hill," said Farmer Oak, with an aspect excessively knowing with regard to some matter in his mind, as he gazed at a remote point in the direction named, and then turned back to meet his colloquist's eyes.

A perception caused him to withdraw his own eyes from hers as suddenly as if he had been caught in a theft. Recollection of the strange antics she had indulged in when passing through the trees was succeeded in the girl by a nettled palpitation, and that by a hot face. It was a time to see a woman redden who was not given to reddening as a rule; not a point in the milkmaid but was of the deepest rose color. From the Maiden's Blush, through all varieties of the Provence down to the Crimson Tuscany the countenance of Oak's acquaintance quickly graduated; whereupon he, in considerateness, turned away his head.

The sympathetic man still looked the other way, and wondered when she would recover coolness sufficient to justify him in facing her again. He heard what seemed to be the flitting of a dead leaf upon the breeze, and looked. She had gone away.

With an air between that of Tragedy and Comedy, Gabriel returned to his work.

Five mornings and evenings passed. The young woman came regularly to milk the healthy cow or to attend to the sick one, but never allowed her vision to stray in the direction of Oak's person. His want of tact had deeply offended her—not by seeing what he could not help, but by letting her know that he had seen it. For, as without law there is no sin, without eyes there is no indecorum; and she appeared to feel that Gabriel's espial had made her

an indecorous woman without her own con-
nivance. It was food for great regret with him; it
was also a *contretemps* which touched into life a
latent heat he had experienced in that direction.

The acquaintanceship might, however, have
ended in a slow forgetting but for an incident
which occurred at the end of the same week. One
afternoon it began to freeze, and the frost increased
with evening, which drew on like a stealthy tightening of bonds. It was a time when in cottages the
breath of the sleepers freezes to the sheets; when
round the drawing-room fire of a thick-walled mansion the sitters' backs are cold, even whilst their
faces are all aglow. Many a small bird went to bed
supperless that night among the bare boughs.

As the milking hour drew near Oak kept his
usual watch upon the cowshed. At last he felt cold,
and shaking an extra quantity of bedding round
the yeaning ewes he entered the hut and heaped
more fuel upon the stove. The wind came in at the
bottom of the door, and to prevent it Oak laid a
sack there and wheeled the cot round a little more
to the south. Then the wind spouted in at a
ventilating hole—of which there was one on each
side of the hut.

Gabriel had always known that when the fire was
lighted and the door closed one of these must be
kept open—that chosen being always on the side
away from the wind. Closing the slide to windward
he turned to open the other; on second thoughts
the farmer considered that he would first sit down,
leaving both closed for a minute or two, till the
temperature of the hut was a little raised. He sat
down.

His head began to ache in an unwonted manner and, fancying himself weary by reason of the
broken rests of the preceding nights, Oak decided
to get up, open the slide, and then allow himself

to fall asleep. He fell asleep, however, without having performed the necessary preliminary.

How long he remained unconscious Gabriel never knew. During the first stages of his return to perception peculiar deeds seemed to be in course of enactment. His dog was howling, his head was aching fearfully—somebody was pulling him about, hands were loosening his neckerchief.

On opening his eyes he found that evening had sunk to dusk in a strange manner of unexpectedness. The young girl with the remarkably pleasant lips and white teeth was beside him. More than this —astonishingly more—his head was upon her lap, his face and neck were disagreeably wet, and her fingers were unbuttoning his collar.

"Whatever is the matter?" said Oak vacantly.

She seemed to experience mirth, but of too insignificant a kind to start enjoyment.

"Nothing now," she answered, "since you are not dead. It is a wonder you were not suffocated in this hut of yours."

"Ah, the hut!" murmured Gabriel. "I gave ten pounds for that hut. But I'll sell it, and sit under thatched hurdles as they did in old times, and curl up to sleep in a lock of straw! It played me nearly the same trick the other day!" Gabriel, by way of emphasis, brought down his fist upon the floor.

"It was not exactly the fault of the hut," she observed in a tone which showed her to be that novelty among women—one who finished a thought before beginning the sentence which was to convey it. "You should, I think, have considered, and not have been so foolish as to leave the slides closed."

"Yes, I suppose I should," said Oak absently. He was endeavoring to catch and appreciate the sensation of being thus with her, his head upon her dress, before the event passed on into the heap of bygone things. He wished she knew his impressions;

but he would as soon have thought of carrying an odor in a net as of attempting to convey the intangibilities of his feeling in the coarse meshes of language. So he remained silent.

She made him sit up, and then Oak began wiping his face and shaking himself like a Samson. "How can I thank 'ee?" he said at last gratefully, some of the natural rusty red having returned to his face.

"Oh, never mind that," said the girl, smiling, and allowing her smile to hold good for Gabriel's next remark, whatever that might prove to be.

"How did you find me?"

"I heard your dog howling and scratching at the door of the hut when I came to the milking (it was so lucky, Daisy's milking is almost over for the season, and I shall not come here after this week or the next). The dog saw me, and jumped over to me, and laid hold of my skirt. I came across and looked round the hut the very first thing to see if the slides were closed. My uncle has a hut like this one, and I have heard him tell his shepherd not to go to sleep without leaving a slide open. I opened the door, and there you were like dead. I threw the milk over you, as there was no water, forgetting it was warm, and no use."

"I wonder if I should have died?" Gabriel said in a low voice, which was rather meant to travel back to himself than to her.

"Oh, no!" the girl replied. She seemed to prefer a less tragic probability; to have saved a man from death involved talk that should harmonize with the dignity of such a deed—and she shunned it.

"I believe you saved my life, Miss—I don't know your name. I know your aunt's, but not yours."

"I would just as soon not tell it—rather not. There is no reason either why I should, as you probably will never have much to do with me."

"Still I should like to know."

"You can inquire at my aunt's—she will tell you."

"My name is Gabriel Oak."

"And mine isn't. You seem fond of yours in speaking it so decisively, Gabriel Oak."

"You see, it is the only one I shall ever have, and I must make the most of it."

"I always think mine sounds odd and disagreeable."

"I should think you might soon get a new one."

"Mercy!—how many opinions you keep about you concerning other people, Gabriel Oak."

"Well, Miss—excuse the words—I thought you would like them. But I can't match you, I know, in mapping out my mind upon my tongue. I never was very clever in my inside. But I thank you. Come, give me your hand!"

She hesitated, somewhat disconcerted at Oak's old-fashioned earnest conclusion to a dialogue lightly carried on. "Very well," she said, and gave him her hand, compressing her lips to a demure impassivity. He held it but an instant, and in his fear of being too demonstrative, swerved to the opposite extreme, touching her fingers with the lightness of a small-hearted person.

"I am sorry," he said the instant after.

"What for?"

"Letting your hand go so quick."

"You may have it again if you like; there it is." She gave him her hand again.

Oak held it longer this time—indeed, curiously long. "How soft it is—being winter time, too—not chapped or rough, or anything!" he said.

"There—that's long enough," said she, though without pulling it away. "But I suppose you are thinking you would like to kiss it? You may if you want to."

"I wasn't thinking of any such thing," said Gabriel simply, "but I will—"

"That you won't!" She snatched back her hand.

Gabriel felt himself guilty of another want of tact.

"Now find out my name," she said teasingly; and withdrew.

4. *Gabriel's Resolve — The Visit — The Mistake*

THE ONLY SUPERIORITY in women that is tolerable to the rival sex is, as a rule, that of the unconscious kind; but a superiority which recognizes itself may sometimes please by suggesting possibilities of capture to the subordinated man.

This well-favored and comely girl soon made appreciable inroads upon the emotional constitution of young Farmer Oak.

Love being an extremely exacting usurer (a sense of exorbitant profit, spiritually, by an exchange of hearts, being at the bottom of pure passions, as that of exorbitant profit, bodily or materially, is at the bottom of those of lower atmosphere), every morning Oak's feelings were as sensitive as the money market in calculations upon his chances. His dog waited for his meals in a way so like that in which Oak waited for the girl's presence that the farmer was quite struck with the resemblance, felt it lowering, and would not look at the dog. However, he continued to watch through the hedge for her regular coming, and thus his sentiments toward her were deepened without any corresponding effect being produced upon herself. Oak had nothing finished and ready to say as yet, and not being able to frame love phrases which end where they begin, passionate tales—

—Full of sound and fury
—Signifying nothing—

he said no word at all.

By making inquiries he found that the girl's name was Bathsheba Everdene, and that the cow would go dry in about seven days. He dreaded the eighth day.

At last the eighth day came. The cow had ceased to give milk for that year, and Bathsheba Everdene came up the hill no more. Gabriel had reached a pitch of existence he never could have anticipated a short time before. He liked saying "Bathsheba" as a private enjoyment instead of whistling; turned over his taste to black hair, though he had sworn by brown ever since he was a boy, isolated himself till the space he filled in the public eye was contemptibly small. Love is a possible strength in an actual weakness. Marriage transforms a distraction into a support, the power of which should be, and happily often is, in direct proportion to the degree of imbecility it supplants. Oak began now to see light in this direction, and said to himself, "I'll make her my wife, or upon my soul I shall be good for nothing!"

All this while he was perplexing himself about an errand on which he might consistently visit the cottage of Bathsheba's aunt.

He found his opportunity in the death of a ewe, mother of a living lamb. On a day which had a summer face and a winter constitution—a fine January morning, when there was just enough blue sky visible to make cheerfully disposed people wish for more, and an occasional gleam of silvery sunshine, Oak put the lamb into a respectable Sunday basket, and stalked across the fields to the house of Mrs. Hurst, the aunt—George, the dog, walking behind, with a countenance of great concern at the serious turn pastoral affairs seemed to be taking.

Gabriel had watched the blue woodsmoke curling from the chimney with strange meditation. At evening he had fancifully traced it down the chimney to the spot of its origin—seen the hearth and Bathsheba beside it—beside it in her outdoor dress; for the clothes she had worn on the hill were by association equally with her person included in the compass of his affection; they seemed at this early time of his love a necessary ingredient of the sweet mixture called Bathsheba Everdene.

He had made a toilet of a nicely adjusted kind— of a nature between the carefully neat and the carelessly ornate—of a degree between fine-market-day and wet-Sunday selection. He thoroughly cleaned his silver watch chain with whiting, put new lacing straps to his boots, looked to the brass eyelet holes, went to the inmost heart of the plantation for a new walking stick, and trimmed it vigorously on his way back; took a new handkerchief from the bottom of his clothes box, put on the light waistcoat patterned all over with sprigs of an elegant flower uniting the beauties of both rose and lily without the defects of either, and used all the hair oil he possessed upon his usually dry, sandy, and inextricably curly hair, till he had deepened it to a splendidly novel color, between that of guano and Roman cement, making it stick to his head like mace round a nutmeg, or wet seaweed round a boulder after the ebb.

Nothing disturbed the stillness of the cottage save the chatter of a knot of sparrows on the eaves; one might fancy scandal and rumor to be no less the staple topic of these little coteries on roofs than of those under them. It seemed that the omen was an unpropitious one, for as the rather untoward commencement of Oak's overtures, just as he arrived by the garden gate he saw a cat inside, going into various arched shapes and fiendish convulsions at the sight of his dog George. The dog took no notice, for he had arrived at an age at which all superfluous barking was cynically avoided as a waste of breath —in fact, he never barked even at the sheep except to order, when it was done with an absolutely neutral countenance, as a sort of Commination-service which, though offensive, had to be gone through once now and then to frighten the flock for their own good.

A voice came from behind some laurel bushes into which the cat had run:

"Poor dear! Did a nasty brute of a dog want to kill it—did he, poor dear!"

"I beg yer pardon," said Oak to the voice, "but George was walking on behind me with a temper as mild as milk."

Almost before he had ceased speaking Oak was seized with a misgiving as to whose ear was the recipient of his answer. Nobody appeared, and he heard the person retreat among the bushes.

Gabriel meditated, and so deeply that he brought small furrows into his forehead by sheer force of reverie. Where the issue of an interview is as likely to be a vast change for the worse as for the better, any initial difference from expectation causes nipping sensations of failure. Oak went up to the door a little abashed: his mental rehearsal and the reality had had no common grounds of opening.

Bathsheba's aunt was indoors. "Will you tell Miss Everdene that somebody would be glad to speak to her?" said Mr. Oak. (Calling one's self merely Somebody, without giving a name, is not to be taken as an example of the ill-breeding of the rural world: it springs from a refined modesty of which towns-

people, with their cards and announcements, have
no notion whatever.)

Bathsheba was out. The voice had evidently been
hers.

"Will you come in, Mr. Oak?"

"Oh, thank 'ee," said Gabriel, following her to
the fireplace. "I've brought a lamb for Miss Everdene. I thought she might like one to rear; girls do."

"She might," said Mrs. Hurst musingly, "though
she's only a visitor here. If you will wait a minute
Bathsheba will be in."

"Yes, I will wait," said Gabriel, sitting down.
"The lamb isn't really the business I came about,
Mrs. Hurst. In short, I was going to ask her if she'd
like to be married."

"And were you indeed?"

"Yes. Because if she would I should be very glad
to marry her. D'ye know if she's got any other young
man hanging about her at all?"

"Let me think," said Mrs. Hurst, poking the fire
superfluously. . . . "Yes—bless you, ever so many
young men. You see, Farmer Oak, she's so good-
looking, and an excellent scholar besides—she was
going to be a governess once, you know, only she
was too wild. Not that her young men ever come
here—but, Lord, in the nature of women, she must
have a dozen!"

"That's unfortunate," said Farmer Oak, contemplating a crack in the stone floor with sorrow. "I'm
only an everyday sort of man, and my only chance
was in being the first comer. . . . Well, there's no
use in my waiting, for that was all I came about: so
I'll take myself off home-along, Mrs. Hurst."

When Gabriel had gone about two hundred yards
along the down, he heard a "hoi-hoi!" uttered behind him, in a piping note of more treble quality
than that in which the exclamation usually em-
bodies itself when shouted across a field. He looked

round, and saw a girl racing after him, waving a white handkerchief.

Oak stood still—and the runner drew nearer. It was Bathsheba Everdene. Gabriel's color deepened: hers was already deep, not, as it appeared, from emotion, but from running.

"Farmer Oak—I—" she said, pausing for want of breath, pulling up in front of him with a slanted face, and putting her hand to her side.

"I have just called to see you," said Gabriel pending her further speech.

"Yes—I know that," she said, panting like a robin, her face red and moist from her exertions, like a peony petal before the sun dries off the dew. "I didn't know you had come to ask to have me, or I should have come in from the garden instantly. I ran after you to say—that my aunt made a mistake in sending you away from courting me."

Gabriel expanded. "I'm sorry to have made you run so fast, my dear," he said, with a grateful sense of favors to come. "Wait a bit till you've found your breath."

"—It was quite a mistake—aunt's telling you I had a young man already," Bathsheba went on. "I haven't a sweetheart at all—and I never had one, and I thought that, as times go with women, it was *such* a pity to send you away thinking that I had several."

"Really and truly I am glad to hear that!" said Farmer Oak, smiling one of his long special smiles, and blushing with gladness. He held out his hand to take hers, which, when she had eased her side by pressing it there, was prettily extended upon her bosom to still her loud-beating heart. Directly he seized it she put it behind her, so that it slipped through his fingers like an eel.

"I have a nice snug little farm," said Gabriel, with half a degree less assurance than when he had seized her hand.

"Yes; you have."

"A man has advanced me money to begin with, but still, it will soon be paid off, and though I am only an everyday sort of man I have got on a little since I was a boy." Gabriel uttered "a little" in a tone to show her that it was the complacent form of "a great deal." He continued: "When we be married, I am quite sure I can work twice as hard as I do now."

He went forward and stretched out his arm again. Bathsheba had overtaken him at a point beside which stood a low stunted holly bush, now laden with red berries. Seeing his advance take the form of an attitude threatening a possible enclosure, if not compression, of her person, she edged off round the bush.

"Why, Farmer Oak," she said over the top, looking at him with rounded eyes, "I never said I was going to marry you."

"Well—that *is* a tale!" said Oak with dismay. "To run after anybody like this, and then say you don't want him!"

"What I meant to tell you was only this," she said eagerly, and yet half-conscious of the absurdity of the position she had made for herself—"that nobody has got me yet as a sweetheart, instead of my having a dozen, as my aunt said; I *hate* to be thought men's property in that way, though possibly I shall be had some day. Why, if I'd wanted you I shouldn't have run after you like this; 'twould have been the *forwardest* thing! But there was no harm in hurrying to correct a piece of false news that had been told you."

"Oh, no—no harm at all." But there is such a thing as being too generous in expressing a judgment impulsively, and Oak added with a more appreciative sense of all the circumstances—"Well, I am not quite certain it was no harm."

"Indeed, I hadn't time to think before starting

whether I wanted to marry or not, for you'd have been gone over the hill."

"Come," said Gabriel, freshening again, "think a minute or two. I'll wait a while, Miss Everdene. Will you marry me? Do, Bathsheba. I love you far more than common!"

"I'll try to think," she observed rather more timorously; "if I can think out of doors; my mind spreads away so."

"But you can give a guess."

"Then give me time," Bathsheba looked thoughtfully into the distance, away from the direction in which Gabriel stood.

"I can make you happy," said he to the back of her head, across the bush. "You shall have a piano in a year or two—farmers' wives are getting to have pianos now—and I'll practice up the flute right well to play with you in the evenings."

"Yes; I should like that."

"And have one of those little ten-pound gigs for market—and nice flowers, and birds—cocks and hens I mean, because they be useful," continued Gabriel, feeling balanced between poetry and practicality.

"I should like it very much."

"And a frame for cucumbers—like a gentleman and lady."

"Yes."

"And when the wedding was over, we'd have it put in the newspaper list of marriages."

"Dearly I should like that!"

"And the babies in the births—every man jack of 'em! And at home by the fire, whenever you look up, there I shall be—and whenever I look up, there will be you."

"Wait, wait, and don't be improper!"

Her countenance fell, and she was silent awhile. He regarded the red berries between them over and over again, to such an extent that holly seemed in his after life to be a cypher signifying a proposal of marriage. Bathsheba decisively turned to him.

"No; 'tis no use," she said. "I don't want to marry you."

"Try."

"I've tried hard all the time I've been thinking; for a marriage would be very nice in one sense. People would talk about me and think I had won my battle, and I should feel triumphant, and all that. But a husband—"

"Well!"

"Why, he'd always be there, as you say; whenever I looked up, there he'd be."

"Of course he would—I, that is."

"Well, what I mean is that I shouldn't mind being a bride at a wedding, if I could be one without having a husband. But since a woman can't show off in that way by herself, I shan't marry—at least yet."

"That's a terrible wooden story!"

At this criticism of her statement Bathsheba made an addition to her dignity by a slight sweep away from him.

"Upon my heart and soul I don't know what a maid can say stupider than that," said Oak. "But dearest," he continued in a palliative voice, "don't be like it!" Oak sighed a deep honest sigh—none the less so in that, being like the sigh of a pine plantation, it was rather noticeable as a disturbance of the atmosphere. "Why won't you have me?" he appealed, creeping round the holly to reach her side.

"I cannot," she said, retreating.

"But why?" he persisted, standing still at last in despair of ever reaching her, and facing over the bush.

"Because I don't love you."

"Yes, but—"

She contracted a yawn to an inoffensive smallness, so that it was hardly ill-mannered at all. "I don't love you," she said.

"But I love you—and, as for myself, I am content to be liked."

"Oh, Mr. Oak—that's very fine! You'd get to despise me."

"Never," said Mr. Oak, so earnestly that he seemed to be coming, by the force of his words, straight through the bush and into her arms. "I shall do one thing in this life—one thing certain—that is, love you, and long for you, and *keep wanting you* till I die." His voice had a genuine pathos now, and his large brown hands perceptibly trembled.

"It seems dreadfully wrong not to have you when you feel so much!" she said with a little distress, and looking hopelessly around for some means of escape from her moral dilemma. "How I wish I hadn't run after you!" However, she seemed to have a short cut for getting back to cheerfulness and set her face to signify archness. "It wouldn't do, Mr. Oak. I want somebody to tame me; I am too independent; and you would never be able to, I know."

Oak cast his eyes down the field in a way of implying that it was useless to attempt argument.

"Mr. Oak," she said, with luminous distinctness and common sense, "you are better off than I. I have hardly a penny in the world—I am staying with my aunt for my bare sustenance. I am better educated than you—and I don't love you a bit: that's my side of the case. Now yours: you are a farmer just beginning, and you ought in common prudence, if you marry at all (which you should certainly not think of doing at present) to marry a woman with money, who would stock a larger farm for you than you have now."

Gabriel looked at her with a little surprise and much admiration.

"That's the very thing I had been thinking myself!" he naïvely said.

Farmer Oak had one-and-a-half Christian characteristics too many to succeed with Bathsheba: his humility, and a superfluous moiety of honesty. Bathsheba was decidedly disconcerted.

"Well, then, why did you come and disturb me?" she said, almost angrily, if not quite, an enlarging red spot rising in each cheek.

"I can't do what I think would be—would be—"

"Right?"

"No: wise."

"You have made an admission *now*, Mr. Oak," she exclaimed with even more hauteur, and rocking her head disdainfully. "After that, do you think I could marry you? Not if I know it."

He broke in passionately: "But don't mistake me like that! Because I am open enough to own what every man in my shoes would have thought of, you make your colors come up your face and get crabbed with me. That about you not being good enough for me is nonsense. You speak like a lady—all the parish notice it, and your uncle at Weatherbury is, I've heard, a large farmer—much larger than ever I shall be. May I call in the evening, or will you walk along with me o' Sundays? I don't want you to make up your mind at once, if you'd rather not."

"No—no—I cannot. Don't press me any more—don't. I don't love you—so 'twould be ridiculous," she said, with a laugh.

No man likes to see his emotions the sport of a merry-go-round of skittishness. "Very well," said Oak firmly, with the bearing of one who was going to give his days and nights to Ecclesiastes for ever. "Then I'll ask you no more."

5. *Departure of Bathsheba*
— *A Pastoral Tragedy*

THE NEWS which one day reached Gabriel that Bathsheba Everdene had left the neighborhood had an influence upon him which might have surprised any who never suspected that the more emphatic the renunciation the less absolute its character.

It may have been observed that there is no regular path for getting out of love as there is for getting in. Some people look upon marriage as a short cut that way, but it has been known to fail. Separation, which was the means that chance offered to Gabriel Oak by Bathsheba's disappearance, though effectual with people of certain humors, is apt to idealize the removed object with others—notably those whose affection, placid and regular as it may be, flows deep and long. Oak belonged to the even-tempered order of humanity, and felt the secret fusion of himself in Bathsheba to be burning with a finer flame now that she was gone—that was all.

His incipient friendship with her aunt had been nipped by the failure of his suit, and all that Oak learnt of Bathsheba's movements was done indirectly. It appeared that she had gone to a place called Weatherbury, more than twenty miles off, but in what capacity—whether as a visitor or permanently, he could not discover.

Gabriel had two dogs. George, the elder, exhibited an ebony-tipped nose, surrounded by a narrow margin of pink flesh, and a coat marked in random splotches approximating in color to white and slate gray; but the gray, after years of sun and rain, had been scorched and washed out of the more prominent locks, leaving them of a reddish-brown, as if the blue component of the gray had faded, like the indigo from the same kind of color in Turner's pictures. In substance it had originally been hair, but long contact with sheep seemed to be turning it by degrees into wool of a poor quality and staple.

This dog had originally belonged to a shepherd of inferior morals and dreadful temper, and the result was that George knew the exact degrees of condemnation signified by cursing and swearing of all descriptions better than the wickedest old man in the neighborhood. Long experience had so precisely taught the animal the difference between such exclamations as "Come in!" and "D— ye, come in!" that he knew to a hair's breadth the rate of trotting back from the ewes' tails that each call involved, if a staggerer with the sheep crook was to be escaped. Though old, he was clever and trustworthy still.

The young dog, George's son, might possibly have been the image of his mother, for there was not much resemblance between him and George. He was learning the sheep-keeping business, so as to follow on at the flock when the other should die, but had got no further than the rudiments as yet— still finding an insuperable difficulty in distinguishing between doing a thing well enough and doing it well. So earnest and yet so wrong-headed was this young dog (he had no name in particular, and answered with perfect readiness to any pleasant interjection) that if sent behind the flock to help them on he did it so thoroughly that he would have chased them across the whole county with the greatest pleasure if not called off, or reminded when to stop by the example of old George.

Thus much for the dogs. On the further side of Norcombe Hill was a chalk pit, from which chalk had been drawn for generations, and spread over adjacent farms. Two hedges converged upon it in the form of a V, but without quite meeting. The narrow opening left, which was immediately over the brow of the pit, was protected by a rough railing.

One night, when Farmer Oak had returned to his house, believing there would be no further necessity for his attendance on the down, he called as usual to the dogs, previously to shutting them up in the outhouse till next morning. Only one responded—old George; the other could not be found, either in the house, lane, or garden. Gabriel then remembered that he had left the two dogs on the hill eating a dead lamb (a kind of meat he usually kept from them, except when other food ran short), and concluding that the young one had not finished his meal he went indoors to the luxury of a bed, which latterly he had only enjoyed on Sundays.

It was a still, moist night. Just before dawn he was assisted in waking by the abnormal reverberation of familiar music. To the shepherd, the note of the sheep bell, like the ticking of the clock to other people, is a chronic sound that only makes itself noticed by ceasing or altering in some unusual manner from the well-known idle tinkle which signifies to the accustomed ear, however distant, that all is well in the fold. In the solemn calm of the awakening morn that note was heard by Gabriel, beating with unusual violence and rapidity. This exceptional ringing may be caused in two ways—by the rapid feeding of the sheep bearing the bell as when the flock breaks into new pasture, which gives it an intermittent rapidity, or by the sheep starting off in a run, when the sound has a regular palpitation. The experienced ear of Oak knew the sound he now heard to be caused by the running of the flock with great velocity.

He jumped out of bed, dressed, tore down the lane through a foggy dawn, and ascended the hill. The forward ewes were kept apart from those among which the fall of lambs would be later, there being two hundred of the latter class in Gabriel's flock. These two hundred seemed to have absolutely vanished from the hill. There were the fifty with their lambs, enclosed at the other end as he had left them, but the rest, forming the bulk of the flock, were nowhere. Gabriel called at the top of his voice the shepherd's call:

"Ovey, ovey, ovey!"

Not a single bleat. He went to the hedge; a gap had been broken through it, and in the gap were the footprints of the sheep. Rather surprised to find them break fence at this season, yet putting it down instantly to their great fondness for ivy in wintertime, of which a great deal grew in the plantation, he followed through the hedge. They were not in the plantation. He called again: the valleys and furthest hills resounded as when the sailors invoked the lost Hylas on the Mysian shore; but no sheep. He passed through the trees and along the ridge of the hill. On the extreme summit, where the ends of the two converging hedges of which we have spoken were stopped short by meeting the brow of the chalk pit, he saw the younger dog standing against the sky—dark and motionless as Napoleon at St. Helena.

A horrible conviction darted through Oak. With a sensation of bodily faintness he advanced: at one point the rails were broken through, and there he saw the footprints of his ewes. The dog came up, licked his hand, and made signs implying that he expected some great reward for signal services

rendered. Oak looked over the precipice. The ewes
lay dead and dying at its foot—a heap of two hundred mangled carcasses, representing in their condition just now at least two hundred more.

Oak was an intensely humane man: indeed, his
humanity often tore in pieces any politic intentions
of his which bordered on strategy, and carried him
on as by gravitation. A shadow in his life had always been that his flock ended in mutton—that a
day came and found every shepherd an arrant
traitor to his defenseless sheep. His first feeling now
was one of pity for the untimely fate of these gentle
ewes and their unborn lambs.

It was a second to remember another phase of the
matter. The sheep were not insured. All the sav-
ings of a frugal life had been dispersed at a blow;
his hopes of being an independent farmer were
laid low—possibly for ever. Gabriel's energies, patience, and industry had been so severely taxed during the years of his life between eighteen and eight-
and-twenty, to reach his present stage of progress,
that no more seemed to be left in him. He leant
down upon a rail, and covered his face with his
hands.

Stupors, however, do not last forever, and Farmer
Oak recovered from his. It was as remarkable as it
was characteristic that the one sentence he uttered
was in thankfulness:

"Thank God I am not married: what would *she*
have done in the poverty now coming upon me!"

Oak raised his head, and wondering what he
could do, listlessly surveyed the scene. By the outer
margin of the pit was an oval pond, and over it
hung the attenuated skeleton of a chrome-yellow
moon, which had only a few days to last—the morning star dogging her on the left hand. The pool
glittered like a dead man's eye, and as the world
awoke a breeze blew, shaking and elongating the
reflection of the moon without breaking it, and

turning the image of the star to a phosphoric streak upon the water. All this Oak saw and remembered.

As far as could be learnt it appeared that the poor young dog, still under the impression that since he was kept for running after sheep, the more he ran after them the better, had at the end of his meal off the dead lamb, which may have given him additional energy and spirits, collected all the ewes into a corner, driven the timid creatures through the hedge, across the upper field, and by main force of worrying had given them momentum enough to break down a portion of the rotten railing, and so hurled them over the edge.

George's son had done his work so thoroughly that he was considered too good a workman to live, and was, in fact, taken and tragically shot at twelve o'clock that same day—another instance of the untoward fate which so often attends dogs and other philosophers who follow out a train of reasoning to its logical conclusion, and attempt perfectly consistent conduct in a world made up so largely of compromise.

Gabriel's farm had been stocked by a dealer—on the strength of Oak's promising look and character —who was receiving a percentage from the farmer till such time as the advance should be cleared off. Oak found that the value of stock, plant, and implements which were really his own would be about sufficient to pay his debts, leaving himself a free man with the clothes he stood up in, and nothing more.

6.   The Fair — The Journey — The Fire

Two MONTHS passed away. We are brought on to a day in February, on which was held the yearly statute or hiring fair in the county town of Casterbridge.

At one end of the street stood from two to three hundred blithe and hearty laborers waiting upon Chance—all men of the stamp to whom labor suggests nothing worse than a wrestle with gravitation, and pleasure nothing better than a renunciation of the same. Among these, carters and wagoners were distinguished by having a piece of whipcord twisted round their hats; thatchers wore a fragment of woven straw; shepherds held their sheep crooks in their hands; and thus the situation required was known to the hirers at a glance.

In the crowd was an athletic young fellow of somewhat superior appearance to the rest—in fact, his superiority was marked enough to lead several ruddy peasants standing by to speak to him inquiringly, as to a farmer, and to use "Sir" as a finishing word. His answer always was—

"I am looking for a place myself—a bailiff's. Do ye know of anybody who wants one?"

Gabriel was paler now. His eyes were more meditative, and his expression was more sad. He had passed through an ordeal of wretchedness which had given him more than it had taken away. He had sunk from his modest elevation as pastoral king into

the very slime-pits of Siddim; but there was left
to him a dignified calm he had never before known,
and that indifference to fate which, though it often
makes a villain of a man, is the basis of his sub-
limity when it does not. And thus the abasement
had been exaltation, and the loss gain.

In the morning a regiment of cavalry had left
the town, and a sergeant and his party had been
beating up for recruits through the four streets. As
the end of the day drew on, and he found himself
not hired, Gabriel almost wished that he had
joined them, and gone off to serve his country.
Weary of standing in the marketplace, and not
much minding the kind of work he turned his hand
to, he decided to offer himself in some other capacity
than that of bailiff.

All the farmers seemed to be wanting shepherds.
Sheeptending was Gabriel's speciality. Turning
down an obscure street and entering an obscurer
lane, he went up to a smith's shop.

"How long would it take you to make a shepherd's
crook?"

"Twenty minutes."

"How much?"

"Two shillings."

He sat on a bench and the crook was made, a stem
being given him into the bargain.

He then went to a ready-made clothes shop, the
owner of which had a large rural connection. As
the crook had absorbed most of Gabriel's money,
he attempted, and carried out, an exchange of his
overcoat for a shepherd's regulation smock-frock.

This transaction having been completed he again
hurried off to the center of the town, and stood
on the curb of the pavement, as a shepherd, crook
in hand.

Now that Oak had turned himself into a shepherd it seemed that bailiffs were most in demand.
However, two or three farmers noticed him and

drew near. Dialogues followed, more or less in the subjoined form:

"Where do you come from?"

"Norcombe."

"That's a long way."

"Fifteen miles."

"Whose farm were you upon last?"

"My own."

This reply invariably operated like a rumor of cholera. The inquiring farmer would edge away and shake his head dubiously. Gabriel, like his dog, was too good to be trustworthy, and he never made advance beyond this point.

It is safer to accept any chance that offers itself, and extemporize a procedure to fit it, than to get a good plan matured, and wait for a chance of using it. Gabriel wished he had not nailed up his colors as a shepherd, but had laid himself out for anything in the whole cycle of labor that was required in the fair. It grew dusk. Some merry men were whistling and singing by the corn exchange. Gabriel's hand, which had lain for some time idle in his smock-frock pocket, touched his flute, which he carried there. Here was an opportunity for putting his dearly brought wisdom into practice.

He drew out his flute and began to play "Jockey to the Fair" in the style of a man who had never known a moment's sorrow. Oak could pipe with Arcadian sweetness, and the sound of the well-known notes cheered his own heart as well as those of the loungers. He played on with spirit, and in half an hour had earned in pence what was a small fortune to a destitute man.

By making inquiries he learnt that there was another fair at Shottsford the next day.

"How far is Shottsford?"

"Ten miles t'other side of Weatherbury."

Weatherbury! It was where Bathsheba had gone

two months before. This information was like coming from night into noon.

"How far is it to Weatherbury?"

"Five or six miles."

Bathsheba had probably left Weatherbury long
before this time, but the place had enough interest
attaching to it to lead Oak to choose Shottsford fair
as his next field of inquiry, because it lay in the
Weatherbury quarter. Moreover, the Weatherbury
folk were by no means uninteresting intrinsically.
If report spoke truly they were as hardy, merry,
thriving, wicked a set as any in the whole county.
Oak resolved to sleep at Weatherbury that night on
his way to Shottsford, and struck out at once into
the high road which had been recommended as the
direct route to the village in question.

The road stretched through water meadows traversed by little brooks, whose quivering surfaces
were braided along their centers, and folded into
creases at the sides; or, where the flow was more
rapid, the stream was pied with spots of white
froth, which rode on in undisturbed serenity. On
the higher levels the dead and dry carcasses of leaves
tapped the ground as they bowled along helter-
skelter upon the shoulders of the wind, and little
birds in the hedges were rustling their feathers and
tucking themselves in comfortably for the night, retaining their places if Oak kept moving, but flying away if he stopped to look at them. He passed
by Yalbury Wood where the game birds were rising to their roosts, and heard the crack-voiced cock-
pheasants' "cu-uck, cuck," and the wheezy whistle
of the hens.

By the time he had walked three or four miles
every shape in the landscape had assumed a uniform
hue of blackness. He descended Yalbury Hill and
could just discern ahead of him a wagon, drawn up
under a great overhanging tree by the roadside.

On coming close, he found there were no horses

attached to it, the spot being apparently quite deserted. The wagon, from its position, seemed to have been left there for the night, for beyond about half a truss of hay which was heaped in the bottom, it was quite empty. Gabriel sat down on the shafts of the vehicle and considered his position. He calculated that he had walked a very fair proportion of the journey; and having been on foot since daybreak, he felt tempted to lie down upon the hay in the wagon instead of pushing on to the village of Weatherbury, and having to pay for a lodging.

Eating his last slices of bread and ham, and drinking from the bottle of cider he had taken the precaution to bring with him, he got into the lonely wagon. Here he spread half of the hay as a bed, and as well as he could in the darkness, pulled the other half over him by way of bedclothes, covering himself entirely, and feeling, physically, as comfortable as ever he had been in his life. Inward melancholy it was impossible for a man like Oak, introspective far beyond his neighbors, to banish quite, whilst conning the present untoward page of his history. So, thinking of his misfortunes, amorous and pastoral, he fell asleep, shepherds enjoying, in common with sailors, the privilege of being able to summon the god instead of having to wait for him.

On somewhat suddenly awakening, after a sleep of whose length he had no idea, Oak found that the wagon was in motion. He was being carried along the road at a rate rather considerable for a vehicle without springs, and under circumstances of physical uneasiness, his head being dandled up and down on the bed of the wagon like a kettledrumstick. He then distinguished voices in conversation, coming from the forepart of the wagon. His concern at this dilemma (which would have been alarm, had he been a thriving man; but misfortune is a fine opiate to personal terror) led him to peer cautiously from the hay, and the first sight he beheld was the stars above him. Charles's Wain was getting toward a right angle with the Pole star, and Gabriel concluded that it must be about nine o'clock—in other words, that he had slept two hours. This small astronomical calculation was made without any positive effort, and whilst he was stealthily turning to discover, if possible, into whose hands he had fallen.

Two figures were dimly visible in front, sitting with their legs outside the wagon, one of whom was driving. Gabriel soon found that this was the wagoner, and it appeared they had come from Casterbridge fair, like himself.

A conversation was in progress, which continued thus:

"Be as 'twill, she's a fine handsome body as far's looks be concerned. But that's only the skin of the woman, and these dandy cattle be as proud as a lucifer in their insides."

"Aye—so 'a do seem, Billy Smallbury—so 'a do seem." This utterance was very shaky by nature, and more so by circumstance, the jolting of the wagon not being without its effect upon the speaker's larynx. It came from the man who held the reins.

"She's a very vain feymell—so 'tis said here and there."

"Ah, now. If so be 'tis like that, I can't look her in the face. Lord, no: not I—heh-heh-heh! Such a shy man as I be!"

"Yes—she's very vain. 'Tis said that every night at going to bed she looks in the glass to put on her nightcap properly."

"And not a married woman. Oh, the world!"

"And 'a can play the peanner, so 'tis said. Can play so clever that 'a can make a psalm tune sound as well as the merriest loose song a man can wish for."

"D'ye tell o't! A happy time for us, and I feel quite a new man! And how do she pay?"

"That I don't know, Master Poorgrass."

On hearing these and other similar remarks, a wild thought flashed into Gabriel's mind that they might be speaking of Bathsheba. There were, however, no grounds for retaining such a supposition, for the wagon, though going in the direction of Weatherbury, might be going beyond it, and the woman alluded to seemed to be the mistress of some estate. They were now apparently close upon Weatherbury, and not to alarm the speakers unnecessarily Gabriel slipped out of the wagon unseen.

He turned to an opening in the hedge, which he found to be a gate, and mounting thereon he sat meditating whether to seek a cheap lodging in the village, or to ensure a cheaper one by lying under some hay or corn stack. The crunching jangle of the wagon died upon his ear. He was about to walk on, when he noticed on his left hand an unusual light—appearing about half a mile distant. Oak watched it, and the glow increased. Something was on fire.

Gabriel again mounted the gate, and, leaping down on the other side upon what he found to be ploughed soil, made across the field in the exact direction of the fire. The blaze, enlarging in a double ratio by his approach and its own increase, showed him as he drew nearer the outlines of ricks beside it, lighted up to great distinctness. A rickyard was the source of the fire. His weary face now began to be painted over with a rich orange glow, and the whole front of his smock-frock and gaiters was covered with a dancing shadow pattern of thorn-twigs—the light reaching him through a leafless intervening hedge—and the metallic curve of his sheep crook shone silver-bright in the same abounding rays. He came up to the boundary fence and stood

to regain breath. It seemed as if the spot were unoccupied by a living soul.

The fire was issuing from a long strawstack, which
was so far gone as to preclude a possibility of saving
it. A rick burns differently from a house. As the
wind blows the fire inward, the portion in flames
completely disappears like melting sugar, and the
outline is lost to the eye. However, a hay or a wheat
rick, well put together, will resist combustion for a
length of time if it begins on the outside.

This before Gabriel's eyes was a rick of straw,
loosely put together, and the flames darted into it
with lightning swiftness. It glowed on the windward
side, rising and falling in intensity like the coal of a
cigar. Then a superincumbent bundle rolled down
with a whisking noise; flames elongated, and bent
themselves about with a quiet roar, but no crackle.
Banks of smoke went off horizontally at the back
like passing clouds, and behind these burned hidden pyres, illuminating the semitransparent sheet
of smoke to a lustrous yellow uniformity. Individual
straws in the foreground were consumed in a creeping movement of ruddy heat, as if they were knots
of red worms, and above shone imaginary fiery
faces, tongues hanging from lips, glaring eyes, and
other impish forms, from which at intervals sparks
flew in clusters like birds from a nest.

Oak suddenly ceased from being a mere spectator
by discovering the case to be more serious than he
had at first imagined. A scroll of smoke blew aside
and revealed to him a wheat rick in startling juxtaposition with the decaying one, and behind this a
series of others, composing the main corn produce
of the farm; so that instead of the strawstack standing, as he had imagined, comparatively isolated,
there was a regular connection between it and the
remaining stacks of the group.

Gabriel leapt over the hedge and saw that he
was not alone. The first man he came to was run-

ning about in a great hurry, as if his thoughts were several yards in advance of his body, which they could never drag on fast enough.

"Oh, man—fire, fire! A good master and a bad servant is fire, fire!—I mane a bad servant and a good master. Oh Mark Clark—come! And you, Billy Smallbury—and you, Maryann Money—and you, Jan Coggan, and Matthew there!" Other figures now appeared behind this shouting man and among the smoke, and Gabriel found that, far from being alone, he was in a great company—whose shadows danced merrily up and down, timed by the jigging of the flames, and not at all by their owners' movements. The assemblage—belonging to that class of society which casts its thought into the form of feeling, and its feelings into the form of commotion—set to work with a remarkable confusion of purpose.

"Stop the draught under the wheat rick!" cried Gabriel to those nearest to him. The corn stood on stone staddles, and between these, tongues of yellow hue from the burning straw licked and darted playfully. If the fire once got *under* this stack, all would be lost.

"Get a tarpaulin—quick!" said Gabriel.

A rickcloth was brought, and they hung it like a curtain across the channel. The flames immediately ceased to go under the bottom of the cornstack, and stood up vertical.

"Stand here with a bucket of water and keep the cloth wet," said Gabriel again.

The flames, now driven upward, began to attack the angles of the huge roof covering the wheatstack.

"A ladder," cried Gabriel.

"The ladder was against the straw rick and is burnt to a cinder," said a specterlike form in the smoke.

Oak seized the cut ends of the sheaves, as if he were going to engage in the operation of "reed-drawing," and digging in his feet, and occasionally sticking in the stem of his sheep crook, he clambered up the beetling face. He at once sat astride the very apex, and began with his crook to beat off the fiery fragments which had lodged thereon, shouting to the others to get him a bough and a ladder, and some water.

Billy Smallbury—one of the men who had been on the wagon—by this time had found a ladder, which Mark Clark ascended, holding on beside Oak upon the thatch. The smoke at this corner was stifling, and Clark, a nimble fellow, having been handed a bucket of water, bathed Oak's face and sprinkled him generally, whilst Gabriel, now with a long beech bough in one hand, in addition to his crook in the other, kept sweeping the stack and dislodging all fiery particles.

On the ground the groups of villagers were still occupied in doing all they could to keep down the conflagration, which was not much. They were all tinged orange, and backed up by shadows of varying pattern. Round the corner of the largest stack, out of the direct rays of the fire, stood a pony, bearing a young woman on its back. By her side was another woman, on foot. These two seemed to keep at a distance from the fire, that the horse might not become restive.

"He's a shepherd," said the woman on foot. "Yes —he is. See how his crook shines as he beats the rick with it. And his smock-frock is burnt in two holes, I declare! A fine young shepherd he is too, ma'am."

"Whose shepherd is he?" said the equestrian in a clear voice.

"Don't know, ma'am."

"Don't any of the others know?"

"Nobody at all—I've asked 'em. Quite a stranger, they say."

The young woman on the pony rode out from the shade and looked anxiously around.

"Do you think the barn is safe?" she said.

"D'ye think the barn is safe, Jan Coggan?" said the second woman, passing on the question to the nearest man in that direction.

"Safe now—leastwise I think so. If this rick had gone the barn would have followed. 'Tis that bold shepherd up there that have done the most good— he sitting on the top o' rick, whizzing his great long arms about like a windmill."

"He does work hard," said the young woman on horseback, looking up at Gabriel through her thick woolen veil. "I wish he was shepherd here. Don't any of you know his name?"

"Never heard the man's name in my life, or seed his form afore."

The fire began to get worsted, and Gabriel's elevated position being no longer required of him, he made as if to descend.

"Maryann," said the girl on horseback, "go to him as he comes down and say that the farmer wishes to thank him for the great service he has done."

Maryann stalked off toward the rick and met Oak at the foot of the ladder. She delivered her message.

"Where is your master the farmer?" asked Gabriel, kindling with the idea of getting employment that seemed to strike him now.

" 'Tisn't a master; 'tis a mistress, shepherd."

"A woman farmer?"

"Aye, 'a b'lieve, and a rich one too!" said a bystander. "Lately 'a came here from a distance. Took on her uncle's farm, who died suddenly. Used to measure his money in half-pint cups. They say now that she've business in every bank in Casterbridge and thinks no more of playing pitch-and-toss sovereign than you and I do pitch-halfpenny—not a bit in the world, shepherd."

"That's she, back there upon the pony," said

Maryann; "wi' her face a-covered up in that black cloth with holes in it."

Oak, his features smudged, grimy, and undiscoverable from the smoke and heat, his smock-frock burnt into holes and dripping with water, the ash stem of his sheep crook charred six inches shorter, advanced with the humility stern adversity had thrust upon him up to the slight female form in the saddle. He lifted his hat with respect, and not without gallantry: stepping close to her hanging feet he said in a hesitating voice—

"Do you happen to want a shepherd, ma'am?"

She lifted the wool veil tied round her face and looked all astonishment. Gabriel and his cold-hearted darling, Bathsheba Everdene, were face to face.

Bathsheba did not speak, and he mechanically repeated in an abashed and sad voice—

"Do you want a shepherd, ma'am?"

7. Recognition — A Timid Girl

BATHSHEBA WITHDREW into the shade. She scarcely knew whether most to be amused at the singularity of the meeting or to be concerned at its awkwardness. There was room for a little pity, also for a very little exultation: the former at his position, the latter at her own. Embarrassed she was not, and she remembered Gabriel's declaration of love to her at Norcombe only to think she had nearly forgotten it.

"Yes," she murmured, putting on an air of dignity, and turning again to him with a little warmth of cheek, "I do want a shepherd. But—"

"He's the very man, ma'am," said one of the villagers, quietly.

Conviction breeds conviction. "Aye, that 'a is," said a second, decisively.

"The man, truly!" said a third, with heartiness.

"He's all there!" said number four, fervidly.

"Then will you tell him to speak to the bailiff?" said Bathsheba.

All was practical again now. A summer eve and loneliness would have been necessary to give the meeting its proper fullness of romance.

The bailiff was pointed out to Gabriel, who, checking the palpitation within his breast at discovering that this Ashtoreth of strange report was only a modification of Venus the well-known and admired, retired with him to talk over the necessary preliminaries of hiring.

The fire before them wasted away. "Men," said Bathsheba, "you shall take a little refreshment after this extra work. Will you come to the house?"

"We could knock in a bit and a drop a good deal freer, Miss, if so be ye'd send it to Warren's Malthouse," replied the spokesman.

Bathsheba then rode off into the darkness, and the men straggled on to the village in twos and threes—Oak and the bailiff being left by the rick alone.

"And now," said the bailiff, finally, "all is settled, I think, about your coming, and I am going home-along. Goodnight to ye, shepherd."

"Can you get me a lodging?" inquired Gabriel.

"That I can't, indeed," he said, moving past Oak as a Christian edges past an offertory plate when he does not mean to contribute. "If you follow on the road till you come to Warren's Malthouse, where they are all gone to have their snap of victuals, I daresay some of 'em, will tell you of a place. Goodnight to ye, shepherd."

The bailiff who showed this nervous dread of loving his neighbor as himself, went up the hill, and Oak walked on to the village, still astonished at the re-encounter with Bathsheba, glad of his nearness to her, and perplexed at the rapidity with which the unpracticed girl of Norcombe had developed into the supervising and cool woman here. But some women only require an emergency to make them fit for one.

Obliged to some extent to forgo dreaming in order to find the way, he reached the churchyard, and passed round it under the wall where several ancient trees grew. There was a wide margin of grass along here, and Gabriel's footsteps were deadened by its softness, even at this indurating period of the year. When abreast of a trunk which appeared to be the oldest of the old, he became aware that a figure was standing behind it. Gabriel did not pause in his walk, and in another moment he accidentally kicked a loose stone. The noise was enough to disturb the motionless stranger, who started and assumed a careless position.

It was a slim girl, rather thinly clad.

"Goodnight to you," said Gabriel heartily.

"Goodnight," said the girl to Gabriel.

The voice was unexpectedly attractive; it was the low and dulcet note suggestive of romance; common in descriptions, rare in experience.

"I'll thank you to tell me if I'm in the way for Warren's Malthouse?" Gabriel resumed, primarily to gain the information, indirectly to get more of the music.

"Quite right. It's at the bottom of the hill. And do you know—" the girl hesitated and then went on again. "Do you know how late they keep open the Buck's Head Inn?" She seemed to be won by

Gabriel's heartiness, as Gabriel had been won by her modulations.

"I don't know where the Buck's Head is, or anything about it. Do you think of going there tonight?"

"Yes—" The woman again paused. There was no necessity for any continuance of speech, and the fact that she did add more seemed to proceed from an unconscious desire to show unconcern by making a remark, which is noticeable in the ingenuous when they are acting by stealth. "You are not a Weatherbury man?" she said timorously.

"I am not. I am the new shepherd—just arrived."

"Only a shepherd—and you seem almost a farmer by your ways."

"Only a shepherd," Gabriel repeated, in a dull cadence of finality. His thoughts were directed to the past, his eyes to the feet of the girl; and for the first time he saw lying there a bundle of some sort. She may have perceived the direction of his face, for she said coaxingly—

"You won't say anything in the parish about having seen me here, will you—at least, not for a day or two?"

"I won't if you wish me not to," said Oak.

"Thank you, indeed," the other replied. "I am rather poor, and I don't want people to know anything about me." Then she was silent and shivered.

"You ought to have a cloak on such a cold night," Gabriel observed. "I would advise 'ee to get indoors."

"Oh, no! Would you mind going on and leaving me? I thank you much for what you have told me."

"I will go on," he said, adding hesitatingly, "since you are not very well off, perhaps you would accept this trifle from me. It is only a shilling, but it is all I have to spare."

"Yes, I will take it," said the stranger gratefully. She extended her hand; Gabriel his. In feeling for each other's palm in the gloom before the money could be passed, a minute incident occurred which told much. Gabriel's fingers alighted on the young woman's wrist. It was beating with a throb of tragic intensity. He had frequently felt the same quick, hard beat in the femoral artery of his lambs when overdriven. It suggested a consumption too great of a vitality which, to judge from her figure and stature, was already too little.

"What is the matter?"

"Nothing."

"But there is?"

"No, no, no! Let your having seen me be a secret!"

"Very well; I will. Goodnight, again."

"Goodnight."

The young girl remained motionless by the tree, and Gabriel descended into the village of Weatherbury, or Lower Longpuddle as it was sometimes called. He fancied that he had felt himself in the penumbra of a very deep sadness when touching that slight and fragile creature. But wisdom lies in moderating mere impressions, and Gabriel endeavored to think little of this.

8. The Malthouse — The Chat — News

WARREN'S MALTHOUSE was enclosed by an old wall enwrapped with ivy, and though not much of the exterior was visible at this hour, the character and purposes of the building were clearly enough shown by its outline upon the sky. From the walls an over-

hanging thatched roof sloped up to a point in the
center, upon which rose a small wooden lantern,
fitted with louver boards on all the four sides, and
from these openings a mist was dimly perceived to
be escaping into the night air. There was no window in front; but a square hole in the door was
glazed with a single pane, through which red, comfortable rays now stretched out upon the ivied wall
in front. Voices were to be heard inside.

Oak's hand skimmed the surface of the door with
fingers extended to an Elymas-the-Sorcerer pattern,
till he found a leathern strap, which he pulled. This
lifted a wooden latch, and the door swung open.

The room inside was lighted only by the ruddy
glow from the kiln mouth, which shone over the
floor with the streaming horizon of the setting sun
and threw upward the shadows of all facial irregularities in those assembled around. The stone-
flag floor was worn into a path from the doorway
to the kiln, and into undulations everywhere. A
curved settle of unplaned oak stretched along one
side, and in a remote corner was a small bed and
bedstead, the owner and frequent occupier of which
was the maltster.

This aged man was now sitting opposite the fire,
his frosty white hair and beard overgrowing his
gnarled figure like the gray moss and lichen upon a
leafless apple tree. He wore breeches and the
laced-up shoes called anklejacks; he kept his eyes
fixed upon the fire.

Gabriel's nose was greeted by an atmosphere
laden with the sweet smell of new malt. The conversation (which seemed to have been concerning
the origin of the fire) immediately ceased, and
everyone ocularly criticized him to the degree expressed by contracting the flesh of their foreheads
and looking at him with narrowed eyelids, as if
he had been a light too strong for their sight.

Several exclaimed meditatively, after this operation
had been completed:

"Oh, 'tis the new shepherd, 'a b'lieve."

"We thought we heard a hand pawing about the
door for the bobbin, but weren't sure 'twere not a
dead leaf blowed across," said another. "Come in,
shepherd; sure ye be welcome, though we don't
know yer name."

"Gabriel Oak, that's my name, neighbors."

The ancient maltster sitting in the midst turned
at this—his turning being as the turning of a rusty
crane.

"That's never Gable Oak's grandson over at Norcombe—never!" he said, as a formula expressive of
surprise, which nobody was supposed to take literally.

"My father and my grandfather were old men of
the name of Gabriel," said the shepherd placidly.

"Thought I knowed the man's face as I seed him
on the rick!—thought I did! And where be ye trading o't to now, shepherd?"

"I'm thinking of biding here," said Mr. Oak.

"Knowed yer grandfather for years and years!"
continued the maltster, the words coming forth of
their own accord as if the momentum previously
imparted had been sufficient.

"Ah—and did you!"

"Knowed yer grandmother."

"And her too!"

"Likewise knowed yer father when he was a
child. Why, my boy Jacob there and your father
were sworn brothers—that they were sure—weren't
ye, Jacob?"

"Aye, sure," said his son, a young man about
sixty-five, with a semibald head and one tooth in
the left center of his upper jaw, which made much
of itself by standing prominent, like a milestone in
a bank. "But 'twas Joe had most to do with him.
However, my son William must have knowed the

very man afore us—didn't ye, Billy, afore ye left
Norcombe?"

"No, 'twas Andrew," said Jacob's son Billy, a
child of forty or thereabouts, who manifested the
peculiarity of possessing a cheerful soul in a gloomy
body, and whose whiskers were assuming a chin-
chilla shade here and there.

"I can mind Andrew," said Oak, "as being a man
in the place when I was quite a child."

"Aye—the other day I and my youngest daughter,
Liddy, were over at my grandson's christening," continued Billy. "We were talking about this very
family, and 'twas only last Purification Day in this
very world, when the use-money is gied away to the
second-best poorfolk, you know, shepherd, and I
can mind the day because they all had to traipse
up to the vestry—yes, this very man's family."

"Come, shepherd, and drink. 'Tis gape and swaller with us—a drap of sommit, but not of much account," said the maltster, removing from the fire his
eyes, which were vermillion-red and bleared by
gazing into it for so many years. "Take up the
God-forgive-me, Jacob. See if 'tis warm, Jacob."

Jacob stooped to the God-forgive-me, which was a
two-handled tall mug standing in the ashes, cracked
and charred with heat: it was rather furred with
extraneous matter about the outside, especially
in the crevices of the handles, the innermost curves
of which may not have seen daylight for several
years by reason of this encrustation thereon—
formed of ashes accidentally wetted with cider and
baked hard; but to the mind of any sensible drinker
the cup was no worse for that, being incontestably
clean on the inside and about the rim. It may be
observed that such a class of mug is called a God-
forgive-me in Weatherbury and its vicinity for uncertain reasons; probably because its size makes any
given toper feel ashamed of himself when he sees its
bottom in drinking it empty.

Jacob, on receiving the order to see if the liquor was warm enough, placidly dipped his forefinger into it by way of thermometer, and having pronounced it nearly of the proper degree, raised the cup and very civilly attempted to dust some of the ashes from the bottom with the skirt of his smock-frock, because Shepherd Oak was a stranger.

"A clane cup for the shepherd," said the maltster commandingly.

"No—not at all," said Gabriel, in a reproving tone of considerateness. "I never fuss about dirt in its pure state, and when I know what sort it is." Taking the mug he drank an inch or more from the depth of its contents, and duly passed it to the next man. "I wouldn't think of giving such trouble to neighbors in washing up when there's so much work to be done in the world already," continued Oak in a moister tone, after recovering from the stoppage of breath which is occasioned by pulls at large mugs.

"A right sensible man," said Jacob.

"True, true; it can't be gainsaid!" observed a brisk young man—Mark Clark by name, a genial and pleasant gentleman, whom to meet anywhere in your travels was to know, to know was to drink with, and to drink with was, unfortunately, to pay for.

"And here's a mouthful of bread and bacon that mis'ess have sent, shepherd. The cider will go down better with a bit of victuals. Don't ye chaw quite close, shepherd, for I let the bacon fall in the road outside as I was bringing it along, and may be 'tis rather gritty. There, 'tis clane dirt; and we all know what that is, as you say, and you bain't a particular man we see, shepherd."

"True, true—not at all," said the friendly Oak.

"Don't let your teeth quite meet, and you won't feel the sandiness at all. Ah! 'tis wonderful what can be done by contrivance!"

"My own mind exactly, neighbor."

"Ah, he's his grandfer's own grandson!—his grandfer were just such a nice unparticular man!" said the maltster.

"Drink, Henry Fray—drink," magnanimously said Jan Coggan, a person who held Saint-Simonian notions of share and share alike where liquor was concerned, as the vessel showed signs of approaching him in its gradual revolution among them.

Having at this moment reached the end of a wistful gaze into mid-air, Henry did not refuse. He was a man of more than middle age, with eyebrows high up in his forehead, who laid it down that the law of the world was bad, with a long-suffering look through his listeners at the world alluded to, as it presented itself to his imagination. He always signed his name "Henery"—strenuously insisting upon that spelling, and if any passing schoolmaster ventured to remark that the second "e" was superfluous and old-fashioned, he received the reply that "H-e-n-e-r-y" was the name he was christened and the name he would stick to—in the tone of one to whom orthographical differences were matters which had a great deal to do with personal character.

Mr. Jan Coggan, who had passed the cup to Henery, was a crimson man with a spacious countenance and private glimmer in his eye, whose name had appeared on the marriage register of Weatherbury and neighboring parishes as best man and chief witness in countless unions of the previous twenty years; he also very frequently filled the post of head godfather in baptisms of the subtly jovial kind.

"Come, Mark Clark—come. There's plenty more in the barrel," said Jan.

"Aye—that I will; 'tis my only doctor," replied Mr. Clark, who, twenty years younger than Jan Coggan, revolved in the same orbit. He secreted mirth on all occasions for special discharge at popular parties.

"Why, Joseph Poorgrass, ye han't had a drop!" said Mr. Coggan to a self-conscious man in the background, thrusting the cup toward him.

"Such a modest man as he is!" said Jacob Small-bury. "Why, ye've hardly had strength of eye enough to look in our young mis'ess's face, so I hear, Joseph?"

All looked at Joseph Poorgrass with pitying reproach.

"No—I've hardly looked at her at all," simpered Joseph, reducing his body smaller whilst talking, apparently from a meek sense of undue prominence. "And when I seed her, 'twas nothing but blushes with me!"

"Poor feller," said Mr. Clark.

"'Tis a curious nature for a man," said Jan Coggan.

"Yes," continued Joseph Poorgrass—his shyness, which was so painful as a defect, filling him with a mild complacency now that it was regarded as an interesting study. "'Twere blush, blush, blush with me every minute of the time, when she was speaking to me."

"I believe ye, Joseph Poorgrass, for we all know ye to be a very bashful man."

"'Tis a' awkward gift for a man, poor soul," said the maltster. "And ye have suffered from it a long time, we know."

"Aye, ever since I was a boy. Yes—mother was concerned to her heart about it—yes. But 'twas all for nought."

"Did ye ever go into the world to try and stop it, Joseph Poorgrass?"

"Oh aye, tried all sorts o' company. They took me to Greenhill Fair, and into a great gay jerry-go-nimble show, where there were womenfolk riding round—standing upon horses, with hardly anything on but their smocks; but it didn't cure me a morsel. And then I was put errandman at the Women's Skittle Alley at the back of the Tailor's Arms in Casterbridge. 'Twas a horrible sinful situation, and a very curious place for a good man. I had to stand and look ba'dy people in the face from morning till night; but 'twas no use—I was just as bad as ever after all. Blushes hev been in the family for generations. There, 'tis a happy providence that I be no worse."

"True," said Jacob Smallbury, deepening his thoughts to a profounder view of the subject. " 'Tis a thought to look at, that ye might have been worse; but even as you be, 'tis a very bad affliction for 'ee, Joseph. For ye see, shepherd, though 'tis very well for a woman, dang it all, 'tis awkward for a man like him, poor feller!"

" 'Tis—'tis," said Gabriel, recovering from a meditation. "Yes, very awkward for the man."

"Aye, and he's very timid, too," observed Jan Coggan. "Once he had been working late at Yalbury Bottom, and had had a drap of drink, and lost his way as he was coming home-along through Yalbury Wood, didn't ye, Master Poorgrass?"

"No, no, no; not that story!" expostulated the modest man, forcing a laugh to bury his concern.

"—And so 'a lost himself quite," continued Mr. Coggan, with an impassive face, implying that a true narrative, like time and tide, must run its course and would respect no man. "And as he was coming along in the middle of the night, much afeared, and not able to find his way out of the trees nohow, 'a cried out, 'Man-a-lost! man-a-lost!' A owl in a tree happened to be crying 'Whoo-whoo-whoo!' as owls do, you know, shepherd" (Gabriel nodded), "and Joseph, all in a tremble, said, 'Joseph Poorgrass, of Weatherbury, sir!' "

"No, no, now—that's too much!" said the timid man, becoming a man of brazen courage all of a sudden. "I didn't say *sir*. I'll take my oath I didn't say 'Joseph Poorgrass o' Weatherbury, sir.' No, no; what's right is right, and I never said sir to the bird, knowing very well that no man of a gentleman's rank would be hollering there at that time o' night. 'Joseph Poorgrass of Weatherbury,' that's every word I said, and I shouldn't ha' said that if 't hadn't been for Keeper Day's metheglin. . . . There, 'twas a merciful thing it ended where it did."

The question of which was right being tacitly waived by the company, Jan went on meditatively:

"And he's the fearfullest man, bain't ye, Joseph? Aye, another time ye were lost by Lambing-Down Gate, weren't ye, Joseph?"

"I was," replied Poorgrass, as if there were some conditions too serious even for modesty to remember itself under, this being one.

"Yes; that were the middle of the night, too. The gate would not open, try how he would, and knowing there was the Devil's hand in it, he kneeled down."

"Aye," said Joseph, acquiring confidence from the warmth of the fire, the cider, and a perception of the narrative capabilities of the experience alluded to. "My heart died within me, that time; but I kneeled down and said the Lord's Prayer, and then the Belief right through, and then the Ten Commandments, in earnest prayer. But no, the gate wouldn't open; and then I went on with Dearly Beloved Brethren, and, thinks I, this makes four, and 'tis all I know out of book, and if this don't do it nothing will, and I'm a lost man. Well, when I got to Saying After Me, I rose from my knees and found the gate would open—yes, neighbors, the gate opened the same as ever."

A meditation on the obvious inference was indulged in by all, and during its continuance each directed his vision into the ashpit, which glowed like a desert in the tropics under a vertical sun, shaping their eyes long and liny, partly because of the light, partly from the depth of the subject discussed.

Gabriel broke the silence. "What sort of a place is this to live at, and what sort of a mis'ess is she to work under?" Gabriel's bosom thrilled gently as he thus slipped under the notice of the assembly the innermost subject of his heart.

"We d' know little of her—nothing. She only showed herself a few days ago. Her uncle was took bad, and the doctor was called with his worldwide skill; but he couldn't save the man. As I take it, she's going to keep on the farm."

"That's about the shape o't, 'a b'lieve," said Jan Coggan. "Aye, 'tis a very good family. I'd as soon be under 'em as under one here and there. Her uncle was a very fair sort of man. Did ye know en, shepherd—a bachelor-man?"

"Not at all."

"I used to go to his house a-courting my first wife, Charlotte, who was his dairymaid. Well, a very good-hearted man were Farmer Everdene, and I being a respectable young fellow was allowed to call and see her and drink as much ale as I liked, but not to carry away any—outside my skin I mane, of course."

"Aye, aye, Jan Coggan; we know yer maning."

"And so you see 'twas beautiful ale, and I wished to value his kindness as much as I could, and not to be so ill-mannered as to drink only a thimble-ful, which would have been insulting the man's generosity—"

"True, Master Coggan, 'twould so," corroborated Mark Clark.

"—And so I used to eat a lot of salt fish afore going, and then by the time I got there I were as dry as a lime-basket—so thorough dry that that ale would slip down—ah, 'twould slip down sweet! Happy times! Heavenly times! Such lovely drunks as I used to have at that house! You can mind, Jacob? You used to go wi' me sometimes."

"I can—I can," said Jacob. "That one, too, that we had at Buck's Head on a White Monday was a pretty tipple."

" 'Twas. But for a wet of the better class, that brought you no nearer to the horned man than you were afore you begun, there was none like those in Farmer Everdene's kitchen. Not a single damn allowed; no, not a bare poor one, even at the most cheerful moment when all were blindest, though the good old word of sin thrown in here and there at such times is a great relief to a merry soul."

"True," said the maltster. "Nater requires her swearing at the regular times, or she's not herself; and unholy exclamations is a necessity of life."

"But Charlotte," continued Coggan—"not a word of the sort would Charlotte allow, nor the smallest item of taking in vain. . . . Aye, poor Charlotte, I wonder if she had the good fortune to get into Heaven when 'a died! But 'a was never much in luck's way and perhaps 'a went downward after all, poor soul."

"And did any of you know Miss Everdene's father and mother?" inquired the shepherd, who found some difficulty in keeping the conversation in the desired channel.

"I knew them a little," said Jacob Smallbury, "but they were townsfolk, and didn't live here. They've been dead for years. Father, what sort of people were mis'ess' father and mother?"

"Well," said the maltster, "he wasn't much to look at; but she was a lovely woman. He was fond enough of her as his sweetheart."

"Used to kiss her scores and long-hundreds o' times, so 'twas said," observed Coggan.

"He was very proud of her, too, when they were married, as I've been told," said the maltster.

"Aye," said Coggan. "He admired her so much that he used to light the candle three times a night to look at her."

"Boundless love; I shouldn't have supposed it in the universe!" murmured Joseph Poorgrass, who habitually spoke on a large scale in his moral reflections.

"Well, to be sure," said Gabriel.

"Oh, 'tis true enough. I knowed the man and woman both well. Levi Everdene—that was the man's name, sure. 'Man,' saith I in my hurry, but he were of a higher circle of life than that—'a was a gentleman tailor really, worth scores of pounds. And he became a very celebrated bankrupt two or three times."

"Oh, I thought he was quite a common man!" said Joseph.

"Oh, no, no! That man failed for heaps of money; hundreds in gold and silver."

The maltster being rather short of breath, Mr. Coggan, after absently scrutinizing a coal which had fallen among the ashes, took up the narrative, with a private twirl of his eye:

"Well, now, you'd hardly believe it, but that man —our Miss Everdene's father—was one of the ficklest husbands alive, after a while. Understand, 'a didn't want to be fickle, but he couldn't help it. The poor feller were faithful and true enough to her in his wish, but his heart would rove, do what he would. He spoke to me in real tribulation about it once. 'Coggan,' he said, 'I could never wish for a handsomer woman than I've got, but feeling she's ticketed as my lawful wife, I can't help my wicked heart wandering, do what I will.' But at last I believe he cured it by making her take off her wedding ring and calling her by her maiden name as they sat together after the shop was shut, and so 'a would get to fancy she was only his sweetheart, and not married to him at all. And as soon as he could thoroughly fancy he was doing wrong and committing the seventh, 'a got to like her as well as ever, and they lived on a perfect picture of mutel love."

"Well, 'twas a most ungodly remedy," murmured Joseph Poorgrass; "but we ought to feel deep cheerfulness that a happy Providence kept it from being any worse. You see, he might have gone the bad road and given his eyes to unlawfulness entirely—yes, gross unlawfulness, so to say it."

"You see," said Billy Smallbury, "the man's will was to do right, sure enough, but his heart didn't chime in."

"He got so much better that he was quite godly in his later years, wasn't he, Jan?" said Joseph Poorgrass. "He got himself confirmed over again in a more serious way, and took to saying 'Amen' almost as loud as the clerk, and he liked to copy comforting verses from the tombstones. He used, too, to hold the moneyplate at Let Your Light So Shine, and stand godfather to poor little come-by-chance children; and he kept a missionary box upon his table to nab folks unawares when they called; yes, and he would box the charity boys' ears, if they laughed in church, till they could hardly stand upright, and do other deeds of piety natural to the saintly inclined."

"Aye, at that time he thought of nothing but high things," added Billy Smallbury. "One day Parson Thirdly met him and said, 'Good morning, Mister Everdene; 'tis a fine day!' 'Amen,' said Everdene, quite absentlike, thinking only of religion when he seed a parson. Yes, he was a very Christian man."

"Their daughter was not at all a pretty chiel at that time," said Henery Fray. "Never should have thought she'd have growed up such a handsome body as she is."

"'Tis to be hoped her temper is as good as her face."

"Well, yes; but the baily will have most to do with the business and ourselves. Ah!" Henery gazed into the ashpit and smiled volumes of ironical knowledge.

"A queer Christian, like the Devil's head in a cowl,[1] as the saying is," volunteered Mark Clark.

"He is," said Henery, implying that irony must cease at a certain point. "Between we two, man and man, I believe that man would as soon tell a lie Sundays as working days—that I do so."

"Good faith, you do talk!" said Gabriel.

"True enough," said the man of bitter moods, looking round upon the company with the antithetic laughter that comes from a keener appreciation of the miseries of life than ordinary men are capable of. "Ah, there's people of one sort, and people of another, but that man—bless your souls!"

Gabriel thought fit to change the subject. "You must be a very aged man, malter, to have sons growed up so old and ancient," he remarked.

"Father's so old that 'a can't mind his age, can ye, father?" interposed Jacob. "And he's growed terrible crooked, too, lately," Jacob continued, surveying his father's figure, which was rather more bowed than his own. "Really, one may say that father there is three-double."

"Crooked folk will last a long while," said the maltster, grimly, and not in the best humor.

"Shepherd would like to hear the pedigree of yer life, father—wouldn't ye, shepherd?"

"Aye, that I should," said Gabriel, with the heartiness of a man who had longed to hear it for several months. "What may your age be, malter?"

The maltster cleared his throat in an exag-

---

[1] This phrase is a conjectural emendation of the unintelligible expression, "as the Devil said to the Owl," used by the natives.

gerated form for emphasis, and elongating his gaze
to the remotest point of the ashpit, said, in the slow
speech justifiable when the importance of a subject
is so generally felt that any mannerism must be tol-
erated in getting at it, "Well, I don't mind the year
I were born in, but perhaps I can reckon up the
places I've lived at, and so get it that way. I bode at
Upper Longpuddle across there" (nodding to the
north) "till I were eleven. I bode seven at Kingsbere" (nodding to the east) "where I took to malting. I went therefrom to Norcombe, and malted
there two-and-twenty years, and two-and-twenty
years I was there turnip hoeing and harvesting. Ah,
I knowed that old place, Norcombe, years afore you
were thought of, Master Oak" (Oak smiled sin-
cere belief in the fact). "Then I malted at Durnover four year, and four year turnip hoeing; and I
was fourteen times eleven months at Millpond St.
Jude's" (nodding northwest-by-north). "Old Twills
wouldn't hire me for more than eleven months at
a time, to keep me from being chargeable to the
parish if so be I was disabled. Then I was
three year at Mellstock, and I've been here one-
and-thirty year come Candlemas. How much is
that?"

"Hundred and seventeen," chuckled another old
gentleman, given to mental arithmetic and little
conversation, who had hitherto sat unobserved in
a corner.

"Well, then, that's my age," said the maltster emphatically.

"Oh, no, father!" said Jacob. "Your turnip hoeing were in the summer and your malting in the
winter of the same years, and ye don't ought
to count both halves, father."

"Chok' it all! I lived through the summers, didn't
I? That's my question. I suppose ye'll say next I be
no age at all to speak of?"

"Sure we shan't," said Gabriel soothingly.

"Ye be a very old aged person, malter," attested Jan Coggan, also soothingly. "We all know that, and ye must have a wonderful talented constitution to be able to live so long, mustn't he, neighbors?"

"True, true; ye must, malter, wonderful," said the meeting unanimously.

The maltster, being now pacified, was even generous enough to voluntarily disparage in a slight degree the virtue of having lived a great many years, by mentioning that the cup they were drinking out of was three years older than he.

While the cup was being examined, the end of Gabriel Oak's flute became visible over his smock-frock pocket, and Henery Fray exclaimed, "Surely, shepherd, I seed you blowing into a great flute by now at Casterbridge?"

"You did," said Gabriel, blushing faintly. "I've been in great trouble, neighbors, and was driven to it. I used not to be so poor as I be now."

"Never mind, heart!" said Mark Clark. "You should take it carelesslike, shepherd, and your time will come. But we could thank ye for a tune, if ye bain't too tired?"

"Neither drum nor trumpet have I heard since Christmas," said Jan Coggan. "Come, raise a tune, Master Oak!"

"That I will," said Gabriel, pulling out his flute and putting it together. "A poor tool, neighbors; but such as I can do ye shall have and welcome."

Oak then struck up "Jockey to the Fair," and played that sparkling melody three times through, accenting the notes in the third round in a most artistic and lively manner by bending his body in small jerks and tapping with his foot to beat time.

"He can blow the flute very well—that 'a can," said a young married man, who having no individuality worth mentioning was known as "Susan

Tall's husband." He continued, "I'd as lief as not be able to blow into a flute as well as that."

"He's a clever man, and 'tis a true comfort for us to have such a shepherd," murmured Joseph Poorgrass, in a soft cadence. "We ought to feel full o' thanksgiving that he's not a player of ba'dy songs instead of these merry tunes; for 'twould have been just as easy for God to have made the shepherd a loose low man—a man of iniquity, so to speak it—as what he is. Yes, for our wives' and daughters' sakes we should feel real thanksgiving."

"True, true—real thanksgiving!" dashed in Mark Clark conclusively, not feeling it to be of any consequence to his opinion that he had only heard about a word and three-quarters of what Joseph had said.

"Yes," added Joseph, beginning to feel like a man in the Bible; "for evil do thrive so in these times that ye may be as much deceived in the clanest-shaved and whitest-shirted man as in the raggedest tramp upon the turnpike, if I may term it so."

"Aye, I can mind yer face now, shepherd," said Henery Fray, criticizing Gabriel with misty eyes as he entered upon his second tune. "Yes—now I see 'ee blowing into the flute I know 'ee to be the same man I see play at Casterbridge, for yer mouth were scrimped up and yer eyes a-staring out like a strangled man's—just as they be now."

"'Tis a pity that playing the flute should make a man look such a scarecrow," observed Mr. Mark Clark, with additional criticism of Gabriel's countenance, the latter person jerking out, with the ghastly grimace required by the instrument, the chorus of "Dame Durden":

'Twas Moll' and Bet', and Doll and Kate',
    And Dor'-othy Drag'gle Tail'.

"I hope you don't mind that young man's bad

manners in naming your features?" whispered Joseph to Gabriel.

"Not at all," said Mr. Oak.

"For by nature ye be a very handsome man, shepherd," continued Joseph Poorgrass with winning suavity.

"Aye, that ye be, shepherd," said the company.

"Thank you very much," said Oak, in the modest tone good manners demanded, thinking, however, that he would never let Bathsheba see him playing the flute; in this resolve showing a discretion equal to that related of its sagacious inventress, the divine Minerva herself.

"Ah, when I and my wife were married at Norcombe Church," said the old maltster, not pleased at finding himself left out of the subject, "we were called the handsomest couple in the neighborhood —everybody said so."

"Danged if ye bain't altered now, malter," said a voice with the vigor natural to the enunciation of a remarkably evident truism. It came from the old man in the background, whose offensiveness and spiteful ways were barely atoned for by the occasional chuckle he contributed to general laughs.

"Oh, no, no," said Gabriel.

"Don't ye play no more, shepherd," said Susan Tall's husband, the young married man who had spoken once before. "I must be moving, and when there's tunes going on I seem as if hung in wires. If I thought after I'd left that music was still playing, and I not there, I should be quite melancholy-like."

"What's yer hurry then, Laban?" inquired Coggan. "You used to bide as late as the latest."

"Well, ye see, neighbors, I was lately married to a woman, and she's my vocation now, and so ye see —" The young man halted lamely.

"New lords new laws, as the saying is, I suppose," remarked Coggan.

"Aye, 'a b'lieve—ha, ha!" said Susan Tall's husband, in a tone intended to imply his habitual reception of jokes without minding them at all. The young man then wished them goodnight and withdrew.

Henery Fray was the first to follow. Then Gabriel arose and went off with Jan Coggan, who had offered him a lodging. A few minutes later, when the remaining ones were on their legs and about to depart, Fray came back again in a hurry. Flourishing his finger ominously he threw a gaze teeming with tidings just where his eye alighted by accident, which happened to be in Joseph Poorgrass' face.

"Oh—what's the matter, what's the matter, Henery?" said Joseph, starting back.

"What's a-brewing, Henery?" asked Jacob and Mark Clark.

"Baily Pennyways—Baily Pennyways—I said so; yes, I said so!"

"What, found out stealing anything?"

"Stealing it is. The news is, that after Miss Everdene got home she went out again to see all was safe, as she usually do, and coming in found Baily Pennyways creeping down the granary steps with half a bushel of barley. She fleed at him like a cat—never such a tomboy as she is—of course I speak with closed doors?"

"You do—you do, Henery."

"She fleed at him, and, to cut a long story short, he owned to having carried off five sack altogether, upon her promising not to persecute him. Well, he's turned out neck and crop, and my question is, who's going to be baily now?"

The question was such a profound one that Henery was obliged to drink there and then from the large cup till the bottom was distinctly visible inside. Before he had replaced it on the table, in came the young man, Susan Tall's husband, in a still greater hurry.

"Have ye heard the news that's all over parish?"

"About Baily Pennyways?"

"But besides that?"

"No—not a morsel of it!" they replied, looking into the very midst of Laban Tall as if to meet his words halfway down his throat.

"What a night of horrors!" murmured Joseph Poorgrass, waving his hands spasmodically. "I've had the newsbell ringing in my left ear quite bad enough for a murder, and I've seen a magpie all alone!"

"Fanny Robin—Miss Everdene's youngest servant—can't be found. They've been wanting to lock up the door these two hours, but she isn't come in. And they don't know what to do about going to bed for fear of locking her out. They wouldn't be so concerned if she hadn't been noticed in such low spirits these last few days, and Maryann d' think the beginning of a crowner's inquest has happened to the poor girl."

"Oh—'tis burned—'tis burned!" came from Joseph Poorgrass' dry lips.

"No—'tis drowned!" said Tall.

"Or 'tis her father's razor!" suggested Billy Smallbury with a vivid sense of detail.

"Well—Miss Everdene wants to speak to one or two of us before we go to bed. What with this trouble about the baily, and now about the girl, mis'ess is almost wild."

They all hastened up the lane to the farmhouse, excepting the old maltster, whom neither news, fire, rain, nor thunder could draw from his hole. There, as the others' footsteps died away, he sat down again, and continued gazing as usual into the furnace with his red, bleared eyes.

From the bedroom window above their heads

Bathsheba's head and shoulders, robed in mystic white, were dimly seen extended into the air.

"Are any of my men among you?" she said anxiously.

"Yes, ma'am, several," said Susan Tall's husband.

"Tomorrow morning I wish two or three of you to make inquiries in the villages round if they have seen such a person as Fanny Robin. Do it quietly; there is no reason for alarm as yet. She must have left whilst we were all at the fire."

"I beg your pardon, but had she any young man courting her in the parish, ma'am?" asked Jacob Smallbury.

"I don't know," said Bathsheba.

"I've never heard of any such thing, ma'am," said two or three.

"It is hardly likely, either," continued Bathsheba. "For any lover of hers might have come to the house if he had been a respectable lad. The most mysterious matter connected with her absence —indeed, the only thing which gives me serious alarm—is that she was seen to go out of the house by Maryann with only her indoor working gown on—not even a bonnet."

"And you mean, ma'am, excusing my words, that a young woman would hardly go to see her young man without dressing up," said Jacob, turning his mental vision upon past experiences. "That's true —she would not, ma'am."

"She had, I think, a bundle, though I couldn't see very well," said a female voice from another window, which seemed that of Maryann. "But she had no young man about here. Hers lives in Casterbridge, and I believe he's a soldier."

"Do you know his name?" Bathsheba said.

"No, mistress; she was very close about it."

"Perhaps I might be able to find out if I went to Casterbridge barracks," said William Smallbury.

"Very well; if she doesn't return tomorrow, mind you go there and try to discover which man it is, and see him. I feel more responsible than I should if she had had any friends or relations alive. I do hope she has come to no harm through a man of that kind. . . . And then there's this disgraceful affair of the bailiff—but I can't speak of him now."

Bathsheba had so many reasons for uneasiness that it seemed she did not think it worthwhile to dwell upon any particular one. "Do as I told you, then," she said in conclusion, closing the casement.

"Aye, aye, mistress; we will," they replied, and moved away.

That night at Coggan's Gabriel Oak, beneath the screen of closed eyelids, was busy with fancies, and full of movement, like a river flowing rapidly under its ice. Night had always been the time at which he saw Bathsheba most vividly, and through the slow hours of shadow he tenderly regarded her image now. It is rarely that the pleasures of the imagination will compensate for the pain of sleeplessness, but they possibly did with Oak tonight, for the delight of merely seeing her effaced for the time his perception of the great difference between seeing and possessing.

He also thought of plans for fetching his few utensils and books from Norcombe. *The Young Man's Best Companion*, *The Farrier's Sure Guide*, *The Veterinary Surgeon*, *Paradise Lost*, *The Pilgrim's Progress*, *Robinson Crusoe*, Ash's *Dictionary*, and Walkingame's *Arithmetic* constituted his library; and though a limited series, it was one from which he had acquired more sound information by diligent perusal than many a man of opportunities has done from a furlong of laden shelves.

9.   The Homestead — A Visitor
— Half-confidences

BY DAYLIGHT, the bower of Oak's newfound mistress, Bathsheba Everdene, presented itself as a hoary building, of the early stage of Classic Renaissance as regards its architecture, and of a proportion which told at a glance that, as is so frequently the case, it had once been the manorial hall upon a small estate around it, now altogether effaced as a distinct property, and merged in the vast tract of a nonresident landlord, which comprised several such modest demesnes.

Fluted pilasters, worked from the solid stone, decorated its front, and above the roof the chimneys were paneled or columnar, some coped gables with finials and like features still retaining traces of their Gothic extraction. Soft brown mosses, like faded velveteen, formed cushions upon the stone tiling, and tufts of the houseleek or sengreen sprouted from the eaves of the low surrounding buildings. A gravel walk leading from the door to the road in front was encrusted at the sides with more moss—here it was a silver-green variety, the nutbrown of the gravel being visible to the width of only a foot or two in the center. This circumstance, and the generally sleepy air of the whole prospect here, together with the animated and contrasting state of the reverse façade, suggested to the imagination that on the adaptation of the building

for farming purposes the vital principle of the
house had turned round inside its body to face the
other way. Reversals of this kind, strange deformities, tremendous paralyses, are often seen to
be inflicted by trade upon edifices—either individual or in the aggregate as streets and towns
—which were originally planned for pleasure
alone.

Lively voices were heard this morning in the upper rooms, the main staircase to which was of hard
oak, the balusters, heavy as bedposts, being turned
and molded in the quaint fashion of their century,
the handrail as stout as a parapet top, and the stairs
themselves continually twisting round like a person trying to look over his shoulder. Going up, the
floors above were found to have a very irregular
surface, rising to ridges, sinking into valleys; and
being just then uncarpeted, the face of the boards
was seen to be eaten into innumerable vermicula-
tions. Every window replied by a clang to the opening and shutting of every door, a tremble followed
every bustling movement, and a creak accompanied
a walker about the house, like a spirit, wherever he
went.

In the room from which the conversation proceeded Bathsheba and her servant-companion,
Liddy Smallbury, were to be discovered sitting
upon the floor, and sorting a complication of papers, books, bottles, and rubbish spread out thereon
—remnants from the household stores of the late
occupier. Liddy, the maltster's great-granddaughter,
was about Bathsheba's equal in age, and her face
was a prominent advertisement of the lighthearted
English country girl. The beauty her features
might have lacked in form was amply made up for
by perfection of hue, which at this wintertime was
the softened ruddiness on a surface of high rotun-
dity that we meet with in a Terburg or a Gerard
Douw; and, like the presentations of those great

colorists, it was a face which kept well back from the boundary between comeliness and the ideal. Though elastic in nature she was less daring than Bathsheba, and occasionally showed some earnestness, which consisted half of genuine feeling, and half of mannerliness superadded by way of duty.

Through a partly opened door the noise of a scrubbing brush led up to the charwoman, Maryann Money, a person who for a face had a circular disk, furrowed less by age than by long gazes of perplexity at distant objects. To think of her was to get good-humored; to speak of her was to raise the image of a dried Normandy pippin.

"Stop your scrubbing a moment," said Bathsheba through the door to her. "I hear something."

Maryann suspended the brush.

The tramp of a horse was apparent, approaching the front of the building. The paces slackened, turned in at the wicket, and, what was most unusual, came up the mossy path close to the door. The door was tapped with the end of a crop or stick.

"What impertinence!" said Liddy, in a low voice. "To ride up the footpath like that! Why didn't he stop at the gate? Lord! 'tis a gentleman! I see the top of his hat."

"Be quiet!" said Bathsheba.

The further expression of Liddy's concern was continued by aspect instead of narrative.

"Why doesn't Mrs. Coggan go to the door?" Bathsheba continued.

Rat-tat-tat-tat resounded more decisively from Bathsheba's oak.

"Maryann, you go!" said she, fluttering under the onset of a crowd of romantic possibilities.

"Oh, ma'am—see, here's a mess!"

The argument was unanswerable after a glance at Maryann.

"Liddy—you must," said Bathsheba.

Liddy held up her hands and arms, coated with dust from the rubbish they were sorting, and looked imploringly at her mistress.

"There—Mrs. Coggan is going!" said Bathsheba, exhaling her relief in the form of a long breath which had lain in her bosom a minute or more.

The door opened, and a deep voice said—

"Is Miss Everdene at home?"

"I'll see, sir," said Mrs. Coggan, and in a minute appeared in the room.

"Dear, what a thirtover place this world is!" continued Mrs. Coggan (a wholesome-looking lady who had a voice for each class of remark according to the emotion involved; who could toss a pancake or twirl a mop with the accuracy of pure mathematics, and who at this moment showed hands shaggy with fragments of dough and arms encrusted with flour). "I am never up to my elbows, Miss, in making a pudding but one of two things do happen—either my nose must needs begin tickling, and I can't live without scratching it, or somebody knocks at the door. Here's Mr. Boldwood wanting to see you, Miss Everdene."

A woman's dress being a part of her countenance, and any disorder in the one being of the same nature with a malformation or wound in the other, Bathsheba said at once—

"I can't see him in this state. Whatever shall I do?"

Not-at-homes were hardly naturalized in Weatherbury farmhouses, so Liddy suggested—"Say you're a fright with dust and can't come down."

"Yes—that sounds very well," said Mrs. Coggan critically.

"Say I can't see him—that will do."

Mrs. Coggan went downstairs and returned the answer as requested, adding, however, on her own responsibility, "Miss is dusting bottles, sir, and is quite a object—that's why 'tis."

"Oh, very well," said the deep voice indifferently. "All I wanted to ask was if anything had been heard of Fanny Robin."

"Nothing, sir—but we may know tonight. William Smallbury is gone to Casterbridge, where her young man lives, as is supposed, and the other men be inquiring about everywhere."

The horse's tramp then recommenced and retreated, and the door closed.

"Who is Mr. Boldwood?" said Bathsheba.

"A gentleman-farmer at Little Weatherbury."

"Married?"

"No, miss."

"How old is he?"

"Forty, I should say—very handsome—rather stern-looking—and rich."

"What a bother this dusting is! I am always in some unfortunate plight or other," Bathsheba said complainingly. "Why should he inquire about Fanny?"

"Oh, because, as she had no friends in her childhood, he took her and put her to school, and got her her place here under your uncle. He's a very kind man that way, but Lord—there!"

"What?"

"Never was such a hopeless man for a woman! He's been courted by sixes and sevens—all the girls, gentle and simple, for miles round, have tried him. Jane Perkins worked at him for two months like a slave, and the two Miss Taylors spent a year upon him, and he cost Farmer Ives's daughter nights of tears and twenty pounds' worth of new clothes; but Lord—the money might as well have been thrown out of the window."

A little boy came up at this moment and looked in upon them. This child was one of the Coggans, who, with the Smallburys, were as common among

the families of this district as the Avons and Der-
wents among our rivers. He always had a loosened
tooth or a cut finger to show to particular friends,
which he did with an air of being thereby elevated
above the common herd of afflictionless humanity
—to which exhibition people were expected to say
"Poor child!" with a dash of congratulation as well
as pity.

"I've got a pen-nee!" said Master Coggan in a
scanning measure.

"Well—who gave it you, Teddy?" said Liddy.

"Mis-terr Bold-wood! He gave it to me for opening the gate."

"What did he say?"

"He said, 'Where are you going, my little man?'
and I said, 'To Miss Everdene's, please,' and he
said, 'She is a staid woman, isn't she, my little man?'
and I said, 'Yes.' "

"You naughty child! What did you say that for?"

" 'Cause he gave me the penny!"

"What a pucker everything is in!" said Bathsheba discontentedly, when the child had gone.
"Get away, Maryann, or go on with your scrubbing,
or do something! You ought to be married by this
time, and not here troubling me!"

"Aye, mistress—so I did. But what between the
poor men I won't have and the rich men who won't
have me, I stand as a pelican in the wilderness!"

"Did anybody ever want to marry you, miss?"
Liddy ventured to ask when they were again alone.
"Lots of 'em, I daresay?"

Bathsheba paused, as if about to refuse a reply,
but the temptation to say yes, since it really was in
her power, was irresistible by aspiring virginity,
in spite of her spleen at having been published as
old.

"A man wanted to once," she said, in a highly experienced tone, and the image of Gabriel Oak, as
the farmer, rose before her.

"How nice it must seem!" said Liddy, with the
fixed features of mental realization. "And you
wouldn't have him?"

"He wasn't quite good enough for me."

"How sweet to be able to disdain, when most of
us are glad to say, 'Thank you!' I seem to hear it.
'No, sir—I'm your better,' or 'Kiss my foot, sir; my
face is for mouths of consequence.' And did you
love him, miss?"

"Oh, no. But I rather liked him."

"Do you now?"

"Of course not—what footsteps are those I
hear?"

Liddy looked from a back window into the court-
yard behind, which was now getting low-toned
and dim with the earliest films of night. A crooked
file of men was approaching the back door. The
whole string of trailing individuals advanced in the
completest balance of intention, like the remarkable creatures known as Chain Salpæ, which, distinctly organized in other respects, have one will
common to a whole family. Some were, as usual, in
snow-white smock-frocks of Russia duck, and some
in whitey-brown ones of drabbet—marked on the
wrists, breasts, backs, and sleeves with honeycomb-
work. Two or three women in pattens brought up
the rear.

"The Philistines be upon us," said Liddy, making her nose white against the glass.

"Oh, very well. Maryann, go down and keep
them in the kitchen till I am dressed, and then
show them in to me in the hall."

10. Mistress and Men

HALF-AN-HOUR LATER Bathsheba, in finished dress, and followed by Liddy, entered the upper end of the old hall to find that her men had all deposited themselves on a long form and a settle at the lower extremity. She sat down at a table and opened the time book, pen in her hand, with a canvas money-bag beside her. From this she poured a small heap of coins. Liddy chose a position at her elbow and began to sew, sometimes pausing and looking round, or, with the air of a privileged person, taking up one of the half sovereigns lying before her, and surveying it merely as a work of art, while strictly preventing her countenance from expressing any wish to possess it as money.

"Now, before I begin, men," said Bathsheba, "I have two matters to speak of. The first is that the bailiff is dismissed for thieving, and that I have formed a resolution to have no bailiff at all, but to manage everything with my own head and hands."

The men breathed an audible breath of amazement.

"The next matter is, have you heard anything of Fanny?"

"Nothing, ma'am."

"Have you done anything?"

"I met Farmer Boldwood," said Jacob Smallbury, "and I went with him and two of his men, and dragged Newmill Pond, but we found nothing."

"And the new shepherd have been to Buck's Head, by Yalbury, thinking she had gone there, but nobody had seed her," said Laban Tall.

"Hasn't William Smallbury been to Casterbridge?"

"Yes, ma'am, but he's not yet come home. He promised to be back by six."

"It wants a quarter to six at present," said Bathsheba, looking at her watch. "I daresay he'll be in directly. Well, now then"—she looked into the book—"Joseph Poorgrass, are you there?"

"Yes, sir—ma'am I mane," said the person addressed. "I be the personal name of Poorgrass."

"And what are you?"

"Nothing in my own eye. In the eye of other people—well, I don't say it; though public thought will out."

"What do you do on the farm?"

"I do do carting things all the year, and in seed time I shoots the rooks and sparrows, and helps at pig killing, sir."

"How much to you?"

"Please nine and ninepence and a good half-penny where 'twas a bad one, sir—ma'am I mane."

"Quite correct. Now here are ten shillings in addition as a small present, as I am a newcomer."

Bathsheba blushed slightly at the sense of being generous in public, and Henery Fray, who had drawn up toward her chair, lifted his eyebrows and fingers to express amazement on a small scale.

"How much do I owe you—that man in the corner—what's your name?" continued Bathsheba.

"Matthew Moon, ma'am," said a singular framework of clothes with nothing of any consequence inside them, which advanced with the toes in no definite direction forward, but turned in or out as they chanced to swing.

"Matthew Mark, did you say?—speak out—I

shall not hurt you," inquired the young farmer kindly.

"Matthew Moon, mem," said Henery Fray, correctingly, from behind her chair, to which point he had edged himself.

"Matthew Moon," murmured Bathsheba, turning her bright eyes to the book. "Ten and twopence halfpenny is the sum put down to you, I see."

"Yes, mis'ess," said Matthew, as the rustle of wind among dead leaves.

"Here it is, and ten shillings. Now the next— Andrew Randle, you are a new man, I hear. How came you to leave your last farm?"

"P-p-p-p-p-pl-pl-pl-pl-l-l-l-l-ease, ma'am, p-p-p-p-pl-pl-pl-pl-please, ma'am, please'm-please'm—"

"'A's a stammering man, mem," said Henery Fray in an undertone, "and they turned him away because the only time he ever did speak plain he said his soul was his own, and other iniquities, to the squire. 'A can cuss, mem, as well as you or I, but 'a can't speak a common speech to save his life."

"Andrew Randle, here's yours—finish thanking me in a day or two. Temperance Miller—oh, here's another, Soberness—both women, I suppose?"

"Yes'm. Here we be, 'a b'lieve," was echoed in shrill unison.

"What have you been doing?"

"Tending thrashing machine, and wimbling hay bonds, and saying 'Hoosh!' to the cocks and hens when they go upon your seeds, and planting Early Flourballs and Thompson's Wonderfuls with a dibble."

"Yes—I see. Are they satisfactory women?" she inquired softly of Henery Fray.

"Oh, mem—don't ask me! yielding women—as scarlet a pair as ever was!" groaned Henery under his breath.

"Sit down."

"Who, mem?"

"Sit down."

Joseph Poorgrass, in the background, twitched, and his lips became dry with fear of some terrible consequences, as he saw Bathsheba summarily speaking, and Henery slinking off to a corner.

"Now the next. Laban Tall, you'll stay on working for me?"

"For you or anybody that pays me well, ma'am," replied the young married man.

"True—the man must live!" said a woman in the back quarter, who had just entered with clicking pattens.

"What woman is that?" Bathsheba asked.

"I be his lawful wife!" continued the voice with greater prominence of manner and tone. This lady called herself five-and-twenty, looked thirty, passed as thirty-five, and was forty. She was a woman who never, like some newly married, showed conjugal tenderness in public, perhaps because she had none to show.

"Oh, you are," said Bathsheba. "Well, Laban, will you stay on?"

"Yes, he'll stay, ma'am!" said again the shrill tongue of Laban's lawful wife.

"Well, he can speak for himself, I suppose."

"O Lord, not he, ma'am! A simple tool. Well enough, but a poor gawkhammer mortal," the wife replied.

"Heh-heh-heh!" laughed the married man, with a hideous effort of appreciation, for he was as irrepressibly good-humored under ghastly snubs as a parliamentary candidate on the hustings.

The names remaining were called in the same manner.

"Now I think I have done with you," said Bathsheba, closing the book and shaking back a stray twine of hair. "Has William Smallbury returned?"

"No, ma'am."

"The new shepherd will want a man under him," suggested Henery Fray, turning to make himself official again by a sideway approach toward her chair.

"Oh—he will. Who can he have?"

"Young Cain Ball is a very good lad," Henery said, "and Shepherd Oak don't mind his youth?" he added, turning with an apologetic smile to the shepherd, who had just appeared on the scene, and was now leaning against the doorpost with his arms folded.

"No, I don't mind that," said Gabriel.

"How did Cain come by such a name?" asked Bathsheba.

"Oh, you see, mem, his pore mother, not being a Scripture-read woman, made a mistake at his christening, thinking 'twas Abel killed Cain, and called en Cain, meaning Abel all the time. The parson put it right, but 'twas too late, for the name could never be got rid of in the parish. 'Tis very unfortunate for the boy."

"It is rather unfortunate."

"Yes. However, we soften it down as much as we can, and call him Cainy. Ah, pore widow woman! she cried her heart out about it almost. She was brought up by a very heathen father and mother, who never sent her to church or school, and it shows how the sins of the parents are visited upon the children, mem."

Mr. Fray here drew up his features to the mild degree of melancholy required when the persons involved in the given misfortune do not belong to your own family.

"Very well then, Cainy Ball to be undershepherd. And you quite understand your duties? —you I mean, Gabriel Oak?"

"Quite well, I thank you, Miss Everdene," said Shepherd Oak from the doorpost. "If I don't, I'll inquire." Gabriel was rather staggered by the remarkable coolness of her manner. Certainly nobody without previous information would have dreamt that Oak and the handsome woman before whom he stood had ever been other than strangers. But perhaps her air was the inevitable result of the social rise which had advanced her from a cottage to a large house and fields. The case is not unexampled in high places. When, in the writings of the later poets, Jove and his family are found to have moved from their cramped quarters on the peak of Olympus into the wide sky above it, their words show a proportionate increase of arrogance and reserve.

Footsteps were heard in the passage, combining in their character the qualities both of weight and measure, rather at the expense of velocity.

(All.) "Here's Billy Smallbury come from Casterbridge."

"And what's the news?" said Bathsheba, as William, after marching to the middle of the hall, took a handkerchief from his hat and wiped his forehead from its center to its remoter boundaries.

"I should have been sooner, miss," he said, "if it hadn't been for the weather." He then stamped with each foot severely, and on looking down his boots were perceived to be clogged with snow.

"Come at last, is it?" said Henery.

"Well, what about Fanny?" said Bathsheba.

"Well, ma'am, in round numbers, she's run away with the soldiers," said William.

"No; not a steady girl like Fanny!"

"I'll tell ye all particulars. When I got to Casterbridge Barracks, they said, 'The Eleventh Dragoon Guards be gone away, and new troops have come.' The Eleventh left last week for Melchester and onward. The Route came from Government like a thief in the night, as is his nature to, and afore the Eleventh knew it almost, they were on the march. They passed near here."

Gabriel had listened with interest. "I saw them go," he said.

"Yes," continued William, "they pranced down the street playing 'The Girl I Left Behind Me,' so 'tis said, in glorious notes of triumph. Every looker-on's inside shook with the blows of the great drum to his deepest vitals, and there was not a dry eye throughout the town among the public-house people and the nameless women!"

"But they're not gone to any war?"

"No, ma'am; but they be gone to take the places of them who may, which is very close connected. And so I said to myself, Fanny's young man was one of the regiment, and she's gone after him. There, ma'am, that's it in black and white."

"Did you find out his name?"

"No; nobody knew it. I believe he was higher in rank than a private."

Gabriel remained musing and said nothing, for he was in doubt.

"Well, we are not likely to know more tonight, at any rate," said Bathsheba. "But one of you had better run across to Farmer Boldwood's and tell him that much."

She then rose; but before retiring, addressed a few words to them with a pretty dignity, to which her mourning dress added a soberness that was hardly to be found in the words themselves:

"Now mind, you have a mistress instead of a master. I don't yet know my powers or my talents in farming; but I shall do my best, and if you serve me well, so shall I serve you. Don't any unfair ones among you (if there are any such, but I hope not) suppose that because I'm a woman I don't understand the difference between bad goings-on and good."

(All.) "No'm!"

(Liddy.) "Excellent well said."

"I shall be up before you are awake; I shall be

afield before you are up; and I shall have break-
fasted before you are afield. In short, I shall
astonish you all."

(All.) "Yes'm!"

"And so goodnight."

(All.) "Goodnight, ma'am."

Then this small thesmothete stepped from the
table, and surged out of the hall, her black silk
dress licking up a few straws and dragging them
along with a scratching noise upon the floor. Liddy,
elevating her feelings to the occasion from a sense
of grandeur, floated off behind Bathsheba with a
milder dignity not entirely free from travesty, and
the door was closed.

11. Outside the Barracks
— Snow — A Meeting

FOR DREARINESS nothing could surpass a prospect in
the outskirts of a certain town and military station,
many miles north of Weatherbury, at a later hour
on this same snowy evening—if that may be called
a prospect of which the chief constituent was darkness.

It was a night when sorrow may come to the
brightest without causing any great sense of incongruity: when, with impressible persons, love becomes solicitousness, hope sinks to misgiving, and
faith to hope: when the exercise of memory does
not stir feelings of regret at opportunities for ambition that have been passed by, and anticipation
does not prompt to enterprise.

The scene was a public path, bordered on the left hand by a river, behind which rose a high wall. On the right was a tract of land, partly meadow and partly moor, reaching, at its remote verge, to a wide undulating upland.

The changes of the seasons are less obtrusive on spots of this kind than amid woodland scenery. Still, to a close observer, they are just as perceptible; the difference is that their media of manifestation are less trite and familiar than such well-known ones as the bursting of the buds or the fall of the leaf. Many are not so stealthy and gradual as we may be apt to imagine in considering the general torpidity of a moor or waste. Winter, in coming to the country hereabout, advanced in well-marked stages, wherein might have been successively observed the retreat of the snakes, the transformation of the ferns, the filling of the pools, a rising of fogs, the embrowning by frost, the collapse of the fungi, and an obliteration by snow.

This climax of the series had been reached tonight on the aforesaid moor, and for the first time in the season its irregularities were forms without features; suggestive of anything, proclaiming nothing, and without more character than that of being the limit of something else—the lowest layer of a firmament of snow. From this chaotic skyful of crowding flakes the mead and moor momentarily received additional clothing, only to appear momentarily more naked thereby. The vast arch of cloud above was strangely low, and formed as it were the roof of a large dark cavern, gradually sinking in upon its floor; for the instinctive thought was that the snow lining the heavens and that encrusting the earth would soon unite into one mass without any intervening stratum of air at all.

We turn our attention to the left-hand characteristics; which were flatness in respect of the river, verticality in respect of the wall behind it, and darkness as to both. These features made up the mass. If anything could be darker than the sky, it was the wall, and if anything could be gloomier than the wall it was the river beneath. The indistinct summit of the façade was notched and pronged by chimneys here and there, and upon its face were faintly signified the oblong shapes of windows, though only in the upper part. Below, down to the water's edge, the flat was unbroken by hole or projection.

An indescribable succession of dull blows, perplexing in their regularity, sent their sound with difficulty through the fluffy atmosphere. It was a neighboring clock striking ten. The bell was in the open air, and being overlaid with several inches of muffling snow, had lost its voice for the time.

About this hour the snow abated: ten flakes fell where twenty had fallen, then one had the room of ten. Not long after a form moved by the brink of the river.

By its outline upon the colorless background a close observer might have seen that it was small. This was all that was positively discoverable, though it seemed human.

The shape went slowly along, but without much exertion, for the snow, though sudden, was not as yet more than two inches deep. At this time some words were spoken aloud:

"One. Two. Three. Four. Five."

Between each utterance the little shape advanced about half-a-dozen yards. It was evident now that the windows high in the wall were being counted. The word "Five" represented the fifth window from the end of the wall.

Here the spot stopped and dwindled smaller. The figure was stooping. Then a morsel of snow flew across the river toward the fifth window. It smacked against the wall at a point several yards from its mark. The throw was the idea of a man conjoined with the execution of a woman. No man who had ever seen bird, rabbit, or squirrel in his childhood, could possibly have thrown with such utter imbecility as was shown here.

Another attempt, and another; till by degrees the wall must have become pimpled with the adhering lumps of snow. At last one fragment struck the fifth window.

The river would have been seen by day to be of that deep smooth sort which races middle and sides with the same gliding precision, any irregularities of speed being immediately corrected by a small whirlpool. Nothing was heard in reply to the signal but the gurgle and cluck of one of these invisible wheels—together with a few small sounds which a sad man would have called moans, and a happy man laughter—caused by the flapping of the waters against trifling objects in other parts of the stream.

The window was struck again in the same manner.

Then a noise was heard, apparently produced by the opening of the window. This was followed by a voice from the same quarter:

"Who's there?"

The tones were masculine, and not those of surprise. The high wall being that of a barrack, and marriage being looked upon with disfavor in the army, assignations and communications had probably been made across the river before tonight.

"Is it Sergeant Troy?" said the blurred spot in the snow, tremulously.

This person was so much like a mere shade upon the earth, and the other speaker so much a part of the building, that one would have said the wall was holding a conversation with the snow.

"Yes," came suspiciously from the shadow. "What girl are you?"

"Oh, Frank—don't you know me?" said the spot. "Your wife, Fanny Robin."

"Fanny!" said the wall, in utter astonishment.

"Yes," said the girl, with a half-suppressed gasp of emotion.

There was something in the woman's tone which is not that of the wife, and there was a manner in the man which is rarely a husband's. The dialogue went on:

"How did you come here?"

"I asked which was your window. Forgive me!"

"I did not expect you tonight. Indeed, I did not think you would come at all. It was a wonder you found me here. I am orderly tomorrow."

"You said I was to come."

"Well—I said that you might."

"Yes, I mean that I might. You are glad to see me, Frank?"

"Oh, yes—of course."

"Can you—come to me?"

"My dear Fan, no! The bugle has sounded, the barrack gates are closed, and I have no leave. We are all of us as good as in the county jail till tomorrow morning."

"Then I shan't see you till then!" The words were in a faltering tone of disappointment.

"How did you get here from Weatherbury?"

"I walked—some part of the way—the rest by the carriers."

"I am surprised."

"Yes—so am I. And Frank, when will it be?"

"What?"

"That you promised."

"I don't quite recollect."

"Oh, you do! Don't speak like that. It weighs me to the earth. It makes me say what ought to be said first by you."

"Never mind—say it."

"Oh, must I?—it is, when shall we be married, Frank?"

"Oh, I see. Well—you have to get proper clothes."

"I have money. Will it be by banns or license?"

"Banns, I should think."

"And we live in two parishes."

"Do we? What then?"

"My lodgings are in St. Mary's, and this is not. So they will have to be published in both."

"Is that the law?"

"Yes. Oh Frank—you think me forward, I am afraid! Don't, dear Frank—will you—for I love you so. And you said lots of times you would marry me, and—and—I—I—I—"

"Don't cry, now! It is foolish. If I said so, of course I will."

"And shall I put up the banns in my parish, and will you in yours?"

"Yes."

"Tomorrow?"

"Not tomorrow. We'll settle in a few days."

"You have the permission of the officers?"

"No—not yet."

"Oh—how is it? You said you almost had before you left Casterbridge."

"The fact is, I forgot to ask. Your coming like this is so sudden and unexpected."

"Yes—yes—it is. It was wrong of me to worry you. I'll go away now. Will you come and see me tomorrow, at Mrs. Twills's, in North Street? I don't like to come to the Barracks. There are bad women about, and they think me one."

"Quite so. I'll come to you, my dear. Goodnight."

"Goodnight, Frank—goodnight!"

And the noise was again heard of a window closing. The little spot moved away. When she passed the corner a subdued exclamation was heard inside the wall.

"Ho—ho. Sergeant—ho—ho!" An expostulation

followed, but it was indistinct; and it became lost amid a low peal of laughter, which was hardly distinguishable from the gurgle of the tiny whirlpools outside.

12.   *Farmers — A Rule — An Exception*

THE FIRST PUBLIC EVIDENCE of Bathsheba's decision to be a farmer in her own person and by proxy no more was her appearance the following market day in the cornmarket at Casterbridge.

The low though extensive hall, supported by beams and pillars, and latterly dignified by the name of Corn Exchange, was thronged with hot men who talked among each other in twos and threes, the speaker of the minute looking sideways into his auditor's face and concentrating his argument by a contraction of one eyelid during delivery. The greater number carried in their hands ground ash saplings, using them partly as walking sticks and partly for poking up pigs, sheep, neighbors with their backs turned, and restful things in general, which seemed to require such treatment in the course of their peregrinations. During conversations each subjected his sapling to great varieties of usage—bending it round his back, forming an arch of it between his two hands, overweighting it on the ground till it reached nearly a semicircle; or perhaps it was hastily tucked under the arm whilst the sample bag was pulled forth and a handful of corn poured into the palm, which, after criticism,

was flung upon the floor, an issue of events perfectly well known to half-a-dozen acute townbred
fowls which had as usual crept into the building
unobserved, and waited the fulfillment of their anticipations with a high-stretched neck and oblique
eye.

Among these heavy yeomen a feminine figure
glided, the single one of her sex that the room contained. She was prettily and even daintily dressed.
She moved between them as a chaise between carts,
was heard after them as a romance after sermons,
was felt among them like a breeze among furnaces.
It had required a little determination—far more
than she had at first imagined—to take up a position here, for at her first entry the lumbering dialogues had ceased, nearly every face had been
turned toward her, and those that were already
turned rigidly fixed there.

Two or three only of the farmers were personally
known to Bathsheba, and to these she had made
her way. But if she was to be the practical woman
she had intended to show herself, business must be
carried on, introductions or none, and she ultimately acquired confidence enough to speak and
reply boldly to men merely known to her by hear-
say. Bathsheba too had her sample bags, and by
degrees adopted the professional pour into the
hand—holding up the grains in her narrow palm
for inspection, in perfect Casterbridge manner.

Something in the exact arch of her upper unbroken row of teeth, and in the keenly pointed corners of her red mouth when, with parted lips, she
somewhat defiantly turned up her face to argue a
point with a tall man, suggested that there was po-
tentiality enough in that lithe slip of humanity for
alarming exploits of sex, and daring enough to
carry them out. But her eyes had a softness—invariably a softness—which, had they not been dark,
would have seemed mistiness; as they were, it low-

ered an expression that might have been piercing
to simple clearness.

Strange to say of a woman in full bloom and
vigor, she always allowed her interlocutors to finish
their statements before rejoining with hers. In arguing on prices she held to her own firmly, as was
natural in a dealer, and reduced theirs persistently,
as was inevitable in a woman. But there was
an elasticity in her firmness which removed it from
obstinacy, as there was a naïveté in her cheapening
which saved it from meanness.

Those of the farmers with whom she had no
dealings (by far the greater part) were continually
asking each other, "Who is she?" The reply would
be—

"Farmer Everdene's niece; took on Weatherbury Upper Farm; turned away the baily, and
swears she'll do everything herself."

The other man would then shake his head.

"Yes, 'tis a pity she's so headstrong," the first
would say. "But we ought to be proud of her here
—she lightens up the old place. 'Tis such a shapely
maid, however, that she'll soon get picked up."

It would be ungallant to suggest that the novelty
of her engagement in such an occupation had almost as much to do with the magnetism as had the
beauty of her face and movements. However, the
interest was general, and this Saturday's debut in
the forum, whatever it may have been to Bathsheba as the buying and selling farmer, was unques-
tionably a triumph to her as the maiden. Indeed,
the sensation was so pronounced that her instinct
on two or three occasions was merely to walk as a
queen among these gods of the fallow, like a little
sister of a little Jove, and to neglect closing prices
altogether.

The numerous evidences of her power to attract
were only thrown into greater relief by a marked
exception. Women seem to have eyes in their rib-

bons for such matters as these. Bathsheba, without looking within a right angle of him, was conscious of a black sheep among the flock.

It perplexed her first. If there had been a respectable minority on either side, the case would have been most natural. If nobody had regarded her, she would have taken the matter indifferently—such cases had occurred. If everybody, this man included, she would have taken it as a matter of course—people had done so before. But the smallness of the exception made the mystery.

She soon knew thus much of the recusant's appearance. He was a gentlemanly man, with full and distinctly outlined Roman features, the prominences of which glowed in the sun with a bronze-like richness of tone. He was erect in attitude, and quiet in demeanor. One characteristic preeminently marked him—dignity.

Apparently he had some time ago reached that entrance to middle age at which a man's aspect naturally ceases to alter for the term of a dozen years or so; and, artificially, a woman's does likewise. Thirty-five and fifty were his limits of variation—he might have been either, or anywhere between the two.

It may be said that married men of forty are usually ready and generous enough to fling passing glances at any specimen of moderate beauty they may discern by the way. Probably, as with persons playing whist for love, the consciousness of a certain immunity under any circumstances from that worst possible ultimate, the having to pay, makes them unduly speculative. Bathsheba was convinced that this unmoved person was not a married man.

When marketing was over, she rushed off to Liddy, who was waiting for her beside the yellow gig in which they had driven to town. The horse was put in, and on they trotted—Bathsheba's sugar, tea, and drapery parcels being packed behind, and expressing in some indescribable manner, by their color, shape, and general lineaments, that they were that young lady-farmer's property, and the grocer's and draper's no more.

"I've been through it, Liddy, and it is over. I shan't mind it again, for they will all have grown accustomed to seeing me there; but this morning it was as bad as being married—eyes everywhere!"

"I knowed it would be," Liddy said. "Men be such a terrible class of society to look at a body."

"But there was one man who had more sense than to waste his time upon me." The information was put in this form that Liddy might not for a moment suppose her mistress was at all piqued. "A very good-looking man," she continued, "upright; about forty, I should think. Do you know at all who he could be?"

Liddy couldn't think.

"Can't you guess at all?" said Bathsheba with some disappointment.

"I haven't a notion; besides, 'tis no difference, since he took less notice of you than any of the rest. Now, if he'd taken more, it would have mattered a great deal."

Bathsheba was suffering from the reverse feeling just then, and they bowled along in silence. A low carriage, bowling along still more rapidly behind a horse of unimpeachable breed, overtook and passed them.

"Why, there he is," she said.

Liddy looked. "That! That's Farmer Boldwood —of course 'tis—the man you couldn't see the other day when he called."

"Oh, Farmer Boldwood," murmured Bathsheba, and looked at him as he outstripped them. The farmer had never turned his head once, but with eyes fixed on the most advanced point along the road, passed as unconsciously and abstractedly as if Bathsheba and her charms were thin air.

"He's an interesting man—don't you think so?" she remarked.

"Oh, yes, very. Everybody owns it," replied Liddy.

"I wonder why he is so wrapt up and indifferent, and seemingly so far away from all he sees around him."

"It is said—but not known for certain—that he met with some bitter disappointment when he was a young man and merry. A woman jilted him, they say."

"People always say that—and we know very well women scarcely ever jilt men; 'tis the men who jilt us. I expect it is simply his nature to be so reserved."

"Simply his nature—I expect so, miss—nothing else in the world."

"Still, 'tis more romantic to think he has been served cruelly, poor thing! Perhaps, after all, he has."

"Depend upon it he has. Oh, yes, miss, he has! I feel he must have."

"However, we are very apt to think extremes of people. I shouldn't wonder after all if it wasn't a little of both—just between the two—rather cruelly used and rather reserved."

"Oh, dear no, miss—I can't think it between the two!"

"That's most likely."

"Well, yes, so it is. I am convinced it is most likely. You may take my word, miss, that that's what's the matter with him."

13. *Sortes Sanctorum — The Valentine*

It was Sunday afternoon in the farmhouse, on
the thirteenth of February. Dinner being over,
Bathsheba, for want of a better companion, had
asked Liddy to come and sit with her. The moldy
pile was dreary in wintertime before the candles
were lighted and the shutters closed; the atmosphere of the place seemed as old as the walls; every
nook behind the furniture had a temperature of its
own, for the fire was not kindled in this part of the
house early in the day; and Bathsheba's new piano,
which was an old one in other annals, looked particularly sloping and out of level on the warped
floor before night threw a shade over its less prominent angles and hid the unpleasantness. Liddy, like
a little brook, though shallow, was always rippling;
her presence had not so much weight as to task
thought, and yet enough to exercise it.

On the table lay an old quarto Bible, bound in
leather. Liddy looking at it said—

"Did you ever find out, miss, who you are going
to marry by means of the Bible and key?"

"Don't be so foolish, Liddy. As if such things
could be."

"Well, there's a good deal in it, all the same."

"Nonsense, child."

"And it makes your heart beat fearful. Some believe in it; some don't; I do."

"Very well, let's try it," said Bathsheba, bounding from her seat with that total disregard of consistency which can be indulged in toward a
dependent, and entering into the spirit of divination at once. "Go and get the front door key."

Liddy fetched it. "I wish it wasn't Sunday," she said on returning. "Perhaps 'tis wrong."

"What's right weekdays is right Sundays," replied her mistress in a tone which was a proof in itself.

The book was opened—the leaves, drab with age, being quite worn away at much-read verses by the forefingers of unpracticed readers in former days, where they were moved along under the line as an aid to the vision. The special verse in the Book of Ruth was sought out by Bathsheba, and the sublime words met her eye. They slightly thrilled and abashed her. It was Wisdom in the abstract facing Folly in the concrete. Folly in the concrete blushed, persisted in her intention, and placed the key on the book. A rusty patch immediately upon the verse, caused by previous pressure of an iron substance thereon, told that this was not the first time the old volume had been used for the purpose.

"Now keep steady, and be silent," said Bathsheba.

The verse was repeated; the book turned round; Bathsheba blushed guiltily.

"Who did you try?" said Liddy curiously.

"I shall not tell you."

"Did you notice Mr. Boldwood's doings in church this morning, miss?" Liddy continued, adumbrating by the remark the track her thoughts had taken.

"No, indeed," said Bathsheba, with serene indifference.

"His pew is exactly opposite yours, miss."

"I know it."

"And you did not see his goings on!"

"Certainly I did not, I tell you."

Liddy assumed a smaller physiognomy and shut her lips decisively.

This move was unexpected, and proportionately disconcerting. "What did he do?" Bathsheba said perforce.

"Didn't turn his head to look at you once all the service."

"Why should he?" again demanded her mistress, wearing a nettled look. "I didn't ask him to."

"Oh, no. But everybody else was noticing you; and it was odd he didn't. There, 'tis like him. Rich and gentlemanly, what does he care?"

Bathsheba dropped into a silence intended to express that she had opinions on the matter too abstruse for Liddy's comprehension, rather than that she had nothing to say.

"Dear me—I had nearly forgotten the valentine I bought yesterday," she exclaimed at length.

"Valentine! who for, miss?" said Liddy. "Farmer Boldwood?"

It was the single name among all possible wrong ones that just at this moment seemed to Bathsheba more pertinent than the right.

"Well, no. It is only for little Teddy Coggan. I have promised him something, and this will be a pretty surprise for him. Liddy, you may as well bring me my desk and I'll direct it at once."

Bathsheba took from her desk a gorgeously illuminated and embossed design in post-octavo, which had been bought on the previous marketday at the chief stationer's in Casterbridge. In the center was a small oval enclosure; this was left blank, that the sender might insert tender words more appropriate to the special occasion than any generalities by a printer could possibly be.

"Here's a place for writing," said Bathsheba. "What shall I put?"

"Something of this sort, I should think," returned Liddy promptly:

> The rose is red,
> The violet blue,
> Carnation's sweet,
> And so are you.

"Yes, that shall be it. It just suits itself to a chubby-faced child like him," said Bathsheba. She inserted the words in a small though legible handwriting; enclosed the sheet in an envelope, and dipped her pen for the direction.

"What fun it would be to send it to the stupid old Boldwood, and how he would wonder!" said the irrepressible Liddy, lifting her eyebrows, and indulging in an awful mirth on the verge of fear as she thought of the moral and social magnitude of the man contemplated.

Bathsheba paused to regard the idea at full length. Boldwood's had begun to be a troublesome image—a species of Daniel in her kingdom who persisted in kneeling eastward when reason and common sense said that he might just as well follow suit with the rest, and afford her the official glance of admiration which cost nothing at all. She was far from being seriously concerned about his nonconformity. Still, it was faintly depressing that the most dignified and valuable man in the parish should withhold his eyes, and that a girl like Liddy should talk about it. So Liddy's idea was at first rather harassing than piquant.

"No, I won't do that. He wouldn't see any humor in it."

"He'd worry to death," said the persistent Liddy.

"Really, I don't care particularly to send it to Teddy," remarked her mistress. "He's rather a naughty child sometimes."

"Yes—that he is."

"Let's toss, as men do," said Bathsheba idly. "Now, then, head, Boldwood; tail, Teddy. No, we won't toss money on a Sunday, that would be tempting the devil indeed."

"Toss this hymnbook; there can't be no sinfulness in that, miss."

"Very well. Open, Boldwood—shut, Teddy. No;

it's more likely to fall open. Open, Teddy—shut, Boldwood."

The book went fluttering in the air and came down shut.

Bathsheba, a small yawn upon her mouth, took the pen, and with offhand serenity directed the missive to Boldwood.

"Now light a candle, Liddy. Which seal shall we use? Here's a unicorn's head—there's nothing in that. What's this—two doves—no. It ought to be something extraordinary, ought it not, Liddy? Here's one with a motto—I remember it is some funny one, but I can't read it. We'll try this, and if it doesn't do we'll have another."

A large red seal was duly affixed. Bathsheba looked closely at the hot wax to discover the words.

"Capital!" she exclaimed, throwing down the letter frolicsomely. " 'Twould upset the solemnity of a parson and clerk too."

Liddy looked at the words of the seal, and read—

MARRY ME.

The same evening the letter was sent, and was duly sorted in Casterbridge post office that night, to be returned to Weatherbury again in the morning.

So very idly and unreflectingly was this deed done. Of love as a spectacle Bathsheba had a fair knowledge; but of love subjectively she knew nothing.

14. Effect of the Letter — Sunrise

AT DUSK on the evening of St. Valentine's Day Boldwood sat down to supper as usual, by a beaming fire of aged logs. Upon the mantel shelf before him was a timepiece, surmounted by a spread eagle, and upon the eagle's wings was the letter Bathsheba had sent. Here the bachelor's gaze was continually fastening itself, till the large red seal became as a blot of blood on the retina of his eye; and as he ate and drank he still read in fancy the words thereon, although they were too remote for his sight—

MARRY ME.

The pert injunction was like those crystal substances, which, colorless themselves, assume the tone of objects about them. Here, in the quiet of Boldwood's parlor, where everything that was not grave was extraneous, and where the atmosphere was that of a Puritan Sunday lasting all the week, the letter and its dictum changed their tenor from the thoughtlessness of their origin to deep solemnity, imbibed from their accessories now.

Since the receipt of the missive in the morning, Boldwood had felt the symmetry of his existence to be slowly getting distorted in the direction of an ideal passion. The disturbance was as the first floating weed to Columbus—the contemptibly little suggesting possibilities of the infinitely great.

The letter must have had an origin and a motive. That the latter was of the smallest magnitude compatible with its existence at all, Boldwood, of course, did not know. And such an explanation did not strike him as a possibility even. It is foreign to a mystified condition of mind to realize of the mystifier that the processes of approving a course suggested by circumstance, and of striking out a course from inner impulse, would look the same in the result. The vast difference between starting a train of events, and directing into a particular groove a series already started, is rarely apparent to the person confounded by the issue.

When Boldwood went to bed he placed the valentine in the corner of the looking glass. He was conscious of its presence, even when his back was turned upon it. It was the first time in Boldwood's life that such an event had occurred. The same fascination that caused him to think it an act which had a deliberate motive prevented him from regarding it as an impertinence. He looked again at the direction. The mysterious influences of night invested the writing with the presence of the unknown writer. Somebody's—some *woman's*—hand had traveled softly over the paper bearing his name; her unrevealed eyes had watched every curve as she formed it; her brain had seen him in imagination the while. Why should she have imagined him? Her mouth—were the lips red or pale, plump or creased? —had curved itself to a certain expression as the pen went on—the corners had moved with all their natural tremulousness: what had been the expression?

The vision of the woman writing, as a supplement to the words written, had no individuality. She was a misty shape, and well she might be, considering that her original was at that moment sound asleep and oblivious of all love and letterwriting under the sky. Whenever Boldwood dozed she took a form, and comparatively ceased to be a vision: when he awoke there was the letter justifying the dream.

The moon shone tonight, and its light was not of a customary kind. His window admitted only a reflection of its rays, and the pale sheen had that reversed direction which snow gives, coming upward and lighting up his ceiling in an unnatural way, casting shadows in strange places, and putting lights where shadows had used to be.

The substance of the epistle had occupied him but little in comparison with the fact of its arrival. He suddenly wondered if anything more might be found in the envelope than what he had withdrawn. He jumped out of bed in the weird light, took the letter, pulled out the flimsy sheet, shook the envelope—searched it. Nothing more was there. Boldwood looked, as he had a hundred times the preceding day, at the insistent red seal: "Marry me," he said aloud.

The solemn and reserved yeoman again closed the letter, and stuck it in the frame of the glass. In doing so he caught sight of his reflected features, wan in expression, and insubstantial in form. He saw how closely compressed was his mouth, and that his eyes were wide-spread and vacant. Feeling uneasy and dissatisfied with himself for this nervous excitability, he returned to bed.

Then the dawn drew on. The full power of the clear heaven was not equal to that of a cloudy sky at noon, when Boldwood arose and dressed himself. He descended the stairs and went out toward the gate of a field to the east, leaning over which he paused and looked around.

It was one of the usual slow sunrises of this time of the year, and the sky, pure violet in the zenith, was leaden to the northward, and murky to the east, where, over the snowy down or ewe lease on Weatherbury Upper Farm, and apparently resting upon the ridge, the only half of the sun yet visible burnt rayless, like a red and flameless fire shining over a white hearthstone. The whole effect resembled a sunset as childhood resembles age.

In other directions the fields and sky were so much of one color by the snow that it was difficult in a hasty glance to tell whereabouts the horizon occurred; and in general there was here, too, that before mentioned preternatural inversion of light and shade which attends the prospect when the garish brightness commonly in the sky is found on the earth, and the shades of earth are in the sky. Over the west hung the wasting moon, now dull and greenish-yellow, like tarnished brass.

Boldwood was listlessly noting how the frost had hardened and glazed the surface of the snow, till it shone in the red eastern light with the polish of marble; how, in some portions of the slope, withered grass bents, encased in icicles, bristled through the smooth wan coverlet in the twisted and curved shapes of old Venetian glass; and how the footprints of a few birds which had hopped over the snow whilst it lay in the state of a soft fleece, were now frozen to a short permanency. A half-muffled noise of light wheels interrupted him. Boldwood turned back into the road. It was the mailcart—a crazy two-wheeled vehicle, hardly heavy enough to resist a puff of wind. The driver held out a letter. Boldwood seized it and opened it, expecting another anonymous one—so greatly are people's ideas of probability a mere sense that precedent will repeat itself.

"I don't think it is for you, sir," said the man, when he saw Boldwood's action. "Though there is no name, I think it is for your shepherd."

Boldwood looked then at the address—

To the New Shepherd,
Weatherbury Farm,
Near Casterbridge

"Oh—what a mistake!—it is not mine. Nor is it for my shepherd. It is for Miss Everdene's. You had better take it on to him—Gabriel Oak—and say I opened it in mistake."

At this moment on the ridge, up against the blazing sky, a figure was visible, like the black snuff in the midst of a candle flame. Then it moved and began to bustle about vigorously from place to place, carrying square skeleton masses, which were riddled by the same rays. A small figure on all fours followed behind. The tall form was that of Gabriel Oak; the small one that of George; the articles in course of transit were hurdles.

"Wait," said Boldwood. "That's the man on the hill. I'll take the letter to him myself."

To Boldwood it was now no longer merely a letter to another man. It was an opportunity. Exhibiting a face pregnant with intention, he entered the snowy field.

Gabriel, at that minute, descended the hill toward the right. The glow stretched down in this direction now, and touched the distant roof of Warren's Malthouse—whither the shepherd was apparently bent. Boldwood followed at a distance.

15. A Morning Meeting — The Letter Again

THE SCARLET AND ORANGE LIGHT outside the malthouse did not penetrate to its interior, which was, as usual, lighted by a rival glow of similar hue, radiating from the hearth.

The maltster, after having lain down in his clothes for a few hours, was now sitting beside a

three-legged table, breakfasting off bread and
bacon. This was eaten on the plateless system,
which is performed by placing a slice of bread
upon the table, the meat flat upon the bread, a mustard plaster upon the meat, and a pinch of salt upon
the whole, then cutting them vertically downward
with a large pocketknife till wood is reached, when
the severed lump is impaled on the knife, elevated,
and sent the proper way of food.

The maltster's lack of teeth appeared not to sensibly diminish his powers as a mill. He had been
without them for so many years that toothlessness
was felt less to be a defect than hard gums an ac-
quisition. Indeed, he seemed to approach the grave
as a hyperbolic curve approaches a straight line—
less directly as he got nearer, till it was doubtful if
he would ever reach it at all.

In the ashpit was a heap of potatoes roasting,
and a boiling pipkin of charred bread, called
"coffee," for the benefit of whomsoever should
call, for Warren's was a sort of clubhouse, used as an
alternative to the inn.

"I say, says I, we get a fine day, and then down
comes a snapper at night," was a remark now suddenly heard spreading into the malthouse from the
door, which had been opened the previous moment. The form of Henery Fray advanced to the
fire, stamping the snow from his boots when about
halfway there. The speech and entry had not seemed
to be at all an abrupt beginning to the maltster, in-
troductory matter being often omitted in this neighborhood, both from word and deed, and the maltster having the same latitude allowed him, did not
hurry to reply. He picked up a fragment of cheese
by pecking upon it with his knife, as a butcher picks
up skewers.

Henery appeared in a drab kerseymere greatcoat, buttoned over his smock-frock, the white skirts
of the latter being visible to the distance of about a

foot below the coattails, which, when you got used to the style of dress, looked natural enough, and even ornamental—it certainly was comfortable.

Matthew Moon, Joseph Poorgrass, and other carters and wagoners followed at his heels, with great lanterns dangling from their hands, which showed that they had just come from the cart-horse stables, where they had been busily engaged since four o'clock that morning.

"And how is she getting on without a baily?" the maltster inquired.

Henery shook his head, and smiled one of the bitter smiles, dragging all the flesh of his forehead into a corrugated heap in the center.

"She'll rue it—surely, surely!" he said. "Benjy Pennyways were not a true man or an honest baily —as big a betrayer as Joey Iscariot himself. But to think she can carr' on alone!" He allowed his head to swing laterally three or four times in silence. "Never in all my creeping up—never!"

This was recognized by all as the conclusion of some gloomy speech which had been expressed in thought alone during the shake of the head; Henery meanwhile retained several marks of despair upon his face, to imply that they would be required for use again directly he should go on speaking.

"All will be ruined, and ourselves too, or there's no meat in gentlemen's houses!" said Mark Clark.

"A headstrong maid, that's what she is—and won't listen to no advice at all. Pride and vanity have ruined many a cobbler's dog. Dear, dear, when I think o' it, I sorrows like a man in travel!"

"True, Henery, you do, I've heard ye," said Joseph Poorgrass, in a voice of thorough attestation, and with a wire-drawn smile of misery.

" 'Twould do a martel man no harm to have what's under her bonnet," said Bill Smallbury, who had just entered, bearing his one tooth before him. "She can spaik real language, and must have some sense somewhere. Do ye foller me?"

"I do; but no baily—I deserved that place," wailed Henery, signifying wasted genius by gazing blankly at visions of a high destiny apparently visible to him on Billy Smallbury's smock-frock. "There, 'twas to be, I suppose. Your lot is your lot, and Scripture is nothing; for if you do good you don't get rewarded according to your works, but be cheated in some mean way out of your recompense."

"No, no; I don't agree with'ee there," said Mark Clark. "God's a perfect gentleman in that respect."

"Good works good pay, so to speak it," attested Joseph Poorgrass.

A short pause ensued, and as a sort of *entr'acte* Henery turned and blew out the lanterns, which the increase of daylight rendered no longer necessary even in the malthouse, with its one pane of glass.

"I wonder what a farmer-woman can want with a harpsichord, dulcimer, pianner, or whatever 'tis they d'call it?" said the maltster. "Liddy saith she've a new one."

"Got a pianner?"

"Aye. Seems her old uncle's things were not good enough for her. She've bought all but everything new. There's heavy chairs for the stout, weak and wiry ones for the slender; great watches, getting on to the size of the clocks, to stand upon the chimbley-piece."

"Pictures, for the most part wonderful frames."

"And long horsehair settles for the drunk, with horsehair pillows at each end," said Mr. Clark. "Likewise looking glasses for the pretty, and lying books for the wicked."

A firm loud tread was now heard stamping outside; the door was opened about six inches, and somebody on the other side exclaimed—

"Neighbors, have ye got room for a few newborn lambs?"

"Aye, sure, shepherd," said the conclave.

The door was flung back till it kicked the wall and trembled from top to bottom with the blow. Mr. Oak appeared in the entry with a steaming face, haybands wound about his ankles to keep out the snow, a leather strap round his waist outside the smock-frock, and looking altogether an epitome of the world's health and vigor. Four lambs hung in various embarrassing attitudes over his shoulders, and the dog George, whom Gabriel had contrived to fetch from Norcombe, stalked solemnly behind.

"Well, Shepherd Oak, and how's lambing this year, if I mid say it?" inquired Joseph Poorgrass.

"Terribly trying," said Oak. "I've been wet through twice a day, either in snow or rain, this last fortnight. Cainy and I haven't tined our eyes tonight."

"A good few twins, too, I hear?"

"Too many by half. Yes; 'tis a very queer lambing this year. We shan't have done by Lady Day."

"And last year 'twer all over by Sexajessamine Sunday," Joseph remarked.

"Bring on the rest, Cain," said Gabriel, "and then turn back to the ewes. I'll follow you soon."

Cainy Ball—a cheery-faced young lad, with a small circular orifice by way of mouth, advanced and deposited two others, and retired as he was bidden. Oak lowered the lambs from their unnatural elevation, wrapped them in hay, and placed them round the fire.

"We've no lambing hut here, as I used to have at Norcombe," said Gabriel, "and 'tis such a plague to bring the weakly ones to a house. If 'twasn't for your place here, malter, I don't know what I should do, this keen weather. And how is it with you today, malter?"

"Oh, neither sick nor sorry, shepherd; but no younger."

"Aye—I understand."

"Sit down, Shepherd Oak," continued the ancient man of malt. "And how was the old place at Norcombe, when ye went for your dog? I should like to see the old familiar spot; but faith, I shouldn't know a soul there now."

"I suppose you wouldn't. 'Tis altered very much."

"Is it true that Dicky Hill's wooden ciderhouse is pulled down?"

"Oh, yes—years ago, and Dicky's cottage just above it."

"Well, to be sure!"

"Yes; and Tompkin's old apple tree is rooted that used to bear two hogsheads of cider, and no help from other trees."

"Rooted?—you don't say it! Ah! stirring times we live in—stirring times."

"And you can mind the old well that used to be in the middle of the place? That's turned into a solid iron pump with a large stone trough, and all complete."

"Dear, dear—how the face of nations alter, and what we live to see nowadays! Yes—and 'tis the same here. They've been talking but now of the mis'ess's strange doings."

"What have you been saying about her?" inquired Oak, sharply turning to the rest, and getting very warm.

"Those middle-aged men have been pulling her over the coals for pride and vanity," said Mark Clark; "but I say, let her have rope enough. Bless her pretty face—shouldn't I like to do so—upon her cherry lips!" The gallant Mark Clark here made a peculiar and well-known sound with his own.

"Mark," said Gabriel sternly, "now you mind this: none of that dalliance talk—that smack-and-coddle style of yours—about Miss Everdene. I don't allow it. Do you hear?"

"With all my heart, as I've got no chance," replied Mr. Clark cordially.

"I suppose you've been speaking against her?" said Oak, turning to Joseph Poorgrass with a very grim look.

"No, no—not a word I—'tis a real joyful thing that she's no worse, that's what I say," said Joseph, trembling and blushing with terror. "Matthew just said—"

"Matthew Moon, what have you been saying?" asked Oak.

"I? Why ye know I wouldn't harm a worm—no, not one underground worm," said Matthew Moon, looking very uneasy.

"Well, somebody has—and look here, neighbors." Gabriel, though one of the quietest and most gentle men on earth, rose to the occasion, with martial promptness and vigor. "That's my fist." Here he placed his fist, rather smaller in size than a common loaf, in the mathematical center of the maltster's little table, and with it gave a bump or two thereon, as if to ensure that their eyes all thoroughly took in the idea of fistiness before he went further. "Now—the first man in the parish that I hear prophesying bad of our mistress, why" (here the fist was raised and let fall, as Thor might have done with his hammer in assaying it)—"he'll smell and taste that—or I'm a Dutchman."

All earnestly expressed by their features that their minds did not wander to Holland for a moment on account of this statement, but were deploring the difference which gave rise to the figure; and Mark Clark cried, "Hear, hear; just what I should ha' said." The dog George looked up at the same time after the shepherd's menace, and, though he understood English but imperfectly, began to growl.

"Now, don't ye take on so, shepherd, and sit

down!" said Henery, with a deprecating peacefulness equal to anything of the kind in Christianity.

"We hear that ye be a extraordinary good and
clever man, shepherd," said Joseph Poorgrass with
considerable anxiety from behind the maltster's
bedstead, whither he had retired for safety. " 'Tis a
great thing to be clever, I'm sure," he added, making movements associated with states of mind
rather than body; "we wish we were, don't we,
neighbors?"

"Aye, that we do, sure," said Matthew Moon,
with a small anxious laugh toward Oak, to show
how very friendly disposed he was likewise.

"Who's been telling you I'm clever?" said Oak.

" 'Tis blowed about from pillar to post quite common," said Matthew. "We hear that ye can tell
the time as well by the stars as we can by the sun
and moon, shepherd."

"Yes, I can do a little that way," said Gabriel, as
a man of medium sentiments on the subject.

"And that ye can make sundials, and prent folks'
names upon their wagons almost like copperplate,
with beautiful flourishes, and great long tails. A
excellent fine thing for ye to be such a clever man,
shepherd. Joseph Poorgrass used to prent to Farmer
James Everdene's wagons before you came, and 'a
could never mind which way to turn the J's and E's
—could ye, Joseph?" Joseph shook his head to express how absolute was the fact that he couldn't.
"And so you used to do 'em the wrong way, like
this, didn't ye, Joseph?" Matthew marked on the
dusty floor with his whiphandle.

⅃AMƎꙄ

"And how Farmer James would cuss, and call thee
a fool, wouldn't he, Joseph, when 'a seed his name
looking so inside-out-like?" continued Matthew
Moon, with feeling.

"Aye—'a would," said Joseph meekly. "But, you see, I wasn't so much to blame, for them J's and E's be such trying sons o' witches for the memory to mind whether they face backward or forward; and I always had such a forgetful memory, too."

" 'Tis a bad affliction for ye, being such a man of calamities in other ways."

"Well, 'tis; but a happy Providence ordered that it should be no worse, and I feel my thanks. As to shepherd, there, I'm sure mis'ess ought to have made ye her baily—such a fitting man for't as you be."

"I don't mind owning that I expected it," said Oak frankly. "Indeed, I hoped for the place. At the same time, Miss Everdene has a right to be her own baily if she choose—and to keep me down to be a common shepherd only." Oak drew a slow breath, looked sadly into the bright ashpit, and seemed lost in thoughts not of the most hopeful hue.

The genial warmth of the fire now began to stimulate the nearly lifeless lambs to bleat and move their limbs briskly upon the hay, and to recognize for the first time the fact that they were born. Their noise increased to a chorus of baas, upon which Oak pulled the milkcan from before the fire, and taking a small teapot from the pocket of his smock-frock, filled it with milk, and taught those of the helpless creatures which were not to be restored to their dams how to drink from the spout—a trick they acquired with astonishing aptitude.

"And she don't even let ye have the skins of the dead lambs, I hear," resumed Joseph Poorgrass, his eyes lingering on the operations of Oak with the necessary melancholy.

"I don't have them," said Gabriel.

"Ye be very badly used, shepherd," hazarded Joseph again, in the hope of getting Oak as an ally in lamentation after all. "I think she's took against ye—that I do."

"Oh, no—not at all," replied Gabriel hastily, and a sigh escaped him, which the deprivation of lamb skins could hardly have caused.

Before any further remark had been added a shade darkened the door, and Boldwood entered the malthouse, bestowing upon each a nod of a quality between friendliness and condescension.

"Ah! Oak, I thought you were here," he said. "I met the mailcart ten minutes ago, and a letter was put into my hand, which I opened without reading the address. I believe it is yours. You must excuse the accident, please."

"Oh, yes—not a bit of difference, Mr. Boldwood —not a bit," said Gabriel readily. He had not a correspondent on earth, nor was there a possible letter coming to him whose contents the whole parish would not have been welcome to peruse.

Oak stepped aside, and read the following in an unknown hand:

DEAR FRIEND—I do not know your name, but I think these few lines will reach you, which I write to thank you for your kindness to me the night I left Weatherbury in a reckless way. I also return the money I owe you, which you will excuse my not keeping as a gift. All has ended well, and I am happy to say I am going to be married to the young man who has courted me for some time—Sergeant Troy, of the 11th Dragoon Guards, now quartered in this town. He would, I know, object to my having received anything except a loan, being a man of great respectability and high honor— indeed, a nobleman by blood.

I should be much obliged to you if you would keep the contents of this letter a secret for the present, dear friend. We mean to surprise Weatherbury by coming there soon as husband and wife, though I blush to state it to one nearly a

stranger. The sergeant grew up in Weatherbury. Thanking you again for your kindness,

    I am, your sincere well-wisher,

                FANNY ROBIN.

"Have you read it, Mr. Boldwood?" said Gabriel.
"If not you had better do so. I know you are interested in Fanny Robin."

Boldwood read the letter and looked grieved.

"Fanny—poor Fanny! the end she is so confident
of has not yet come, she should remember—and
may never come. I see she gives no address."

"What sort of a man is this Sergeant Troy?" said
Gabriel.

"H'm—I'm afraid not one to build much hope
upon in such a case as this," the farmer murmured,
"though he's a clever fellow, and up to everything.
A slight romance attaches to him, too. His mother
was a French governess, and it seems that a secret
attachment existed between her and the late Lord
Severn. She was married to a poor medical man,
and soon after an infant was born; and while money
was forthcoming all went on well. Unfortunately
for her boy, his best friends died; and he got then a
situation as second clerk at a lawyer's in Casterbridge. He stayed there for some time, and might
have worked himself into a dignified position of
some sort had he not indulged in the wild freak of
enlisting. I have much doubt if ever little Fanny
will surprise us in the way she mentions—very
much doubt. A silly girl—silly girl!"

The door was hurriedly burst open again, and in
came running Cainy Ball out of breath, his mouth
red and open, like the bell of a penny trumpet,
from which he coughed with noisy vigor and great
distension of face.

"Now, Cain Ball," said Oak sternly, "why will
you run so fast and lose your breath so? I'm always
telling you of it."

"Oh—I—a puff of mee breath—went—the wrong way, please, Mister Oak, and made me cough—hok —hok!"

"Well—what have you come for?"

"I've run to tell ye," said the junior shepherd, supporting his exhausted youthful frame against the doorpost, "that you must come directly. Two more ewes have twinned—that's what's the matter, Shepherd Oak."

"Oh, that's it," said Oak, jumping up, and dismissing for the present his thoughts on poor Fanny. "You are a good boy to run and tell me, Cain, and you shall smell a large plum pudding some day as a treat. But, before we go, Cainy, bring the tarpot, and we'll mark this lot and have done with 'em."

Oak took from his illimitable pockets a marking iron, dipped it into the pot, and imprinted on the buttocks of the infant sheep the initials of her he delighted to muse on—"B.E.," which signified to all the region round that henceforth the lambs belonged to Farmer Bathsheba Everdene, and to no one else.

"Now, Cainy, shoulder your two, and off. Good morning, Mr. Boldwood." The shepherd lifted the sixteen large legs and four small bodies he had himself brought, and vanished with them in the direction of the lambing field hard by—their frames being now in a sleek and hopeful state, pleasantly contrasting with their death's-door plight of half an hour before.

Boldwood followed him a little way up the field, hesitated, and turned back. He followed him again with a last resolve, annihilating return. On approaching the nook in which the fold was constructed, the farmer drew out his pocketbook, unfastened it, and allowed it to lie open on his hand. A letter was revealed—Bathsheba's.

"I was going to ask you, Oak," he said, with unreal carelessness, "if you know whose writing this is?"

Oak glanced into the book, and replied instantly, with a flushed face, "Miss Everdene's."

Oak had colored simply at the consciousness of sounding her name. He now felt a strangely distressing qualm from a new thought. The letter could of course be no other than anonymous, or the inquiry would not have been necessary.

Boldwood mistook his confusion: sensitive persons are always ready with their "Is it I?" in preference to objective reasoning.

"The question was perfectly fair," he returned— and there was something incongruous in the serious earnestness with which he applied himself to an argument on a valentine. "You know it is always expected that privy inquiries will be made: that's where the—fun lies." If the word "fun" had been "torture," it could not have been uttered with a more constrained and restless countenance than was Boldwood's then.

Soon parting from Gabriel, the lonely and reserved man returned to his house to breakfast—feeling twinges of shame and regret at having so far exposed his mood by those fevered questions to a stranger. He again placed the letter on the mantelpiece, and sat down to think of the circumstances attending it by the light of Gabriel's information.

16. All Saints' and All Souls'

ON A WEEKDAY MORNING a small congregation, consisting mainly of women and girls, rose from its knees in the moldy nave of a church called All Saints', in the distant barrack town before-mentioned, at the end of a service without a sermon. They were about to disperse, when a smart footstep, entering the porch and coming up the central passage, arrested their attention. The step echoed with a ring unusual in a church; it was the clink of spurs. Everybody looked. A young cavalry soldier in a red uniform, with the three chevrons of a sergeant upon his sleeve, strode up the aisle, with an embarrassment which was only the more marked by the intense vigor of his step, and by the determination upon his face to show none. A slight flush had mounted his cheek by the time he had run the gauntlet between these women; but, passing on through the chancel arch, he never paused till he came close to the altar railing. Here for a moment he stood alone.

The officiating curate, who had not yet doffed his surplice, perceived the newcomer, and followed him to the communion space. He whispered to the soldier, and then beckoned to the clerk, who in his turn whispered to an elderly woman, apparently his wife, and they also went up the chancel steps.

" 'Tis a wedding!" murmured some of the women, brightening. "Let's wait!"

The majority again sat down.

There was a creaking of machinery behind, and some of the young ones turned their heads. From the interior face of the west wall of the tower projected a little canopy with a quarterjack and small bell beneath it, the automaton being driven by the same clock machinery that struck the large bell in the tower. Between the tower and the church was a close screen, the door of which was kept shut during services, hiding this grotesque clockwork from sight. At present, however, the door was open, and the egress of the jack, the blows on the bell, and the mannikin's retreat into the nook again, were visible to many, and audible throughout the church.

The jack had struck half-past eleven.

"Where's the woman?" whispered some of the spectators.

The young sergeant stood still with the abnormal rigidity of the old pillars around. He faced the southeast, and was as silent as he was still.

The silence grew to be a noticeable thing as the minutes went on, and nobody else appeared, and not a soul moved. The rattle of the quarterjack again from its niche, its blows for three-quarters, its fussy retreat, were almost painfully abrupt, and caused many of the congregation to start palpably.

"I wonder where the woman is!" a voice whispered again.

There began now that slight shifting of feet, that artificial coughing among several, which betrays a nervous suspense. At length there was a titter. But the soldier never moved. There he stood, his face to the southeast, upright as a column, his cap in his hand.

The clock ticked on. The women threw off their nervousness, and titters and giggling became more frequent. Then came a dead silence. Every one was waiting for the end. Some persons may have noticed

how extraordinarily the striking of quarters seems
to quicken the flight of time. It was hardly credible
that the jack had not got wrong with the minutes
when the rattle began again, the puppet emerged,
and the four quarters were struck fitfully as before.
One could almost be positive that there was a mali-
cious leer upon the hideous creature's face, and a
mischievous delight in its twitchings. Then followed
the dull and remote resonance of the twelve heavy
strokes in the tower above. The women were impressed, and there was no giggle this time.

The clergyman glided into the vestry, and the
clerk vanished. The sergeant had not yet turned;
every woman in the church was waiting to see his
face, and he appeared to know it. At last he did
turn, and stalked resolutely down the nave, braving
them all, with a compressed lip. Two bowed and
toothless old almsmen then looked at each other
and chuckled, innocently enough; but the sound
had a strange weird effect in that place.

Opposite to the church was a paved square,
around which several overhanging wood buildings
of old time cast a picturesque shade. The young
man on leaving the door went to cross the square,
when, in the middle, he met a little woman. The expression of her face, which had been one of intense anxiety, sank at the sight of his nearly to
terror.

"Well?" he said, in a suppressed passion, fixedly
looking at her.

"Oh, Frank—I made a mistake!—I thought that
church with the spire was All Saints', and I was at
the door at half-past eleven to a minute as you said.
I waited till a quarter to twelve, and found then
that I was in All Souls'. But I wasn't much frightened, for I thought it could be tomorrow as well."

"You fool, for so fooling me! But say no more."

"Shall it be tomorrow, Frank?" she asked blankly.

"Tomorrow!" and he gave vent to a hoarse

laugh. "I don't go through that experience again for some time, I warrant you!"

"But after all," she expostulated in a trembling voice, "the mistake was not such a terrible thing! Now, dear Frank, when shall it be?"

"Ah, when? God knows!" he said, with a light irony, and turning from her walked rapidly away.

17. *In the Marketplace*

ON SATURDAY Boldwood was in Casterbridge markethouse as usual, when the disturber of his dreams entered, and became visible to him. Adam had awakened from his deep sleep, and behold! there was Eve. The farmer took courage, and for the first time really looked at her.

Material causes and emotional effects are not to be arranged in regular equation. The result from capital employed in the production of any movement of a mental nature is sometimes as tremendous as the cause itself is absurdly minute. When women are in a freakish mood their usual intuition, either from carelessness or inherent defect, seemingly fails to teach them this, and hence it was that Bathsheba was fated to be astonished today.

Boldwood looked at her—not slyly, critically, or understandingly, but blankly at gaze, in the way a reaper looks up at a passing train—as something foreign to his element, and but dimly understood. To Boldwood women had been remote phenomena rather than necessary complements—comets of such uncertain aspect, movement, and permanence, that whether their orbits were as geometrical, unchangeable, and as subject to laws as his own, or as absolutely erratic as they superficially appeared, he had not deemed it his duty to consider.

He saw her black hair, her correct facial curves and profile, and the roundness of her chin and throat. He saw then the side of her eyelids, eyes, and lashes, and the shape of her ear. Next he noticed her figure, her skirt, and the very soles of her shoes.

Boldwood thought her beautiful, but wondered whether he was right in his thought, for it seemed impossible that this romance in the flesh, if so sweet as he imagined, could have been going on long without creating a commotion of delight among men, and provoking more inquiry than Bathsheba had done, even though that was not a little. To the best of his judgment neither nature nor art could improve this perfect one of an imperfect many. His heart began to move within him. Boldwood, it must be remembered, though forty years of age, had never before inspected a woman with the very center and force of his glance; they had struck upon all his senses at wide angles.

Was she really beautiful? He could not assure himself that his opinion was true even now. He furtively said to a neighbor, "Is Miss Everdene considered handsome?"

"Oh, yes; she was a good deal noticed the first time she came, if you remember. A very handsome girl indeed."

A man is never more credulous than in receiving favorable opinions on the beauty of a woman he is half, or quite, in love with; a mere child's word on the point has the weight of an R.A.'s. Boldwood was satisfied now.

And this charming woman had in effect said to him, "Marry me." Why should she have done that strange thing? Boldwood's blindness to the difference between approving of what circumstances suggest, and originating what they do not suggest, was well matched by Bathsheba's insensibility to the possibly great issues of little beginnings.

She was at this moment coolly dealing with a dashing young farmer, adding up accounts with him as indifferently as if his face had been the pages of a ledger. It was evident that such a nature as his had no attraction for a woman of Bathsheba's taste. But Boldwood grew hot down to his hands with an incipient jealousy; he trod for the first time the threshold of "the injured lover's hell." His first impulse was to go and thrust himself between them. This could be done, but only in one way—by asking to see a sample of her corn. Boldwood renounced the idea. He could not make the request; it was debasing loveliness to ask it to buy and sell, and jarred with his conceptions of her.

All this time Bathsheba was conscious of having broken into that dignified stronghold at last. His eyes, she knew, were following her everywhere. This was a triumph; and had it come naturally, such a triumph would have been the sweeter to her for this piquing delay. But it had been brought about by misdirected ingenuity, and she valued it only as she valued an artificial flower or a wax fruit.

Being a woman with some good sense in reasoning on subjects wherein her heart was not involved, Bathsheba genuinely repented that a freak which had owed its existence as much to Liddy as to herself, should ever have been undertaken, to disturb the placidity of a man she respected too highly to deliberately tease.

She that day nearly formed the intention of begging his pardon on the very next occasion of their meeting. The worst features of this arrangement were that, if he thought she ridiculed him, an apology would increase the offense by being disbelieved; and if he thought she wanted him to woo her, it would read like additional evidence of her forwardness.

18. Boldwood in Meditation — Regret

BOLDWOOD was tenant of what was called Little
Weatherbury Farm, and his person was the nearest approach to aristocracy that this remoter quarter
of the parish could boast of. Genteel strangers,
whose god was their town, who might happen to be
compeled to linger about this nook for a day, heard
the sound of light wheels, and prayed to see good
society, to the degree of a solitary lord, or squire at
the very least, but it was only Mr. Boldwood going
out for the day. They heard the sound of wheels
yet once more, and were reanimated to expectancy:
it was only Mr. Boldwood coming home again.

His house stood recessed from the road, and the
stables, which are to a farm what a fireplace is to a
room, were behind, their lower portions being lost
amid bushes of laurel. Inside the blue door, open
halfway down, were to be seen at this time the backs
and tails of half-a-dozen warm and contented horses
standing in their stalls; and as thus viewed, they
presented alternations of roan and bay, in shapes
like a Moorish arch, the tail being a streak down the
midst of each. Over these, and lost to the eye gazing in from the outer light, the mouths of the same
animals could be heard busily sustaining the above-
named warmth and plumpness by quantities of
oats and hay. The restless and shadowy figure of a
colt wandered about a loose-box at the end, whilst
the steady grind of all the eaters was occasionally

diversified by the rattle of a rope or the stamp of a foot.

Pacing up and down at the heels of the animals was Farmer Boldwood himself. This place was his almonry and cloister in one: here, after looking to the feeding of his four-footed dependents, the celibate would walk and meditate of an evening till the moon's rays streamed in through the cobwebbed windows, or total darkness enveloped the scene.

His square-framed perpendicularity showed more fully now than in the crowd and bustle of the markethouse. In this meditative walk his foot met the floor with heel and toe simultaneously, and his fine reddish-fleshed face was bent downward just enough to render obscure the still mouth and the well-rounded though rather prominent and broad chin. A few clear and threadlike horizontal lines were the only interruption to the otherwise smooth surface of his large forehead.

The phases of Boldwood's life were ordinary enough, but his was not an ordinary nature. That stillness, which struck casual observers more than anything else in his character and habit, and seemed so precisely like the rest of inanition, may have been the perfect balance of enormous antagonistic forces —positives and negatives in fine adjustment. His equilibrium disturbed, he was in extremity at once. If an emotion possessed him at all, it ruled him; a feeling not mastering him was entirely latent. Stagnant or rapid, it was never slow. He was always hit mortally, or he was missed.

He had no light and careless touches in his constitution, either for good or for evil. Stern in the outlines of action, mild in the details, he was serious throughout all. He saw no absurd sides to the follies of life, and thus, though not quite companionable in the eyes of merry men and scoffers, and those to whom all things show life as a jest, he was not intolerable to the earnest and those acquainted with grief. Being a man who read all the dramas of life seriously, if he failed to please when they were comedies, there was no frivolous treatment to reproach him for when they chanced to end tragically.

Bathsheba was far from dreaming that the dark and silent shape upon which she had so carelessly thrown a seed was a hotbed of tropic intensity. Had she known Boldwood's moods her blame would have been fearful, and the stain upon her heart ineradicable. Moreover, had she known her present power for good or evil over this man, she would have trembled at her responsibility. Luckily for her present, unluckily for her future tranquility, her understanding had not yet told her what Boldwood was. Nobody knew entirely; for though it was possible to form guesses concerning his wild capabilities from old floodmarks faintly visible, he had never been seen at the high tides which caused them.

Farmer Boldwood came to the stable door and looked forth across the level fields. Beyond the first enclosure was a hedge, and on the other side of this a meadow belonging to Bathsheba's farm.

It was now early spring—the time of going to grass with the sheep, when they have the first feed of the meadows, before these are laid up for mowing. The wind, which had been blowing east for several weeks, had veered to the southward, and the middle of spring had come abruptly—almost without a beginning. It was that period in the vernal quarter when we may suppose the dryads to be waking for the season. The vegetable world begins to move and swell and the saps to rise, till in the completest silence of lone gardens and trackless plantations, where everything seems helpless and still after the bond and slavery of frost, there are bustlings, strainings, united thrusts, and pulls-all-together, in comparison with which the powerful tugs of cranes and pulleys in a noisy city are but pigmy efforts.

Boldwood, looking into the distant meadows, saw there three figures. They were those of Miss Everdene, Shepherd Oak, and Cainy Ball.

When Bathsheba's figure shone upon the farmer's eyes it lighted him up as the moon lights up a great tower. A man's body is as the shell, or the tablet, of his soul, as he is reserved or ingenuous, overflowing or self-contained. There was a change in Boldwood's exterior from its former impassibleness; and his face showed that he was now living outside his defenses for the first time, and with a fearful sense of exposure. It is the usual experience of strong natures when they love.

At last he arrived at a conclusion. It was to go across and inquire boldly of her.

The insulation of his heart by reserve during these many years, without a channel of any kind for disposable emotion, had worked its effect. It has been observed more than once that the causes of love are chiefly subjective, and Boldwood was a living testimony to the truth of the proposition. No mother existed to absorb his devotion, no sister for his tenderness, no idle ties for sense. He became surcharged with the compound, which was genuine lover's love.

He approached the gate of the meadow. Beyond it the ground was melodious with ripples, and the sky with larks; the low bleating of the flock mingling with both. Mistress and man were engaged in the operation of making a lamb "take," which is performed whenever an ewe has lost her own offspring, one of the twins of another ewe being given her as a substitute. Gabriel had skinned the dead lamb, and was tying the skin over the body of the live lamb in the customary manner, whilst Bathsheba was holding open a little pen of four hurdles, into which the mother and foisted lamb were driven, where they would remain till the old sheep conceived an affection for the young one.

Bathsheba looked up at the completion of the maneuver and saw the farmer by the gate, where he was overhung by a willow tree in full bloom. Gabriel, to whom her face was as the uncertain glory of an April day, was ever regardful of its faintest changes, and instantly discerned thereon the mark of some influence from without, in the form of a keenly self-conscious reddening. He also turned and beheld Boldwood.

At once connecting these signs with the letter Boldwood had shown him, Gabriel suspected her of some coquettish procedure begun by that means, and carried on since, he knew not how.

Farmer Boldwood had read the pantomime denoting that they were aware of his presence, and the perception was as too much light turned upon his new sensibility. He was still in the road, and by moving on he hoped that neither would recognize that he had originally intended to enter the field. He passed by with an utter and overwhelming sensation of ignorance, shyness, and doubt. Perhaps in her manner there were signs that she wished to see him—perhaps not—he could not read a woman. The cabala of this erotic philosophy seemed to consist of the subtlest meanings expressed in misleading ways. Every turn, look, word, and accent contained a mystery quite distinct from its obvious import, and not one had ever been pondered by him until now.

As for Bathsheba, she was not received into the belief that Farmer Boldwood had walked by on business or in idleness. She collected the probabilities of the case, and concluded that she was herself responsible for Boldwood's appearance there. It troubled her much to see what a great flame a little wildfire was likely to kindle. Bathsheba was no schemer for marriage, nor was she deliberately a trifler with the affections of men, and a censor's experience on seeing an actual flirt after observing her would have been a feeling of surprise that Bathsheba could be so different from such a one, and yet so like what a flirt is supposed to be.

She resolved never again, by look or by sign, to interrupt the steady flow of this man's life. But a resolution to avoid an evil is seldom framed till the evil is so far advanced as to make avoidance impossible.

19.   The Sheep Washing — The Offer

BOLDWOOD did eventually call upon her. She was not at home. "Of course not," he murmured. In contemplating Bathsheba as a woman, he had forgotten the accidents of her position as an agriculturist—that being as much of a farmer, and as extensive a farmer, as himself, her probable whereabouts was out-of-doors at this time of the year. This, and the other oversights Boldwood was guilty of, were natural to the mood, and still more natural to the circumstances. The great aids to idealization in love were present here: occasional observation of her from a distance, and the absence of social intercourse with her—visual familiarity, oral strangeness. The smaller human elements were kept out of sight; the pettinesses that enter so largely into all earthly living and doing were disguised by the accident of lover and loved one not being on visiting terms; and there was hardly awakened a thought in Boldwood that sorry household realities appertained to her, or that she, like all others, had moments of commonplace, when to be least plainly seen was to be most prettily remembered. Thus a mild sort of apotheosis took place in his fancy, whilst she still lived and breathed within his own horizon, a troubled creature like himself.

It was the end of May when the farmer determined to be no longer repulsed by trivialities or distracted by suspense. He had by this time grown used to being in love; the passion now startled him less even when it tortured him more, and he felt himself adequate to the situation. On inquiring for her at her house they had told him she was at the sheep washing, and he went off to seek her there.

The sheep-washing pool was a perfectly circular basin of brickwork in the meadows, full of the clearest water. To birds on the wing its glassy surface, reflecting the light sky, must have been visible for miles around as a glistening cyclops' eye in a green face. The grass about the margin at this season was a sight to remember long—in a minor sort of way. Its activity in sucking the moisture from the rich damp sod was almost a process observable by the eye. The outskirts of this level water-meadow were diversified by rounded and hollow pastures, where just now every flower that was not a buttercup was a daisy. The river slid along noiselessly as a shade, the swelling reeds and sedge forming a flexible palisade upon its moist brink. To the north of the mead were trees, the leaves of which were new, soft, and moist, not yet having stiffened and darkened under summer sun and drought, their color being yellow beside a green—green beside a yellow. From the recesses of this knot of foliage the loud notes of three cuckoos were resounding through the still air.

Boldwood went meditating down the slopes with

his eyes on his boots, which the yellow pollen from the buttercups had bronzed in artistic gradations. A tributary of the main stream flowed through the basin of the pool by an inlet and outlet at opposite points of its diameter. Shepherd Oak, Jan Coggan, Moon, Poorgrass, Cain Ball, and several others were assembled here, all dripping wet to the very roots of their hair, and Bathsheba was standing by in a new riding habit—the most elegant she had ever worn—the reins of her horse being looped over her arm. Flagons of cider were rolling about upon the green. The meek sheep were pushed into the pool by Coggan and Matthew Moon, who stood by the lower hatch, immersed to their waists; then Gabriel, who stood on the brink, thrust them under as they swam along, with an instrument like a crutch, formed for the purpose, and also for assisting the exhausted animals when the wool became saturated and they began to sink. They were let out against the stream, and through the upper opening, all impurities flowing away below. Cainy Ball and Joseph, who performed this latter operation, were if possible wetter than the rest; they resembled dolphins under a fountain, every protuberance and angle of their clothes dribbling forth a small rill.

Boldwood came close and bade her good morning with such constraint that she could not but think he had stepped across to the washing for its own sake, hoping not to find her there; more, she fancied his brow severe and his eye slighting. Bathsheba immediately contrived to withdraw, and glided along by the river till she was a stone's throw off. She heard footsteps brushing the grass, and had a consciousness that love was encircling her like a perfume. Instead of turning or waiting, Bathsheba went further among the high sedges, but Boldwood seemed determined, and pressed on till they were completely past the bend of the river.

Here, without being seen, they could hear the splashing and shouts of the washers above.

"Miss Everdene!" said the farmer.

She trembled, turned, and said "Good morning." His tone was so utterly removed from all she had expected as a beginning. It was lowness and quiet accentuated: an emphasis of deep meanings, their form, at the same time, being scarcely expressed. Silence has sometimes a remarkable power of showing itself as the disembodied soul of feeling wandering without its carcass, and it is then more impressive than speech. In the same way, to say a little is often to tell more than to say a great deal. Boldwood told everything in that word.

As the consciousness expands on learning that what was fancied to be the rumble of wheels is the reverberation of thunder, so did Bathsheba's at her intuitive conviction.

"I feel—almost too much—to think," he said, with a solemn simplicity. "I have come to speak to you without preface. My life is not my own since I have beheld you clearly, Miss Everdene—I come to make you an offer of marriage."

Bathsheba tried to preserve an absolutely neutral countenance, and all the motion she made was that of closing lips which had previously been a little parted.

"I am now forty-one years old," he went on. "I may have been called a confirmed bachelor, and I was a confirmed bachelor. I had never any views of myself as a husband in my earlier days, nor have I made any calculation on the subject since I have been older. But we all change, and my change, in this matter, came with seeing you. I have felt lately, more and more, that my present way of living is bad in every respect. Beyond all things, I want you as my wife."

"I feel, Mr. Boldwood, that though I respect you

much, I do not feel—what would justify me to—in accepting your offer," she stammered.

This giving back of dignity for dignity seemed to open the sluices of feeling that Boldwood had as yet kept closed.

"My life is a burden without you," he exclaimed, in a low voice. "I want you—I want you to let me say I love you again and again!"

Bathsheba answered nothing, and the mare upon her arm seemed so impressed that instead of cropping the herbage she looked up.

"I think and hope you care enough for me to listen to what I have to tell!"

Bathsheba's momentary impulse at hearing this was to ask why he thought that, till she remembered that, far from being a conceited assumption on Boldwood's part, it was but the natural conclusion of serious reflection based on deceptive premises of her own offering.

"I wish I could say courteous flatteries to you," the farmer continued in an easier tone, "and put my rugged feeling into a graceful shape: but I have neither power nor patience to learn such things. I want you for my wife—so wildly that no other feeling can abide in me; but I should not have spoken out had I not been led to hope."

"The valentine again! O that valentine!" she said to herself, but not a word to him.

"If you can love me say so, Miss Everdene. If not —don't say no!"

"Mr. Boldwood, it is painful to have to say I am surprised, so that I don't know how to answer you with propriety and respect—but am only just able to speak out my feeling—I mean my meaning; that I am afraid I can't marry you, much as I respect you. You are too dignified for me to suit you, sir."

"But, Miss Everdene!"

"I—I didn't—I know I ought never to have

dreamt of sending that valentine—forgive me, sir —it was a wanton thing which no woman with any self-respect should have done. If you will only pardon my thoughtlessness, I promise never to—"

"No, no, no. Don't say thoughtlessness! Make me think it was something more—that it was a sort of prophetic instinct—the beginning of a feeling that you would like me. You torture me to say it was done in thoughtlessness—I never thought of it in that light, and I can't endure it. Ah! I wish I knew how to win you! but that I can't do—I can only ask if I have already got you. If I have not, and it is not true that you have come unwittingly to me as I have to you, I can say no more."

"I have not fallen in love with you, Mr. Boldwood—certainly I must say that." She allowed a very small smile to creep for the first time over her serious face in saying this, and the white row of upper teeth, and keenly cut lips already noticed, suggested an idea of heartlessness, which was immediately contradicted by the pleasant eyes.

"But you will just think—in kindness and condescension think—if you cannot bear with me as a husband! I fear I am too old for you, but believe me I will take more care of you than would many a man of your own age. I will protect and cherish you with all my strength—I will indeed! You shall have no cares—be worried by no household affairs, and live quite at ease, Miss Everdene. The dairy superintendence shall be done by a man—I can afford it well—you shall never have so much as to look out of doors at haymaking time, or to think of weather in the harvest. I rather cling to the chaise, because it is the same my poor father and mother drove, but if you don't like it I will sell it, and you shall have a pony carriage of your own. I cannot say how far above every other idea and object on earth you seem to me—nobody knows—God only knows—how much you are to me!"

Bathsheba's heart was young, and it swelled with sympathy for the deep-natured man who spoke so simply.

"Don't say it: don't! I cannot bear you to feel so much, and me to feel nothing. And I am afraid they will notice us, Mr. Boldwood. Will you let the matter rest now? I cannot think collectedly. I did not know you were going to say this to me. Oh, I am wicked to have made you suffer so!" She was frightened as well as agitated at his vehemence.

"Say then, that you don't absolutely refuse. Do not quite refuse?"

"I can do nothing. I cannot answer."

"I may speak to you again on the subject?"

"Yes."

"I may think of you?"

"Yes, I suppose you may think of me."

"And hope to obtain you?"

"No—do not hope! Let us go on."

"I will call upon you again tomorrow."

"No—please not. Give me time."

"Yes—I will give you any time," he said earnestly and gratefully. "I am happier now."

"No—I beg you! Don't be happier if happiness only comes from my agreeing. Be neutral, Mr. Boldwood! I must think."

"I will wait," he said.

And then she turned away. Boldwood dropped his gaze to the ground, and stood long like a man who did not know where he was. Realities then returned upon him like the pain of a wound received in an excitement which eclipses it, and he, too, then went on.

20. Perplexity — Grinding the Shears — A Quarrel

"HE IS SO DISINTERESTED and kind to offer me all that I can desire," Bathsheba mused.

Yet Farmer Boldwood, whether by nature kind or the reverse to kind, did not exercise kindness here. The rarest offerings of the purest loves are but a self-indulgence, and no generosity at all.

Bathsheba, not being the least in love with him, was eventually able to look calmly at his offer. It was one which many women of her own station in the neighborhood, and not a few of higher rank, would have been wild to accept and proud to publish. In every point of view, ranging from politic to passionate, it was desirable that she, a lonely girl, should marry, and marry this earnest, well-to-do, and respected man. He was close to her doors: his standing was sufficient: his qualities were even supererogatory. Had she felt, which she did not, any wish whatever for the married state in the abstract, she could not reasonably have rejected him, being a woman who frequently appealed to her understanding for deliverance from her whims. Boldwood as a means to marriage was unexceptionable: she esteemed and liked him, yet she did not want him. It appears that ordinary men take wives because possession is not possible without marriage, and that ordinary women accept husbands because marriage is not possible without possession; with totally differing aims the method is the same on both sides. But the understood incentive on the woman's part was wanting here. Besides, Bathsheba's position as absolute mistress of a farm and house was a novel one, and the novelty had not yet begun to wear off.

But a disquiet filled her which was somewhat to her credit, for it would have affected few. Beyond the mentioned reasons with which she combated her objections, she had a strong feeling that, having been the one who began the game, she ought in honesty to accept the consequences. Still the reluctance remained. She said in the same breath that it would be ungenerous not to marry Boldwood, and that she couldn't do it to save her life.

Bathsheba's was an impulsive nature under a deliberative aspect. An Elizabeth in brain and a Mary Stuart in spirit, she often performed actions of the greatest temerity with a manner of extreme discretion. Many of her thoughts were perfect syllogisms; unluckily they always remained thoughts. Only a few were irrational assumptions; but, unfortunately, they were the ones which most frequently grew into deeds.

The next day to that of the declaration she found Gabriel Oak at the bottom of her garden, grinding his shears for the sheep shearing. All the surrounding cottages were more or less scenes of the same operation; the scurr of whetting spread into the sky from all parts of the village as from an armory previous to a campaign. Peace and war kiss each other at their hours of preparation—sickles, scythes, shears, and pruning hooks ranking with swords, bayonets, and lances, in their common necessity for point and edge.

Cainy Ball turned the handle of Gabriel's grindstone, his head performing a melancholy seesaw up and down with each turn of the wheel. Oak stood somewhat as Eros is represented when in the act of sharpening his arrows: his figure slightly bent, the weight of his body thrown over on the shears, and his head balanced sideways, with a critical compression of the lips and contraction of the eyelids to crown the attitude.

His mistress came up and looked upon them in silence for a minute or two; then she said—

"Cain, go to the lower mead and catch the bay mare. I'll turn the winch of the grindstone. I want to speak to you, Gabriel."

Cain departed, and Bathsheba took the handle. Gabriel had glanced up in intense surprise, quelled its expression, and looked down again. Bathsheba turned the winch, and Gabriel applied the shears.

The peculiar motion involved in turning a wheel has a wonderful tendency to benumb the mind. It is a sort of attenuated variety of Ixion's punishment, and contributes a dismal chapter to the history of jails. The brain gets muddled, the head grows heavy, and the body's center of gravity seems to settle by degrees in a leaden lump somewhere between the eyebrows and the crown. Bathsheba felt the unpleasant symptoms after two or three dozen turns.

"Will you turn, Gabriel, and let me hold the shears?" she said. "My head is in a whirl, and I can't talk."

Gabriel turned. Bathsheba then began, with some awkwardness, allowing her thoughts to stray occasionally from her story to attend to the shears, which required a little nicety in sharpening.

"I wanted to ask you if the men made any observations on my going behind the sedge with Mr. Boldwood yesterday."

"Yes, they did," said Gabriel. "You don't hold the shears right, miss—I knew you wouldn't know the way—hold like this."

He relinquished the winch, and enclosing her two hands completely in his own (taking each as we sometimes clasp a child's hand in teaching him to write), grasped the shears with her. "Incline the edge so," he said.

Hands and shears were inclined to suit the words, and held thus for a peculiarly long time by the instructor as he spoke.

"That will do," exclaimed Bathsheba. "Loose my hands. I won't have them held! Turn the winch."

Gabriel freed her hands quietly, retired to his handle, and the grinding went on.

"Did the men think it odd?" she said again.

"Odd was not the idea, miss."

"What did they say?"

"That Farmer Boldwood's name and your own were likely to be flung over pulpit together before the year was out."

"I thought so by the look of them! Why, there's nothing in it. A more foolish remark was never made, and I want you to contradict it: that's what I came for."

Gabriel looked incredulous and sad, but between his moments of incredulity, relieved.

"They must have heard our conversation," she continued.

"Well, then, Bathsheba!" said Oak, stopping the handle, and gazing into her face with astonishment.

"Miss Everdene, you mean," she said, with dignity.

"I mean this, that if Mr. Boldwood really spoke of marriage, I bain't going to tell a story and say he didn't to please you. I have already tried to please you too much for my own good!"

Bathsheba regarded him with round-eyed perplexity. She did not know whether to pity him for disappointed love of her, or to be angry with him for having got over it—his tone being ambiguous.

"I said I wanted you just to mention that it was not true I was going to be married to him," she murmured, with a slight decline in her assurance.

"I can say that to them if you wish, Miss Everdene. And I could likewise give an opinion to 'ee on what you have done."

"I daresay. But I don't want your opinion."

"I suppose not," said Gabriel bitterly, and going on with his turning; his words rising and falling in a regular swell and cadence as he stooped or rose with the winch, which directed them, according to his position, perpendicularly into the earth, or horizontally along the garden, his eyes being fixed on a leaf upon the ground.

With Bathsheba a hastened act was a rash act; but, as does not always happen, time gained was prudence ensured. It must be added, however, that time was very seldom gained. At this period the single opinion in the parish on herself and her doings that she valued as sounder than her own was Gabriel Oak's. And the outspoken honesty of his character was such that on any subject, even that of her love for, or marriage with, another man, the same disinterestedness of opinion might be calculated on, and be had for the asking. Thoroughly convinced of the impossibility of his own suit, a high resolve constrained him not to injure that of another. This is a lover's most stoical virtue, as the lack of it is a lover's most venial sin. Knowing he would reply truly she asked the question, painful as she must have known the subject would be. Such is the selfishness of some charming women. Perhaps it was some excuse for her thus torturing honesty to her own advantage, that she had absolutely no other sound judgment within easy reach.

"Well, what is your opinion of my conduct?" she said quietly.

"That it is unworthy of any thoughtful, and meek, and comely woman."

In an instant Bathsheba's face colored with the angry crimson of a Danby sunset. But she forbore to utter this feeling, and the reticence of her tongue only made the loquacity of her face the more noticeable.

The next thing Gabriel did was to make a mistake.

"Perhaps you don't like the rudeness of my reprimanding you, for I know it is rudeness; but I thought it would do good."

She instantly replied sarcastically—

"On the contrary, my opinion of you is so low, that I see in your abuse the praise of discerning people!"

"I am glad you don't mind it, for I said it honestly and with every serious meaning."

"I see. But, unfortunately, when you try not to speak in jest you are amusing—just as when you wish to avoid seriousness you sometimes say a sensible word."

It was a hard hit, but Bathsheba had unmistakably lost her temper, and on that account Gabriel had never in his life kept his own better. He said nothing. She then broke out—

"I may ask, I suppose, where in particular my unworthiness lies? In my not marrying you, perhaps!"

"Not by any means," said Gabriel quietly. "I have long given up thinking of that matter."

"Or wishing it, I suppose," she said; and it was apparent that she expected an unhesitating denial of this supposition.

Whatever Gabriel felt, he coolly echoed her words—

"Or wishing it either."

A woman may be treated with a bitterness which is sweet to her, and with a rudeness which is not offensive. Bathsheba would have submitted to an indignant chastisement for her levity had Gabriel protested that he was loving her at the same time; the impetuosity of passion unrequited is bearable, even if it stings and anathematizes—there is a triumph in the humiliation, and a tenderness in the strife. This was what she had been expecting, and what she had not got. To be lectured because the lecturer saw her in the cold morning light of open-shuttered disillusion was exasperating. He had not finished, either. He continued in a more agitated voice:

"My opinion is (since you ask it) that you are greatly to blame for playing pranks upon a man like Mr. Boldwood, merely as a pastime. Leading on a man you don't care for is not a praiseworthy action. And even, Miss Everdene, if you seriously inclined toward him, you might have let him find it out in some way of true loving kindness, and not by sending him a valentine's letter."

Bathsheba laid down the shears.

"I cannot allow any man to—to criticize my private conduct!" she exclaimed. "Nor will I for a minute. So you'll please leave the farm at the end of the week!"

It may have been a peculiarity—at any rate it was a fact—that when Bathsheba was swayed by an emotion of an earthly sort her lower lip trembled: when by a refined emotion, her upper or heavenward one. Her nether lip quivered now.

"Very well, so I will," said Gabriel calmly. He had been held to her by a beautiful thread which it pained him to spoil by breaking, rather than by a chain he could not break. "I should be even better pleased to go at once," he added.

"Go at once then, in Heaven's name!" said she, her eyes flashing at his, though never meeting them. "Don't let me see your face any more."

"Very well, Miss Everdene—so it shall be."

And he took his shears and went away from her in placid dignity, as Moses left the presence of Pharaoh.

21. Troubles in the Fold — A Message

GABRIEL OAK had ceased to feed the Weatherbury flock for about four-and-twenty hours, when on Sunday afternoon the elderly gentlemen Joseph Poorgrass, Matthew Moon, Fray, and half-a-dozen others, came running up to the house of the mistress of the Upper Farm.

"Whatever *is* the matter, men?" she said, meeting them at the door just as she was coming out on her way to church, and ceasing in a moment from the close compression of her two red lips, with which she had accompanied the exertion of pulling on a tight glove.

"Sixty!" said Joseph Poorgrass.

"Seventy!" said Moon.

"Fifty-nine!" said Susan Tall's husband.

"—Sheep have broke fence," said Fray.

"—And got into a field of young clover," said Tall.

"—Young clover!" said Moon.

"—Clover!" said Joseph Poorgrass.

"And they be getting blasted," said Henery Fray.

"That they be," said Joseph.

"And will all die as dead as nits, if they bain't got out and cured!" said Tall.

Joseph's countenance was drawn into lines and puckers by his concern. Fray's forehead was wrinkled both perpendicularly and crosswise, after the pattern of a portcullis, expressive of a double

despair. Laban Tall's lips were thin, and his face
was rigid. Matthew's jaws sank, and his eyes
turned whichever way the strongest muscle happened to pull them.

"Yes," said Joseph, "and I was sitting at home
looking for Ephesians, and says I to myself, ' 'Tis
nothing but Corinthians and Thessalonians in this
danged Testament,' when who should come in but
Henery there: 'Joseph,' he said, 'the sheep have
blasted theirselves——' "

With Bathsheba it was a moment when thought
was speech and speech exclamation. Moreover, she
had hardly recovered her equanimity since the disturbance which she had suffered from Oak's remarks.

"That's enough—that's enough!—Oh, you fools!"
she cried, throwing the parasol and prayerbook
into the passage, and running out of doors in the
direction signified. "To come to me, and not go
and get them out directly! Oh, the stupid numb-
skulls!"

Her eyes were at their darkest and brightest now.
Bathsheba's beauty belonging rather to the de-
monian than to the angelic school, she never looked
so well as when she was angry—and particularly
when the effect was heightened by a rather dashing
velvet dress, carefully put on before a glass.

All the ancient men ran in a jumbled throng
after her to the cloverfield, Joseph sinking down in
the midst when about halfway, like an individual
withering in a world which was more and more in-
supportable. Having once received the stimulus
that her presence always gave them they went round
among the sheep with a will. The majority of the
afflicted animals were lying down, and could not
be stirred. These were bodily lifted out, and the
others driven into the adjoining field. Here, after
the lapse of a few minutes, several more fell down,
and lay helpless and livid as the rest.

Bathsheba, with a sad, bursting heart, looked at these primest specimens of her prime flock as they rolled there—

Swoln with wind and the rank mist they drew.

Many of them foamed at the mouth, their breathing being quick and short, whilst the bodies of all were fearfully distended.

"Oh, what can I do, what can I do!" said Bathsheba, helplessly. "Sheep are such unfortunate animals!—there's always something happening to them! I never knew a flock pass a year without getting into some scrape or other."

"There's only one way of saving them," said Tall.

"What way? Tell me quick!"

"They must be pierced in the side with a thing made on purpose."

"Can you do it? Can I?"

"No, ma'am. We can't, nor you neither. It must be done in a particular spot. If ye go to the right or left but an inch you stab the ewe and kill her. Not even a shepherd can do it, as a rule."

"Then they must die," she said, in a resigned tone.

"Only one man in the neighborhood knows the way," said Joseph, now just come up. "He could cure 'em all if he were here."

"Who is he? Let's get him!"

"Shepherd Oak," said Matthew. "Ah, he's a clever man in talents!"

"Ah, that he is so!" said Joseph Poorgrass.

"True—he's the man," said Laban Tall.

"How dare you name that man in my presence!" she said excitedly. "I told you never to allude to him, nor shall you if you stay with me. Ah!" she added, brightening, "Farmer Boldwood knows!"

"Oh, no, ma'am," said Matthew. "Two of his store ewes got into some vetches t' other day, and were just like these. He sent a man on horseback here posthaste for Gable, and Gable went and saved 'em. Farmer Boldwood hev got the thing they do it with. 'Tis a holler pipe, with a sharp pricker inside. Isn't it, Joseph?"

"Aye—a holler pipe," echoed Joseph. "That's what 'tis."

"Aye, sure—that's the machine," chimed in Henery Fray reflectively, with an Oriental indifference to the flight of time.

"Well," burst out Bathsheba, "don't stand there with your 'ayes' and your 'sures,' talking at me! Get somebody to cure the sheep instantly!"

All then stalked off in consternation, to get somebody as directed, without any idea of who it was to be. In a minute they had vanished through the gate, and she stood alone with the dying flock.

"Never will I send for him—never!" she said firmly.

One of the ewes here contracted its muscles horribly, extended itself, and jumped high into the air. The leap was an astonishing one. The ewe fell heavily, and lay still.

Bathsheba went up to it. The sheep was dead.

"Oh, what shall I do—what shall I do!" she again exclaimed, wringing her hands. "I won't send for him. No, I won't!"

The most vigorous expression of a resolution does not always coincide with the greatest vigor of the resolution itself. It is often flung out as a sort of prop to support a decaying conviction which, whilst strong, required no enunciation to prove it so. The "No, I won't" of Bathsheba meant virtually, "I think I must."

She followed her assistants through the gate, and lifted her hand to one of them. Laban answered to her signal.

"Where is Oak staying?"

"Across the valley at Nest Cottage."

"Jump on the bay mare, and ride across, and say he must return instantly—that I say so."

Tall scrambled off to the field, and in two minutes was on Poll, the bay, barebacked, and with only a halter by way of rein. He diminished down the hill.

Bathsheba watched. So did all the rest. Tall cantered along the bridle path through Sixteen Acres, Sheeplands, Middle Field, The Flats, Cappel's Piece, shrank almost to a point, crossed the bridge, and ascended from the valley through Springmead and Whitepits on the other side. The cottage to which Gabriel had retired before taking his final departure from the locality was visible as a white spot on the opposite hill, backed by blue firs. Bathsheba walked up and down. The men entered the field and endeavored to ease the anguish of the dumb creatures by rubbing them. Nothing availed.

Bathsheba continued walking. The horse was seen descending the hill, and the wearisome series had to be repeated in reverse order: Whitepits, Springmead, Cappel's Piece, The Flats, Middle Field, Sheeplands, Sixteen Acres. She hoped Tall had had presence of mind enough to give the mare up to Gabriel, and return himself on foot. The rider neared them. It was Tall.

"Oh what folly!" said Bathsheba.

Gabriel was not visible anywhere.

"Perhaps he is already gone!" she said.

Tall came into the enclosure, and leapt off, his face tragic as Morton's after the battle of Shrewsbury.

"Well?" said Bathsheba, unwilling to believe that her verbal *lettre de cachet* could possibly have miscarried.

"He says *beggars mustn't be choosers,*" replied Laban.

"What!" said the young farmer, opening her

eyes and drawing in her breath for an outburst. Joseph Poorgrass retired a few steps behind a hurdle.

"He says he shall not come onless you request en to come civilly and in a proper manner, as becomes any 'ooman begging a favor."

"Oh, oh, that's his answer! Where does he get his airs? Who am I, then, to be treated like that? Shall I beg to a man who has begged to me?"

Another of the flock sprang into the air, and fell dead.

The men looked grave, as if they suppressed opinion.

Bathsheba turned aside, her eyes full of tears. The strait she was in through pride and shrewishness could not be disguised longer: she burst out crying bitterly; they all saw it; and she attempted no further concealment.

"I wouldn't cry about it, miss," said William Smallbury compassionately. "Why not ask him softer like? I'm sure he'd come then. Gable is a true man in that way."

Bathsheba checked her grief and wiped her eyes. "Oh, it is a wicked cruelty to me—it is—it is!" she murmured. "And he drives me to do what I wouldn't; yes, he does!—Tall, come indoors."

After this collapse, not very dignified for the head of an establishment, she went into the house, Tall at her heels. Here she sat down and hastily scribbled a note between the small convulsive sobs of convalescence which follow a fit of crying as a ground swell follows a storm. The note was none the less polite for being written in a hurry. She held it at a distance, was about to fold it, then added these words at the bottom:

Do not desert me, Gabriel!

She looked a little redder in refolding it, and closed her lips, as if thereby to suspend till too late the action of conscience in examining whether such strategy were justifiable. The note was despatched as the message had been, and Bathsheba waited indoors for the result.

It was an anxious quarter of an hour that intervened between the messenger's departure and the sound of the horse's tramp again outside. She could not watch this time, but, leaning over the old bureau at which she had written the letter, closed her eyes, as if to keep out both hope and fear.

The case, however, was a promising one. Gabriel was not angry: he was simply neutral, although her first command had been so haughty. Such imperiousness would have damned a little less beauty; and on the other hand, such beauty would have redeemed a little less imperiousness.

She went out when the horse was heard, and looked up. A mounted figure passed between her and the sky, and drew on toward the field of sheep, the rider turning his face in receding. Gabriel looked at her. It was a moment when a woman's eyes and tongue tell distinctly opposite tales. Bathsheba looked full of gratitude, and she said:

"Oh, Gabriel, how could you serve me so unkindly!"

Such a tenderly shaped reproach for his previous delay was the one speech in the language that he could pardon for not being commendation of his readiness now.

Gabriel murmured a confused reply and hastened on. She knew from the look which sentence in her note had brought him. Bathsheba followed to the field.

Gabriel was already among the turgid, prostrate forms. He had flung off his coat, rolled up his shirt sleeves, and taken from his pocket the instrument of salvation. It was a small tube or trochar, with a lance passing down the inside; and Gabriel began to use it with a dexterity that would have graced a hospital surgeon. Passing his hand over the sheep's left flank, and selecting the proper point, he punctured the skin and rumen with the lance as it stood in the tube; then he suddenly withdrew the lance, retaining the tube in its place. A current of air rushed up the tube, forcibly enough to have extinguished a candle held at the orifice.

It has been said that mere ease after torment is delight for a time; and the countenances of these poor creatures expressed it now. Forty-nine operations were successfully performed. Owing to the great hurry necessitated by the far-gone state of some of the flock, Gabriel missed his aim in one case, and in one only—striking wide of the mark, and inflicting a mortal blow at once upon the suffering ewe. Four had died; three recovered without an operation. The total number of sheep which had thus strayed and injured themselves so dangerously was fifty-seven.

When the love-led man had ceased from his labors Bathsheba came and looked him in the face.

"Gabriel, will you stay on with me?" she said, smiling winningly, and not troubling to bring her lips quite together again at the end, because there was going to be another smile soon.

"I will," said Gabriel.

And she smiled on him again.

22. *The Great Barn and the Sheep Shearers*

MEN THIN AWAY to insignificance and oblivion
quite as often by not making the most of good
spirits when they have them as by lacking good
spirits when they are indispensable. Gabriel lately,
for the first time since his prostration by misfortune, had been independent in thought and
vigorous in action to a marked extent—conditions
which, powerless without an opportunity as an opportunity without them is barren, would have
given him a sure lift upward when the favorable
conjunction should have occurred. But this incur-
able loitering beside Bathsheba Everdene stole his
time ruinously. The spring tides were going by
without floating him off, and the neap might soon
come which could not.

It was the first day of June, and the sheep-shear-
ing season culminated, the landscape, even to the
leanest pasture, being all health and color. Every
green was young, every pore was open, and every
stalk was swollen with racing currents of juice. God
was palpably present in the country, and the devil
had gone with the world to town. Flossy catkins of
the later kinds, fern sprouts like bishops' croziers,
the square-headed moschatel, the odd cuckoo-pint
—like an apoplectic saint in a niche of malachite—
snow-white ladies'-smocks, the toothwort, approximating to human flesh, the enchanter's nightshade,
and the black-petaled doleful-bells were among the

quainter objects of the vegetable world in and about
Weatherbury at this teeming time; and of the animal, the metamorphosed figures of Mr. Jan Coggan, the master shearer; the second and third shearers, who traveled in the exercise of their calling, and
do not require definition by name; Henery Fray the
fourth shearer, Susan Tall's husband the fifth, Joseph Poorgrass the sixth, young Cain Ball as assist-
ant shearer, and Gabriel Oak as general supervisor.
None of these were clothed to any extent worth
mentioning, each appearing to have hit in the matter of raiment the decent mean between a high and
low caste Hindu. An angularity of lineament, and
a fixity of facial machinery in general, proclaimed
that serious work was the order of the day.

They sheared in the great barn, called for the
nonce the shearing barn, which on ground plan
resembled a church with transepts. It not only
emulated the form of the neighboring church of
the parish, but vied with it in antiquity. Whether
the barn had ever formed one of a group of con-
ventual buildings nobody seemed to be aware; no
trace of such surroundings remained. The vast
porches at the sides, lofty enough to admit a wagon
laden to its highest with corn in the sheaf, were
spanned by heavy-pointed arches of stone, broadly
and boldly cut, whose very simplicity was the
origin of a grandeur not apparent in erections
where more ornament has been attempted. The
dusky, filmed, chestnut roof, braced and tied in
by huge collars, curves, and diagonals, was far
nobler in design, because more wealthy in material,
than nine-tenths of those in our modern churches.
Along each side wall was a range of striding but-
tresses, throwing deep shadows on the spaces between them, which were perforated by lancet openings, combining in their proportions the precise
requirements both of beauty and ventilation.

One could say about this barn, what could hardly

be said of either the church or the castle, akin to it
in age and style, that the purpose which had dictated its original erection was the same with that to
which it was still applied. Unlike and superior to
either of those two typical remnants of medievalism, the old barn embodied practices which had
suffered no mutilation at the hands of time. Here
at least the spirit of the ancient builders was at one
with the spirit of the modern beholder. Standing
before this abraded pile, the eye regarded its present usage, the mind dwelt upon its past history
with a satisfied sense of functional continuity
throughout—a feeling almost of gratitude, and
quite of pride, at the permanence of the idea which
had heaped it up. The fact that four centuries had
neither proved it to be founded on a mistake, inspired any hatred of its purpose, nor given rise to
any reaction that had battered it down, invested
this simple gray effort of old minds with a repose,
if not a grandeur, which a too curious reflection
was apt to disturb in its ecclesiastical and military
compeers. For once medievalism and modernism
had a common standpoint. The lanceolate windows, the time-eaten archstones and chamfers, the
orientation of the axis, the misty chestnut work of
the rafters, referred to no exploded fortifying art
or wornout religious creed. The defense and salvation of the body by daily bread is still a study, a
religion, and a desire.

Today the large side doors were thrown open
toward the sun to admit a bountiful light to the immediate spot of the shearers' operations, which was
the wood threshing floor in the center, formed of
thick oak, black with age and polished by the beating of flails for many generations, till it had grown
as slippery and as rich in hue as the stateroom floors
of an Elizabethan mansion. Here the shearers
knelt, the sun slanting in upon their bleached
shirts, tanned arms, and the polished shears they

flourished, causing these to bristle with a thousand rays strong enough to blind a weak-eyed man. Beneath them a captive sheep lay panting, quickening its pants as misgiving merged in terror, till it quivered like the hot landscape outside.

This picture of today in its frame of four hundred years ago did not produce that marked contrast between ancient and modern which is implied by the contrast of date. In comparison with cities, Weatherbury was immutable. The citizen's *Then* is the rustic's *Now*. In London, twenty or thirty years ago are old times; in Paris ten years, or five; in Weatherbury three or four score years were included in the mere present, and nothing less than a century set a mark on its face or tone. Five decades hardly modified the cut of a gaiter, the embroidery of a smock-frock, by the breadth of a hair. Ten generations failed to alter the turn of a single phrase. In these Wessex nooks the busy outsider's ancient times are only old; his old times are still new; his present is futurity.

So the barn was natural to the shearers, and the shearers were in harmony with the barn.

The spacious ends of the building, answering ecclesiastically to nave and chancel extremities, were fenced off with hurdles, the sheep being all collected in a crowd within these two enclosures; and in one angle a catching pen was formed, in which three or four sheep were continuously kept ready for the shearers to seize without loss of time. In the background, mellowed by tawny shade, were the three women, Maryann Money, and Temperance and Soberness Miller, gathering up the fleeces and twisting ropes of wool with a wimble for tying them round. They were indifferently well assisted by the old maltster, who, when the malting season from October to April had passed, made himself useful upon any of the bordering farmsteads.

Behind all was Bathsheba, carefully watching

the men to see that there was no cutting or wounding through carelessness, and that the animals were shorn close. Gabriel, who flitted and hovered under her bright eyes like a moth, did not shear continuously, half his time being spent in attending to the others and selecting the sheep for them. At the present moment he was engaged in handing round a mug of mild liquor, supplied from a barrel in the corner, and cut pieces of bread and cheese.

Bathsheba, after throwing a glance here, a caution there, and lecturing one of the younger operators who had allowed his last finished sheep to go off among the flock without restamping it with her initials, came again to Gabriel, as he put down the luncheon to drag a frightened ewe to his shear station, flinging it over upon its back with a dexterous twist of the arm. He lopped off the tresses about its head, and opened up the neck and collar, his mistress quietly looking on.

"She blushes at the insult," murmured Bathsheba, watching the pink flush which arose and overspread the neck and shoulders of the ewe where they were left bare by the clicking shears—a flush which was enviable, for its delicacy, by many queens of coteries, and would have been creditable, for its promptness, to any woman in the world.

Poor Gabriel's soul was fed with a luxury of content by having her over him, her eyes critically regarding his skillful shears, which apparently were going to gather up a piece of the flesh at every close, and yet never did so. Like Guildenstern, Oak was happy in that he was not over happy. He had no wish to converse with her: that his bright lady and himself formed one group, exclusively their own, and containing no others in the world, was enough.

So the chatter was all on her side. There is a loquacity that tells nothing, which was Bathsheba's; and there is a silence which says much: that was Gabriel's. Full of this dim and temperate bliss

he went on to fling the ewe over upon her other
side, covering her head with his knee, gradually
running the shears line after line round her dew-
lap, thence about her flank and back, and finishing
over the tail.

"Well done, and done quickly!" said Bathsheba,
looking at her watch at the last snip resounded.

"How long, miss?" said Gabriel, wiping his brow.

"Three-and-twenty minutes and a half since you
took the first lock from its forehead. It is the first
time that I have ever seen one done in less than
half an hour."

The clean, sleek creature arose from its fleece—
how perfectly like Aphrodite rising from the
foam should have been seen to be realized—looking startled and shy at the loss of its garment, which
lay on the floor in one soft cloud, united throughout, the portion visible being the inner surface
only, which, never before exposed, was white as
snow, and without flaw or blemish of the minutest
kind.

"Cain Ball!"

"Yes, Mister Oak; here I be!"

Cainy now runs forward with the tarpot. "B.E."
is newly stamped upon the shorn skin, and away
the simple dam leaps, panting, over the board into
the shirtless flock outside. Then up comes Maryann; throws the loose locks into the middle of the
fleece, rolls it up, and carries it into the background
as three-and-a-half pounds of unadulterated warmth
for the winter enjoyment of persons unknown and
far away, who will, however, never experience the
superlative comfort derivable from the wool as it
here exists, new and pure—before the unctuousness
of its nature whilst in a living state has dried, stiffened, and been washed out—rendering it just now
as superior to anything *woolen* as cream is superior
to milk and water.

But heartless circumstance could not leave entire

Gabriel's happiness of this morning. The rams, old ewes, and two-shear ewes had duly undergone their stripping, and the men were proceeding with the shearlings and hogs, when Oak's belief that she was going to stand pleasantly by and time him through another performance was painfully interrupted by Farmer Boldwood's appearance in the extremest corner of the barn. Nobody seemed to have perceived his entry, but there he certainly was. Boldwood always carried with him a social atmosphere of his own, which everybody felt who came near him; and the talk, which Bathsheba's presence had somewhat suppressed, was now totally suspended.

He crossed over toward Bathsheba, who turned to greet him with a carriage of perfect ease. He spoke to her in low tones, and she instinctively modulated her own to the same pitch, and her voice ultimately even caught the inflection of his. She was far from having a wish to appear mysteriously connected with him; but woman at the impressionable age gravitates to the larger body not only in her choice of words, which is apparent every day, but even in her shades of tone and humor when the influence is great.

What they conversed about was not audible to Gabriel, who was too independent to get near, though too concerned to disregard. The issue of their dialogue was the taking of her hand by the courteous farmer to help her over the spreading board into the bright June sunlight outside. Standing beside the sheep already shorn, they went on talking again. Concerning the flock? Apparently not. Gabriel theorized, not without truth, that in quiet discussion of any matter within reach of the speakers' eyes, these are usually fixed upon it. Bathsheba demurely regarded a contemptible straw lying upon the ground, in a way which suggested less ovine criticism than womanly embarrassment. She became more or less red in the cheek, the blood wavering in uncertain flux and reflux over the sensitive space between ebb and flood. Gabriel sheared on, constrained and sad.

She left Boldwood's side, and he walked up and down alone for nearly a quarter of an hour. Then she reappeared in her new riding habit of myrtle green, which fitted her to the waist as a rind fits its fruit; and young Bob Coggan led on her mare, Boldwood fetching his own horse from the tree under which it had been tied.

Oak's eyes could not forsake them; and in endeavoring to continue his shearing at the same time that he watched Boldwood's manner, he snipped the sheep in the groin. The animal plunged; Bathsheba instantly gazed toward it, and saw the blood.

"Oh, Gabriel!" she exclaimed, with severe remonstrance, "you who are so strict with the other men—see what you are doing yourself!"

To an outsider there was not much to complain of in this remark; but to Oak, who knew Bathsheba to be well aware that she herself was the cause of the poor ewe's wound, because she had wounded the ewe's shearer in a still more vital part, it had a sting which the abiding sense of his inferiority to both herself and Boldwood was not calculated to heal. But a manly resolve to recognize boldly that he had no longer a lover's interest in her, helped him occasionally to conceal a feeling.

"Bottle!" he shouted, in an unmoved voice of routine. Cainy Ball ran up, the wound was anointed, and the shearing continued.

Boldwood gently tossed Bathsheba into the saddle, and before they turned away she again spoke out to Oak with the same dominative and tantalizing graciousness.

"I am going now to see Mr. Boldwood's Leicesters. Take my place in the barn, Gabriel, and keep the men carefully to their work."

The horses' heads were put about, and they trotted away.

Boldwood's deep attachment was a matter of great interest among all around him; but, after having been pointed out for so many years as the perfect exemplar of thriving bachelorship, his lapse was an anticlimax somewhat resembling that of St. John Long's death by consumption in the midst of his proofs that it was not a fatal disease.

"That means matrimony," said Temperance Miller, following them out of sight with her eyes.

"I reckon that's the size o't," said Coggan, working along without looking up.

"Well, better wed over the mixen than over the moor," said Laban Tall, turning his sheep.

Henery Fray spoke, exhibiting miserable eyes at the same time: "I don't see why a maid should take a husband when she's bold enough to fight her own battles, and don't want a home; for 'tis keeping another woman out. But let it be, for 'tis a pity he and she should trouble two houses."

As usual with decided characters, Bathsheba invariably provoked the criticism of individuals like Henery Fray. Her emblazoned fault was to be too pronounced in her objections, and not sufficiently overt in her likings. We learn that it is not the rays which bodies absorb, but those which they reject, that give them the colors they are known by; and in the same way people are specialized by their dislikes and antagonisms, whilst their goodwill is looked upon as no attribute at all.

Henery continued in a more complaisant mood: "I once hinted my mind to her on a few things, as nearly as a battered frame dared to do so to such a froward piece. You all know, neighbors, what a man I be, and how I come down with my powerful words when my pride is boiling wi' scarn?"

"We do, we do, Henery."

"So I said, 'Mistress Everdene, there's places

empty, and there's gifted men willing; but the spite'—no, not the spite—I didn't say spite—'but the villainy of the contrarikind,' I said (meaning womankind), 'keeps 'em out.' That wasn't too strong for her, say?"

"Passably well put."

"Yes; and I would have said it, had death and salvation overtook me for it. Such is my spirit when I have a mind."

"A true man, and proud as a lucifer."

"You see the artfulness? Why, 'twas about being baily really; but I didn't put it so plain that she could understand my meaning, so I could lay it on all the stronger. That was my depth! . . . However, let her marry an she will. Perhaps 'tis high time. I believe Farmer Boldwood kissed her behind the spearbed at the sheep washing t'other day—that I do."

"What a lie!" said Gabriel.

"Ah, neighbor Oak—how'st know?" said Henery mildly.

"Because she told me all that passed," said Oak, with a pharisaical sense that he was not as other shearers in this matter.

"Ye have a right to believe it," said Henery, with dudgeon; "a very true right. But I mid see a little distance into things! To be long-headed enough for a baily's place is a poor mere trifle—yet a trifle more than nothing. However, I look round upon life quite cool. Do you heed me, neighbors? My words, though made as simple as I can, mid be rather deep for some heads."

"Oh, yes, Henery, we quite heed ye."

"A strange old piece, goodmen—whirled about from here to yonder, as if I were nothing! A little warped, too. But I have my depths; ha, and even my great depths! I might gird at a certain shepherd, brain to brain. But no—oh, no!"

"A strange old piece, ye say!" interposed the

maltster, in a querulous voice. "At the same time ye be no old man worth naming—no old man at all. Yer teeth bain't half gone yet; and what's a old man's standing if so be his teeth bain't gone? Weren't I stale in wedlock afore ye were out of arms? 'Tis a poor thing to be sixty, when there's people far past four-score—a boast weak as water."

It was the unvarying custom in Weatherbury to sink minor differences when the maltster had to be pacified.

"Weak as water! yes," said Jan Coggan. "Malter, we feel ye to be a wonderful veteran man, and nobody can gainsay it."

"Nobody," said Joseph Poorgrass. "Ye be a very rare old spectacle, malter, and we all admire ye for that gift."

"Aye, and as a young man, when my senses were in prosperity, I was likewise liked by a good-few who knowed me," said the maltster.

" 'Ithout doubt you was—'ithout doubt."

The bent and hoary man was satisfied, and so apparently was Henery Fray. That matters should continue pleasant Maryann spoke, who, what with her brown complexion, and the working wrapper of rusty linsey, had at present the mellow hue of an old sketch in oils—notably some of Nicholas Poussin's—

"Do anybody know of a crooked man, or a lame, or any secondhand fellow at all that would do for poor me?" said Maryann. "A perfect one I don't expect to get at my time of life. If I could hear of such a thing 'twould do me more good than toast and ale."

Coggan furnished a suitable reply. Oak went on with his shearing, and said not another word. Pestilent moods had come, and teased away his quiet. Bathsheba had shown indications of anointing him above his fellows by installing him as the bailiff that the farm imperatively required. He did not

covet the post relatively to the farm: in relation to
herself, as beloved by him and unmarried to
another, he had coveted it. His readings of her
seemed now to be vapory and indistinct. His lec-
ture to her was, he thought, one of the absurdest
mistakes. Far from coquetting with Boldwood, she
had trifled with himself in thus feigning that she
had trifled with another. He was inwardly convinced that, in accordance with the anticipations
of his easygoing and worse-educated comrades, that
day would see Boldwood the accepted husband of
Miss Everdene. Gabriel at this time of his life had
outgrown the instinctive dislike which every Christian boy has for reading the Bible, perusing it now
quite frequently, and he inwardly said, " 'I find
more bitter than death the woman whose heart is
snares and nets!' " This was mere exclamation—
the froth of the storm. He adored Bathsheba just
the same.

"We workfolk shall have some lordly junketing
tonight," said Cainy Ball, casting forth his thoughts
in a new direction. "This morning I see 'em making the great puddens in the milking pails—lumps
of fat as big as yer thumb, Mister Oak! I've never
seed such splendid large knobs of fat before in the
days of my life—they never used to be bigger than
a horsebean. And there was a great black crock
upon the brandise with his legs a-sticking out, but
I don't know what was in within."

"And there's two bushels of biffins for apple
pies," said Maryann.

"Well, I hope to do my duty by it all," said
Joseph Poorgrass, in a pleasant, masticating manner of anticipation. "Yes; victuals and drink is a
cheerful thing, and gives nerves to the nerveless, if
the form of words may be used. 'Tis the gospel of
the body, without which we perish, so to speak it."

23. Eventide — A Second Declaration

FOR THE SHEARING SUPPER a long table was placed
on the grassplot beside the house, the end of the
table being thrust over the sill of the wide parlor
window and a foot or two into the room. Miss Everdene sat inside the window, facing down the table.
She was thus at the head without mingling with
the men.

This evening Bathsheba was unusually excited,
her red cheeks and lips contrasting lustrously with
the mazy skeins of her shadowy hair. She seemed
to expect assistance, and the seat at the bottom of
the table was at her request left vacant until after
they had begun the meal. She then asked Gabriel
to take the place and the duties appertaining to
that end, which he did with great readiness.

At this moment Mr. Boldwood came in at the
gate, and crossed the green to Bathsheba at the
window. He apologized for his lateness: his arrival
was evidently by arrangement.

"Gabriel," said she, "will you move again,
please, and let Mr. Boldwood come there?"

Oak moved in silence back to his original seat.

The gentleman-farmer was dressed in cheerful
style, in a new coat and white waistcoat, quite contrasting with his usual sober suits of gray. Inwardly,
too, he was blithe, and consequently chatty to an
exceptional degree. So also was Bathsheba now
that he had come, though the uninvited presence

of Pennyways, the bailiff who had been dismissed for theft, disturbed her equanimity for a while.

Supper being ended, Coggan began on his own private account, without reference to listeners:

> I've lost my love, and I care not,
> I've lost my love, and I care not;
>   I shall soon have another
>   That's better than t'other;
> I've lost my love, and I care not.

This lyric, when concluded, was received with a silently appreciative gaze at the table, implying that the performance, like a work by those established authors who are independent of notices in the papers, was a well-known delight which required no applause.

"Now, Master Poorgrass, your song!" said Coggan.

"I be all but in liquor, and the gift is wanting in me," said Joseph, diminishing himself.

"Nonsense; wou'st never be so ungrateful, Joseph—never!" said Coggan, expressing hurt feelings by an inflection of voice. "And mistress is looking hard at ye, as much as to say, 'Sing at once, Joseph Poorgrass.'"

"Faith, so she is; well, I must suffer it! . . . Just eye my features, and see if the telltale blood overheats me much, neighbors?"

"No, yer blushes be quite reasonable," said Coggan.

"I always tries to keep my colors from rising when a beauty's eyes get fixed on me," said Joseph diffidently, "but if so be 'tis willed they do, they must."

"Now, Joseph, your song, please," said Bathsheba from the window.

"Well, really, ma'am," he replied in a yielding tone, "I don't know what to say. It would be a poor plain ballet of my own composure."

"Hear, hear!" said the supper party.

Poorgrass, thus assured, trilled forth a flickering yet commendable piece of sentiment, the tune of which consisted of the keynote and another, the latter being the sound chiefly dwelt upon. This was so successful that he rashly plunged into a second in the same breath, after a few false starts:

> I sow'-ed th'-e . . . . .
> I sow'-ed . . . . .
> I sow'-ed th'-e seeds' of' love',
>   I-it was' all' i'-in the'-e spring',
> I-in A'-pril', Ma'-ay, a'-nd sun'-ny' June',
>   When sma'-all bi'-irds they' do' sing.

"Well put out of hand," said Coggan, at the end of the verse. " 'They do sing' was a very taking paragraph."

"Aye; and there was a pretty place at 'seeds of love,' and 'twas well heaved out. Though 'love' is a nasty high corner when a man's voice is getting crazed. Next verse, Master Poorgrass."

But during this rendering young Bob Coggan exhibited one of those anomalies which will afflict little people when other persons are particularly serious: in trying to check his laughter, he pushed down his throat as much of the tablecloth as he could get hold of, when, after continuing hermetically sealed for a short time, his mirth burst out through his nose. Joseph perceived it, and with hectic cheeks of indignation instantly ceased singing. Coggan boxed Bob's ears immediately.

"Go on, Joseph—go on, and never mind the young scamp," said Coggan. " 'Tis a very catching ballet. Now then again—the next bar; I'll help ye to flourish up the shrill notes where yer wind is rather wheezy:

> Oh, the wi'-il-lo' tree' will' twist',
> And the wil'-low' tre'-ee wi'-ill twine'."

But the singer could not be set going again. Bob Coggan was sent home for his ill manners, and tranquility was restored by Jacob Smallbury, who volunteered a ballad as inclusive and interminable as that with which the worthy toper old Silenus amused on a similar occasion the swains Chromis and Mnasylus, and other jolly dogs of his day.

It was still the beaming time of evening, though night was stealthily making itself visible low down upon the ground, the western lines of light raking the earth without alighting upon it to any extent, or illuminating the dead levels at all. The sun had crept round the tree as a last effort before death, and then began to sink, the shearers' lower parts becoming steeped in embrowning twilight, whilst their heads and shoulders were still enjoying day, touched with a yellow of self-sustained brilliancy that seemed inherent rather than acquired.

The sun went down in an ochreous mist; but they sat, and talked on, and grew as merry as the gods in Homer's heaven. Bathsheba still remained enthroned inside the window, and occupied herself in knitting, from which she sometimes looked up to view the fading scene outside. The slow twilight expanded and enveloped them completely before the signs of moving were shown.

Gabriel suddenly missed Farmer Boldwood from his place at the bottom of the table. How long he had been gone Oak did not know; but he had apparently withdrawn into the encircling dusk. Whilst he was thinking of this Liddy brought candles into the back part of the room overlooking the shearers, and their lively new flames shone down the table and over the men, and dispersed among the green shadows behind. Bathsheba's form, still in its original position, was now again distinct between their eyes and the light, which revealed that Boldwood had gone inside the room, and was sitting near her.

Next came the question of the evening. Would

Miss Everdene sing to them the song she always sang so charmingly—"The Banks of Allan Water" —before they went home?

After a moment's consideration Bathsheba assented, beckoning to Gabriel, who hastened up into the coveted atmosphere.

"Have you brought your flute?" she whispered.

"Yes, miss."

"Play to my singing, then."

She stood up in the window opening, facing the men, the candles behind her, Gabriel on her right hand, immediately outside the sash frame. Boldwood had drawn up on her left, within the room. Her singing was soft and rather tremulous at first, but it soon swelled to a steady clearness. Subsequent events caused one of the verses to be remembered for many months, and even years, by more than one of those who were gathered there:

> For his bride a soldier sought her,
>   And a winning tongue had he:
> On the banks of Allan Water
>   None was gay as she!

In addition to the dulcet piping of Gabriel's flute Boldwood supplied a bass in his customary profound voice, uttering his notes so softly, however, as to abstain entirely from making anything like an ordinary duet of the song; they rather formed a rich unexplored shadow, which threw her tones into relief. The shearers reclined against each other as at suppers in the early ages of the world, and so silent and absorbed were they that her breathing could almost be heard between the bars; and at the end of the ballad, when the last tone loitered on to an inexpressible close, there arose that buzz of pleasure which is the attar of applause.

It is scarcely necessary to state that Gabriel could not avoid noting the farmer's bearing tonight toward their entertainer. Yet there was nothing exceptional in his actions beyond what appertained to his time of performing them. It was when the rest were all looking away that Boldwood observed her; when they regarded her he turned aside; when they thanked or praised he was silent; when they were inattentive he murmured his thanks. The meaning lay in the difference between actions none of which had any meaning of itself; and the necessity of being jealous, which lovers are troubled with, did not lead Oak to underestimate these signs.

Bathsheba then wished them goodnight, withdrew from the window, and retired to the back part of the room, Boldwood thereupon closing the sash and the shutters, and remaining inside with her. Oak wandered away under the quiet and scented trees. Recovering from the softer impressions produced by Bathsheba's voice, the shearers rose to leave, Coggan turning to Pennyways as he pushed back the bench to pass out:

"I like to give praise where praise is due, and the man deserves it—that 'a do so," he remarked, looking at the worthy thief as if he were the masterpiece of some world-renowned artist.

"I'm sure I should never have believed it if we hadn't proved it, so to allude," hiccuped Joseph Poorgrass, "that every cup, every one of the best knives and forks, and every empty bottle be in their place as perfect now as at the beginning, and not one stole at all."

"I'm sure I don't deserve half the praise you give me," said the virtuous thief grimly.

"Well, I'll say this for Pennyways," added Coggan, "that whenever he do really make up his mind to do a noble thing in the shape of a good action, as I could see by his face he did tonight afore sitting down, he's generally able to carry it out. Yes, I'm proud to say, neighbors, that he's stole nothing at all."

"Well, 'tis an honest deed, and we thank ye for it, Pennyways," said Joseph; to which opinion the remainder of the company subscribed unanimously.

At this time of departure, when nothing more was visible of the inside of the parlor than a thin and still chink of light between the shutters, a passionate scene was in course of enactment there.

Miss Everdene and Boldwood were alone. Her cheeks had lost a great deal of their healthful fire from the very seriousness of her position; but her eye was bright with the excitement of a triumph—though it was a triumph which had rather been contemplated than desired.

She was standing behind a low armchair, from which she had just risen, and he was kneeling in it —inclining himself over its back toward her, and holding her hand in both his own. His body moved restlessly, and it was with what Keats daintily calls a too happy happiness. This unwonted abstraction by love of all dignity from a man of whom it had ever seemed the chief component was, in its distressing incongruity, a pain to her which quenched much of the pleasure she derived from the proof that she was idolized.

"I will try to love you," she was saying, in a trembling voice quite unlike her usual self-confidence. "And if I can believe in any way that I shall make you a good wife I shall indeed be willing to marry you. But, Mr. Boldwood, hesitation on so high a matter is honorable in any woman, and I don't want to give a solemn promise tonight. I would rather ask you to wait a few weeks till I can see my situation better."

"But you have every reason to believe that then—"

"I have every reason to hope that at the end of the five or six weeks, between this time and harvest, that you say you are going to be away from home, I shall be able to promise to be your wife," she said

firmly. "But remember this distinctly, I don't promise yet."

"It is enough; I don't ask more. I can wait on
those dear words. And now, Miss Everdene, goodnight!"

"Goodnight," she said graciously—almost tenderly; and Boldwood withdrew with a serene smile.

Bathsheba knew more of him now; he had entirely bared his heart before her, even until he had
almost worn in her eyes the sorry look of a grand
bird without the feathers that make it grand. She
had been awestruck at her past temerity, and was
struggling to make amends without thinking
whether the sin quite deserved the penalty she was
schooling herself to pay. To have brought all this
about her ears was terrible; but after a while the
situation was not without a fearful joy. The facility
with which even the most timid women sometimes
acquire a relish for the dreadful when that is amal-
gamated with a little triumph is marvelous.

24. *The Same Night — The Fir Plantation*

AMONG THE MULTIFARIOUS DUTIES which Bathsheba
had voluntarily imposed upon herself by dispensing
with the services of a bailiff was the particular one
of looking round the homestead before going to
bed, to see that all was right and safe for the night.
Gabriel had almost constantly preceded her in this
tour every evening, watching her affairs as carefully

as any specially appointed officer of surveillance
could have done; but this tender devotion was to a
great extent unknown to his mistress, and as much
as was known was somewhat thanklessly received.
Women are never tired of bewailing man's fickle-
ness in love, but they only seem to snub his constancy.

As watching is best done invisibly, she usually
carried a dark lantern in her hand, and every now
and then turned on the light to examine nooks and
corners with the coolness of a metropolitan po.ice-
man. This coolness may have owed its existence
not so much to her fearlessness of expected danger
as to her freedom from the suspicion of any; her
worst anticipated discovery being that a horse might
not be well bedded, the fowls not all in, or a door
not closed.

This night the buildings were inspected as usual,
and she went round to the farm paddock. Here the
only sounds disturbing the stillness were steady
munchings of many mouths, and stentorian breathings from all but invisible noses, ending in snores
and puffs like the blowing of bellows slowly. Then
the munching would recommence, when the lively
imagination might assist the eye to discern a group
of pink-white nostrils shaped as caverns, and very
clammy and humid on their surfaces, not exactly
pleasant to the touch until one got used to them;
the mouths beneath having a great partiality for
closing upon any loose end of Bathsheba's apparel
which came within reach of their tongues. Above
each of these a stil. keener vision suggested a brown
forehead and two staring though not unfriendly
eyes, and above all a pair of whitish crescent-shaped
horns like two particularly new moons, an occasional stolid "moo!" proclaiming beyond the shade
of a doubt that these phenomena were the features and persons of Daisy, Whitefoot, Bonny-lass,
Jolly-O, Spot, Twinkle-eye, etc., etc.—the respect-

able dairy of Devon cows belonging to Bathsheba aforesaid.

Her way back to the house was by a path through a young plantation of tapering firs, which had been planted some years earlier to shelter the premises from the north wind. By reason of the density of the interwoven foliage overhead it was gloomy there at cloudless noontide, twilight in the evening, dark as midnight at dusk, and black as the ninth plague of Egypt at midnight. To describe the spot is to call it a vast, low, naturally formed hall, the plumy ceiling of which was supported by slender pillars of living wood, the floor being covered with a soft dun carpet of dead spikelets and mildewed cones, with a tuft of grass blades here and there.

This bit of the path was always the crux of the night's ramble, though, before starting, her apprehensions of danger were not vivid enough to lead her to take a companion. Slipping along here covertly as Time, Bathsheba fancied she could hear footsteps entering the track at the opposite end. It was certainly a rustle of footsteps. Her own instantly fell as gently as snowflakes. She reassured herself by a remembrance that the path was public, and that the traveler was probably some villager returning home; regretting, at the same time, that the meeting should be about to occur in the darkest point of her route, even though only just outside her own door.

The noise approached, came close, and a figure was apparently on the point of gliding past her when something tugged at her skirt and pinned it forcibly to the ground. The instantaneous check nearly threw Bathsheba off her balance. In recovering she struck against warm clothes and buttons.

"A rum start, upon my soul!" said a masculine voice, a foot or so above her head. "Have I hurt you, mate?"

"No," said Bathsheba, attempting to shrink away.

"We have got hitched together somehow, I think."

"Yes."

"Are you a woman?"

"Yes."

"A lady, I should have said."

"It doesn't matter."

"I am a man."

"Oh!"

Bathsheba softly tugged again, but to no purpose.

"Is that a dark lantern you have? I fancy so," said the man.

"Yes."

"If you'll allow me I'll open it, and set you free."

A hand seized the lantern, the door was opened, the rays burst out from their prison, and Bathsheba beheld her position with astonishment.

The man to whom she was hooked was brilliant in brass and scarlet. He was a soldier. His sudden appearance was to darkness what the sound of a trumpet is to silence. Gloom, the *genius loci* at all times hitherto, was now totally overthrown, less by the lantern light than by what the lantern lighted. The contrast of this revelation with her anticipations of some sinister figure in somber garb was so great that it had upon her the effect of a fairy transformation.

It was immediately apparent that the military man's spur had become entangled in the gimp which decorated the skirt of her dress. He caught a view of her face.

"I'll unfasten you in one moment, miss," he said, with newborn gallantry.

"Oh, no—I can do it, thank you," she hastily replied, and stooped for the performance.

The unfastening was not such a trifling affair. The rowel of the spur had so wound itself among the gimp cords in those few moments, that separation was likely to be a matter of time.

He too stooped, and the lantern standing on the ground betwixt them threw the gleam from its open side among the fir tree needles and the blades of long damp grass with the effect of a large glow-worm. It radiated upward into their faces, and sent over half the plantation gigantic shadows of both man and woman, each dusky shape becoming distorted and mangled upon the tree trunks till it wasted to nothing.

He looked hard into her eyes when she raised them for a moment; Bathsheba looked down again, for his gaze was too strong to be received point-blank with her own. But she had obliquely noticed that he was young and slim, and that he wore three chevrons upon his sleeve.

Bathsheba pulled again.

"You are a prisoner, miss; it is no use blinking the matter," said the soldier drily. "I must cut your dress if you are in such a hurry."

"Yes—please do!" she exclaimed helplessly.

"It wouldn't be necessary if you could wait a moment," and he unwound a cord from the little wheel. She withdrew her own hand, but, whether by accident or design, he touched it. Bathsheba was vexed; she hardly knew why.

His unraveling went on, but it nevertheless seemed coming to no end. She looked at him again.

"Thank you for the sight of such a beautiful face!" said the young sergeant, without ceremony.

She colored with embarrassment. " 'Twas unwillingly shown," she replied stiffly, and with as much dignity—which was very little—as she could infuse into a position of captivity.

"I like you the better for that incivility, miss," he said.

"I should have liked—I wish—you had never shown yourself to me by intruding here!" She pulled again, and the gathers of her dress began to give way like lilliputian musketry.

"I deserve the chastisement your words give me. But why should such a fair and dutiful girl have such an aversion to her father's sex?"

"Go on your way, please."

"What, Beauty, and drag you after me? Do but look; I never saw such a tangle!"

"Oh, 'tis shameful of you; you have been making it worse on purpose to keep me here—you have!"

"Indeed, I don't think so," said the sergeant, with a merry twinkle.

"I tell you you have!" she exclaimed, in high temper. "I insist upon undoing it. Now, allow me!"

"Certainly, miss; I am not of steel." He added a sigh which had as much archness in it as a sigh could possess without losing its nature altogether. "I am thankful for beauty, even when 'tis thrown to me like a bone to a dog. These moments will be over too soon!"

She closed her lips in a determined silence.

Bathsheba was revolving in her mind whether by a bold and desperate rush she could free herself at the risk of leaving her skirt bodily behind her. The thought was too dreadful. The dress—which she had put on to appear stately at the supper—was the head and front of her wardrobe; not another in her stock became her so well. What woman in Bathsheba's position, not naturally timid, and within call of her retainers, would have bought escape from a dashing soldier at so dear a price?

"All in good time; it will soon be done, I perceive," said her cool friend.

"This trifling provokes, and—and—"

"Not too cruel!"

"—Insults me!"

"It is done in order that I may have the pleasure of apologizing to so charming a woman, which I straightway do most humbly, madam," he said, bowing low.

Bathsheba really knew not what to say.

"I've seen a good many women in my time," continued the young man in a murmur, and more thoughtfully than hitherto, critically regarding her bent head at the same time; "but I've never seen a woman so beautiful as you. Take it or leave it—be offended or like it—I don't care."

"Who are you, then, who can so well afford to despise opinion?"

"No stranger. Sergeant Troy. I am staying in this place. There! it is undone at last, you see. Your light fingers were more eager than mine. I wish it had been the knot of knots, which there's no untying!"

This was worse and worse. She started up, and so did he. How to decently get away from him—that was her difficulty now. She sidled off inch by inch, the lantern in her hand, till she could see the redness of his coat no longer.

"Ah, Beauty; good-bye!" he said.

She made no reply, and, reaching a distance of twenty or thirty yards, turned about, and ran indoors.

Liddy had just retired to rest. In ascending to her own chamber, Bathsheba opened the girl's door an inch or two, and, panting, said—

"Liddy, is any soldier staying in the village—sergeant somebody—rather gentlemanly for a sergeant, and good-looking—a red coat with blue facings?"

"No, miss . . . No, I say; but really it might be Sergeant Troy home on furlough, though I have not seen him. He was here once in that way when the regiment was at Casterbridge."

"Yes; that's the name. Had he a moustache—no whiskers or beard?"

"He had."

"What kind of a person is he?"

"Oh! miss—I blush to name it—a gay man! But I know him to be very quick and trim, who might have made his thousands, like a squire. Such a clever young dand as he is! He's a doctor's son by name, which is a great deal; and he's an earl's son by nature!"

"Which is a great deal more. Fancy! Is it true?"

"Yes. And he was brought up so well, and sent to Casterbridge Grammar School for years and years. Learnt all languages while he was there; and it was said he got on so far that he could take down Chinese in shorthand; but that I don't answer for, as it was only reported. However, he wasted his gifted lot, and listed a soldier; but even then he rose to be a sergeant without trying at all. Ah! such a blessing it is to be highborn; nobility of blood will shine out even in the ranks and files. And is he really come home, miss?"

"I believe so. Goodnight, Liddy."

After all, how could a cheerful wearer of skirts be permanently offended with the man? There are occasions when girls like Bathsheba will put up with a great deal of unconventional behavior. When they want to be praised, which is often; when they want to be mastered, which is sometimes; and when they want no nonsense, which is seldom. Just now the first feeling was in the ascendant with Bathsheba, with a dash of the second. Moreover, by chance or by devilry, the ministrant was antecedently made interesting by being a handsome stranger who had evidently seen better days.

So she could not clearly decide whether it was her opinion that he had insulted her or not.

"Was ever anything so odd!" she at last exclaimed to herself, in her own room. "And was ever anything so meanly done as what I did—to skulk away like that from a man who was only civil and kind!" Clearly she did not think his barefaced praise of her person an insult now.

It was a fatal omission of Boldwood's that he had never once told her she was beautiful.

25. *The New Acquaintance Described*

IDIOSYNCRASY AND VICISSITUDE had combined to stamp Sergeant Troy as an exceptional being.

He was a man to whom memories were an incumbrance, and anticipations a superfluity. Simply feeling, considering, and caring for what was before his eyes, he was vulnerable only in the present. His outlook upon time was as a transient flash of the eye now and then: that projection of consciousness into days gone by and to come, which makes the past a synonym for the pathetic and the future a word for circumspection, was foreign to Troy. With him the past was yesterday; the future, tomorrow; never, the day after.

On this account he might, in certain lights, have been regarded as one of the most fortunate of his order. For it may be argued with great plausibility that reminiscence is less an endowment than a disease, and that expectation in its only comfortable form—that of absolute faith—is practically an impossibility; whilst in the form of hope and the secondary compounds, patience, impatience, resolve, curiosity, it is a constant fluctuation between pleasure and pain.

Sergeant Troy, being entirely innocent of the practice of expectation, was never disappointed. To set against this negative gain there may have been some positive losses from a certain narrowing of the higher tastes and sensations which it entailed.

But limitation of the capacity is never recognized as a loss by the loser therefrom: in this attribute moral or æsthetic poverty contrasts plausibly with material, since those who suffer do not mind it, whilst those who mind it soon cease to suffer. It is not a denial of anything to have been always without it, and what Troy had never enjoyed he did not miss; but, being fully conscious that what sober people missed he enjoyed, his capacity, though really less, seemed greater than theirs.

He was moderately truthful toward men, but to women lied like a Cretan—a system of ethics above all others calculated to win popularity at the first flush of admission into lively society; and the possibility of the favor gained being transitory had reference only to the future.

He never passed the line which divides the spruce vices from the ugly; and hence, though his morals had hardly been applauded, disapproval of them had frequently been tempered with a smile. This treatment had led to his becoming a sort of regrater of other men's gallantries, to his own aggrandizement as a Corinthian, rather than to the moral profit of his hearers.

His reason and his propensities had seldom any reciprocating influence, having separated by mutual consent long ago: thence it sometimes happened that, while his intentions were as honorable as could be wished, any particular deed formed a dark background which threw them into fine relief. The sergeant's vicious phases being the offspring of impulse, and his virtuous phases of cool meditation, the latter had a modest tendency to be oftener heard of than seen.

Troy was full of activity, but his activities were less of a locomotive than a vegetative nature; and, never being based upon any original choice of foundation or direction, they were exercised on whatever object chance might place in their way.

Hence, whilst he sometimes reached the brilliant in speech because that was spontaneous, he fell below the commonplace in action, from inability to guide incipient effort. He had a quick comprehension and considerable force of character; but, being without the power to combine them, the comprehension became engaged with trivialities whilst waiting for the will to direct it, and the force wasted itself in useless grooves through unheeding the comprehension.

He was a fairly well-educated man for one of middle class—exceptionally well educated for a common soldier. He spoke fluently and unceasingly. He could in this way be one thing and seem another; for instance, he could speak of love and think of dinner; call on the husband to look at the wife; be eager to pay and intend to owe.

The wondrous power of flattery in *passados* at woman is a perception so universal as to be remarked upon by many people almost as automatically as they repeat a proverb, or say that they are Christians and the like, without thinking much of the enormous corollaries which spring from the proposition. Still less is it acted upon for the good of the complemental being alluded to. With the majority such an opinion is shelved with all those trite aphorisms which require some catastrophe to bring their tremendous meanings thoroughly home. When expressed with some amount of reflectiveness it seems coordinate with a belief that this flattery must be reasonable to be effective. It is to the credit of men that few attempt to settle the question by experiment, and it is for their happiness, perhaps, that accident has never settled it for them. Nevertheless, that a male dissembler who by deluging her with untenable fictions charms the female wisely, may acquire powers reaching to the extremity of perdition, is a truth taught to many by unsought and wringing occurrences. And some pro-

fess to have attained to the same knowledge by experiment as aforesaid, and jauntily continue their
indulgence in such experiments with terrible effect.
Sergeant Troy was one.

He had been known to observe casually that in
dealing with womankind the only alternative to
flattery was cursing and swearing. There was no
third method. "Treat them fairly, and you are a
lost man," he would say.

This philosopher's public appearance in Weatherbury promptly followed his arrival there. A week or
two after the shearing Bathsheba, feeling a nameless relief of spirits on account of Boldwood's absence, approached her hayfields and looked over
the hedge toward the haymakers. They consisted in
about equal proportions of gnarled and flexuous
forms, the former being the men, the latter the
women, who wore tilt bonnets covered with nan-
keen, which hung in a curtain upon their shoulders.
Coggan and Mark Clark were mowing in a less forward meadow, Clark humming a tune to the strokes
of his scythe, to which Jan made no attempt to keep
time with his. In the first mead they were already
loading hay, the women raking it into cocks and
windrows, and the men tossing it upon the wagon.

From behind the wagon a bright scarlet spot
emerged, and went on lodging unconcernedly with
the rest. It was the gallant sergeant, who had come
haymaking for pleasure; and nobody could deny
that he was doing the mistress of the farm real
knight service by this voluntary contribution of his
labor at a busy time.

As soon as she had entered the field Troy saw her,
and sticking his pitchfork into the ground and
picking up his crop or cane, he came forward.
Bathsheba blushed with half-angry embarrassment,
and adjusted her eyes as well as her feet to the
direct line of her path.

26. *Scene on the Verge of the Hay Mead*

"AH, MISS EVERDENE!" said the sergeant, touching his diminutive cap. "Little did I think it was you I was speaking to the other night. And yet, if I had reflected, the 'Queen of the Cornmarket' (truth is truth at any hour of the day or night, and I heard you so named in Casterbridge yesterday), the 'Queen of the Cornmarket,' I say, could be no other woman. I step across now to beg your forgiveness a thousand times for having been led by my feelings to express myself too strongly for a stranger. To be sure I am no stranger to the place—I am Sergeant Troy, as I told you, and I have assisted your uncle in these fields no end of times when I was a lad. I have been doing the same for you today."

"I suppose I must thank you for that, Sergeant Troy," said the Queen of the Cornmarket in an indifferently grateful tone.

The sergeant looked hurt and sad. "Indeed you must not, Miss Everdene," he said. "Why could you think such a thing necessary?"

"I am glad it is not."

"Why? if I may ask without offence."

"Because I don't much want to thank you for anything."

"I am afraid I have made a hole with my tongue that my heart will never mend. O these intolerable times: that ill luck should follow a man for honestly telling a woman she is beautiful! 'Twas the most I

said—you must own that; and the least I could say
—that I own myself."

"There is some talk I could do without more
easily than money."

"Indeed. That remark is a sort of digression."

"No. It means that I would rather have your
room than your company."

"And I would rather have curses from you than
kisses from any other woman; so I'll stay here."

Bathsheba was absolutely speechless. And yet she
could not help feeling that the assistance he was
rendering forbade a harsh repulse.

"Well," continued Troy, "I suppose there is a
praise which is rudeness, and that may be mine. At
the same time there is a treatment which is injustice,
and that may be yours. Because a plain blunt man,
who has never been taught concealment, speaks out
his mind without exactly intending it, he's to be
snapped off like the son of a sinner."

"Indeed there's no such case between us," she said,
turning away. "I don't allow strangers to be bold
and impudent—even in praise of me."

"Ah—it is not the fact but the method which
offends you," he said carelessly. "But I have the sad
satisfaction of knowing that my words, whether
pleasing or offensive, are unmistakably true. Would
you have had me look at you, and tell my acquaintance that you are quite a commonplace
woman, to save you the embarrassment of being
stared at if they come near you? Not I. I couldn't
tell any such ridiculous lie about a beauty to en-
courage a single woman in England in too exces-
sive a modesty."

"It is all pretence—what you are saying!" exclaimed Bathsheba, laughing in spite of herself
at the sergeant's sly method. "You have a rare invention, Sergeant Troy. Why couldn't you have
passed by me that night, and said nothing?—
that was all I meant to reproach you for."

"Because I wasn't going to. Half the pleasure of a feeling lies in being able to express it on the spur of the moment, and I let out mine. It would have been just the same if you had been the reverse person—ugly and old—I should have exclaimed about it in the same way."

"How long is it since you have been so afflicted with strong feeling, then?"

"Oh, ever since I was big enough to know loveliness from deformity."

"'Tis to be hoped your sense of the difference you speak of doesn't stop at faces, but extends to morals as well."

"I won't speak of morals or religion—my own or anybody else's. Though perhaps I should have been a very good Christian if you pretty women hadn't made me an idolater."

Bathsheba moved on to hide the irrepressible dimplings of merriment. Troy followed, whirling his crop.

"But—Miss Everdene—you do forgive me?"

"Hardly."

"Why?"

"You say such things."

"I said you were beautiful, and I'll say so still, for, by—so you are! The most beautiful ever I saw, or may I fall dead this instant! Why, upon my—"

"Don't—don't! I won't listen to you—you are so profane!" she said, in a restless state between distress at hearing him and a penchant to hear more.

"I again say you are a most fascinating woman. There's nothing remarkable in my saying so, is there? I'm sure the fact is evident enough. Miss Everdene, my opinion may be too forcibly let out to please you, and, for the matter of that, too insignificant to convince you, but surely it is honest, and why can't it be excused?"

"Because it—it isn't a correct one," she femininely murmured.

"Oh, fie—fie! Am I any worse for breaking the third of that Terrible Ten than you for breaking the ninth?"

"Well, it doesn't seem *quite* true to me that I am fascinating," she replied evasively.

"Not so to you: then I say with all respect that, if so, it is owing to your modesty, Miss Everdene. But surely you must have been told by everybody of what everybody notices? And you should take their words for it."

"They don't say so exactly."

"Oh, yes, they must!"

"Well, I mean to my face, as you do," she went on, allowing herself to be further lured into a conversation that intention had rigorously forbidden.

"But you know they think so?"

"No—that is—I certainly have heard Liddy say they do, but—" She paused.

Capitulation—that was the purport of the simple reply, guarded as it was—capitulation, unknown to herself. Never did a fragile tail-less sentence convey a more perfect meaning. The careless sergeant smiled within himself, and probably too the devil smiled from a loophole in Tophet, for the moment was the turning point of a career. Her tone and mien signified beyond mistake that the seed which was to lift the foundation had taken root in the chink: the remainder was a mere question of time and natural changes.

"There the truth comes out!" said the soldier, in reply. "Never tell me that a young lady can live in a buzz of admiration without knowing something about it. Ah, well, Miss Everdene, you are—pardon my blunt way—you are rather an injury to our race than otherwise."

"How—indeed?" she said, opening her eyes.

"Oh, it is true enough. I may as well be hung for

a sheep as a lamb (an old country saying, not of much account, but it will do for a rough soldier), and so I will speak my mind, regardless of your pleasure, and without hoping or intending to get your pardon. Why, Miss Everdene, it is in this manner that your good looks may do more harm than good in the world." The sergeant looked down the mead in critical abstraction. "Probably some one man on an average falls in love with each ordinary woman. She can marry him: he is content, and leads a useful life. Such women as you a hundred men always covet—your eyes will bewitch scores on scores into an unavailing fancy for you—you can only marry one of that many. Out of these say twenty will endeavor to drown the bitterness of despised love in drink; twenty more will mope away their lives without a wish or attempt to make a mark in the world, because they have no ambition apart from their attachment to you; twenty more—the susceptible person myself possibly among them—will be always draggling after you, getting where they may just see you, doing desperate things. Men are such constant fools! The rest may try to get over their passion with more or less success. But all these men will be saddened. And not only those ninety-nine men, but the ninety-nine women they might have married are saddened with them. There's my tale. That's why I say that a woman so charming as yourself, Miss Everdene, is hardly a blessing to her race."

The handsome sergeant's features were during this speech as rigid and stern as John Knox's in addressing his gay young queen.

Seeing she made no reply, he said, "Do you read French?"

"No; I began, but when I got to the verbs, father died," she said simply.

"I do—when I have an opportunity, which latterly has not been often (my mother was a Pari-

sienne)—and there's a proverb they have, *Qui aime
bien châtie bien*—'He chastens who loves well.'
Do you understand me?"

"Ah!" she replied, and there was even a little
tremulousness in the usually cool girl's voice; "if
you can only fight half as winningly as you can talk,
you are able to make a pleasure of a bayonet
wound!" And then poor Bathsheba instantly perceived her slip in making this admission: in hastily
trying to retrieve it, she went from bad to worse.
"Don't, however, suppose that *I* derive any pleasure
from what you tell me."

"I know you do not—I know it perfectly," said
Troy, with much hearty conviction on the exterior
of his face: and altering the expression to moodi-
ness; "when a dozen men are ready to speak tenderly to you, and give the admiration you deserve
without adding the warning you need, it stands to
reason that my poor rough-and-ready mixture of
praise and blame cannot convey much pleasure.
Fool as I may be, I am not so conceited as to suppose that!"

"I think you—are conceited, nevertheless," said
Bathsheba, looking askance at a reed she was fitfully
pulling with one hand, having lately grown feverish
under the soldier's system of procedure—not because the nature of his cajolery was entirely unperceived, but because its vigor was overwhelming.

"I would not own it to anybody else—nor do I
exactly to you. Still, there might have been some
self-conceit in my foolish supposition the other
night. I knew that what I said in admiration might
be an opinion too often forced upon you to give any
pleasure, but I certainly did think that the kindness
of your nature might prevent you judging an un-
controlled tongue harshly—which you have done—
and thinking badly of me and wounding me this
morning, when I am working hard to save your
hay."

"Well, you need not think more of that: perhaps you did not mean to be rude to me by speaking out your mind: indeed, I believe you did not," said the shrewd woman, in painfully innocent earnest. "And I thank you for giving help here. But—but mind you don't speak to me again in that way, or in any other, unless I speak to you."

"Oh, Miss Bathsheba! That is too hard!"

"No, it isn't. Why is it?"

"You will never speak to me; for I shall not be here long. I am soon going back again to the miserable monotony of drill—and perhaps our regiment will be ordered out soon. And yet you take away the one little ewe lamb of pleasure that I have in this dull life of mine. Well, perhaps generosity is not a woman's most marked characteristic."

"When are you going from here?" she asked with some interest.

"In a month."

"But how can it give you pleasure to speak to me?"

"Can you ask, Miss Everdene—knowing as you do—what my offence is based on?"

"If you do care so much for a silly trifle of that kind, then, I don't mind doing it," she uncertainly and doubtingly answered. "But you can't really care for a word from me? You only say so—I think you only say so."

"That's unjust—but I won't repeat the remark. I am too gratified to get such a mark of your friendship at any price to cavil at the tone. I *do,* Miss Everdene, care for it. You may think a man foolish to want a mere word—just a good morning. Perhaps he is—I don't know. But you have never been a man looking upon a woman, and that woman yourself."

"Well."

"Then you know nothing of what such an experience is like—and Heaven forbid that you ever should!"

"Nonsense, flatterer! What is it like? I am interested in knowing."

"Put shortly, it is not being able to think, hear, or look in any direction except one without wretchedness, nor there without torture."

"Ah, sergeant, it won't do—you are pretending!" she said, shaking her head. "Your words are too dashing to be true."

"I am not, upon the honor of a soldier."

"But *why* is it so?—Of course I ask for mere pasttime."

"Because you are so distracting—and I am so distracted."

"You look like it."

"I am indeed."

"Why, you only saw me the other night!"

"That makes no difference. The lightning works instantaneously. I loved you then, at once—as I do now."

Bathsheba surveyed him curiously, from the feet upward, as high as she liked to venture her glance, which was not quite so high as his eyes.

"You cannot and you don't," she said demurely. "There is no such sudden feeling in people. I won't listen to you any longer. Dear me, I wish I knew what o'clock it is—I am going—I have wasted too much time here already!"

The sergeant looked at his watch and told her. "What, haven't you a watch, miss?" he inquired.

"I have not just at present—I am about to get a new one."

"No. You shall be given one. Yes—you shall. A gift, Miss Everdene—a gift."

And before she knew what the young man was intending, a heavy gold watch was in her hand.

"It is an unusually good one for a man like me

to possess," he quietly said. "That watch has a history. Press the spring and open the back."

She did so.

"What do you see?"

"A crest and a motto."

"A coronet with five points, and beneath, *Cedit amor rebus*—'Love yields to circumstance.' It's the motto of the Earls of Severn. That watch belonged to the last lord, and was given to my mother's husband, a medical man, for his use till I came of age, when it was to be given to me. It was all the fortune that ever I inherited. That watch has regulated imperial interests in its time—the stately ceremonial, the courtly assignation, pompous travels, and lordly sleeps. Now it is yours."

"But, Sergeant Troy, I cannot take this—I cannot!" she exclaimed with round-eyed wonder. "A gold watch! What are you doing? Don't be such a dissembler!"

The sergeant retreated to avoid receiving back his gift, which she held out persistently toward him. Bathsheba followed as he retired.

"Keep it—do, Miss Everdene—keep it!" said the erratic child of impulse. "The fact of your possessing it makes it worth ten times as much to me. A more plebian one will answer my purpose just as well, and the pleasure of knowing whose heart my old one beats against—well, I won't speak of that. It is in far worthier hands than ever it has been in before."

"But indeed I can't have it!" she said, in a perfect simmer of distress. "Oh, how can you do such a thing; that is, if you really mean it! Give me your dead father's watch, and such a valuable one! You should not be so reckless, indeed, Sergeant Troy!"

"I love my father: good; but better, I love you more. That's how I can do it," said the sergeant with an intonation of such exquisite fidelity to nature that it was evidently not all acted now. Her beauty, which, whilst it had been quiescent, he had praised in jest, had in its animated phases moved him to earnest; and though his seriousness was less than she imagined, it was probably more than he imagined himself.

Bathsheba was brimming with agitated bewilderment, and she said, in half-suspicious accents of feeling, "Can it be! Oh, how can it be, that you care for me, and so suddenly! You have seen so little of me: I may not be really so—so nice-looking as I seem to you. Please, do take it; Oh, do! I cannot and will not have it. Believe me, your generosity is too great. I have never done you a single kindness, and why should you be so kind to me?"

A factitious reply had been again upon his lips, but it was again suspended, and he looked at her with an arrested eye. The truth was, that as she now stood—excited, wild, and honest as the day— her alluring beauty bore out so fully the epithets he had bestowed upon it that he was quite startled at his temerity in advancing them as false. He said mechanically, "Ah, why?" and continued to look at her.

"And my workfolk see me following you about the field, and are wondering. Oh, this is dreadful!" she went on, unconscious of the transmutation she was effecting.

"I did not quite mean you to accept it at first, for it was my one poor patent of nobility," he broke out bluntly; "but, upon my soul, I wish you would now. Without any shamming, come! Don't deny me the happiness of wearing it for my sake? But you are too lovely even to care to be kind as others are."

"No, no; don't say so! I have reasons for reserve which I cannot explain."

"Let it be, then, let it be," he said, receiving back the watch at last; "I must be leaving you now.

And will you speak to me for these few weeks of my stay?"

"Indeed I will. Yet, I don't know if I will! Oh, why did you come and disturb me so!"

"Perhaps in setting a gin, I have caught myself. Such things have happened. Well, will you let me work in your fields?" he coaxed.

"Yes, I suppose so; if it is any pleasure to you."

"Miss Everdene, I thank you."

"No, no."

"Good-bye!"

The sergeant brought his hand to the cap on the slope of his head, saluted, and returned to the distant group of haymakers.

Bathsheba could not face the haymakers now. Her heart erratically flitting hither and thither from perplexed excitement, hot, and almost tearful, she retreated homeward, murmuring. "Oh, what have I done! What does it mean! I wish I knew how much of it was true!"

27. Hiving the Bees

THE WEATHERBURY BEES were late in their swarming this year. It was in the latter part of June, and the day after the interview with Troy in the hayfield, that Bathsheba was standing in her garden, watching a swarm in the air and guessing their probable setting place. Not only were they late this year, but unruly. Sometimes throughout a whole

season all the swarms would alight on the lowest
attainable bough—such as part of a currant bush
or espalier apple tree; next year they would, with
just the same unanimity, make straight off to the
uppermost member of some tall, gaunt costard, or
quarrender, and there defy all invaders who did
not come armed with ladders and staves to take
them.

This was the case at present. Bathsheba's eyes,
shaded by one hand, were following the ascending
multitude against the unexplorable stretch of blue
till they ultimately halted by one of the unwieldy
trees spoken of. A process somewhat analogous to
that of alleged formations of the universe, time and
times ago, was observable. The bustling swarm had
swept the sky in a scattered and uniform haze, which
now thickened to a nebulous center: this glided on
to a bough and grew still denser, till it formed a
solid black spot upon the light.

The men and women being all busily engaged in
saving the hay—even Liddy had left the house for
the purpose of lending a hand—Bathsheba resolved
to hive the bees herself, if possible. She had dressed
the hive with herbs and honey, fetched a ladder,
brush, and crook, made herself impregnable with
armor of leather gloves, straw hat, and large gauze
veil—once green but now faded to snuff color—and
ascended a dozen rungs of the ladder. At once she
heard, not ten yards off, a voice that was beginning
to have a strange power in agitating her.

"Miss Everdene, let me assist you; you should
not attempt such a thing alone."

Troy was just opening the garden gate.

Bathsheba flung down the brush, crook, and
empty hive, pulled the skirt of her dress tightly
round her ankles in a tremendous flurry, and as
well as she could slid down the ladder. By the time
she reached the bottom Troy was there also, and he
stooped to pick up the hive.

"How fortunate I am to have dropped in at this moment!" exclaimed the sergeant.

She found her voice in a minute. "What! and will you shake them in for me?" she asked, in what, for a defiant girl, was a faltering way; though, for a timid girl, it would have seemed a brave way enough.

"Will I!" said Troy. "Why, of course I will. How blooming you are today!" Troy flung down his cane and put his foot on the ladder to ascend.

"But you must have on the veil and gloves, or you'll be stung fearfully!"

"Ah, yes. I must put on the veil and gloves. Will you kindly show me how to fix them properly?"

"And you must have the broad brimmed hat, too; for your cap has no brim to keep the veil off, and they'd reach your face."

"The broad brimmed hat, too, by all means."

So a whimsical fate ordered that her hat should be taken off—veil and all attached—and placed upon his head, Troy tossing his own into a gooseberry bush. Then the veil had to be tied at its lower edge round his collar and the gloves put on him.

He looked such an extraordinary object in this guise that, flurried as she was, she could not avoid laughing outright. It was the removal of yet another stake from the palisade of cold manners which had kept him off.

Bathsheba looked on from the ground whilst he was busy sweeping and shaking the bees from the tree, holding up the hive with the other hand for them to fall into. She made use of an unobserved minute whilst his attention was absorbed in the operation to arrange her plumes a little. He came down holding the hive at arm's length, behind which trailed a cloud of bees.

"Upon my life," said Troy, through the veil, "holding up this hive makes one's arm ache worse than a week of sword exercise." When the maneuver was complete he approached her. "Would you be good enough to untie me and let me out? I am nearly stifled inside this silk cage."

To hide her embarrassment during the unwonted process of untying the string about his neck, she said:

"I have never seen that you spoke of."

"What?"

"The sword exercise."

"Ah! would you like to?" said Troy.

Bathsheba hesitated. She had heard wondrous reports from time to time by dwellers in Weatherbury, who had by chance sojourned awhile in Casterbridge, near the barracks, of this strange and glorious performance, the sword exercise. Men and boys who had peeped through chinks or over walls into the barrackyard returned with accounts of its being the most flashing affair conceivable; accouterments and weapons glistening like stars— here, there, around—yet all by rule and compass. So she said mildly what she felt strongly:

"Yes: I should like to see it very much."

"And so you shall; you shall see me go through it."

"No! How?"

"Let me consider."

"Not with a walking stick—I don't care to see that. It must be a real sword."

"Yes, I know; and I have no sword here; but I think I could get one by the evening. Now, will you do this?"

Troy bent over her and murmured some suggestion in a low voice.

"Oh, no, indeed!" said Bathsheba, blushing. "Thank you very much, but I couldn't on any account."

"Surely you might? Nobody would know."

She shook her head, but with a weakened negation. "If I were to," she said, "I must bring Liddy too. Might I not?"

Troy looked far away. "I don't see why you want to bring her," he said coldly.

An unconscious look of assent in Bathsheba's eyes betrayed that something more than his coldness had made her also feel that Liddy would be superfluous in the suggested scene. She had felt it, even whilst making the proposal.

"Well, I won't bring Liddy—and I'll come. But only for a very short time," she added; "a very short time."

"It will not take five minutes," said Troy.

28.   The Hollow Amid the Ferns

THE HILL opposite Bathsheba's dwelling extended, a mile off, into an uncultivated tract of land, dotted at this season with tall thickets of brake fern, plump and diaphanous from recent rapid growth, and radiant in hues of clear and untainted green.

At eight o'clock this midsummer evening, whilst the bristling ball of gold in the west still swept the tips of the ferns with its long, luxuriant rays, a soft brushing by of garments might have been heard among them, and Bathsheba appeared in their midst, their soft, feathery arms caressing her up to her shoulders. She paused, turned, went back over the hill and halfway to her own door, whence she cast a farewell glance upon the spot she had just left, having resolved not to remain near the place after all.

She saw a dim spot of artificial red moving round the shoulder of the rise. It disappeared on the other side.

She waited one minute—two minutes—thought of Troy's disappointment at her nonfulfillment of a promised engagement, till she again ran along the field, clambered over the bank, and followed the original direction. She was now literally trembling and panting at this her temerity in such an errant undertaking; her breath came and went quickly, and her eyes shone with an infrequent light. Yet go she must. She reached the verge of a pit in the middle of the ferns. Troy stood in the bottom, looking up toward her.

"I heard you rustling through the fern before I saw you," he said, coming up and giving her his hand to help her down the slope.

The pit was a saucer-shaped concave, naturally formed, with a top diameter of about thirty feet, and shallow enough to allow the sunshine to reach their heads. Standing in the center, the sky overhead was met by a circular horizon of fern: this grew nearly to the bottom of the slope and then abruptly ceased. The middle within the belt of verdure was floored with a thick flossy carpet of moss and grass intermingled, so yielding that the foot was half-buried within it.

"Now," said Troy, producing the sword, which, as he raised it into the sunlight, gleamed a sort of greeting, like a living thing; "first, we have four right and four left cuts; four right and four left thrusts. Infantry cuts and guards are more interesting than ours, to my mind; but they are not so swashing. They have seven cuts and three thrusts. So much as a preliminary. Well, next, our cut one is as if you were sowing your corn—so." Bathsheba saw a sort of rainbow, upside down in the air, and Troy's arm was still again. "Cut two, as if you were hedging—so. Three, as if you were reaping—so. Four, as if you were threshing—in that way. Then the same on the left. The thrusts are these: one, two, three, four, right; one, two, three, four, left." He repeated them. "Have 'em again?" he said. "One, two—"

She hurriedly interrupted: "I'd rather not; though I don't mind your twos and fours; but your ones and threes are terrible!"

"Very well. I'll let you off the ones and threes. Next, cuts, points and guards altogether." Troy duly exhibited them. "Then there's pursuing practice, in this way." He gave the movements as before. "There, those are the stereotyped forms. The infantry have two most diabolical upward cuts, which we are too humane to use. Like this—three, four."

"How murderous and bloodthirsty!"

"They are rather deathy. Now I'll be more interesting, and let you see some loose play—giving all the cuts and points, infantry and cavalry, quicker than lightning, and as promiscuously—with just enough rule to regulate instinct and yet not to fetter it. You are my antagonist, with this difference from real warfare, that I shall miss you every time by one hair's breadth, or perhaps two. Mind you don't flinch, whatever you do."

"I'll be sure not to!" she said invincibly.

He pointed to about a yard in front of him.

Bathsheba's adventurous spirit was beginning to find some grains of relish in these highly novel proceedings. She took up her position as directed, facing Troy.

"Now just to learn whether you have pluck enough to let me do what I wish, I'll give you a preliminary test."

He flourished the sword by way of introduction number two, and the next thing of which she was conscious was that the point and blade of the sword were darting with a gleam toward her left side, just above her hip; then of their reappearance on her right side, emerging as it were from between her ribs, having apparently passed through her body. The third item of consciousness was that of seeing the same sword, perfectly clean and free from blood held vertically in Troy's hand (in the position technically called "recover swords"). All was as quick as electricity.

"Oh!" she cried out in affright, pressing her hand to her side. "Have you run me through?— no, you have not! Whatever have you done!"

"I have not touched you," said Troy quietly. "It was mere sleight of hand. The sword passed behind you. Now you are not afraid, are you? Because if you are I can't perform. I give my word that I will not only not hurt you, but not once touch you."

"I don't think I am afraid. You are quite sure you will not hurt me?"

"Quite sure."

"Is the sword very sharp?"

"Oh, no—only stand as still as a statue. Now!"

In an instant the atmosphere was transformed to Bathsheba's eyes. Beams of light caught from the low sun's rays, above, around, in front of her, well-nigh shut out earth and heaven—all emitted in the marvelous evolutions of Troy's reflecting blade, which seemed everywhere at once, and yet nowhere specially. These circling gleams were accompanied by a keen rush that was almost a whistling —also springing from all sides of her at once. In short, she was enclosed in a firmament of light, and of sharp hisses, resembling a skyful of meteors close at hand.

Never since the broadsword became the national weapon had there been more dexterity shown in its management than by the hands of Sergeant Troy, and never had he been in such splendid temper for the performance as now in the evening sunshine among the ferns with Bathsheba. It may safely be asserted with respect to the closeness of his cuts, that had it been possible for the edge of the sword to leave in the air a permanent substance wherever it flew past, the space left untouched would have been almost a mold of Bathsheba's figure.

Behind the luminous streams of this *aurora militaris,* she could see the hue of Troy's sword arm, spread in a scarlet haze over the space covered by its motions, like a twanged harpstring, and behind all Troy himself, mostly facing her; sometimes, to show the rear cuts, half turned away, his eye nevertheless always keenly measuring her breadth and outline, and his lips tightly closed in sustained effort. Next, his movements lapsed slower, and she could see them individually. The hissing of the sword had ceased, and he stopped entirely.

"That outer loose lock of hair wants tidying," he said, before she had moved or spoken. "Wait: I'll do it for you."

An arc of silver shone on her right side: the sword had descended. The lock dropped to the ground.

"Bravely borne!" said Troy. "You didn't flinch a shade's thickness. Wonderful in a woman!"

"It was because I didn't expect it. Oh, you have spoilt my hair!"

"Only once more."

"No—no! I am afraid of you—indeed I am!" she cried.

"I won't touch you at all—not even your hair. I am only going to kill that caterpillar settling on you. Now: still!"

It appeared that a caterpillar had come from the fern and chosen the front of her bodice as his resting place. She saw the point glisten toward her bosom, and seemingly enter it. Bathsheba closed her eyes in the full persuasion that she was killed at last. However, feeling just as usual, she opened them again.

"There it is, look," said the sergeant, holding his sword before her eyes.

The caterpillar was spitted upon its point.

"Why, it is magic!" said Bathsheba, amazed.

"Oh, no—dexterity. I merely gave point to your bosom where the caterpillar was, and instead of running you through checked the extension a thousandth of an inch short of your surface."

"But how could you chop off a curl of my hair with a sword that has no edge?"

"No edge! This sword will shave like a razor. Look here."

He touched the palm of his hand with the blade, and then, lifting it, showed her a thin shaving of scarfskin dangling therefrom.

"But you said before beginning that it was blunt and couldn't cut me!"

"That was to get you to stand still, and so make sure of your safety. The risk of injuring you through your moving was too great not to force me to tell you a fib to escape it."

She shuddered. "I have been within an inch of my life, and didn't know it!"

"More precisely speaking, you have been within half an inch of being pared alive two hundred and ninety-five times."

"Cruel, cruel, 'tis of you!"

"You have been perfectly safe, nevertheless. My sword never errs." And Troy returned the weapon to the scabbard.

Bathsheba, overcome by a hundred tumultuous feelings resulting from the scene, abstractedly sat down on a tuft of heather.

"I must leave you now," said Troy softly. "And I'll venture to take and keep this in remembrance of you."

She saw him stoop to the grass, pick up the winding lock which he had severed from her manifold tresses, twist it round his fingers, unfasten a button in the breast of his coat, and carefully put it inside. She felt powerless to withstand or deny him. He was altogether too much for her, and Bathsheba seemed as one who, facing a reviving wind, finds it blow so strongly that it stops the breath.

He drew near and said, "I must be leaving you." He drew nearer still. A minute later and she saw his scarlet form disappear amid the ferny thicket, almost in a flash, like a brand swiftly waved.

That minute's interval had brought the blood beating into her face, set her stinging as if aflame to the very hollows of her feet, and enlarged emotion to a compass which quite swamped thought. It had brought upon her a stroke resulting, as did that of Moses in Horeb, in a liquid stream—here a stream of tears. She felt like one who has sinned a great sin.

The circumstance had been the gentle dip of Troy's mouth downward upon her own. He had kissed her.

29. *Particulars of a Twilight Walk*

WE NOW SEE the element of folly distinctly mingling with the many varying particulars which made up the character of Bathsheba Everdene. It was almost foreign to her intrinsic nature. Introduced as lymph on the dart of Eros it eventually permeated and colored her whole constitution. Bathsheba, though she had too much understanding to be entirely governed by her womanliness, had too much womanliness to use her understanding to the best advantage. Perhaps in no minor point does woman astonish her helpmate more than in the strange power she possesses of believing cajoleries that she knows to be false—except, indeed, in that of being utterly sceptical on strictures that she knows to be true.

Bathsheba loved Troy in the way that only self-reliant women love when they abandon their self-reliance. When a strong woman recklessly throws away her strength she is worse than a weak woman who has never had any strength to throw away. One source of her inadequacy is the novelty of the occasion. She has never had practice in making the best of such a condition. Weakness is doubly weak by being new.

Bathsheba was not conscious of guile in this matter. Though in one sense a woman of the world, it was, after all, that world of daylight coteries and green carpets wherein cattle form the passing crowd and winds the busy hum; where a quiet family of rabbits or hares live on the other side of your party wall, where your neighbor is everybody in the tything, and where calculation is confined to marketdays. Of the fabricated tastes of good fashionable society she knew but little, and of the formulated self-indulgence of bad, nothing at all. Had her utmost thoughts in this direction been distinctly worded (and by herself they never were), they would only have amounted to such a matter as that she felt her impulses to be pleasanter guides than her discretion. Her love was entire as a child's, and though warm as summer it was fresh as spring. Her culpability lay in her making no attempt to control feeling by subtle and careful inquiry into consequences. She could show others the steep and thorny way, but "reck'd not her own rede."

And Troy's deformities lay deep down from a woman's vision, whilst his embellishments were upon the very surface; thus contrasting with homely Oak, whose defects were patent to the blindest, and whose virtues were as metals in a mine.

The difference between love and respect was markedly shown in her conduct. Bathsheba had spoken of her interest in Boldwood with the greatest freedom to Liddy, but she had only communed with her own heart concerning Troy.

All this infatuation Gabriel saw, and was troubled thereby from the time of his daily journey a-field to the time of his return, and on to the small hours of many a night. That he was not beloved had hitherto been his great sorrow; that Bathsheba was getting into the toils was now a sorrow greater than the first, and one which nearly obscured it. It was a result which paralleled the oft-quoted observation of Hippocrates concerning physical pains.

That is a noble though perhaps an unpromising love which not even the fear of breeding aversion in the bosom of the one beloved can deter from combating his or her errors. Oak determined to speak to his mistress. He would base his appeal on what he considered her unfair treatment of Farmer Boldwood, now absent from home.

An opportunity occurred one evening when she had gone for a short walk by a path through the neighboring cornfields. It was dusk when Oak, who had not been far a-field that day, took the same path and met her returning, quite pensively, as he thought.

The wheat was now tall, and the path was narrow; thus the way was quite a sunken groove between the embowing thicket on either side. Two persons could not walk abreast without damaging the crop, and Oak stood aside to let her pass.

"Oh, is it Gabriel?" she said. "You are taking a walk too. Goodnight."

"I thought I would come to meet you, as it is rather late," said Oak, turning and following at her heels when she had brushed somewhat quickly by him.

"Thank you, indeed, but I am not very fearful."

"Oh, no; but there are bad characters about."

"I never meet them."

Now Oak, with marvelous ingenuity, had been going to introduce the gallant sergeant through the channel of "bad characters." But all at once the scheme broke down, it suddenly occurring to him that this was rather a clumsy way, and too barefaced to begin with. He tried another preamble.

"And as the man who would naturally come to meet you is away from home, too—I mean Farmer Boldwood—why, thinks I, I'll go," he said.

"Ah, yes." She walked on without turning her head, and for many steps nothing further was heard from her quarter than the rustle of her dress against the heavy corn ears. Then she resumed rather tartly—

"I don't quite understand what you meant by saying that Mr. Boldwood would naturally come to meet me."

"I meant on account of the wedding which they say is likely to take place between you and him, miss. Forgive my speaking plainly."

"They say what is not true," she returned quickly. "No marriage is likely to take place between us."

Gabriel now put forth his unobscured opinion, for the moment had come. "Well, Miss Everdene," he said, "putting aside what people say, I never in my life saw any courting if his is not a courting of you."

Bathsheba would probably have terminated the

conversation there and then by flatly forbidding the subject, had not her conscious weakness of position allured her to palter and argue in endeavors to better it.

"Since this subject has been mentioned," she said very emphatically, "I am glad of the opportunity of clearing up a mistake which is very common and very provoking. I didn't definitely promise Mr. Boldwood anything. I have never cared for him. I respect him, and he has urged me to marry him. But I have given him no distinct answer. As soon as he returns I shall do so; and the answer will be that I cannot think of marrying him."

"People are full of mistakes, seemingly."

"They are."

"The other day they said you were trifling with him, and you almost proved that you were not; lately they have said that you be not, and you straightway begin to show—"

"That I am, I suppose you mean."

"Well, I hope they speak the truth."

"They do, but wrongly applied. I don't trifle with him; but then, I have nothing to do with him."

Oak was unfortunately led on to speak of Boldwood's rival in a wrong tone to her after all. "I wish you had never met that young Sergeant Troy, miss," he sighed.

Bathsheba's steps became faintly spasmodic. "Why?" she asked.

"He is not good enough for 'ee."

"Did any one tell you to speak to me like this?"

"Nobody at all."

"Then it appears to me that Sergeant Troy does not concern us here," she said intractably. "Yet I must say that Sergeant Troy is an educated man, and quite worthy of any woman. He is well born."

"His being higher in learning and birth than

the ruck o' soldiers is anything but a proof of his worth. It shows his course to be down'ard."

"I cannot see what this has to do with our conversation. Mr. Troy's course is not by any means downward; and his superiority *is* a proof of his worth!"

"I believe him to have no conscience at all. And I cannot help begging you, miss, to have nothing to do with him. Listen to me this once—only this once! I don't say he's such a bad man as I have fancied—I pray to God he is not. But since we don't exactly know what he is, why not behave as if he *might* be bad, simply for your own safety? Don't trust him, mistress; I ask you not to trust him so."

"Why, pray?"

"I like soldiers, but this one I do not like," he said sturdily. "His cleverness in his calling may have tempted him astray, and what is mirth to the neighbors is ruin to the woman. When he tries to talk to 'ee again, why not turn away with a short 'Good day'; and when you see him coming one way, turn the other. When he says anything laughable, fail to see the point and don't smile, and speak of him before those who will report your talk as 'that fantastical man,' or 'that Sergeant What's-his-name.' 'That man of a family that has come to the dogs.' Don't be unmannerly toward en, but harmless uncivil, and so get rid of the man."

No Christmas robin detained by a windowpane ever pulsed as did Bathsheba now.

"I say—I say again—that it doesn't become you to talk about him. Why he should be mentioned passes me quite!" she exclaimed desperately. "I know this, th-th-that he is a thoroughly conscientious man—blunt sometimes even to rudeness—but always speaking his mind about you plain to your face!"

"Oh."

"He is as good as anybody in this parish! He is very particular, too, about going to church—yes, he is!"

"I am afeard nobody ever saw him there. I never did, certainly."

"The reason of that is," she said eagerly, "that he goes in privately by the old tower door, just when the service commences, and sits at the back of the gallery. He told me so."

This supreme instance of Troy's goodness fell upon Gabriel's ears like the thirteenth stroke of a crazy clock. It was not only received with utter incredulity as regarded itself, but threw a doubt on all the assurances that had preceded it.

Oak was grieved to find how entirely she trusted him. He brimmed with deep feeling as he replied in a steady voice, the steadiness of which was spoilt by the palpableness of his great effort to keep it so:

"You know, mistress, that I love you, and shall love you always. I only mention this to bring to your mind that at any rate I would wish to do you no harm: beyond that I put it aside. I have lost in the race for money and good things, and I am not such a fool as to pretend to 'ee now. I am poor, and you have got altogether above me. But Bathsheba, dear mistress, this I beg you to consider—that, both to keep yourself well honored among the workfolk, and in common generosity to an honorable man who loves you as well as I, you should be more discreet in your bearing toward this soldier."

"Don't, don't, don't!" she exclaimed, in a choking voice.

"Are ye not more to me than my own affairs, and even life!" he went on. "Come, listen to me! I am six years older than you, and Mr. Boldwood is ten years older than I, and consider—I do beg of 'ee to consider before it is too late—how safe you would be in his hands!"

Oak's allusion to his own love for her lessened, to some extent, her anger at his interference; but she could not really forgive him for letting his wish to marry her be eclipsed by his wish to do her good, any more than for his slighting treatment of Troy.

"I wish you to go elsewhere," she commanded, a paleness of face invisible to the eye being suggested by the trembling words. "Do not remain on this farm any longer. I don't want you—I beg you to go!"

"That's nonsense," said Oak calmly. "This is the second time you have pretended to dismiss me; and what's the use o' it?"

"Pretended! You shall go, sir—your lecturing I will not hear! I am mistress here."

"Go, indeed—what folly will you say next? Treating me like Dick, Tom, and Harry when you know that a short time ago my position was as good as yours! Upon my life, Bathsheba, it is too barefaced. You know, too, that I can't go without putting things in such a strait as you wouldn't get out of I can't tell when. Unless, indeed, you'll promise to have an understanding man as bailiff, or manager, or something. I'll go at once if you'll promise that."

"I shall have no bailiff; I shall continue to be my own manager," she said decisively.

"Very well, then; you should be thankful to me for biding. How would the farm go on with nobody to mind it but a woman? But mind this, I don't wish 'ee to feel you owe me anything. Not I. What I do, I do. Sometimes I say I should be as glad as a bird to leave the place—for don't suppose I'm content to be a nobody. I was made for better things. However, I don't like to see your concerns going to ruin, as they must if you keep in this mind. . . . I hate taking my own measure so plain, but, upon my life, your provoking ways make a man say what he wouldn't dream of at other times! I own to being rather interfering. But you know well enough how it is, and who she is that I like too well, and feel too much like a fool about to be civil to her!"

It is more than probable that she privately and unconsciously respected him a little for this grim fidelity, which had been shown in his tone even more than in his words. At any rate she murmured something to the effect that he might stay if he wished. She said more distinctly, "Will you leave me alone now? I don't order it as a mistress—I ask it as a woman, and I expect you not to be so uncourteous as to refuse."

"Certainly I will, Miss Everdene," said Gabriel gently. He wondered that the request should have come at this moment, for the strife was over, and they were on a most desolate hill, far from every human habitation, and the hour was getting late. He stood still and allowed her to get far ahead of him till he could only see her form upon the sky.

A distressing explanation of this anxiety to be rid of him at that point now ensued. A figure apparently rose from the earth beside her. The shape beyond all doubt was Troy's. Oak would not be even a possible listener, and at once turned back till a good two hundred yards were between the lovers and himself.

Gabriel went home by way of the churchyard. In passing the tower he thought of what she had said about the sergeant's virtuous habit of entering the church unperceived at the beginning of service. Believing that the little gallery door alluded to was quite disused, he ascended the external flight of steps at the top of which it stood, and examined it. The pale luster yet hanging in the northwestern heaven was sufficient to show that a sprig of ivy had grown from the wall across the door to a length of more than a foot, delicately tying the panel to the stone jamb. It was a decisive proof that the door had not been opened at least since Troy came back to Weatherbury.

30. Hot Cheeks and Tearful Eyes

HALF AN HOUR LATER Bathsheba entered her own house. There burnt upon her face when she met the light of the candles the flush and excitement which were little less than chronic with her now. The farewell words of Troy, who had accompanied her to the very door, still lingered in her ears. He had bidden her adieu for two days, which were, so he stated, to be spent at Bath in visiting some friends. He had also kissed her a second time.

It is only fair to Bathsheba to explain here a little fact which did not come to light till a long time afterward: that Troy's presentation of himself so aptly at the roadside this evening was not by any distinctly preconcerted arrangement. He had hinted—she had forbidden; and it was only on the chance of his still coming that she had dismissed Oak, fearing a meeting between them just then.

She now sank down into a chair, wild and perturbed by all these new and fevering sequences. Then she jumped up with a manner of decision, and fetched her desk from a side table.

In three minutes, without pause or modification, she had written a letter to Boldwood, at his address beyond Casterbridge, saying mildly but firmly that she had well considered the whole subject he had brought before her and kindly given her time to decide upon; that her final decision was that she could not marry him. She had expressed to Oak an intention to wait till Boldwood came home before communicating to him her conclusive reply. But Bathsheba found that she could not wait.

It was impossible to send this letter till the next day; yet to quell her uneasiness by getting it out of her hands, and so, as it were, setting the act in motion at once, she arose to take it to any one of the women who might be in the kitchen.

She paused in the passage. A dialogue was going on in the kitchen, and Bathsheba and Troy were the subject of it.

"If he marry her, she'll gie up farming."

" 'Twill be a gallant life, but may bring some trouble between the mirth—so say I."

"Well, I wish I had half such a husband."

Bathsheba had too much sense to mind seriously what her servitors said about her; but too much womanly redundance of speech to leave alone what was said till it died the natural death of unminded things. She burst in upon them.

"Who are you speaking of?" she asked.

There was a pause before anybody replied. At last Liddy said frankly, "What was passing was a bit of a word about yourself, miss."

"I thought so! Maryann and Liddy and Temperance—now I forbid you to suppose such things. You know I don't care the least for Mr. Troy—not I. Everybody knows how much I hate him. Yes," repeated the froward young person, "*hate* him!"

"We know you do, miss," said Liddy, "and so do we all."

"I hate him too," said Maryann.

"Maryann—Oh, you perjured woman! How can you speak that wicked story!" said Bathsheba excitedly. "You admired him from your heart only this morning in the very world, you did. Yes, Maryann, you know it!"

"Yes, miss, but so did you. He is a wild scamp now, and you are right to hate him."

"He's *not* a wild scamp! How dare you to my face! I have no right to hate him, nor you, nor anybody. But I am a silly woman! What is it to me what he is? You know it is nothing. I don't care for him; I don't mean to defend his good name, not I. Mind this, if any of you say a word against him you'll be dismissed instantly!"

She flung down the letter and surged back into the parlor, with a big heart and tearful eyes, Liddy following her.

"Oh, miss!" said mild Liddy, looking pitifully into Bathsheba's face. "I am sorry we mistook you so! I did think you cared for him; but I see you don't now."

"Shut the door, Liddy."

Liddy closed the door, and went on: "People always say such foolery, miss. I'll make answer hence-for'ard, 'Of course a lady like Miss Everdene can't love him'; I'll say it out in plain black and white."

Bathsheba burst out: "Oh Liddy, are you such a simpleton? Can't you read riddles? Can't you see? Are you a woman yourself?"

Liddy's clear eyes rounded with wonderment.

"Yes; you must be a blind thing, Liddy!" she said in reckless abandonment and grief. "Oh, I love him to very distraction and misery and agony! Don't be frightened at me, though perhaps I am enough to frighten any innocent woman. Come closer—closer." She put her arms round Liddy's neck. "I must let it out to somebody; it is wearing me away! Don't you yet know enough of me to see through that miserable denial of mine? O God, what a lie it was! Heaven and my Love forgive me. And don't you know that a woman who loves at all thinks nothing of perjury when it is balanced against her love? There, go out of the room; I want to be quite alone."

Liddy went toward the door.

"Liddy, come here. Solemnly swear to me that

he's not a fast man; that it is all lies they say about him!"

"But, miss, how can I say he is not if—"

"You graceless girl! How can you have the cruel heart to repeat what they say? Unfeeling thing that you are. . . . But *I'll* see if you or anybody else in the village, or town either, dare do such a thing!" She started off, pacing from fireplace to door and back again.

"No, miss. I don't—I know it is not true!" said Liddy, frightened at Bathsheba's unwonted vehemence.

"I suppose you only agree with me like that to please me. But, Liddy, he *cannot* be bad, as is said. Do you hear?"

"Yes, miss, yes."

"And you don't believe he is?"

"I don't know what to say, miss," said Liddy, beginning to cry. "If I say No, you don't believe me; and if I say Yes, you rage at me!"

"Say you don't believe it—say you don't!"

"I don't believe him to be so bad as they make out."

"He is not bad at all. . . . My poor life and heart, how weak I am!" she moaned, in a relaxed, desultory way, heedless of Liddy's presence. "Oh, how I wish I had never seen him! Loving is misery for women always. I shall never forgive God for making me a woman, and dearly am I beginning to pay for the honor of owning a pretty face." She freshened and turned to Liddy suddenly. "Mind this, Lydia Smallbury, if you repeat anywhere a single word of what I have said to you inside this closed door, I'll never trust you, or love you, or have you with me a moment longer—not a moment!"

"I don't want to repeat anything," said Liddy, with womanly dignity of a diminutive order; "but I don't wish to stay with you. And, if you please, I'll

go at the end of the harvest, or this week, or today.
. . . I don't see that I deserve to be put upon and
stormed at for nothing!" concluded the small
woman, bigly.

"No, no, Liddy; you must stay!" said Bathsheba,
dropping from haughtiness to entreaty with ca-
pricious inconsequence. "You must not notice my
being in a taking just now. You are not as a servant
—you are a companion to me. Dear, dear—I don't
know what I am doing since this miserable ache o'
my heart has weighted and worn upon me so! What
shall I come to! I suppose I shall get further and
further into troubles. I wonder sometimes if I am
doomed to die in the Union. I am friendless
enough, God knows!"

"I won't notice anything, nor will I leave you!"
sobbed Liddy, impulsively putting up her lips to
Bathsheba's, and kissing her.

Then Bathsheba kissed Liddy, and all was
smooth again.

"I don't often cry, do I, Lidd? but you have made
tears come into my eyes," she said, a smile shining
through the moisture. "Try to think him a good
man, won't you, dear Liddy?"

"I will, miss, indeed."

"He is a sort of steady man in a wild way, you
know. That's better than to be as some are, wild
in a steady way. I am afraid that's how I am. And
promise me to keep my secret—do, Liddy! And do
not let them know that I have been crying about
him, because it will be dreadful for me, and no
good to him, poor thing!"

"Death's head himself shan't wring it from me,
mistress, if I've a mind to keep anything; and I'll
always be your friend," replied Liddy emphatically,
at the same time bringing a few more tears into her
own eyes, not from any particular necessity, but
from an artistic sense of making herself in keeping
with the remainder of the picture, which seems to

influence women at such times. "I think God likes us to be good friends, don't you?"

"Indeed I do."

"And, dear miss, you won't harry me and storm at me, will you? because you seem to swell so tall as a lion then, and it frightens me! Do you know, I fancy you would be a match for any man when you are in one o' your takings."

"Never! do you?" said Bathsheba, slightly laughing, though somewhat seriously alarmed by this Amazonian picture of herself. "I hope I am not a bold sort of maid—mannish?" she continued with some anxiety.

"Oh, no, not mannish; but so almighty womanish that 'tis getting on that way sometimes. Ah! miss," she said, after having drawn her breath very sadly in and sent it very sadly out, "I wish I had half your failing that way. 'Tis a great protection to a poor maid in these illegit'mate days!"

31. Blame — Fury

THE NEXT EVENING Bathsheba, with the idea of getting out of the way of Mr. Boldwood in the event of his returning to answer her note in person, proceeded to fulfill an engagement made with Liddy some few hours earlier. Bathsheba's companion, as a gauge of their reconciliation, had been granted a week's holiday to visit her sister, who was married to a thriving hurdler and cattlecrib-maker living in a delightful labyrinth of hazel copse not far beyond Yalbury. The arrangement was that Miss Everdene should honor them by coming there for a day or two to inspect some ingenious contrivances which this man of the woods had introduced into his wares.

Leaving her instructions with Gabriel and Maryann, that they were to see everything carefully locked up for the night, she went out of the house just at the close of a timely thunder shower, which had refined the air, and daintily bathed the coat of the land, though all beneath was dry as ever. Freshness was exhaled in an essence from the varied contours of bank and hollow, as if the earth breathed maiden breath; and the pleased birds were hymning to the scene. Before her, among the clouds, there was a contrast in the shape of lairs of fierce light which showed themselves in the neighborhood of a hidden sun, lingering on to the farthest northwest corner of the heavens that this midsummer season allowed.

She had walked nearly two miles of her journey, watching how the day was retreating, and thinking how the time of deeds was quietly melting into the time of thought, to give place in its turn to the time of prayer and sleep, when she beheld advancing over Yalbury hill the very man she sought so anxiously to elude. Boldwood was stepping on, not with that quiet tread of reserved strength which was his customary gait, in which he always seemed to be balancing two thoughts. His manner was stunned and sluggish now.

Boldwood had for the first time been awakened to woman's privileges in tergiversation even when it involves another person's possible blight. That Bathsheba was a firm and positive girl, far less inconsequent than her fellows, had been the very lung of his hope; for he had held that these qualities would lead her to adhere to a straight

course for consistency's sake, and accept him,
though her fancy might not flood him with the
iridescent hues of uncritical love. But the argument
now came back as sorry gleams from a broken mirror. The discovery was no less a scourge than a surprise.

He came on looking upon the ground, and did
not see Bathsheba till they were less than a stone's
throw apart. He looked up at the sound of her pit-
pat, and his changed appearance sufficiently de-
noted to her the depth and strength of the feelings
paralyzed by her letter.

"Oh; is it you, Mr. Boldwood?" she faltered, a
guilty warmth pulsing in her face.

Those who have the power of reproaching in
silence may find it a means more effective than
words. There are accents in the eye which are not
on the tongue, and more tales come from pale
lips than can enter an ear. It is both the grandeur
and the pain of the remoter moods that they avoid
the pathway of sound. Boldwood's look was unanswerable.

Seeing she turned a little aside, he said, "What,
are you afraid of me?"

"Why should you say that?" said Bathsheba.

"I fancied you looked so," said he. "And it is
most strange, because of its contrast with my feeling for you."

She regained self-possession, fixed her eyes
calmly, and waited.

"You know what that feeling is," continued Boldwood deliberately. "A thing strong as death. No
dismissal by a hasty letter affects that."

"I wish you did not feel so strongly about me,"
she murmured. "It is generous of you, and more
than I deserve, but I must not hear it now."

"Hear it? What do you think I have to say, then?
I am not to marry you, and that's enough. Your

letter was excellently plain. I want you to hear nothing—not I."

Bathsheba was unable to direct her will into any definite groove for freeing herself from this fearfully awkward position. She confusedly said, "Good evening," and was moving on. Boldwood walked up to her heavily and dully.

"Bathsheba—darling—is it final indeed?"

"Indeed it is."

"Oh, Bathsheba—have pity upon me!" Boldwood burst out. "God's sake, Yes—I am come to that low, lowest stage—to ask a woman for pity! Still, she is you—she is you."

Bathsheba commanded herself well. But she could hardly get a clear voice for what came instinctively to her lips: "There is little honor to the woman in that speech." It was only whispered, for something unutterably mournful no less than distressing in this spectacle of a man showing himself to be so entirely the vane of a passion enervated the feminine instinct for punctilios.

"I am beyond myself about this, and am mad," he said. "I am no stoic at all to be supplicating here; but I do supplicate to you. I wish you knew what is in me of devotion to you; but it is impossible, that. In bare human mercy to a lonely man, don't throw me off now!"

"I don't throw you off—indeed, how can I? I never had you." In her noon-clear sense that she had never loved him she forgot for a moment her thoughtless angle on that day in February.

"But there was a time when you turned to me, before I thought of you! I don't reproach you, for even now I feel that the ignorant and cold darkness that I should have lived in if you had not attracted me by that letter—valentine you call it—would have been worse than my knowledge of you, though it has brought this misery. But, I say, there was a time when I knew nothing of you, and cared nothing for you, and yet you drew me on. And if you say you gave me no encouragement, I cannot but contradict you."

"What you call encouragement was the childish game of an idle minute. I have bitterly repented of it—aye, bitterly, and in tears. Can you still go on reminding me?"

"I don't accuse you of it—I deplore it. I took for earnest what you insist was jest, and now this that I pray to be jest you say is awful, wretched earnest. Our moods meet at wrong places. I wish your feeling was more like mine, or my feeling more like yours! Oh, could I but have foreseen the torture that trifling trick was going to lead me into, how I should have cursed you; but only having been able to see it since, I cannot do that, for I love you too well! But it is weak, idle driveling to go on like this. . . . Bathsheba, you are the first woman of any shade or nature that I have ever looked at to love, and it is the having been so near claiming you for my own that makes this denial so hard to bear. How nearly you promised me! But I don't speak now to move your heart, and make you grieve because of my pain; it is no use, that. I must bear it; my pain would get no less by paining you."

"But I do pity you—deeply—Oh, so deeply!" she earnestly said.

"Do no such thing—do no such thing. Your dear love, Bathsheba, is such a vast thing beside your pity, that the loss of your pity as well as your love is no great addition to my sorrow, nor does the gain of your pity make it sensibly less. O sweet—how dearly you spoke to me behind the spear bed at the washing pool, and in the barn at the shearing, and that dearest last time in the evening at your home! Where are your pleasant words all gone—your earnest hope to be able to love me? Where is your firm conviction that you would get to care for me very much? Really forgotten?—really?"

She checked emotion, looked him quietly and clearly in the face, and said in her low, firm voice, "Mr. Boldwood, I promised you nothing. Would you have had me a woman of clay when you paid me that furthest, highest compliment a man can pay a woman—telling her he loves her? I was bound to show some feeling, if I would not be a graceless shrew. Yet each of those pleasures was just for the day—the day just for the pleasure. How was I to know that what is a pastime to all other men was death to you? Have reason, do, and think more kindly of me!"

"Well, never mind arguing—never mind. One thing is sure: you were all but mine, and now you are not nearly mine. Everything is changed, and that by you alone, remember. You were nothing to me once, and I was contented; you are now nothing to me again, and how different the second nothing is from the first! Would to God you had never taken me up, since it was only to throw me down!"

Bathsheba, in spite of her mettle, began to feel unmistakable signs that she was inherently the weaker vessel. She strove miserably against this femininity which would insist upon supplying unbidden emotions in stronger and stronger current. She had tried to elude agitation by fixing her mind on the trees, sky, any trivial object before her eyes, whilst his reproaches fell, but ingenuity could not save her now.

"I did not take you up—surely I did not!" she answered as heroically as she could. "But don't be in this mood with me. I can endure being told I am in the wrong, if you will only tell it me gently! O sir, will you not kindly forgive me, and look at it cheerfully?"

"Cheerfully! Can a man fooled to utter heart-burning find a reason for being merry? If I have lost, how can I be as if I had won? Heavens, you must be heartless quite! Had I known what a fearfully bitter sweet this was to be, how I would have avoided you, and never seen you, and been deaf to you. I tell you all this, but what do you care! You don't care."

She returned silent and weak denials to his charges, and swayed her head desperately, as if to thrust away the words as they came showering about her ears from the lips of the trembling man in the climax of life, with his bronzed Roman face and fine frame.

"Dearest, dearest, I am wavering even now between the two opposites of recklessly renouncing you, and laboring humbly for you again. Forget that you have said No, and let it be as it was! Say, Bathsheba, that you only wrote that refusal to me in fun—come, say it to me!"

"It would be untrue, and painful to both of us. You overrate my capacity for love. I don't possess half the warmth of nature you believe me to have. An unprotected childhood in a cold world has beaten gentleness out of me."

He immediately said with more resentment: "That may be true, somewhat; but ah, Miss Everdene, it won't do as a reason! You are not the cold woman you would have me believe. No, no! It isn't because you have no feeling in you that you don't love me. You naturally would have me think so— you would hide from me that you have a burning heart like mine. You have love enough, but it is turned into a new channel. I know where."

The swift music of her heart became hubbub now, and she throbbed to extremity. He was coming to Troy. He did then know what had occurred! And the name fell from his lips the next moment.

"Why did Troy not leave my treasure alone?"

he asked fiercely. "When I had no thought of injuring him, why did he force himself upon your notice! Before he worried you your inclination was to have me; when next I should have come to you, your answer would have been Yes. Can you deny it—I ask, can you deny it?"

She delayed the reply, but was too honest to withhold it. "I cannot," she whispered.

"I know you cannot. But he stole in in my absence and robbed me. Why didn't he win you away before, when nobody would have been grieved?— when nobody would have been set talebearing. Now the people sneer at me—the very hills and sky seem to laugh at me till I blush shamefully for my folly. I have lost my respect, my good name, my standing—lost it, never to get it again. Go and marry your man—go on!"

"Oh, sir—Mr. Boldwood!"

"You may as well. I have no further claim upon you. As for me, I had better go somewhere alone, and hide—and pray. I loved a woman once. I am now ashamed. When I am dead they'll say, miserable love-sick man that he was. Heaven—heaven —if I had got jilted secretly, and the dishonor not known, and my position kept! But no matter, it is gone, and the woman not gained. Shame upon him —shame!"

His unreasonable anger terrified her, and she glided from him, without obviously moving, as she said, "I am only a girl—do not speak to me so!"

"All the time you knew—how very well you knew—that your new freak was my misery. Dazzled by brass and scarlet—oh, Bathsheba—this is woman's folly indeed!"

She fired up at once. "You are taking too much upon yourself!" she said vehemently. "Everybody is upon me—everybody. It is unmanly to attack a woman so! I have nobody in the world to fight my battles for me; but no mercy is shown. Yet if a thousand of you sneer and say things against me, I *will not* be put down!"

"You'll chatter with him doubtless about me. Say to him, 'Boldwood would have died for me.' Yes, and you have given way to him, knowing him to be not the man for you. He has kissed you—claimed you as his. Do you hear—he has kissed you. Deny it!"

The most tragic woman is cowed by a tragic man, and although Boldwood was, in vehemence and glow, nearly her own self rendered into another sex, Bathsheba's cheek quivered. She gasped, "Leave me, sir—leave me! I am nothing to you. Let me go on!"

"Deny that he has kissed you."

"I shall not."

"Ha—then he has!" came hoarsely from the farmer.

"He has," she said slowly, and, in spite of her fear, defiantly. "I am not ashamed to speak the truth."

"Then curse him; and curse him!" said Boldwood, breaking into a whispered fury. "Whilst I would have given worlds to touch your hand, you have let a rake come in without right or ceremony and—kiss you! Heaven's mercy—kiss you! . . . Ah, a time of his life shall come when he will have to repent, and think wretchedly of the pain he has caused another man; and then may he ache, and wish, and curse, and yearn—as I do now!"

"Don't, don't, oh, don't pray down evil upon him!" she implored in a miserable cry. "Anything but that—anything. Oh, be kind to him, sir, for I love him true!"

Boldwood's ideas had reached that point of fusion at which outline and consistency entirely disappear. The impending night appeared to concentrate in his eye. He did not hear her at all now.

"I'll punish him—by my soul, that will I! I'll meet him, soldier or no, and I'll horsewhip the untimely stripling for this reckless theft of my one delight. If he were a hundred men I'd horsewhip him—" He dropped his voice suddenly and unnaturally. "Bathsheba, sweet, lost coquette, pardon me! I've been blaming you, threatening you, behaving like a churl to you, when he's the greatest sinner. He stole your dear heart away with his unfathomable lies! . . . It is a fortunate thing for him that he's gone back to his regiment—that he's away up the country, and not here! I hope he may not return here just yet. I pray God he may not come into my sight, for I may be tempted beyond myself. Oh, Bathsheba, keep him away—yes, keep him away from me!"

For a moment Boldwood stood so inertly after this that his soul seemed to have been entirely exhaled with the breath of his passionate words. He turned his face away, and withdrew, and his form was soon covered over by the twilight as his footsteps mixed in with the low hiss of the leafy trees.

Bathsheba, who had been standing motionless as a model all this latter time, flung her hands to her face and wildly attempted to ponder on the exhibition which had just passed away. Such astounding wells of fevered feeling in a still man like Mr. Boldwood were incomprehensible, dreadful. Instead of being a man trained to repression he was —what she had seen him.

The force of the farmer's threats lay in their relation to a circumstance known at present only to herself: her lover was coming back to Weatherbury in the course of the very next day or two. Troy had not returned to his distant barracks as Boldwood and others supposed, but had merely gone to visit some acquaintance in Bath, and had yet a week or more remaining to his furlough.

She felt wretchedly certain that if he revisited her just at this nick of time, and came into contact with Boldwood, a fierce quarrel would be the consequence. She panted with solicitude when she thought of possible injury to Troy. The least spark would kindle the farmer's swift feelings of rage and jealousy; he would lose his selfmastery as he had this evening; Troy's blitheness might become aggressive; it might take the direction of derision, and Boldwood's anger might then take the direction of revenge.

With almost a morbid dread of being thought a gushing girl, this guileless woman too well concealed from the world under a manner of carelessness the warm depths of her strong emotions. But now there was no reserve. In her distraction, instead of advancing further she walked up and down, beating the air with her fingers, pressing her brow, and sobbing brokenly to herself. Then she sat down on a heap of stones by the wayside to think. There she remained long. Above the dark margin of the earth appeared foreshores and promontories of coppery cloud, bounding a green and pellucid expanse in the western sky. Amaranthine glosses came over them then, and the upresting world wheeled her round to a contrasting prospect eastward in the shape of indecisive and palpitating stars. She gazed upon their silent throes amid the shades of space, but realized none at all. Her troubled spirit was far away with Troy.

32. Night — Horses Tramping

THE VILLAGE OF WEATHERBURY was quiet as the graveyard in its midst, and the living were lying well-nigh as still as the dead. The church clock struck eleven. The air was so empty of other sounds that the whirr of the clockwork immediately before the strokes was distinct, and so was also the click of the same at their close. The notes flew forth with the usual blind obtuseness of inanimate things —flapping and rebounding among walls, undulating against the scattered clouds, spreading through their interstices into unexplored miles of space.

Bathsheba's crannied and moldy halls were tonight occupied only by Maryann, Liddy being, as was stated, with her sister, whom Bathsheba had set out to visit. A few minutes after eleven had struck, Maryann turned in her bed with a sense of being disturbed. She was totally unconscious of the nature of the interruption to her sleep. It led to a dream, and the dream to an awakening, with an uneasy sensation that something had happened. She left her bed and looked out of the window. The paddock abutted on this end of the building, and in the paddock she could just discern by the uncertain gray a moving figure approaching the horse that was feeding there. The figure seized the horse by the forelock, and led it to the corner of the field. Here she could see some object which circumstances proved to be a vehicle, for after a few minutes spent apparently in harnessing, she heard the trot of the horse down the road, mingled with the sound of light wheels.

Two varieties only of humanity could have entered the paddock with the ghostlike glide of that mysterious figure. They were a woman and a Gypsy man. A woman was out of the question in such an occupation at this hour, and the comer could be no less than a thief, who might probably have known the weakness of the household on this particular night, and have chosen it on that account for his daring attempt. Moreover, to raise suspicion to conviction itself, there were Gypsies in Weatherbury Bottom.

Maryann, who had been afraid to shout in the robber's presence, having seen him depart had no fear. She hastily slipped on her clothes, stumped down the disjointed staircase with its hundred creaks, ran to Coggan's, the nearest house, and raised an alarm. Coggan called Gabriel, who now again lodged in his house as at first, and together they went to the paddock. Beyond all doubt the horse was gone.

"Hark!" said Gabriel.

They listened. Distinct upon the stagnant air came the sounds of a trotting horse passing up Longpuddle Lane—just beyond the Gypsies' encampment in Weatherbury Bottom.

"That's our Dainty—I'll swear to her step," said Jan.

"Mighty me! Won't mis'ess storm and call us stupids when she comes back!" moaned Maryann. "How I wish it had happened when she was at home, and none of us had been answerable!"

"We must ride after," said Gabriel decisively. "I'll be responsible to Miss Everdene for what we do. Yes, we'll follow."

"Faith, I don't see how," said Coggan. "All our horses are too heavy for that trick except little Poppet, and what's she between two of us?—If we only had that pair over the hedge we might do something."

"Which pair?"

"Mr. Boldwood's Tidy and Moll."

"Then wait here till I come hither again," said Gabriel. He ran down the hill toward Farmer Boldwood's.

"Farmer Boldwood is not at home," said Maryann.

"All the better," said Coggan. "I know what he's gone for."

Less than five minutes brought up Oak again, running at the same pace, with two halters dangling from his hand.

"Where did you find 'em?" said Coggan, turning round and leaping upon the hedge without waiting for an answer.

"Under the eaves. I knew where they were kept," said Gabriel, following him. "Coggan, you can ride barebacked? There's no time to look for saddles."

"Like a hero!" said Jan.

"Maryann, you go to bed," Gabriel shouted to her from the top of the hedge.

Springing down into Boldwood's pastures, each pocketed his halter to hide it from the horses, who, seeing the men empty-handed, docilely allowed themselves to be seized by the mane, when the halters were dextrously slipped on. Having neither bit nor bridle, Oak and Coggan extemporized the former by passing the rope in each case through the animal's mouth and looping it on the other side. Oak vaulted astride, and Coggan clambered up by aid of the bank, when they ascended to the gate and galloped off in the direction taken by Bathsheba's horse and the robber. Whose vehicle the horse had

been harnessed to was a matter of some uncertainty.

Weatherbury Bottom was reached in three or
four minutes. They scanned the shady green
patch by the roadside. The Gypsies were gone.

"The villains!" said Gabriel. "Which way have
they gone, I wonder?"

"Straight on, as sure as God made little apples,"
said Jan.

"Very well; we are better mounted, and must
overtake 'em," said Oak. "Now, on at full speed!"

No sound of the rider in their van could now be
discovered. The road metal grew softer and more
clayey as Weatherbury was left behind, and the late
rain had wetted its surface to a somewhat plastic,
but not muddy state. They came to crossroads. Coggan suddenly pulled up Moll and slipped off.

"What's the matter?" said Gabriel.

"We must try to track 'em, since we can't hear
'em," said Jan, fumbling in his pockets. He struck a
light, and held the match to the ground. The rain
had been heavier here, and all foot and horse tracks
made previous to the storm had been abraded and
blurred by the drops, and they were now so many
little scoops of water, which reflected the flame of
the match like eyes. One set of tracks was fresh and
had no water in them; one pair of ruts was also
empty, and not small canals, like the others. The
footprints forming this recent impression were full
of information as to pace; they were in equidistant
pairs, three or four feet apart, the right and left
foot of each pair being exactly opposite one
another.

"Straight on!" Jan exclaimed. "Tracks like that
mean a stiff gallop. No wonder we don't hear him.
And the horse is harnessed—look at the ruts. Aye,
that's our mare, sure enough!"

"How do you know?"

"Old Jimmy Harris only shoed her last week, and I'd swear to his make among ten thousand."

"The rest of the Gypsies must ha' gone on earlier, or some other way," said Oak. "You saw there were no other tracks?"

"True." They rode along silently for a long weary time. Coggan carried an old pinchbeck repeater which he had inherited from some genius in his family; and it now struck one. He lighted another match, and examined the ground again.

" 'Tis a canter now," he said, throwing away the light. "A twisty, rickety pace for a gig. The fact is, they overdrove her at starting; we shall catch 'em yet."

Again they hastened on, and entered Blackmore Vale. Coggan's watch struck two. When they looked again the hoofmarks were so spaced as to form a sort of zigzag if united, like the lamps along a street.

"That's a trot, I know," said Gabriel.

"Only a trot now," said Coggan cheerfully. "We shall overtake him in time."

They pushed rapidly on for yet two or three miles. "Ah! a moment," said Jan. "Let's see how she was driven up this hill. 'Twill help us." A light was promptly struck upon his gaiters as before, and the examination made.

"Hurrah!" said Coggan. "She walked up here— and well she might. We shall get them in two miles, for a crown."

They rode three, and listened. No sound was to be heard save a millpond trickling hoarsely through a hatch, and suggesting gloomy possibilities of drowning by jumping in. Gabriel dismounted when they came to a turning. The tracks were absolutely the only guide as to the direction that they now had, and great caution was necessary to avoid confusing them with some others which had made their appearance lately.

"What does this mean?—though I guess," said Gabriel, looking up at Coggan as he moved the match over the ground about the turning. Coggan, who, no less than the panting horses, had latterly shown signs of weariness, again scrutinized the mystic characters. This time only three were of the regular horseshoe shape. Every fourth was a dot.

He screwed up his face, and emitted a long "whew-w-w!"

"Lame," said Oak.

"Yes. Dainty is lamed; the near-foot-afore," said Coggan slowly, staring still at the footprints.

"We'll push on," said Gabriel, remounting his humid steed.

Although the road along its greater part had been as good as any turnpike road in the country, it was nominally only a byway. The last turning had brought them into the high road leading to Bath. Coggan recollected himself.

"We shall have him now!" he exclaimed.

"Where?"

"Sherton Turnpike. The keeper of that gate is the sleepiest man between here and London—Dan Randall, that's his name—knowed en for years, when he was at Casterbridge gate. Between the lameness and the gate 'tis a done job."

They now advanced with extreme caution. Nothing was said until, against a shady background of foliage, five white bars were visible, crossing their route a little way ahead.

"Hush—we are almost close!" said Gabriel.

"Amble on upon the grass," said Coggan.

The white bars were blotted out in the midst by a dark shape in front of them. The silence of this lonely time was pierced by an exclamation from that quarter.

"Hoy-a-hoy! Gate!"

It appeared that there had been a previous call

which they had not noticed, for on their close approach the door of the turnpike house opened, and the keeper came out half-dressed, with a candle in his hand. The rays illumined the whole group.

"Keep the gate close!" shouted Gabriel. "He has stolen the horse!"

"Who?" said the turnpike man.

Gabriel looked at the driver of the gig, and saw a woman—Bathsheba, his mistress.

On hearing his voice she had turned her face away from the light. Coggan had, however, caught sight of her in the meanwhile.

"Why, 'tis mistress—I'll take my oath!" he said, amazed.

Bathsheba it certainly was, and she had by this time done the trick she could do so well in crises not of love, namely, mask a surprise by coolness of manner.

"Well, Gabriel," she inquired quietly, "where are you going?"

"We thought—" began Gabriel.

"I am driving to Bath," she said, taking for her own use the assurance that Gabriel lacked. "An important matter made it necessary for me to give up my visit to Liddy, and go off at once. What, then, were you following me?"

"We thought the horse was stole."

"Well—what a thing! How very foolish of you not to know that I had taken the trap and horse. I could neither wake Maryann nor get into the house, though I hammered for ten minutes against her windowsill. Fortunately, I could get the key of the coachhouse, so I troubled no one further. Didn't you think it might be me?"

"Why should we, miss?"

"Perhaps not. Why, those are never Farmer Boldwood's horses! Goodness mercy! what have you been doing—bringing trouble upon me in this way! What! mustn't a lady move an inch from her door without being dogged like a thief?"

"But how was we to know, if you left no account of your doings?" expostulated Coggan, "and ladies don't drive at these hours, miss, as a jineral rule of society."

"I did leave an account—and you would have seen it in the morning. I wrote in chalk on the coach-house doors that I had come back for the horse and gig, and driven off; that I could arouse nobody, and should return soon."

"But you'll consider, ma'am, that we couldn't see that till it got daylight."

"True," she said, and though vexed at first she had too much sense to blame them long or seriously for a devotion to her that was as valuable as it was rare. She added with a very pretty grace, "Well, I really thank you heartily for taking all this trouble; but I wish you had borrowed anybody's horses but Mr. Boldwood's."

"Dainty is lame, miss," said Coggan. "Can ye go on?"

"It was only a stone in her shoe. I got down and pulled it out a hundred yards back. I can manage very well, thank you. I shall be in Bath by daylight. Will you now return, please?"

She turned her head—the gateman's candle shimmering upon her quick, clear eyes as she did so—passed through the gate, and was soon wrapped in the embowering shades of mysterious summer boughs. Coggan and Gabriel put about their horses, and, fanned by the velvety air of this July night, retraced the road by which they had come.

"A strange vagary, this of hers, isn't it, Oak?" said Coggan curiously.

"Yes," said Gabriel shortly.

"She won't be in Bath by no daylight!"

"Coggan, suppose we keep this night's work as quiet as we can?"

"I am of one and the same mind."

"Very well. We shall be home by three o'clock or so, and can creep into the parish like lambs."

Bathsheba's perturbed meditations by the roadside had ultimately evolved a conclusion that there were only two remedies for the present desperate state of affairs. The first was merely to keep Troy away from Weatherbury till Boldwood's indignation had cooled; the second to listen to Oak's entreaties, and Boldwood's denunciations, and give up Troy altogether.

Alas! Could she give up this new love—induce him to renounce her by saying she did not like him—could no more speak to him, and beg him, for her good, to end his furlough in Bath, and see her and Weatherbury no more?

It was a picture full of misery, but for a while she contemplated it firmly, allowing herself, nevertheless, as girls will, to dwell upon the happy life she would have enjoyed had Troy been Boldwood, and the path of love the path of duty—inflicting upon herself gratuitous tortures by imagining him the lover of another woman after forgetting her; for she had penetrated Troy's nature so far as to estimate his tendencies pretty accurately, but unfortunately loved him no less in thinking that he might soon cease to love her—indeed, considerably more.

She jumped to her feet. She would see him at once. Yes, she would implore him by word of mouth to assist her in this dilemma. A letter to keep him away could not reach him in time, even if he should be disposed to listen to it.

Was Bathsheba altogether blind to the obvious fact that the support of a lover's arms is not of a kind best calculated to assist a resolve to renounce him? Or was she sophistically sensible, with a thrill of pleasure, that by adopting this course for getting rid of him she was ensuring a meeting with him, at any rate, once more?

It was now dark, and the hour must have been nearly ten. The only way to accomplish her purpose was to give up her idea of visiting Liddy at Yalbury, return to Weatherbury Farm, put the horse into the gig, and drive at once to Bath. The scheme seemed at first impossible: the journey was a fearfully heavy one, even for a strong horse, at her own estimate; and she much underrated the distance. It was most venturesome for a woman, at night, and alone.

But could she go on to Liddy's and leave things to take their course? No, no; anything but that. Bathsheba was full of a stimulating turbulence, beside which caution vainly prayed for a hearing. She turned back toward the village.

Her walk was slow, for she wished not to enter Weatherbury till the cottagers were in bed, and, particularly, till Boldwood was secure. Her plan was now to drive to Bath during the night, see Sergeant Troy in the morning before he set out to come to her, bid him farewell, and dismiss him: then to rest the horse thoroughly (herself to weep the while, she thought), starting early the next morning on her return journey. By this arrangement she could trot Dainty gently all the day, reach Liddy at Yalbury in the evening, and come home to Weatherbury with her whenever they chose—so nobody would know she had been to Bath at all.

Such was Bathsheba's scheme. But in her topographical ignorance as a latecomer to the place, she misreckoned the distance of her journey as not much more than half what it really was. Her idea, however, she proceeded to carry out, with what initial success we have already seen.

33. In the Sun — A Harbinger

A WEEK PASSED, and there were no tidings of Bathsheba; nor was there any explanation of her Gil-
pin's rig.

Then a note came for Maryann, stating that the
business which had called her mistress to Bath still
detained her there; but that she hoped to return in
the course of another week.

Another week passed. The oat harvest began,
and all the men were a-field under a mono-
chromatic Lammas sky, amid the trembling air and
short shadows of noon. Indoors nothing was to be
heard save the droning of blue bottle flies; out-of-
doors the whetting of scythes and the hiss of tressy
oatears rubbing together as their perpendicular
stalks of amber-yellow fell heavily to each swath.
Every drop of moisture not in the men's bottles and
flagons in the form of cider was raining as perspiration from their foreheads and cheeks. Drought was
everywhere else.

They were about to withdraw for a while into
the charitable shade of a tree in the fence, when
Coggan saw a figure in a blue coat and brass buttons running to them across the field.

"I wonder who that is?" he said.

"I hope nothing is wrong about mistress," said
Maryann, who with some other women was tying
the bundles (oats being always sheafed on this

farm), "but an unlucky token came to me indoors this morning. I went to unlock the door and dropped the key, and it fell upon the stone floor and broke into two pieces. Breaking a key is a dreadful bodement. I wish mis'ess was home."

" 'Tis Cain Ball," said Gabriel, pausing from whetting his reaphook.

Oak was not bound by his agreement to assist in the cornfield; but the harvest month is an anxious time for a farmer, and the corn was Bathsheba's, so he lent a hand.

"He's dressed up in his best clothes," said Matthew Moon. "He hev been away from home for a few days, since he's had that felon upon his finger; for 'a said, since I can't work I'll have a hollerday."

"A good time for one—a' excellent time," said Joseph Poorgrass, straightening his back; for he, like some of the others, had a way of resting a while from his labor on such hot days for reasons preternaturally small; of which Cain Ball's advent on a weekday in his Sunday clothes was one of the first magnitude. " 'Twas a bad leg allowed me to read the *Pilgrim's Progress*, and Mark Clark learnt All-Fours in a whitlow."

"Aye, and my father put his arm out of joint to have time to go courting," said Jan Coggan, in an eclipsing tone, wiping his face with his shirtsleeve and thrusting back his hat upon the nape of his neck.

By this time Cainy was nearing the group of harvesters, and was perceived to be carrying a large slice of bread and ham in one hand, from which he took mouthfuls as he ran, the other being wrapped in a bandage. When he came close, his mouth assumed the bell shape, and he began to cough violently.

"Now, Cainy!" said Gabriel sternly. "How many more times must I tell you to keep from running so fast when you be eating? You'll choke yourself some day, that's what you'll do, Cain Ball."

"Hok-hok-hok!" replied Cain. "A crumb of my victuals went the wrong way—hok-hok! That's what 'tis, Mister Oak! And I've been visiting to Bath because I had a felon on my thumb; yes, and I've seen —ahok-hok!"

Directly Cain mentioned Bath, they all threw down their hooks and forks and drew round him. Unfortunately the erratic crumb did not improve his narrative powers, and a supplementary hindrance was that of a sneeze, jerking from his pocket his rather large watch, which dangled in front of the young man pendulum-wise.

"Yes," he continued, directing his thoughts to Bath and letting his eyes follow, "I've seed the world at last—yes—and I've seed our mis'ess— ahok-hok-hok!"

"Bother the boy!" said Gabriel. "Something is always going the wrong way down your throat, so that you can't tell what's necessary to be told."

"Ahok! there! Please, Mister Oak, a gnat have just fleed into my stomach and brought the cough on again!"

"Yes, that's just it. Your mouth is always open, you young rascal!"

"'Tis terrible bad to have a gnat fly down yer throat, pore boy!" said Matthew Moon.

"Well, at Bath you saw—" prompted Gabriel.

"I saw our mis'ess," continued the junior shepherd, "and a sojer, walking along. And bymeby they got closer and closer, and then they went arm-in-crook, like courting complete—hok-hok! like courting complete—hok!—courting complete—" Losing the thread of his narrative at this point simultaneously with his loss of breath, their informant looked up and down the field apparently for some clue to it. "Well, I see our mis'ess and a soldier—a-ha-a-wk!"

"Damn the boy!" said Gabriel.

" 'Tis only my manner, Mister Oak, if ye'll excuse it," said Cain Ball, looking reproachfully at Oak, with eyes drenched in their own dew.

"Here's some cider for him—that'll cure his throat," said Jan Coggan, lifting a flagon of cider, pulling out the cork, and applying the hole to Cainy's mouth; Joseph Poorgrass in the meantime beginning to think apprehensively of the serious consequences that would follow Cain Ball's strangulation in his cough, and the history of his Bath adventures dying with him.

"For my poor self, I always say 'please God' afore I do anything," said Joseph, in an unboastful voice; "and so should you, Cain Ball. 'Tis a great safeguard, and might perhaps save you from being choked to death some day."

Mr. Coggan poured the liquor with unstinted liberality at the suffering Cain's circular mouth; half of it running down the side of the flagon, and half of what reached his mouth running down outside his throat, and half of what ran in going the wrong way, and being coughed and sneezed around the persons of the gathered reapers in the form of a cider fog, which for a moment hung in the sunny air like a small exhalation.

"There's a great clumsy sneeze! Why can't ye have better manners, you young dog!" said Coggan, withdrawing the flagon.

"The cider went up my nose!" cried Cainy, as soon as he could speak; "and now 'tis gone down my neck, and into my poor dumb felon, and over my shiny buttons and all my best cloze!"

"The poor lad's cough is terrible onfortunate," said Matthew Moon. "And a great history on hand, too. Bump his back, shepherd."

" 'Tis my nater," mourned Cain. "Mother says I always was so excitable when my feelings were worked up to a point!"

"True, true," said Joseph Poorgrass. "The Balls
were allays a very excitable family. I knowed the
boy's grandfather—a truly nervous and modest
man, even to genteel refinery. 'Twas blush, blush
with him, almost as much as 'tis with me—not but
that 'tis a fault in me!"

"Not at all, Master Poorgrass," said Coggan.
" 'Tis a very noble quality in ye."

"Heh-heh! well, I wish to noise nothing abroad
—nothing at all," murmured Poorgrass diffidently.
"But we be born to things—that's true. Yet I would
rather my trifle were hid; though, perhaps, a high
nater is a little high, and at my birth all things were
possible to my Maker, and he may have begrudged
no gifts. . . . But under your bushel, Joseph! under your bushel with 'ee! A strange desire, neighbors, this desire to hide, and no praise due. Yet
there is a Sermon on the Mount with a calendar
of the blessed at the head, and certain meek men
may be named therein."

"Cainy's grandfather was a very clever man,"
said Matthew Moon. "Invented a' apple tree out
of his own head, which is called by his name to this
day—the Early Ball. You know 'em, Jan? A Quar-
renden grafted on a Tom Putt, and a Rathe-ripe
upon top o' that again. 'Tis trew 'a used to bide
about in a public house wi' a 'ooman in a way he
had no business to by rights, but there—'a were a
clever man in the sense of the term."

"Now then," said Gabriel impatiently, "what did
you see, Cain?"

"I seed our mis'ess go into a sort of park place,
where there's seats, and shrubs and flowers, arm-
in-crook with a sojer," continued Cainy firmly, and
with a dim sense that his words were very effective
as regarded Gabriel's emotions. "And I think the
sojer was Sergeant Troy. And they sat there together for more than half-an-hour, talking moving
things, and she once was crying a'most to death.

And when they came out her eyes were shining and she was as white as a lily; and they looked into one another's faces, as far gone friendly as a man and woman can be."

Gabriel's features seemed to get thinner. "Well, what did you see besides?"

"Oh, all sorts."

"White as a lily? You are sure 'twas she?"

"Yes."

"Well, what besides?"

"Great glass windows to the shops, and great clouds in the sky, full of rain, and old wooden trees in the country round."

"You stun-poll! What will ye say next?" said Coggan.

"Let en alone," interposed Joseph Poorgrass. "The boy's maning is that the sky and the earth in the kingdom of Bath is not altogether different from ours here. 'Tis for our good to gain knowledge of strange cities, and as such the boy's words should be suffered, so to speak it."

"And the people of Bath," continued Cain, "never need to light their fires except as a luxury, for the water springs up out of the earth ready boiled for use."

"'Tis true as the light," testified Matthew Moon. "I've heard other navigators say the same thing."

"They drink nothing else there," said Cain, "and seem to enjoy it, to see how they swaller it down."

"Well, it seems a barbarian practice enough to us, but I daresay the natives think nothing o' it," said Matthew.

"And don't victuals spring up as well as drink?" asked Coggan, twirling his eye.

"No—I own to a blot there in Bath—a true blot. God didn't provide 'em with victuals as well as drink, and 'twas a drawback I couldn't get over at all."

"Well, 'tis a curious place, to say the least," ob-

served Moon, "and it must be a curious people that
live therein."

"Miss Everdene and the soldier were walking
about together, you say?" said Gabriel, returning
to the group.

"Aye, and she wore a beautiful gold-color silk
gown, trimmed with black lace, that would have
stood alone 'ithout legs inside if required. 'Twas a
very winsome sight; and her hair was brushed
splendid. And when the sun shone upon the bright
gown and his red coat—my! how handsome they
looked. You could see 'em all the length of
the street."

"And what then?" murmured Gabriel.

"And then I went into Griffin's to hae my boots
hobbed, and then I went to Riggs's batty-cake shop,
and asked 'em for a penneth of the cheapest and
nicest stales, that were all but blue-moldy, but not
quite. And whilst I was chawing 'em down I walked
on and seed a clock with a face as big as a baking
trendle—"

"But that's nothing to do with mistress!"

"I'm coming to that, if you'll leave me alone,
Mister Oak!" remonstrated Cainy. "If you excites
me, perhaps you'll bring on my cough, and then I
shan't be able to tell ye nothing."

"Yes—let him tell it his own way," said Coggan.

Gabriel settled into a despairing attitude of patience, and Cainy went on:

"And there were great large houses, and more
people all the week long than at Weatherbury club-
walking on White Tuesdays. And I went to grand
churches and chapels. And how the parson would
pray! Yes; he would kneel down and put up
his hands together, and make the holy gold rings
on his fingers gleam and twinkle in yer eyes, that
he'd earned by praying so excellent well!—Ah yes,
I wish I lived there."

"Our poor Parson Thirdly can't get no money

to buy such rings," said Matthew Moon thought-fully. "And as good a man as ever walked. I don't believe poor Thirdly have a single one, even of humblest tin or copper. Such a great ornament as they'd be to him on a dull a'ternoon, when he's up in the pulpit lighted by the wax candles! But 'tis impossible, poor man. Ah, to think how unequal things be."

"Perhaps he's made of different stuff than to wear 'em," said Gabriel grimly. "Well, that's enough of this. Go on, Cainy—quick."

"Oh—and the new style of pa'sons wear mous-taches and long beards," continued the illustrious traveler, "and look like Moses and Aaron complete, and make we folks in the congregation feel all over like the children of Israel."

"A very right feeling—very," said Joseph Poor-grass.

"And there's two religions going on in the na-tion now—High Church and High Chapel. And, thinks I, I'll play fair; so I went to High Church in the morning, and High Chapel in the after-noon."

"A right and proper boy," said Joseph Poorgrass.

"Well, at High Church they pray singing, and worship all the colors of the rainbow; and at High Chapel they pray preaching, and worship drab and whitewash only. And then—I didn't see no more of Miss Everdene at all."

"Why didn't you say so afore, then?" exclaimed Oak, with much disappointment.

"Ah," said Matthew Moon, "she'll wish her cake dough if so be she's over intimate with that man."

"She's not over intimate with him," said Gabriel indignantly.

"She would know better," said Coggan. "Our mis'ess has too much sense under they knots of black hair to do such a mad thing."

"You see, he's not a coarse, ignorant man, for he was well brought up," said Matthew dubiously. " 'Twas only wildness that made him a soldier, and maids rather like your man of sin."

"Now, Cain Ball," said Gabriel restlessly, "can you swear in the most awful form that the woman you saw was Miss Everdene?"

"Cain Ball, you be no longner a babe and suckling," said Joseph in the sepulchral tone the circumstances demanded, "and you know what taking an oath is. 'Tis a horrible testament mind ye, which you say and seal with your bloodstone, and the prophet Matthew tells us that on whomsoever it shall fall it will grind him to powder. Now, before all the workfolk here assembled, can you swear to your words as the shepherd asks ye?"

"Please no, Mister Oak!" said Cainy, looking from one to the other with great uneasiness at the spiritual magnitude of the position. "I don't mind saying 'tis true, but I don't like to say 'tis damn true, if that's what you mane."

"Cain, Cain, how can you!" asked Joseph sternly. "You be asked to swear in a holy manner, and you swear like wicked Shimei, the son of Gera, who cursed as he came. Young man, fie!"

"No, I don't! 'Tis you want to squander a pore boy's soul, Joseph Poorgrass—that's what 'tis!" said Cain, beginning to cry. "All I mane is that in common truth 'twas Miss Everdene and Sergeant Troy, but in the horrible so-help-me truth that ye want to make of it perhaps 'twas somebody else!"

"There's no getting at the rights of it," said Gabriel, turning to his work.

"Cain Ball, you'll come to a bit of bread!" groaned Joseph Poorgrass.

Then the reapers' hooks were flourished again, and the old sounds went on. Gabriel, without making any pretence of being lively, did nothing to show that he was particularly dull. However, Coggan knew pretty nearly how the land lay, and when they were in a nook together he said—

"Don't take on about her, Gabriel. What difference does it make whose sweetheart she is, since she can't be yours?"

"That's the very thing I say to myself," said Gabriel.

34. Home Again — A Trickster

THAT SAME EVENING at dusk Gabriel was leaning over Coggan's garden gate, taking an up-and-down survey before retiring to rest.

A vehicle of some kind was softly creeping along the grassy margin of the lane. From it spread the tones of two women talking. The tones were natural and not at all suppressed. Oak instantly knew the voices to be those of Bathsheba and Liddy.

The carriage came opposite and passed by. It was Miss Everdene's gig, and Liddy and her mistress were the only occupants of the seat. Liddy was asking questions about the city of Bath, and her companion was answering them listlessly and unconcernedly. Both Bathsheba and the horse seemed weary.

The exquisite relief of finding that she was here again, safe and sound, overpowered all reflection, and Oak could only luxuriate in the sense of it. All grave reports were forgotten.

He lingered and lingered on, till there was no difference between the eastern and western expanses of sky, and the timid hares began to limp courageously round the dim hillocks. Gabriel might have been there an additional half-hour when a dark form walked slowly by. "Goodnight, Gabriel," the passer said.

It was Boldwood. "Goodnight, sir," said Gabriel.

Boldwood likewise vanished up the road, and Oak shortly afterward turned indoors to bed.

Farmer Boldwood went on toward Miss Everdene's house. He reached the front, and approaching the entrance, saw a light in the parlor. The blind was not drawn down, and inside the room was Bathsheba, looking over some papers or letters. Her back was toward Boldwood. He went to the door, knocked, and waited with tense muscles and an aching brow.

Boldwood had not been outside his garden since his meeting with Bathsheba in the road to Yalbury. Silent and alone, he had remained in moody meditation on woman's ways, deeming as essentials of the whole sex the accidents of the single one of their number he had ever closely beheld. By degrees a more charitable temper had pervaded him, and this was the reason of his sally tonight. He had come to apologize and beg forgiveness of Bathsheba with something like a sense of shame at his violence, having but just now learnt that she had returned—only from a visit to Liddy, as he supposed, the Bath escapade being quite unknown to him.

He inquired for Miss Everdene. Liddy's manner was odd, but he did not notice it. She went in, leaving him standing there, and in her absence the blind of the room containing Bathsheba was pulled down. Boldwood augured ill from that sign. Liddy came out.

"My mistress cannot see you, sir," she said.

The farmer instantly went out by the gate. He was unforgiven—that was the issue of it all. He had seen her who was to him simultaneously a delight and a torture, sitting in the room he had shared with her as a peculiarly privileged guest only a little earlier in the summer, and she had denied him an entrance there now.

Boldwood did not hurry homeward. It was ten o'clock at least, when, walking deliberately through the lower part of Weatherbury, he heard the carrier's spring van entering the village. The van ran to and from a town in a northern direction, and it was owned and driven by a Weatherbury man, at the door of whose house it now pulled up. The lamp fixed to the head of the hood illuminated a scarlet and gilded form, who was the first to alight.

"Ah!" said Boldwood to himself, "come to see her again."

Troy entered the carrier's house, which had been the place of his lodging on his last visit to his native place. Boldwood was moved by a sudden determination. He hastened home. In ten minutes he was back again, and made as if he were going to call upon Troy at the carrier's. But as he approached, someone opened the door and came out. He heard this person say "Goodnight" to the inmates, and the voice was Troy's. This was strange, coming so immediately after his arrival. Boldwood, however, hastened up to him. Troy had what appeared to be a carpetbag in his hand—the same that he had brought with him. It seemed as if he were going to leave again this very night.

Troy turned up the hill and quickened his pace. Boldwood stepped forward.

"Sergeant Troy?"

"Yes—I'm Sergeant Troy."

"Just arrived from up the country, I think?"

"Just arrived from Bath."

"I am William Boldwood."

"Indeed."

The tone in which this word was uttered was all that had been wanted to bring Boldwood to the point.

"I wish to speak a word with you," he said.

"What about?"

"About her who lives just ahead there—and about a woman you have wronged."

"I wonder at your impertinence," said Troy, moving on.

"Now look here," said Boldwood, standing in front of him, "wonder or not, you are going to hold a conversation with me."

Troy heard the dull determination in Boldwood's voice, looked at his stalwart frame, then at the thick cudgel he carried in his hand. He remembered it was past ten o'clock. It seemed worth while to be civil to Boldwood.

"Very well, I'll listen with pleasure," said Troy, placing his bag on the ground, "only speak low, for somebody or other may overhear us in the farmhouse there."

"Well then—I know a good deal concerning your—Fanny Robin's attachment to you. I may say, too, that I believe I am the only person in the village, excepting Gabriel Oak, who does know it. You ought to marry her."

"I suppose I ought. Indeed, I wish to, but I cannot."

"Why?"

Troy was about to utter something hastily; he then checked himself and said, "I am too poor." His voice was changed. Previously it had had a devil-may-care tone. It was the voice of a trickster now.

Boldwood's present mood was not critical enough to notice tones. He continued, "I may as well speak plainly; and understand, I don't wish to enter into the questions of right or wrong, woman's honor and shame, or to express any opinion on your conduct. I intend a business transaction with you."

"I see," said Troy. "Suppose we sit down here."

An old tree trunk lay under the hedge immediately opposite, and they sat down.

"I was engaged to be married to Miss Everdene," said Boldwood, "but you came and—"

"Not engaged," said Troy.

"As good as engaged."

"If I had not turned up she might have become engaged to you."

"Hang might!"

"Would, then."

"If you had not come I should certainly—yes, *certainly*—have been accepted by this time. If you had not seen her you might have been married to Fanny. Well, there's too much difference between Miss Everdene's station and your own for this flirtation with her ever to benefit you by ending in marriage. So all I ask is, don't molest her any more. Marry Fanny. I'll make it worth your while."

"How will you?"

"I'll pay you well now, I'll settle a sum of money upon her, and I'll see that you don't suffer from poverty in the future. I'll put it clearly. Bathsheba is only playing with you: you are too poor for her as I said; so give up wasting your time about a great match you'll never make for a moderate and rightful match you may make tomorrow; take up your carpetbag, turn about, leave Weatherbury now, this night, and you shall take fifty pounds with you. Fanny shall have fifty to enable her to prepare for the wedding, when you have told me where she is living, and she shall have five hundred paid down on her wedding day."

In making this statement Boldwood's voice revealed only too clearly a consciousness of the weakness of his position, his aims, and his method. His manner had lapsed quite from that of the firm and dignified Boldwood of former times; and such a scheme as he had now engaged in he would have condemned as childishly imbecile only a few months ago. We discern a grand force in the lover which he lacks whilst a free man; but there is a breadth of vision in the free man which in the lover we vainly seek. Where there is much bias there must be some narrowness, and love, though added emotion, is subtracted capacity. Boldwood exemplified this to an abnormal degree: he knew nothing of Fanny Robin's circumstances or whereabouts, he knew nothing of Troy's possibilities, yet that was what he said.

"I like Fanny best," said Troy, "and if, as you say, Miss Everdene is out of my reach, why I have all to gain by accepting your money, and marrying Fan. But she's only a servant."

"Never mind—do you agree to my arrangement?"

"I do."

"Ah!" said Boldwood, in a more elastic voice. "Oh, Troy, if you like her best, why then did you step in here and injure my happiness?"

"I love Fanny best now," said Troy. "But Bath—Miss Everdene inflamed me, and displaced Fanny for a time. It is over now."

"Why should it be over so soon? And why then did you come here again?"

"There are weighty reasons. Fifty pounds at once, you said!"

"I did," said Boldwood, "and here they are—fifty sovereigns." He handed Troy a small packet.

"You have everything ready—it seems that you calculated on my accepting them," said the sergeant, taking the packet.

"I thought you might accept them," said Boldwood.

"You've only my word that the program shall be adhered to, whilst I at any rate have fifty pounds."

"I had thought of that, and I have considered that if I can't appeal to your honor I can trust to your—well, shrewdness we'll call it—not to lose five hundred pounds in prospect, and also make a bitter enemy of a man who is willing to be an extremely useful friend."

"Stop, listen!" said Troy in a whisper.

A light pit-pat was audible upon the road just above them.

"By George—'tis she," he continued. "I must go on and meet her."

"She—who?"

"Bathsheba."

"Bathsheba—out alone at this time o' night!" said Boldwood in amazement, and starting up. "Why must you meet her?"

"She was expecting me tonight—and I must now speak to her, and wish her good-bye, according to your wish."

"I don't see the necessity of speaking."

"It can do no harm—and she'll be wandering about looking for me if I don't. You shall hear all I say to her. It will help you in your lovemaking when I am gone."

"Your tone is mocking."

"Oh, no. And remember this, if she does not know what has become of me, she will think more about me than if I tell her flatly I have come to give her up."

"Will you confine your words to that one point? —Shall I hear every word you say?"

"Every word. Now sit still there, and hold my carpetbag for me, and mark what you hear."

The light footstep came closer, halting occasionally, as if the walker listened for a sound. Troy whistled a double note in a soft, fluty tone.

"Come to that, is it!" murmured Boldwood uneasily.

"You promised silence," said Troy.

"I promise again."

Troy stepped forward.

"Frank, dearest, is that you?" The tones were Bathsheba's.

"O God!" said Boldwood.

"Yes," said Troy to her.

"How late you are," she continued tenderly. "Did you come by the carrier? I listened and heard his wheels entering the village, but it was some time ago, and I had almost given you up, Frank."

"I was sure to come," said Frank. "You knew I should, did you not?"

"Well, I thought you would," she said playfully, "and, Frank, it is so lucky! There's not a soul in my house but me tonight. I've packed them all off, so nobody on earth will know of your visit to your lady's bower. Liddy wanted to go to her grandfather's to tell him about her holiday, and I said she might stay with them till tomorrow—when you'll be gone again."

"Capital," said Troy. "But, dear me, I had better go back for my bag, because my slippers and brush and comb are in it; you run home whilst I fetch it, and I'll promise to be in your parlor in ten minutes."

"Yes." She turned and tripped up the hill again.

During the progress of this dialogue there was a nervous twitching of Boldwood's tightly closed lips, and his face became bathed in a clammy dew. He now started forward toward Troy. Troy turned to him and took up the bag.

"Shall I tell her I have come to give her up and cannot marry her?" said the soldier mockingly.

"No, no; wait a minute. I want to say more to you—more to you!" said Boldwood, in a hoarse whisper.

"Now," said Troy, "you see my dilemma. Perhaps I am a bad man—the victim of my impulses—led away to do what I ought to leave undone. I can't, however, marry them both. And I have two reasons for choosing Fanny. First, I like her best upon the whole, and second, you make it worth my while."

At the same instant Boldwood sprang upon him, and held him by the neck. Troy felt Boldwood's grasp slowly tightening. The move was absolutely unexpected.

"A moment," he gasped. "You are injuring her you love!"

"Well, what do you mean?" said the farmer.

"Give me breath," said Troy.

Boldwood loosened his hand, saying, "By Heaven, I've a mind to kill you!"

"And ruin her."

"Save her."

"Oh, how can she be saved now, unless I marry her?"

Boldwood groaned. He reluctantly released the soldier, and flung him back against the hedge. "Devil, you torture me!" said he.

Troy rebounded like a ball, and was about to make a dash at the farmer; but he checked himself, saying lightly—

"It is not worth while to measure my strength with you. Indeed it is a barbarous way of settling a quarrel. I shall shortly leave the army because of the same conviction. Now after that revelation of how the land lies with Bathsheba, 'twould be a mistake to kill me, would it not?"

"'Twould be a mistake to kill you," repeated Boldwood, mechanically, with a bowed head.

"Better kill yourself."

"Far better."

"I'm glad you see it."

"Troy, make her your wife, and don't act upon

what I arranged just now. The alternative is dreadful, but take Bathsheba; I give her up! She must love you indeed to sell soul and body to you so utterly as she has done. Wretched woman—deluded woman—you are, Bathsheba!"

"But about Fanny?"

"Bathsheba is a woman well to do," continued Boldwood, in nervous anxiety, "and, Troy, she will make a good wife; and, indeed, she is worth your hastening on your marriage with her!"

"But she has a will—not to say a temper, and I shall be a mere slave to her. I could do anything with poor Fanny Robin."

"Troy," said Boldwood imploringly, "I'll do anything for you, only don't desert her; pray don't desert her, Troy."

"Which, poor Fanny?"

"No; Bathsheba Everdene. Love her best! Love her tenderly! How shall I get you to see how advantageous it will be to you to secure her at once?"

"I don't wish to secure her in any new way."

Boldwood's arm moved spasmodically toward Troy's person again. He repressed the instinct, and his form dropped as with pain.

Troy went on—

"I shall soon purchase my discharge, and then—"

"But I wish you to hasten on this marriage! It will be better for you both. You love each other, and you must let me help you to do it."

"How?"

"Why, by settling the five hundred on Bathsheba instead of Fanny, to enable you to marry at once. No; she wouldn't have it of me. I'll pay it down to you on the wedding day."

Troy paused in secret amazement at Boldwood's wild infatuation. He carelessly said, "And am I to have anything now?"

"Yes, if you wish to. But I have not much additional money with me. I did not expect this; but all I have is yours."

Boldwood, more like a somnambulist than a wakeful man, pulled out the large canvas bag he carried by way of a purse, and searched it.

"I have twenty-one pounds more with me," he said. "Two notes and a sovereign. But before I leave you I must have a paper signed—"

"Pay me the money, and we'll go straight to her parlor, and make any arrangement you please to secure my compliance with your wishes. But she must know nothing of this cash business."

"Nothing, nothing," said Boldwood hastily. "Here is the sum, and if you'll come to my house we'll write out the agreement for the remainder, and the terms also."

"First we'll call upon her."

"But why? Come with me tonight, and go with me tomorrow to the surrogate's."

"But she must be consulted; at any rate informed."

"Very well; go on."

They went up the hill to Bathsheba's house. When they stood at the entrance, Troy said, "Wait here a moment." Opening the door, he glided inside, leaving the door ajar.

Boldwood waited. In two minutes a light appeared in the passage. Boldwood then saw that the chain had been fastened across the door. Troy appeared inside carrying a bedroom candlestick.

"What, did you think I should break in?" said Boldwood contemptuously.

"Oh, no; it is merely my humor to secure things. Will you read this a moment? I'll hold the light."

Troy handed a folded newspaper through the slit between door and doorpost, and put the candle close. "That's the paragraph," he said, placing his finger on a line.

Boldwood looked and read—

MARRIAGES

On the 17th inst., at St. Ambrose's Church, Bath, by the Rev. G. Mincing, B.A., Francis Troy, only son of the late Edward Troy, Esq., M.D., of Weatherbury, and sergeant 11th Dragoon Guards, to Bathsheba, only surviving daughter of the late Mr. John Everdene, of Casterbridge.

"This may be called Fort meeting Feeble, hey, Boldwood?" A low gurgle of derisive laughter followed the words.

The paper fell from Boldwood's hands. Troy continued—

"Fifty pounds to marry Fanny. Good. Twenty-one pounds not to marry Fanny, but Bathsheba. Boldwood, yours is the ridiculous fate which always attends interference between a man and his wife. And another word. Bad as I am, I am not such a villain as to make the marriage or misery of any woman a matter of huckster and sale. Fanny has long ago left me. I don't know where she is. I have searched everywhere. Another word yet. You say you love Bathsheba; yet on the merest apparent evidence you instantly believe in her dishonor. A fig for such love! Now that I've taught you a lesson, take your money back again."

"I will not; I will not!" said Boldwood, in a hiss.

"Anyhow I won't have it," said Troy contemptuously. He wrapped the packet of gold in the notes, and threw the whole into the road.

Boldwood shook his clenched fist at him. "You juggler of Satan! You black hound! But I'll punish you yet; mark me, I'll punish you yet!"

Another peal of laughter. Troy then closed the door, and locked himself in.

Throughout the whole of that night Boldwood's dark form might have been seen walking about the hills and downs of Weatherbury like an unhappy Shade in the Mournful Fields by Acheron.

35. At an Upper Window

IT WAS VERY EARLY the next morning—a time of sun and dew. The confused beginnings of many birds' songs spread into the healthy air, and the wan blue of the heaven was here and there coated with thin webs of incorporeal cloud which were of no effect in obscuring day. All the lights in the scene were yellow as to color, and all the shadows were attenuated as to form. The creeping plants about the old manor house were bowed with rows of heavy water drops, which had upon objects behind them the effect of minute lenses of high magnifying power.

Just before the clock struck five Gabriel Oak and Coggan passed the village cross, and went on together to the fields. They were yet barely in view of their mistress's house, when Oak fancied he saw the opening of a casement in one of the upper windows. The two men were at this moment partially screened by an elder bush, now beginning to be enriched with black bunches of fruit, and they paused before emerging from its shade.

A handsome man leaned idly from the lattice. He looked east and then west, in the manner of

one who makes a first morning survey. The man
was Sergeant Troy. His red jacket was loosely thrown
on, but not buttoned, and he had altogether the relaxed bearing of a soldier taking his ease.

Coggan spoke first, looking quietly at the window.

"She has married him!" he said.

Gabriel had previously beheld the sight, and he
now stood with his back turned, making no reply.

"I fancied we should know something today,"
continued Coggan. "I heard wheels pass my door
just after dark—you were out somewhere." He
glanced round upon Gabriel. "Good heavens above
us, Oak, how white your face is; you look like a
corpse!"

"Do I?" said Oak, with a faint smile.

"Lean on the gate: I'll wait a bit."

"All right, all right."

They stood by the gate awhile, Gabriel listlessly
staring at the ground. His mind sped into the future, and saw there enacted in years of leisure the
scenes of repentance that would ensue from this
work of haste. That they were married he had instantly decided. Why had it been so mysteriously
managed? It had become known that she had had
a fearful journey to Bath, owing to her miscalculat-
ing the distance: that the horse had broken down,
and that she had been more than two days getting
there. It was not Bathsheba's way to do things furtively. With all her faults she was candor itself.
Could she have been entrapped? The union was
not only an unutterable grief to him: it amazed
him, notwithstanding that he had passed the preceding week in a suspicion that such might be the
issue of Troy's meeting her away from home. Her
quiet return with Liddy had to some extent dispersed the dread. Just as that imperceptible motion
which appears like stillness is infinitely divided in

its properties from stillness itself, so had his hope
undistinguishable from despair differed from despair indeed.

In a few minutes they moved on again toward
the house. The sergeant still looked from the window.

"Morning, comrades!" he shouted, in a cheery
voice, when they came up.

Coggan replied to the greeting. "Bain't ye going
to answer the man?" he then said to Gabriel. "I'd
say good morning—you needn't spend a hapeth of
meaning upon it, and yet keep the man civil."

Gabriel soon decided too that, since the deed was
done, to put the best face upon the matter would be
the greatest kindness to her he loved.

"Good morning, Sergeant Troy," he returned,
in a ghastly voice.

"A rambling, gloomy house this," said Troy, smiling.

"Why—they *may* not be married!" suggested
Coggan. "Perhaps she's not there."

Gabriel shook his head. The soldier turned a little
toward the east, and the sun kindled his scarlet
coat to an orange glow.

"But it is a nice old house," responded Gabriel.

"Yes—I suppose so; but I feel like new wine in
an old bottle here. My notion is that sash windows
should be put throughout, and these old wains-
coted walls brightened up a bit; or the oak cleared
quite away, and the walls papered."

"It would be a pity, I think."

"Well, no. A philosopher once said in my hearing
that the old builders, who worked when art was a
living thing, had no respect for the work of builders
who went before them, but pulled down and altered
as they thought fit; and why shouldn't we? 'Creation
and preservation don't do well together,' says he,
'and a million of antiquarians can't invent a style.'

My mind exactly. I am for making this place more modern, that we may be cheerful whilst we can."

The military man turned and surveyed the interior of the room, to assist his ideas of improvement in this direction. Gabriel and Coggan began to move on.

"Oh, Coggan," said Troy, as if inspired by a recollection, "do you know if insanity has ever appeared in Mr. Boldwood's family?"

Jan reflected for a moment.

"I once heard that an uncle of his was queer in his head, but I don't know the rights o't," he said.

"It is of no importance," said Troy lightly. "Well, I shall be down in the fields with you some time this week; but I have a few matters to attend to first. So good day to you. We shall, of course, keep on just as friendly terms as usual. I'm not a proud man: nobody is ever able to say that of Sergeant Troy. However, what is must be, and here's half-a-crown to drink my health, men."

Troy threw the coin dexterously across the front plot and over the fence toward Gabriel, who shunned it in its fall, his face turning to an angry red. Coggan twirled his eye, edged forward, and caught the money in its ricochet upon the road.

"Very well—you keep it, Coggan," said Gabriel with disdain, and almost fiercely. "As for me, I'll do without gifts from him!"

"Don't show it too much," said Coggan musingly. "For if he's married to her, mark my words, he'll buy his discharge and be our master here. Therefore 'tis well to say 'Friend' outwardly, though you say 'Troublehouse' within."

"Well—perhaps it is best to be silent; but I can't go further than that. I can't flatter, and if my place here is only to be kept by smoothing him down, my place must be lost."

A horseman, whom they had for some time seen

in the distance, now appeared close beside them.

"There's Mr. Boldwood," said Oak. "I wonder what Troy meant by his question."

Coggan and Oak nodded respectfully to the farmer, just checked their paces to discover if they were wanted, and finding they were not, stood back to let him pass on.

The only signs of the terrible sorrow Boldwood had been combating through the night, and was combating now, were the want of color in his well-defined face, the enlarged appearance of the veins in his forehead and temples, and the sharper lines about his mouth. The horse bore him away, and the very step of the animal seemed significant of dogged despair. Gabriel, for a minute, rose above his own grief in noticing Boldwood's. He saw the square figure sitting erect upon the horse, the head turned to neither side, the elbows steady by the hips, the brim of the hat level and undisturbed in its onward glide, until the keen edges of Boldwood's shape sank by degrees over the hill. To one who knew the man and his story there was something more striking in this immobility than in a collapse. The clash of discord between mood and matter here was forced painfully home to the heart; and, as in laughter there are more dreadful phases than in tears, so was there in the steadiness of this agonized man an expression deeper than a cry.

36. Wealth in Jeopardy — The Revel

ONE NIGHT, at the end of August, when Bathsheba's experiences as a married woman were still new, and when the weather was yet dry and sultry, a man stood motionless in the stackyard of Weatherbury Upper Farm, looking at the moon and sky.

The night had a sinister aspect. A heated breeze from the south slowly fanned the summits of lofty objects, and in the sky dashes of buoyant cloud were sailing in a course at right angles to that of another stratum, neither of them in the direction of the breeze below. The moon, as seen through these films, had a lurid metallic look. The fields were sallow with the impure light, and all were tinged in monochrome, as if beheld through stained glass. The same evening the sheep had trailed homeward head to tail, the behavior of the rooks had been confused, and the horses had moved with timidity and caution.

Thunder was imminent, and, taking some secondary appearances into consideration, it was likely to be followed by one of the lengthened rains which mark the close of dry weather for the season. Before twelve hours had passed a harvest atmosphere would be a bygone thing.

Oak gazed with misgiving at eight naked and unprotected ricks, massive and heavy with the rich produce of one-half the farm for that year. He went on to the barn.

This was the night which had been selected by Sergeant Troy—ruling now in the room of his wife—for giving the harvest supper and dance. As Oak approached the building the sound of violins and a tambourine, and the regular jigging of many feet, grew more distinct. He came close to the large doors, one of which stood slightly ajar, and looked in.

The central space, together with the recess at one end, was emptied of all incumbrances, and this area, covering about two-thirds of the whole, was appropriated for the gathering, the remaining end, which was piled to the ceiling with oats, being screened off with sailcloth. Tufts and garlands of green foliage decorated the walls, beams, and extemporized chandeliers, and immediately opposite to Oak a rostrum had been erected, bearing a table and chairs. Here sat three fiddlers, and beside them stood a frantic man with his hair on end, perspiration streaming down his cheeks, and a tambourine quivering in his hand.

The dance ended, and on the black oak floor in the midst a new row of couples formed for another.

"Now, ma'am, and no offence I hope, I ask what dance you would like next?" said the first violin.

"Really, it makes no difference," said the clear voice of Bathsheba, who stood at the inner end of the building, observing the scene from behind a table covered with cups and viands. Troy was lolling beside her.

"Then," said the fiddler, "I'll venture to name that the right and proper thing is 'The Soldier's Joy'—there being a gallant soldier married into the farm—hey, my sonnies, and gentlemen all?"

"It shall be 'The Soldier's Joy,'" exclaimed a chorus.

"Thanks for the compliment," said the sergeant gaily, taking Bathsheba by the hand and leading her to the top of the dance. "For though I have purchased my discharge from Her Most Gracious Majesty's regiment of cavalry the 11th Dragoon Guards, to attend to the new duties awaiting me here, I shall continue a soldier in spirit and feeling as long as I live."

So the dance began. As to the merits of "The Soldier's Joy," there cannot be, and never were, two opinions. It has been observed in the musical circles of Weatherbury and its vicinity that this melody, at the end of three-quarters of an hour of thunderous footing, still possesses more stimulative properties for the heel and toe than the majority of other dances at their first opening. "The Soldier's Joy" has, too, an additional charm, in being so admirably adapted to the tambourine aforesaid—no mean instrument in the hands of a performer who understands the proper convulsions, spasms, St. Vitus' dances, and fearful frenzies necessary when exhibiting its tones in their highest perfection.

The immortal tune ended, a fine DD rolling forth from the bass viol with the sonorousness of a cannonade, and Gabriel delayed his entry no longer. He avoided Bathsheba, and got as near as possible to the platform, where Sergeant Troy was now seated, drinking brandy and water, though the others drank without exception cider and ale. Gabriel could not easily thrust himself within speaking distance of the sergeant, and he sent a message, asking him to come down for a moment. The sergeant said he could not attend.

"Will you tell him, then," said Gabriel, "that I only stepped arth'art to say that heavy rain is sure to fall soon, and that something should be done to protect the ricks?"

"Mr. Troy says it will not rain," returned the

messenger, "and he cannot stop to talk to you about such fidgets."

In juxtaposition with Troy, Oak had a melancholy tendency to look like a candle beside gas, and ill at ease he went out again, thinking he would go home; for, under the circumstances, he had no heart for the scene in the barn. At the door he paused for a moment: Troy was speaking.

"Friends, it is not only the harvest home that we are celebrating tonight; but this is also a wedding feast. A short time ago I had the happiness to lead to the altar this lady, your mistress, and not until now have we been able to give any public flourish to the event in Weatherbury. That it may be thoroughly well done, and that every man may go happy to bed, I have ordered to be brought here some bottles of brandy and kettles of hot water. A treble strong goblet will be handed round to each guest."

Bathsheba put her hand upon his arm, and, with upturned pale face, said imploringly, "No—don't give it to them—pray don't, Frank! It will only do them harm: they have had enough of everything."

"True—we don't wish for no more, thank ye," said one or two.

"Pooh!" said the sergeant contemptuously, and raised his voice as if lighted up by a new idea. "Friends," he said, "we'll send the womenfolk home! 'Tis time they were in bed. Then we cockbirds will have a jolly carouse to ourselves! If any of the men show the white feather, let them look elsewhere for a winter's work."

Bathsheba indignantly left the barn, followed by all the women and children. The musicians, not looking upon themselves as "company," slipped quietly away to their springwagon and put in the horse. Thus Troy and the men on the farm were left sole occupants of the place. Oak, not to appear unnecessarily disagreeable, stayed a little while; then he, too, arose and quietly took his departure, followed by a friendly oath from the sergeant for not staying to a second round of grog.

Gabriel proceeded toward his home. In approaching the door, his toe kicked something which felt and sounded soft, leathery, and distended, like a boxing glove. It was a large toad humbly traveling across the path. Oak took it up, thinking it might be better to kill the creature to save it from pain; but finding it uninjured, he placed it again among the grass. He knew what this direct message from the Great Mother meant. And soon came another.

When he struck a light indoors there appeared upon the table a thin glistening streak, as if a brush of varnish had been lightly dragged across it. Oak's eyes followed the serpentine sheen to the other side, where it led up to a huge brown garden slug, which had come indoors tonight for reasons of its own. It was Nature's second way of hinting to him that he was to prepare for foul weather.

Oak sat down meditating for nearly an hour. During this time two black spiders, of the kind common in thatched houses, promenaded the ceiling, ultimately dropping to the floor. This reminded him that if there was one class of manifestation on this matter that he thoroughly understood, it was the instincts of sheep. He left the room, ran across two or three fields toward the flock, got upon a hedge, and looked over among them.

They were crowded close together on the other side around some furze bushes, and the first peculiarity observable was that, on the sudden appearance of Oak's head over the fence, they did not stir or run away. They had now a terror of something greater than their terror of man. But this was not the most noteworthy feature: they were all grouped in such a way that their tails, without a single exception, were toward that half of the horizon from which the storm threatened. There was an inner circle closely huddled, and outside these they radiated wider apart, the pattern formed by the flock as a whole not being unlike a vandyked lace collar, to which the clump of furze bushes stood in the position of a wearer's neck.

This was enough to reestablish him in his original opinion. He knew now that he was right, and that Troy was wrong. Every voice in nature was unanimous in bespeaking change. But two distinct translations attached to these dumb expressions. Apparently there was to be a thunderstorm, and afterward a cold continuous rain. The creeping things seemed to know all about the later rain, but little of the interpolated thunderstorm; whilst the sheep knew all about the thunderstorm and nothing of the later rain.

This complication of weathers being uncommon, was all the more to be feared. Oak returned to the stackyard. All was silent here, and the conical tips of the ricks jutted darkly into the sky. There were five wheat ricks in this yard, and three stacks of barley. The wheat when threshed would average about thirty quarters to each stack; the barley, at least forty. Their value to Bathsheba, and indeed to anybody, Oak mentally estimated by the following simple calculation:

$$5 \times 30 = 150 \text{ quarters} = 500l.$$
$$3 \times 40 = 120 \text{ quarters} = 250l.$$
$$\text{Total} \quad . \quad . \quad \overline{750l.}$$

Seven hundred and fifty pounds in the divinest form that money can wear—that of necessary food for man and beast: should the risk be run of deteriorating this bulk of corn to less than half its value, because of the instability of a woman? "Never, if I can prevent it!" said Gabriel.

Such was the argument that Oak set outwardly before him. But man, even to himself, is a palimpsest, having an ostensible writing, and another beneath the lines. It is possible that there was this golden legend under the utilitarian one: "I will help to my last effort the woman I have loved so dearly."

He went back to the barn to endeavor to obtain assistance for covering the ricks that very night. All was silent within, and he would have passed on in the belief that the party had broken up, had not a dim light, yellow as saffron by contrast with the greenish whiteness outside, streamed through a knothole in the folding doors.

Gabriel looked in. An unusual picture met his eye.

The candles suspended among the evergreens had burnt down to their sockets, and in some cases the leaves tied about them were scorched. Many of the lights had quite gone out, others smoked and stank, grease dropping from them upon the floor. Here, under the table, and leaning against forms and chairs in every conceivable attitude except the perpendicular, were the wretched persons of all the workfolk, the hair of their heads at such low levels being suggestive of mops and brooms. In the midst of these shone red and distinct the figure of Sergeant Troy, leaning back in a chair. Coggan was on his back, with his mouth open, buzzing forth snores, as were several others; the united breathings of the horizontal assemblage forming a subdued roar like London from a distance. Joseph Poorgrass was curled round in the fashion of a hedgehog, apparently in attempts to present the least possible portion of his surface to the air; and behind him was dimly visible an unimportant remnant of William Smallbury. The glasses and cups still stood upon the table, a water jug being overturned, from which a small rill, after tracing its course with marvelous precision down the center of the long table, fell into the neck of the unconscious Mark Clark, in a steady, monotonous drip, like the dripping of a stalactite in a cave.

Gabriel glanced hopelessly at the group, which, with one or two exceptions, composed all the able-bodied men upon the farm. He saw at once that if the ricks were to be saved that night, or even the next morning, he must save them with his own hands.

A faint "ting-ting" resounded from under Coggan's waistcoat. It was Coggan's watch striking the hour of two.

Oak went to the recumbent form of Matthew Moon, who usually undertook the rough thatching of the homestead, and shook him. The shaking was without effect.

Gabriel shouted in his ear, "Where's your thatching beetle and rick stick and spars?"

"Under the staddles," said Moon mechanically, with the unconscious promptness of a medium.

Gabriel let go his head, and it dropped upon the floor like a bowl. He then went to Susan Tall's husband.

"Where's the key of the granary?"

No answer. The question was repeated, with the same result. To be shouted to at night was evidently less of a novelty to Susan Tall's husband than to Matthew Moon. Oak flung down Tall's head into the corner again and turned away.

To be just, the men were not greatly to blame for this painful and demoralizing termination to the evening's entertainment. Sergeant Troy had so strenuously insisted, glass in hand, that drinking should be the bond of their union, that those who wished to refuse hardly liked to be so unmannerly under the circumstances. Having from their youth up been entirely unaccustomed to any liquor stronger than cider or mild ale, it was no wonder that they had succumbed, one and all, with extraordinary uniformity, after the lapse of about an hour.

Gabriel was greatly depressed. This debauch boded ill for that willful and fascinating mistress whom the faithful man even now felt within him as the embodiment of all that was sweet and bright and hopeless.

He put out the expiring lights, that the barn might not be endangered, closed the door upon the men in their deep and oblivious sleep, and went again into the lone night. A hot breeze, as if breathed from the parted lips of some dragon about to swallow the globe, fanned him from the south while directly opposite in the north rose a grim misshapen body of cloud, in the very teeth of the wind. So unnaturally did it rise that one could fancy it to be lifted by machinery from below. Meanwhile the faint cloudlets had flown back into the southeast corner of the sky, as if in terror of the large cloud, like a young brood gazed in upon by some monster.

Going on to the village, Oak flung a small stone against the window of Laban Tall's bedroom, expecting Susan to open it; but nobody stirred. He went round to the back door, which had been left unfastened for Laban's entry, and passed in to the foot of the staircase.

"Mrs. Tall, I've come for the key of the granary, to get at the rick cloths," said Oak, in a stentorian voice.

"Is that you?" said Mrs. Susan Tall, half-awake.

"Yes," said Gabriel.

"Come along to bed, do, you draw-latching rogue —keeping a body awake like this!"

"It isn't Laban—'tis Gabriel Oak. I want the key of the granary."

"Gabriel! What in the name of fortune did you pretend to be Laban for?"

"I didn't. I thought you meant—"

"Yes you did! What do you want here?"

"The key of the granary."

"Take it then. 'Tis on the nail. People coming disturbing women at this time of night ought—"

Gabriel took the key, without waiting to hear the conclusion of the tirade. Ten minutes later his lonely figure might have been seen dragging four large waterproof coverings across the yard, and soon two of these heaps of treasure in grain were covered snug—two cloths to each. Two hundred pounds were secured. Three wheatstacks remained open, and there were no more cloths. Oak looked under the staddles and found a fork. He mounted the third pile of wealth and began operating, adopting the plan of sloping the upper sheaves one over the other; and, in addition, filling the interstices with the material of some untied sheaves.

So far all was well. By this hurried contrivance Bathsheba's property in wheat was safe for at any rate a week or two, provided always that there was not much wind.

Next came the barley. This it was only possible to protect by systematic thatching. Time went on, and the moon vanished not to reappear. It was the farewell of the ambassador previous to war. The night had a haggard look, like a sick thing; and there came finally an utter expiration of air from the whole heaven in the form of a slow breeze, which might have been likened to a death. And now nothing was heard in the yard but the dull thuds of the beetle which drove in the spars, and the rustle of thatch in the intervals.

37. *The Storm — The Two Together*

A LIGHT FLAPPED OVER the scene, as if reflected from phosphorescent wings crossing the sky, and a rumble filled the air. It was the first move of the approaching storm.

The second peal was noisy, with comparatively little visible lightning. Gabriel saw a candle shining in Bathsheba's bedroom, and soon a shadow swept to and fro upon the blind.

Then there came a third flash. Maneuvers of a most extraordinary kind were going on in the vast firmamental hollows overhead. The lightning now was the color of silver, and gleamed in the heavens like a mailed army. Rumbles became rattles. Gabriel from his elevated position could see over the landscape at least half-a-dozen miles in front. Every hedge, bush, and tree was distinct as in a line engraving. In a paddock in the same direction was a herd of heifers, and the forms of these were visible at this moment in the act of galloping about in the wildest and maddest confusion, flinging their heels and tails high into the air, their heads to earth. A poplar in the immediate foreground was like an ink stroke on burnished tin. Then the picture vanished, leaving the darkness so intense that Gabriel worked entirely by feeling with his hands.

He had stuck his ricking rod, or poniard, as it was indifferently called—a long iron lance, polished by handling—into the stack, used to support the sheaves instead of the support called a groom used on houses. A blue light appeared in the zenith, and in some indescribable manner flickered down near the top of the rod. It was the fourth of the larger flashes. A moment later and there was a smack—smart, clear, and short. Gabriel felt his position to be anything but a safe one, and he resolved to descend.

Not a drop of rain had fallen as yet. He wiped his weary brow, and looked again at the black forms of the unprotected stacks. Was his life so valuable to him after all? What were his prospects that he should be so chary of running risk, when important and urgent labor could not be carried on without such risk? He resolved to stick to the stack. However, he took a precaution. Under the staddles was a long tethering chain, used to prevent the escape of errant horses. This he carried up the ladder, and sticking his rod through the clog at one end, allowed the other end of the chain to trail upon the ground. The spike attached to it he drove in. Under the shadow of this extemporized lightning conductor he felt himself comparatively safe.

Before Oak had laid his hands upon his tools again out leapt the fifth flash, with the spring of a serpent and the shout of a fiend. It was green as an emerald, and the reverberation was stunning. What was this the light revealed to him? In the open ground before him, as he looked over the ridge of the rick, was a dark and apparently female form. Could it be that of the only venturesome woman in the parish—Bathsheba? The form moved on a step: then he could see no more.

"Is that you, ma'am?" said Gabriel to the darkness.

"Who is there?" said the voice of Bathsheba.

"Gabriel. I am on the rick, thatching."

"Oh, Gabriel!—and are you? I have come about them. The weather awoke me, and I thought of the corn. I am so distressed about it—can we save it anyhow? I cannot find my husband. Is he with you?"

"He is not here."

"Do you know where he is?"

"Asleep in the barn."

"He promised that the stacks should be seen to, and now they are all neglected! Can I do anything to help? Liddy is afraid to come out. Fancy finding you here at such an hour! Surely I can do something."

"You can bring up some reed sheaves to me, one by one, ma'am; if you are not afraid to come up the ladder in the dark," said Gabriel. "Every moment is precious now, and that would save a good deal of time. It is not very dark when the lightning has been gone a bit."

"I'll do anything!" she said resolutely. She instantly took a sheaf upon her shoulder, clambered up close to his heels, placed it behind the rod, and descended for another. At her third ascent the rick suddenly brightened with the brazen glare of shining majolica—every knot in every straw was visible. On the slope in front of him appeared two human shapes, black as jet. The rick lost its sheen—the shapes vanished. Gabriel turned his head. It had been the sixth flash which had come from the east behind him, and the two dark forms on the slope had been the shadows of himself and Bathsheba.

Then came the peal. It hardly was credible that such a heavenly light could be the parent of such a diabolic sound.

"How terrible!" she exclaimed, and clutched him by the sleeve. Gabriel turned, and steadied her on her aerial perch by holding her arm. At the same moment, while he was still reversed in his attitude, there was more light, and he saw, as it were, a copy of the tall poplar tree on the hill drawn in black on the wall of the barn. It was the shadow of that tree, thrown across by a secondary flash in the west.

The next flare came. Bathsheba was on the ground now, shouldering another sheaf, and she bore its dazzle without flinching—thunder and all —and again ascended with the load. There was then a silence everywhere for four or five minutes, and the crunch of the spars, as Gabriel hastily drove them in, could again be distinctly heard. He thought the crisis of the storm had passed. But there came a burst of light.

"Hold on!" said Gabriel, taking the sheaf from her shoulder, and grasping her arm again.

Heaven opened then, indeed. The flash was almost too novel for its inexpressibly dangerous nature to be at once realized, and they could only comprehend the magnificence of its beauty. It sprang from east, west, north, south, and was a perfect dance of death. The forms of skeletons appeared in the air, shaped with blue fire for bones —dancing, leaping, striding, racing around, and mingling altogether in unparalleled confusion. With these were intertwined undulating snakes of green, and behind these was a broad mass of lesser light. Simultaneously came from every part of the tumbling sky what may be called a shout; since, though no shout ever came near it, it was more of the nature of a shout than of anything else earthly. In the meantime one of the grisly forms had alighted upon the point of Gabriel's rod, to run invisibly down it, down the chain, and into the earth. Gabriel was almost blinded, and he could feel Bathsheba's warm arm tremble in his hand—a sensation novel and thrilling enough; but love, life, everything human, seemed small and trifling in such close juxtaposition with an infuriated universe.

Oak had hardly time to gather up these impressions into a thought, and to see how strangely the red feather of her hat shone in this light, when the tall tree on the hill before mentioned seemed on fire to a white heat, and a new one among these terrible voices mingled with the last crash of those preceding. It was a stupefying blast, harsh and pitiless, and it fell upon their ears in a dead, flat blow, without that reverberation which lends the tones of a drum to more distant thunder. By the luster reflected from every part of the earth and from the wide domical scoop above it, he saw that the tree was sliced down the whole length of its tall, straight stem, a huge riband of bark being apparently flung off. The other portion remained erect, and revealed the bared surface as a strip of white down the front. The lightning had struck the tree. A sulphurous smell filled the air; then all was silent, and black as a cave in Hinnom.

"We had a narrow escape!" said Gabriel hurriedly. "You had better go down."

Bathsheba said nothing; but he could distinctly hear her rhythmical pants, and the recurrent rustle of the sheaf beside her in response to her frightened pulsations. She descended the ladder, and, on second thoughts, he followed her. The darkness was now impenetrable by the sharpest vision. They both stood still at the bottom, side by side. Bathsheba appeared to think only of the weather—Oak thought only of her just then. At last he said—

"The storm seems to have passed now, at any rate."

"I think so too," said Bathsheba. "Though there are multitudes of gleams, look!"

The sky was now filled with an incessant light, frequent repetition melting into complete continuity, as an unbroken sound results from the successive strokes on a gong.

"Nothing serious," said he. "I cannot understand

no rain falling. But Heaven be praised, it is all the better for us. I am now going up again."

"Gabriel, you are kinder than I deserve! I will stay and help you yet. Oh, why are not some of the others here!"

"They would have been here if they could," said Oak, in a hesitating way.

"Oh, I know it all—all," she said, adding slowly: "They are all asleep in the barn, in a drunken sleep, and my husband among them. That's it, is it not? Don't think I am a timid woman and can't endure things."

"I am not certain," said Gabriel. "I will go and see."

He crossed to the barn, leaving her there alone. He looked through the chinks of the door. All was in total darkness, as he had left it, and there still arose, as at the former time, the steady buzz of many snores.

He felt a zephyr curling about his cheek, and turned. It was Bathsheba's breath—she had followed him, and was looking into the same chink.

He endeavored to put off the immediate and painful subject of their thoughts by remarking gently, "If you'll come back again, miss—ma'am, and hand up a few more, it would save much time."

Then Oak went back again, ascended to the top, stepped off the ladder for greater expedition, and went on thatching. She followed, but without a sheaf.

"Gabriel," she said, in a strange and impressive voice.

Oak looked up at her. She had not spoken since he left the barn. The soft and continual shimmer of the dying lightning showed a marble face high against the black sky of the opposite quarter. Bathsheba was sitting almost on the apex of the stack, her feet gathered up beneath her, and resting on the top round of the ladder.

"Yes, mistress," he said.

"I suppose you thought that when I galloped away to Bath that night it was on purpose to be married?"

"I did at last—not at first," he answered, somewhat surprised at the abruptness with which this new subject was broached.

"And others thought so, too!"

"Yes."

"And you blamed me for it?"

"Well—a little."

"I thought so. Now, I care a little for your good opinion, and I want to explain something—I have longed to do it ever since I returned, and you looked so gravely at me. For if I were to die—and I may die soon—it would be dreadful that you should always think mistakenly of me. Now, listen."

Gabriel ceased his rustling.

"I went to Bath that night in the full intention of breaking off my engagement to Mr. Troy. It was owing to circumstances which occurred after I got there that—that we were married. Now, do you see the matter in a new light?"

"I do—somewhat."

"I must, I suppose, say more, now that I have begun. And perhaps it's no harm, for you are certainly under no delusion that I ever loved you, or that I can have any object in speaking, more than that object I have mentioned. Well, I was alone in a strange city, and the horse was lame. And at last I didn't know what to do. I saw, when it was too late, that scandal might seize hold of me for meeting him alone in that way. But I was coming away, when he suddenly said he had that day seen a woman more beautiful than I, and that his constancy could not be counted on unless I at once became his. . . . And I was grieved and troubled—" She cleared her voice, and waited a moment, as if to gather breath. "And then, between jealousy and distraction, I married him!" she whispered with desperate impetuosity.

Gabriel made no reply.

"He was not to blame, for it was perfectly true about—about his seeing somebody else," she quickly added. "And now I don't wish for a single remark from you upon the subject—indeed, I forbid it. I only wanted you to know that misunderstood bit of my history before a time comes when you could never know it—You want some more sheaves?"

She went down the ladder, and the work proceeded. Gabriel soon perceived a languor in the movements of his mistress up and down, and he said to her, gently as a mother—

"I think you had better go indoors now, you are tired. I can finish the rest alone. If the wind does not change the rain is likely to keep off."

"If I am useless I will go," said Bathsheba, in a flagging cadence. "But oh, if your life should be lost!"

"You are not useless; but I would rather not tire you longer. You have done well."

"And you better!" she said gratefully. "Thank you for your devotion, a thousand times, Gabriel! Goodnight—I know you are doing your very best for me."

She diminished in the gloom, and vanished, and he heard the latch of the gate fall as she passed through. He worked in a reverie now, musing upon her story, and upon the contradictoriness of that feminine heart which had caused her to speak more warmly to him tonight than she ever had done whilst unmarried and free to speak as warmly as she chose.

He was disturbed in his meditation by a grating noise from the coach house. It was the vane on the roof turning round and this change in the wind was the signal for a disastrous rain.

38. Rain — One Solitary Meets Another

IT WAS NOW FIVE O'CLOCK, and the dawn was promising to break in hues of drab and ash.

The air changed its temperature and stirred itself more vigorously. Cool breezes coursed in transparent eddies round Oak's face. The wind shifted yet a point or two and blew stronger. In ten minutes every wind of heaven seemed to be roaming at large. Some of the thatching on the wheatstacks was now whirled fantastically aloft, and had to be replaced and weighted with some rails that lay near at hand. This done, Oak slaved away again at the barley. A huge drop of rain smote his face, the wind snarled round every corner, the trees rocked to the bases of their trunks, and the twigs clashed in strife. Driving in spars at any point and on any system, inch by inch he covered more and more safely from ruin this distracting impersonation of seven hundred pounds. The rain came on in earnest, and Oak soon felt the water to be tracking cold and clammy routes down his back. Ultimately he was reduced well-nigh to a homogeneous sop, and the dyes of his clothes trickled down and stood in a pool at the foot of the ladder. The rain stretched obliquely through the dull atmosphere in liquid spines, unbroken in continuity between their beginnings in the clouds and their points in him.

Oak suddenly remembered that eight months before this time he had been fighting against fire in the same spot as desperately as he was fighting against water now—and for a futile love of the same woman. As for her—But Oak was generous and true, and dismissed his reflections.

It was about seven o'clock in the dark leaden morning when Gabriel came down from the last stack, and thankfully exclaimed, "It is done!" He was drenched, weary, and sad, and yet not so sad as drenched and weary, for he was cheered by a sense of success in a good cause.

Faint sounds came from the barn, and he looked that way. Figures stepped singly and in pairs through the doors—all walking awkwardly, and abashed, save the foremost, who wore a red jacket, and advanced with his hands in his pockets, whistling. The others shambled after with a conscience-stricken air: the whole procession was not unlike Flaxman's group of the suitors tottering on toward the infernal regions under the conduct of Mercury. The gnarled shapes passed into the village, Troy, their leader, entering the farmhouse. Not a single one of them had turned his face to the ricks, or apparently bestowed one thought upon their condition.

Soon Oak too went homeward, by a different route from theirs. In front of him against the wet glazed surface of the lane he saw a person walking yet more slowly than himself under an umbrella. The man turned and plainly started; he was Boldwood.

"How are you this morning, sir?" said Oak.

"Yes, it is a wet day—Oh, I am well, very well, I thank you; quite well."

"I am glad to hear it, sir."

Boldwood seemed to awake to the present by degrees. "You look tired and ill, Oak," he said then, desultorily regarding his companion.

"I am tired. You look strangely altered, sir."

"I? Not a bit of it: I am well enough. What put that into your head?"

"I thought you didn't look quite so topping as you used to, that was all."

"Indeed, then you are mistaken," said Boldwood shortly. "Nothing hurts me. My constitution is an iron one."

"I've been working hard to get our ricks covered, and was barely in time. Never had such a struggle in my life. . . . Yours of course are safe, sir."

"Oh, yes." Boldwood added, after an interval of silence: "What did you ask, Oak?"

"Your ricks are all covered before this time?"

"No."

"At any rate, the large ones upon the stone staddles?"

"They are not."

"Them under the hedge?"

"No. I forgot to tell the thatcher to set about it."

"Nor the little one by the stile?"

"Nor the little one by the stile. I overlooked the ricks this year."

"Then not a tenth of your corn will come to measure, sir."

"Possibly not."

"Overlooked them," repeated Gabriel slowly to himself. It is difficult to describe the intensely dramatic effect that announcement had upon Oak at such a moment. All the night he had been feeling that the neglect he was laboring to repair was abnormal and isolated—the only instance of the kind within the circuit of the county. Yet at this very time, within the same parish, a greater waste had been going on, uncomplained of and disregarded. A few months earlier Boldwood's forgetting his husbandry would have been as preposterous an idea as a sailor forgetting he was in a ship. Oak was just thinking that whatever he himself might have suffered from Bathsheba's marriage, here was a man who had suffered more, when Boldwood spoke in a changed voice—that of one who yearned to make a confidence and relieve his heart by an outpouring.

"Oak, you know as well as I that things have gone wrong with me lately. I may as well own it. I was going to get a little settled in life; but in some way my plan has come to nothing."

"I thought my mistress would have married you," said Gabriel, not knowing enough of the full depths of Boldwood's love to keep silence on the farmer's account, and determined not to evade discipline by doing so on his own. "However, it is so sometimes, and nothing happens that we expect," he added, with the repose of a man whom misfortune had inured rather than subdued.

"I daresay I am a joke about the parish," said Boldwood, as if the subject came irresistibly to his tongue, and with a miserable lightness meant to express his indifference.

"Oh, no—I don't think that."

"—But the real truth of the matter is that there was not, as some fancy, any jilting on—her part. No engagement ever existed between me and Miss Everdene. People say so, but it is untrue: she never promised me!" Boldwood stood still now and turned his wild face to Oak. "Oh, Gabriel," he continued, "I am weak and foolish, and I don't know what, and I can't fend off my miserable grief! . . .

I had some faint belief in the mercy of God till I lost that woman. Yes, He prepared a gourd to shade me, and like the prophet I thanked Him and was glad. But the next day He prepared a worm to smite the gourd and wither it; and I feel it is better to die than to live!"

A silence followed. Boldwood aroused himself from the momentary mood of confidence into which he had drifted, and walked on again, resuming his usual reserve.

"No, Gabriel," he resumed, with a carelessness which was like the smile on the countenance of a skull, "it was made more of by other people than ever it was by us. I do feel a little regret occasionally, but no woman ever had power over me for any length of time. Well, good morning; I can trust you not to mention to others what has passed between us two here."

39. Coming Home — A Cry

ON THE TURNPIKE ROAD, between Casterbridge and Weatherbury, and about three miles from the former place, is Yalbury Hill, one of those steep long ascents which pervade the highways of this undulating part of South Wessex. In returning from market it is usual for the farmers and other gig gentry to alight at the bottom and walk up.

One Saturday evening in the month of October Bathsheba's vehicle was duly creeping up this incline. She was sitting listlessly in the second seat of the gig, whilst walking beside her in a farmer's marketing suit of unusually fashionable cut was an erect, well-made young man. Though on foot, he held the reins and whip, and occasionally aimed light cuts at the horse's ear with the end of the lash, as a recreation. This man was her husband, formerly Sergeant Troy, who, having bought his discharge with Bathsheba's money, was gradually transforming himself into a farmer of a spirited and very modern school. People of unalterable ideas still insisted upon calling him "Sergeant" when they met him, which was in some degree owing to his having still retained the well-shaped moustache of his military days, and the soldierly bearing inseparable from his form and training.

"Yes, if it hadn't been for that wretched rain I should have cleared two hundred as easy as looking, my love," he was saying. "Don't you see, it altered all the chances? To speak like a book I once read, wet weather is the narrative, and fine days are the episodes, of our country's history; now, isn't that true?"

"But the time of year is come for changeable weather."

"Well, yes. The fact is, these autumn races are the ruin of everybody. Never did I see such a day as 'twas! 'Tis a wild open place, just out of Budmouth, and a drab sea rolled in toward us like liquid misery. Wind and rain—good Lord! Dark? Why, 'twas as black as my hat before the last race was run. 'Twas five o'clock, and you couldn't see the horses till they were almost in, leave alone colors. The ground was as heavy as lead, and all judgment from a fellow's experience went for nothing. Horses, riders, people, were all blown about like ships at sea. Three booths were blown over, and the wretched folk inside crawled out upon their hands and knees; and in the next field were as many as a dozen hats at one time. Aye, Pimpernel regularly stuck fast, when about sixty yards off, and when I saw Policy stepping on, it did knock my heart against the lining of my ribs, I assure you, my love!"

"And you mean, Frank," said Bathsheba sadly —her voice was painfully lowered from the fullness and vivacity of the previous summer—"that you have lost more than a hundred pounds in a month by this dreadful horse racing? Oh, Frank, it is cruel; it is foolish of you to take away my money so. We shall have to leave the farm; that will be the end of it!"

"Humbug about cruel. Now, there 'tis again— turn on the waterworks; that's just like you."

"But you'll promise me not to go to Budmouth second meeting, won't you?" she implored. Bathsheba was at the full depth for tears, but she maintained a dry eye.

"I don't see why I should; in fact, if it turns out to be a fine day, I was thinking of taking you."

"Never, never! I'll go a hundred miles the other way first. I hate the sound of the very word!"

"But the question of going to see the race or staying at home has very little to do with the matter. Bets are all booked safely enough before the race begins, you may depend. Whether it is a bad race for me or a good one, will have very little to do with our going there next Monday."

"But you don't mean to say that you have risked anything on this one too!" she exclaimed, with an agonized look.

"There now, don't you be a little fool. Wait till you are told. Why, Bathsheba, you have lost all the pluck and sauciness you formerly had, and upon my life if I had known what a chicken-hearted creature you were under all your boldness, I'd never have—I know what."

A flash of indignation might have been seen in

Bathsheba's dark eyes as she looked resolutely ahead after this reply. They moved on without further speech, some early withered leaves from the trees which hooded the road at this spot occasionally spinning downward across their path to the earth.

A woman appeared on the brow of the hill. The ridge was in a cutting, so that she was very near the husband and wife before she became visible. Troy had turned toward the gig to remount, and whilst putting his foot on the step the woman passed behind him.

Though the overshadowing trees and the approach of eventide enveloped them in gloom, Bathsheba could see plainly enough to discern the extreme poverty of the woman's garb, and the sadness of her face.

"Please, sir, do you know at what time Casterbridge Unionhouse closes at night?"

The woman said these words to Troy over his shoulder.

Troy started visibly at the sound of the voice; yet he seemed to recover presence of mind sufficient to prevent himself from giving way to his impulse to suddenly turn and face her. He said, slowly—

"I don't know."

The woman, on hearing him speak, quickly looked up, examined the side of his face, and recognized the soldier under the yeoman's garb. Her face was drawn into an expression which had gladness and agony both among its elements. She uttered an hysterical cry, and fell down.

"Oh, poor thing!" exclaimed Bathsheba, instantly preparing to alight.

"Stay where you are, and attend to the horse!" said Troy peremptorily, throwing her the reins and the whip. "Walk the horse to the top: I'll see to the woman."

"But I—"

"Do you hear? Clk—Poppet!"

The horse, gig, and Bathsheba moved on.

"How on earth did you come here? I thought you were miles away, or dead! Why didn't you write to me?" said Troy to the woman, in a strangely gentle, yet hurried voice, as he lifted her up.

"I feared to."

"Have you any money?"

"None."

"Good Heaven—I wish I had more to give you! Here's—wretched—the merest trifle. It is every farthing I have left. I have none but what my wife gives me, you know, and I can't ask her now."

The woman made no answer.

"I have only another moment," continued Troy; "and now listen. Where are you going tonight? Casterbridge Union?"

"Yes; I thought to go there."

"You shan't go there; yet, wait. Yes, perhaps for tonight; I can do nothing better—worse luck! Sleep there tonight, and stay there tomorrow. Monday is the first free day I have; and on Monday morning, at ten exactly, meet me on Grey's Bridge, just out of the town. I'll bring all the money I can muster. You shan't want—I'll see that, Fanny; then I'll get you a lodging somewhere. Good-bye till then. I am a brute—but good-bye!"

After advancing the distance which completed the ascent of the hill, Bathsheba turned her head. The woman was upon her feet, and Bathsheba saw her withdrawing from Troy, and going feebly down the hill by the third milestone from Casterbridge. Troy then came on toward his wife, stepped into the gig, took the reins from her hand, and without making any observation whipped the horse into a trot. He was rather agitated.

"Do you know who that woman was?" said Bathsheba, looking searchingly into his face.

"I do," he said, looking boldly back into hers.

"I thought you did," said she, with angry hauteur, and still regarding him. "Who is she?"

He suddenly seemed to think that frankness would benefit neither of the women.

"Nothing to either of us," he said. "I know her by sight."

"What is her name?"

"How should I know her name?"

"I think you do."

"Think if you will, and be—" The sentence was completed by a smart cut of the whip round Poppet's flank, which caused the animal to start forward at a wild pace. No more was said.

40. On Casterbridge Highway

FOR A CONSIDERABLE TIME the woman walked on. Her steps became feebler, and she strained her eyes to look afar upon the naked road, now indistinct amid the penumbrae of night. At length her onward walk dwindled to the merest totter, and she opened a gate within which was a haystack. Underneath this she sat down and presently slept.

When the woman awoke it was to find herself in the depths of a moonless and starless night. A heavy unbroken crust of cloud stretched across the sky, shutting out every speck of heaven; and a distant halo which hung over the town of Casterbridge was visible against the black concave, the luminosity appearing the brighter by its great contrast with the circumscribing darkness. Toward this weak, soft glow the woman turned her eyes.

"If I could only get there!" she said. "Meet him the day after tomorrow: God help me! Perhaps I shall be in my grave before then."

A manor house clock from the far depths of shadow struck the hour, one, in a small, attenuated tone. After midnight the voice of a clock seems to lose in breadth as much as in length, and to diminish its sonorousness to a thin falsetto.

Afterward a light—two lights—arose from the remote shade, and grew larger. A carriage rolled along the road, and passed the gate. It probably contained some late diners-out. The beams from one lamp shone for a moment upon the crouching woman, and threw her face into vivid relief. The face was young in the groundwork, old in the finish; the general contours were flexuous and childlike, but the finer lineaments had begun to be sharp and thin.

The pedestrian stood up, apparently with a revived determination, and looked around. The road appeared to be familiar to her, and she carefully scanned the fence as she slowly walked along. Presently there became visible a dim white shape; it was another milestone. She drew her fingers across its face to feel the marks.

"Two more!" she said.

She leant against the stone as a means of rest for a short interval, then bestirred herself, and again pursued her way. For a slight distance she bore up bravely, afterward flagging as before. This was beside a lone copsewood, wherein heaps of white chips strewn upon the leafy ground showed that woodmen had been faggoting and making hurdles during the day. Now there was not a rustle, not a breeze, not the faintest clash of twigs to keep her company. The woman looked over the gate, opened it, and went in. Close to the entrance stood a row of faggots, bound and unbound, together with stakes of all sizes.

For a few seconds the wayfarer stood with that tense stillness which signifies itself to be not the end, but merely the suspension, of a previous motion. Her attitude was that of a person who listens, either to the external world of sound, or to the imagined discourse of thought. A close criticism might have detected signs proving that she was intent on the latter alternative. Moreover, as was shown by what followed, she was oddly exercising the faculty of invention upon the speciality of the clever Jacquet Droz, the designer of automatic substitutes for human limbs.

By the aid of the Casterbridge aurora, and by feeling with her hands, the woman selected two sticks from the heaps. These sticks were nearly straight to the height of three or four feet, where each branched into a fork like the letter Y. She sat down, snapped off the small upper twigs, and carried the remainder with her into the road. She placed one of these forks under each arm as a crutch, tested them, timidly threw her whole weight upon them—so little that it was—and swung herself forward. The girl had made for herself a material aid.

The crutches answered well. The pat of her feet, and the tap of her sticks upon the highway, were all the sounds that came from the traveler now. She had passed the last milestone by a good long distance, and began to look wistfully toward the bank as if calculating upon another milestone soon. The crutches, though so very useful, had their limits of power. Mechanism only transfers labor, being powerless to supersede it, and the original amount of exertion was not cleared away; it was thrown into the body and arms. She was exhausted, and each swing forward became fainter. At last she swayed sideways, and fell.

Here she lay, a shapeless heap, for ten minutes and more. The morning wind began to boom dully over the flats, and to move afresh dead leaves which had lain still since yesterday. The woman desperately turned round upon her knees, and next rose to her feet. Steadying herself by the help of one crutch, she essayed a step, then another, then a third, using the crutches now as walking sticks only. Thus she progressed till descending Mellstock Hill another milestone appeared, and soon the beginning of an iron-railed fence came into view. She staggered across to the first post, clung to it, and looked around.

The Casterbridge lights were now individually visible. It was getting toward morning, and vehicles might be hoped for, if not expected soon. She listened. There was not a sound of life save that acme and sublimation of all dismal sounds, the bark of a fox, its three hollow notes being rendered at intervals of a minute with the precision of a funeral bell.

"Less than a mile!" the woman murmured. "No; more," she added, after a pause. "The mile is to the county hall, and my resting place is on the other side Casterbridge. A little over a mile, and there I am!" After an interval she again spoke. "Five or six steps to a yard—six perhaps. I have to go seventeen hundred yards. A hundred times six, six hundred. Seventeen times that. Oh, pity me, Lord!"

Holding to the rails, she advanced, thrusting one hand forward upon the rail, then the other, then leaning over it whilst she dragged her feet on beneath.

This woman was not given to soliloquy; but extremity of feeling lessens the individuality of the weak, as it increases that of the strong. She said again in the same tone, "I'll believe that the end lies five posts forward, and no further, and so get strength to pass them."

This was a practical application of the principle that a half-feigned and fictitious faith is better than no faith at all.

She passed five posts and held on to the fifth.

"I'll pass five more by believing my longed-for spot is at the next fifth. I can do it."

She passed five more.

"It lies only five further."

She passed five more.

"But is is five further."

She passed them.

"That stone bridge is the end of my journey," she said, when the bridge over the Froom was in view.

She crawled to the bridge. During the effort each breath of the woman went into the air as if never to return again.

"Now for the truth of the matter," she said, sitting down. "The truth is, that I have less than half a mile." Self-beguilement with what she had known all the time to be false had given her strength to come over half a mile that she would have been powerless to face in the lump. The artifice showed that the woman, by some mysterious intuition, had grasped the paradoxical truth that blindness may operate more vigorously than prescience, and the short-sighted effect more than the far-seeing; that limitation, and not comprehensiveness, is needed for striking a blow.

The half mile stood now before the sick and weary woman like a stolid Juggernaut. It was an impassive King of her world. The road here ran across Durnover Moor, open to the road on either side. She surveyed the wide space, the lights, herself, sighed, and lay down against a guardstone of the bridge.

Never was ingenuity exercised so sorely as the traveler here exercised hers. Every conceivable aid, method, stratagem, mechanism, by which these last desperate eight hundred yards could be overpassed by a human being unperceived, was revolved in her busy brain, and dismissed as impracticable. She thought of sticks, wheels, crawling—she even thought of rolling. But the exertion demanded by either of these latter two was greater than to walk erect. The faculty of contrivance was worn out. Hopelessness had come at last.

"No further!" she whispered, and closed her eyes.

From the stripe of shadow on the opposite side of the bridge a portion of shade seemed to detach itself and move into isolation upon the pale white of the road. It glided noiselessly toward the recumbent woman.

She became conscious of something touching her hand; it was softness and it was warmth. She opened her eyes, and the substance touched her face. A dog was licking her cheek.

He was a huge, heavy, and quiet creature, standing darkly against the low horizon, and at least two feet higher than the present position of her eyes. Whether Newfoundland, mastiff, bloodhound, or what not, it was impossible to say. He seemed to be of too strange and mysterious a nature to belong to any variety among those of popular nomenclature. Being thus assignable to no breed, he was the ideal embodiment of canine greatness—a generalization from what was common to all. Night, in its sad, solemn, and benevolent aspect, apart from its stealthy and cruel side, was personified in this form. Darkness endows the small and ordinary ones among mankind with poetical power, and even the suffering woman threw her idea into figure.

In her reclining position she looked up to him

just as in earlier times she had, when standing, looked up to a man. The animal, who was as homeless as she, respectfully withdrew a step or two when the woman moved, and, seeing that she did not repulse him, he licked her hand again.

A thought moved within her like lightning. "Perhaps I can make use of him—I might do it then!"

She pointed in the direction of Casterbridge, and the dog seemed to misunderstand: he trotted on. Then, finding she could not follow, he came back and whined.

The ultimate and saddest singularity of woman's effort and invention was reached when, with a quickened breathing, she rose to a stooping posture, and, resting her two little arms upon the shoulders of the dog, leant firmly thereon, and murmured stimulating words. Whilst she sorrowed in her heart she cheered with her voice, and what was stranger than that the strong should need encouragement from the weak was that cheerfulness should be so well stimulated by such utter dejection. Her friend moved forward slowly, and she with small mincing steps moved forward beside him, half her weight being thrown upon the animal. Sometimes she sank as she had sunk from walking erect, from the crutches, from the rails. The dog, who now thoroughly understood her desire and her incapacity, was frantic in his distress on these occasions; he would tug at her dress and run forward. She always called him back, and it was now to be observed that the woman listened for human sounds only to avoid them. It was evident that she had an object in keeping her presence on the road and her forlorn state unknown.

Their progress was necessarily very slow. They reached the bottom of the town, and the Casterbridge lamps lay before them like fallen pleiads as they turned to the left into the dense shade of a deserted avenue of chestnuts, and so skirted the borough. Thus the town was passed, and the goal was reached.

On this much desired spot outside the town rose a picturesque building. Originally it had been a mere case to hold people. The shell had been so thin, so devoid of excrescence, and so closely drawn over the accommodation granted, that the grim character of what was beneath showed through it, as the shape of a body is visible under a winding sheet.

Then Nature, as if offended, lent a hand. Masses of ivy grew up, completely covering the walls, till the place looked like an abbey; and it was discovered that the view from the front, over the Casterbridge chimneys, was one of the most magnificent in the county. A neighboring earl once said that he would give up a year's rental to have at his own door the view enjoyed by the inmates from theirs—and very probably the inmates would have given up the view for his year's rental.

This stone edifice consisted of a central mass and two wings, whereon stood as sentinels a few slim chimneys, now gurgling sorrowfully to the slow wind. In the wall was a gate and by the gate a bell-pull formed of a hanging wire. The woman raised herself as high as possible upon her knees, and could just reach the handle. She moved it and fell forward in a bowed attitude, her face upon her bosom.

It was getting on toward six o'clock, and sounds of movement were to be heard inside the building which was the haven of rest to this wearied soul. A little door by the large one was opened, and a man appeared inside. He discerned the panting heap of clothes, went back for a light, and came again. He entered a second time, and returned with two women.

These lifted the prostrate figure and assisted her in through the doorway. The man then closed the door.

"How did she get here?" said one of the women.

"The Lord knows," said the other.

"There is a dog outside," murmured the overcome traveler. "Where is he gone? He helped me."

"I stoned him away," said the man.

The little procession then moved forward—the man in front bearing the light, the two bony women next, supporting between them the small and supple one. Thus they entered the house and disappeared.

41. Suspicion — Fanny Is Sent For

BATHSHEBA SAID VERY LITTLE to her husband all that evening of their return from market, and he was not disposed to say much to her. He exhibited the unpleasant combination of a restless condition with a silent tongue. The next day, which was Sunday, passed nearly in the same manner as regarded their taciturnity, Bathsheba going to church both morning and afternoon. This was the day before the Budmouth races. In the evening Troy said, suddenly—

"Bathsheba, could you let me have twenty pounds?"

Her countenance instantly sank. "Twenty pounds?" she said.

"The fact is, I want it badly." The anxiety upon Troy's face was unusual and very marked. It was a culmination of the mood he had been in all the day.

"Ah! for those races tomorrow."

Troy for the moment made no reply. Her mistake had its advantages to a man who shrank from having his mind inspected as he did now. "Well, suppose I do want it for races?" he said, at last.

"Oh, Frank!" Bathsheba replied, and there was such a volume of entreaty in the words. "Only such a few weeks ago you said that I was far sweeter than all your other pleasures put together, and that you would give them all up for me; and now, won't you give up this one, which is more a worry than a pleasure? Do, Frank. Come, let me fascinate you by all I can do—by pretty words and pretty looks, and every thing I can think of—to stay at home. Say yes to your wife—say yes!"

The tenderest and softest phases of Bathsheba's nature were prominent now—advanced impulsively for his acceptance, without any of the disguises and defences which the wariness of her character when she was cool too frequently threw over them. Few men could have resisted the arch yet dignified entreaty of the beautiful face, thrown a little back and sideways in the well-known attitude that expresses more than the words it accompanies, and which seems to have been designed for these special occasions. Had the woman not been his wife, Troy would have succumbed instantly; as it was, he thought he would not deceive her longer.

"The money is not wanted for racing debts at all," he said.

"What is it for?" she asked. "You worry me a great deal by these mysterious responsibilities, Frank."

Troy hesitated. He did not now love her enough to allow himself to be carried too far by her ways. Yet it was necessary to be civil. "You wrong me by such a suspicious manner," he said. "Such strait-waistcoating as you treat me to is not becoming in you at so early a date."

"I think that I have a right to grumble a little if I pay," she said, with features between a smile and a pout.

"Exactly; and, the former being done, suppose we proceed to the latter. Bathsheba, fun is all very well, but don't go too far, or you may have cause to regret something."

She reddened. "I do that already," she said quickly.

"What do you regret?"

"That my romance has come to an end."

"All romances end at marriage."

"I wish you wouldn't talk like that. You grieve me to my soul by being smart at my expense."

"You are dull enough at mine. I believe you hate me."

"Not you—only your faults. I do hate them."

" 'Twould be much more becoming if you set yourself to cure them. Come, let's strike a balance with the twenty pounds, and be friends."

She gave a sigh of resignation. "I have about that sum here for household expenses. If you must have it, take it."

"Very good. Thank you. I expect I shall have gone away before you are in to breakfast tomorrow."

"And must you go? Ah! there was a time, Frank, when it would have taken a good many promises to other people to drag you away from me. You used to call me darling, then. But it doesn't matter to you how my days are passed now."

"I must go, in spite of sentiment." Troy, as he

spoke, looked at his watch, and, apparently actuated by *non lucendo* principles, opened the case at the back, revealing, snugly stowed within it, a small coil of hair.

Bathsheba's eyes had been accidentally lifted at that moment, and she saw the action and saw the hair. She flushed in pain and surprise, and some words escaped her before she had thought whether or not it was wise to utter them. "A woman's curl of hair!" she said. "Oh, Frank, whose is that?"

Troy had instantly closed his watch. He carelessly replied, as one who cloaked some feelings that the sight had stirred: "Why, yours, of course. Whose should it be? I had quite forgotten that I had it."

"What a dreadful fib, Frank!"

"I tell you I had forgotten it!" he said loudly.

"I don't mean that—it was yellow hair."

"Nonsense."

"That's insulting me. I know it was yellow. Now whose was it? I want to know."

"Very well—I'll tell you, so make no more ado. It is the hair of a young woman I was going to marry before I knew you."

"You ought to tell me her name, then."

"I cannot do that."

"Is she married yet?"

"No."

"Is she alive?"

"Yes."

"Is she pretty?"

"Yes."

"It is wonderful how she can be, poor thing, under such an awful affliction!"

"Affliction—what affliction?" he inquired quickly.

"Having hair of that dreadful color."

"Oh—ho—I like that!" said Troy, recovering himself. "Why, her hair has been admired by everybody who has seen her since she has worn it loose, which has not been long. It is beautiful hair. People used to turn their heads to look at it, poor girl!"

"Pooh! that's nothing—that's nothing!" she exclaimed, in incipient accents of pique. "If I cared for your love as much as I used to I could say people had turned to look at mine."

"Bathsheba, don't be so fitful and jealous. You knew what married life would be like, and shouldn't have entered it if you feared these contingencies."

Troy had by this time driven her to bitterness: her heart was big in her throat, and the ducts to her eyes were painfully full. Ashamed as she was to show emotion, at last she burst out:

"This is all I get for loving you so well! Ah! when I married you your life was dearer to me than my own. I would have died for you—how truly I can say that I would have died for you! And now you sneer at my foolishness in marrying you. Oh! is it kind to me to throw my mistake in my face? Whatever opinion you may have of my wisdom, you should not tell me of it so mercilessly, now that I am in your power."

"I can't help how things fall out," said Troy; "upon my heart, women will be the death of me!"

"Well, you shouldn't keep people's hair. You'll burn it, won't you, Frank?"

Frank went on as if he had not heard her. "There are considerations even before my consideration for you; reparations to be made—ties you know nothing of. If you repent of marrying, so do I."

Trembling now, she put her hand upon his arm, saying, in mingled tones of wretchedness and coaxing, "I only repent it if you don't love me better than any woman in the world! I don't otherwise, Frank. You don't repent because you already love somebody better than you love me, do you?"

"I don't know. Why do you say that?"

"You won't burn that curl. You like the woman who owns that pretty hair—yes; it is pretty—more beautiful than my miserable black mane! Well, it is no use; I can't help being ugly. You must like her best, if you will!"

"Until today, when I took it from a drawer, I have never looked upon that bit of hair for several months—that I am ready to swear."

"But just now you said 'ties'; and then—that woman we met?"

"'Twas the meeting with her that reminded me of the hair."

"Is it hers, then?"

"Yes. There, now that you have wormed it out of me, I hope you are content."

"And what are the ties?"

"Oh! that meant nothing—a mere jest."

"A mere jest!" she said, in mournful astonishment. "Can you jest when I am so wretchedly in earnest? Tell me the truth, Frank. I am not a fool, you know, although I am a woman, and have my woman's moments. Come! treat me fairly," she said, looking honestly and fearlessly into his face. "I don't want much; bare justice—that's all! Ah! once I felt I could be content with nothing less than the highest homage from the husband I should choose. Now, anything short of cruelty will content me. Yes! the independent and spirited Bathsheba is come to this!"

"For Heaven's sake don't be so desperate!" Troy said snappishly, rising as he did so, and leaving the room.

Directly he had gone, Bathsheba burst into great sobs—dry-eyed sobs, which cut as they came, without any softening by tears. But she determined to repress all evidences of feeling. She was conquered; but she would never own it as long as she lived.

Her pride was indeed brought low by despairing discoveries of her spoliation by marriage with a less pure nature than her own. She chafed to and fro in rebelliousness, like a caged leopard; her whole soul was in arms, and the blood fired her face. Until she had met Troy, Bathsheba had been proud of her position as a woman; it had been a glory to her to know that her lips had been touched by no man's on earth—that her waist had never been encircled by a lover's arm. She hated herself now. In those earlier days she had always nourished a secret contempt for girls who were the slaves of the first good-looking young fellow who should choose to salute them. She had never taken kindly to the idea of marriage in the abstract as did the majority of women she saw about her. In the turmoil of her anxiety for her lover she had agreed to marry him; but the perception that had accompanied her happiest hours on this account was rather that of self-sacrifice than of promotion and honor. Although she scarcely knew the divinity's name, Diana was the goddess whom Bathsheba instinctively adored. That she had never, by look, word, or sign, encouraged a man to approach her—that she had felt herself sufficient to herself, and had in the independence of her girlish heart fancied there was a certain degradation in renouncing the simplicity of a maiden existence to become the humbler half of an indifferent matrimonial whole—were facts now bitterly remembered. Oh, if she had never stooped to folly of this kind, respectable as it was, and could only stand again, as she had stood on the hill at Norcombe, and dare Troy or any other man to pollute a hair of her head by his interference!

The next morning she rose earlier than usual, and had the horse saddled for her ride round the farm in the customary way. When she came in at half-past eight—their usual hour for breakfasting

—she was informed that her husband had risen, taken his breakfast, and driven off to Casterbridge with the gig and Poppet.

After breakfast she was cool and collected—quite herself in fact—and she rambled to the gate, intending to walk to another quarter of the farm, which she still personally superintended as well as her duties in the house would permit, continually, however, finding herself preceded in forethought by Gabriel Oak, for whom she began to entertain the genuine friendship of a sister. Of course, she sometimes thought of him in the light of an old lover, and had momentary imaginings of what life with him as a husband would have been like; also of life with Boldwood under the same conditions. But Bathsheba, though she could feel, was not much given to futile dreaming, and her musings under this head were short and entirely confined to the times when Troy's neglect was more than ordinarily evident.

She saw coming up the road a man like Mr. Boldwood. It was Mr. Boldwood. Bathsheba blushed painfully, and watched. The farmer stopped when still a long way off, and held up his hand to Gabriel Oak, who was in a footpath across the field. The two men then approached each other and seemed to engage in earnest conversation.

Thus they continued for a long time. Joseph Poorgrass now passed near them, wheeling a barrow of apples up the hill to Bathsheba's residence. Boldwood and Gabriel called to him, spoke to him for a few minutes, and then all three parted, Joseph immediately coming up the hill with his barrow.

Bathsheba, who had seen this pantomime with some surprise, experienced great relief when Boldwood turned back again. "Well, what's the message, Joseph?" she said.

He set down his barrow, and, putting upon himself the refined aspect that a conversation with a lady required, spoke to Bathsheba over the gate.

"You'll never see Fanny Robin no more—use nor principal—ma'am."

"Why?"

"Because she's dead in the Union."

"Fanny dead—never!"

"Yes, ma'am."

"What did she die from?"

"I don't know for certain; but I should be inclined to think it was from general neshness of constitution. She was such a limber maid that 'a could stand no hardship, even when I knowed her, and 'a went like a candle-snoff, so 'tis said. She was took bad in the morning, and, being quite feeble and worn out, she died in the evening. She belongs by law to our parish; and Mr. Boldwood is going to send a wagon at three this afternoon to fetch her home here and bury her."

"Indeed I shall not let Mr. Boldwood do any such thing—I shall do it! Fanny was my uncle's servant, and, although I only knew her for a couple of days, she belongs to me. How very, very sad this is!—the idea of Fanny being in a workhouse." Bathsheba had begun to know what suffering was, and she spoke with real feeling. . . . "Send across to Mr. Boldwood's, and say that Mrs. Troy will take upon herself the duty of fetching an old servant of the family. . . . We ought not to put her in a wagon; we'll get a hearse."

"There will hardly be time, ma'am, will there?"

"Perhaps not," she said, musingly. "When did you say we must be at the door—three o'clock?"

"Three o'clock this afternoon, ma'am, so to speak it."

"Very well—you go with it. A pretty wagon is better than an ugly hearse, after all. Joseph, have

the new spring wagon with the blue body and red
wheels, and wash it very clean. And, Joseph—"

"Yes, ma'am."

"Carry with you some evergreens and flowers to
put upon her coffin—indeed, gather a great many,
and completely bury her in them. Get some
boughs of laurustinus, and variegated box, and
yew, and boy's-love; aye, and some bunches of chry-
santhemum. And let old Pleasant draw her, because she knew him so well."

"I will, ma'am. I ought to have said that the
Union, in the form of four laboring men, will meet
me when I gets to our churchyard gate, and take
her and bury her according to the rites of the Board
of Guardians, as by law ordained."

"Dear me—Casterbridge Union—and is Fanny
come to this?" said Bathsheba, musing. "I wish I
had known of it sooner. I thought she was far away.
How long has she lived there?"

"On'y been there a day or two."

"Oh!—then she has not been staying there as a
regular inmate?"

"No. She first went to live in a garrison town
t'other side o' Wessex, and since then she's been
picking up a living at seampstering in Melchester
for several months, at the house of a very respectable widow woman who takes in work of that sort.
She only got handy the Unionhouse on Sunday
morning 'a b'lieve, and 'tis supposed here and there
that she had traipsed every step of the way from
Melchester. Why she left her place I can't say, for I
don't know; and as to a lie, why, I wouldn't tell it.
That's the short of the story, ma'am."

"Ah-h!"

No gem ever flashed from a rosy ray to a white
one more rapidly than changed the young wife's
countenance whilst this word came from her in a
long-drawn breath. "Did she walk along our turn-

pike road?" she said, in a suddenly restless and eager voice.

"I believe she did. . . . Ma'am, shall I call Liddy? You bain't well, ma'am, surely? You look like a lily—so pale and fainty!"

"No; don't call her; it is nothing. When did she pass Weatherbury?"

"Last Saturday night."

"That will do, Joseph; now you may go."

"Certainly, ma'am."

"Joseph, come hither a moment. What was the color of Fanny Robin's hair?"

"Really, mistress, now that 'tis put to me so judge-and-jury like, I can't call to mind, if ye'll believe me!"

"Never mind; go on and do what I told you. Stop—well, no, go on."

She turned herself away from him, that he might no longer notice the mood which had set its sign so visibly upon her, and went indoors with a distressing sense of faintness and a beating brow. About an hour after, she heard the noise of the wagon and went out, still with a painful consciousness of her bewildered and troubled look. Joseph, dressed in his best suit of clothes, was putting in the horse to start. The shrubs and flowers were all piled in the wagon, as she had directed. Bathsheba hardly saw them now.

"Whose sweetheart did you say, Joseph?"

"I don't know, ma'am."

"Are you quite sure?"

"Yes, ma'am, quite sure."

"Sure of what?"

"I'm sure that all I know is that she arrived in the morning and died in the evening without further parley. What Oak and Mr. Boldwood told me was only these few words: 'Little Fanny Robin is dead, Joseph,' Gabriel said, looking in my face in his steady old way. I was very sorry, and I said, 'Ah!—and how did she come to die?' 'Well, she's dead in Casterbridge Union,' he said, 'and perhaps 'tisn't much matter about how she came to die. She reached the Union early Sunday morning, and died in the afternoon—that's clear enough.' Then I asked what she'd been doing lately, and Bold-wood turned round to me then, and left off spit-ting a thistle with the end of his stick. He told me about her having lived by seampstering in Melches-ter, as I mentioned to you, and that she walked therefrom at the end of last week, passing near here Saturday night in the dusk. They then said I had better just name a hent of her death to you, and away they went. Her death might have been brought on by biding in the night wind, you know, ma'am; for people used to say she'd go off in a de-cline: she used to cough a good deal in winter time. However, 'tisn't much odds to us about that now, for 'tis all over."

"Have you heard a different story at all?" She looked at him so intently that Joseph's eyes quailed.

"Not a word, mistress, I assure 'ee!" he said. "Hardly anybody in the parish knows the news yet."

"I wonder why Gabriel didn't bring the message to me himself. He mostly makes a point of seeing me upon the most trifling errand." These words were merely murmured, and she was looking upon the ground.

"Perhaps he was busy, ma'am," Joseph suggested. "And sometimes he seems to suffer from things upon his mind, connected with the time when he was better off than 'a is now. 'A's rather a curious item, but a very understanding shepherd, and learned in books."

"Did anything seem upon his mind whilst he was speaking to you about this?"

"I cannot but say that there did, ma'am. He was terrible down, and so was Farmer Boldwood."

"Thank you, Joseph. That will do. Go on now, or you'll be late."

Bathsheba, still unhappy, went indoors again. In the course of the afternoon she said to Liddy, who had been informed of the occurrence, "What was the color of poor Fanny Robin's hair? Do you know? I cannot recollect—I only saw her for a day or two."

"It was light, ma'am; but she wore it rather short, and packed away under her cap, so that you would hardly notice it. But I have seen her let it down when she was going to bed, and it looked beautiful then. Real golden hair."

"Her young man was a soldier, was he not?"

"Yes. In the same regiment as Mr. Troy. He says he knew him very well."

"What, Mr. Troy says so? How came he to say that?"

"One day I just named it to him, and asked him if he knew Fanny's young man. He said, 'Oh, yes, he knew the young man as well as he knew himself, and that there wasn't a man in the regiment he liked better.'"

"Ah! Said that, did he?"

"Yes; and he said there was a strong likeness between himself and the other young man, so that sometimes people mistook them—"

"Liddy, for Heaven's sake stop your talking!" said Bathsheba, with the nervous petulance that comes from worrying perceptions.

42. Joseph and His Burden — Buck's Head

A WALL BOUNDED THE SITE of Casterbridge Union-house, except along a portion of the end. Here a high gable stood prominent, and it was covered like the front with a mat of ivy. In this gable was no window, chimney, ornament, or protuberance of any kind. The single feature appertaining to it, beyond the expanse of dark green leaves, was a small door.

The situation of the door was peculiar. The sill was three or four feet above the ground, and for a moment one was at a loss for an explanation of this exceptional altitude, till ruts immediately beneath suggested that the door was used solely for the passage of articles and persons to and from the level of a vehicle standing on the outside. Upon the whole, the door seemed to advertise itself as a species of Traitor's Gate translated to another sphere. That entry and exit hereby was only at rare intervals became apparent on noting that tufts of grass were allowed to flourish undisturbed in the chinks of the sill.

As the clock over the South Street almshouse pointed to five minutes to three, a blue spring wagon, picked out with red, and containing boughs and flowers, passed the end of the street, and up toward this side of the building. Whilst the chimes were yet stammering out a shattered form of "Mal-

brook," Joseph Poorgrass rang the bell, and
received directions to back his wagon against the
high door under the gable. The door then opened,
and a plain elm coffin was slowly thrust forth, and
laid by two men in fustian along the middle of the
vehicle.

One of the men then stepped up beside it,
took from his pocket a lump of chalk, and wrote
upon the cover the name and a few other words in
a large scrawling hand. (We believe that they do
these things more tenderly now, and provide a
plate.) He covered the whole with a black cloth,
threadbare, but decent, the tailboard of the wagon
was returned to its place, one of the men handed
a certificate of registry to Poorgrass, and both entered the door, closing it behind them. Their connection with her, short as it had been, was over for
ever.

Joseph then placed the flowers as enjoined, and
the evergreens around the flowers, till it was difficult to divine what the wagon contained; he
smacked his whip, and the rather pleasing funeral
car crept down the hill, and along the road to
Weatherbury.

The afternoon drew on apace, and, looking to
the right toward the sea as he walked beside the
horse, Poorgrass saw strange clouds and scrolls of
mist rolling over the long ridges which girt the
landscape in that quarter. They came in yet greater
volumes, and indolently crept across the intervening valleys, and around the withered papery flags
of the moor and river brinks. Then their dank
spongy forms closed in upon the sky. It was a sudden overgrowth of atmospheric fungi which had
their roots in the neighboring sea, and by the time
that horse, man, and corpse entered Yalbury Great
Wood, these silent workings of an invisible hand
had reached them, and they were completely en-

veloped, this being the first arrival of the autumn fogs, and the first fog of the series.

The air was as an eye suddenly struck blind. The wagon and its load rolled no longer on the horizontal division between clearness and opacity, but were imbedded in an elastic body of monotonous pallor throughout. There was no perceptible motion in the air, not a visible drop of water fell upon a leaf of the beeches, birches, and firs composing the wood on either side. The trees stood in an attitude of intentness, as if they waited longingly for a wind to come and rock them. A startling quiet overhung all surrounding things— so completely, that the crunching of the wagon wheels was as a great noise, and small rustles, which had never obtained a hearing except by night, were distinctly individualized.

Joseph Poorgrass looked round upon his sad burden as it loomed faintly through the flowering laurustinus, then at the unfathomable gloom amid the high trees on each hand, indistinct, shadowless, and specterlike in their monochrome of gray. He felt anything but cheerful, and wished he had the company even of a child or dog. Stopping the horse he listened. Not a footstep or wheel was audible anywhere around, and the dead silence was broken only by a heavy particle falling from a tree through the evergreens and alighting with a smart rap upon the coffin of poor Fanny. The fog had by this time saturated the trees, and this was the first dropping of water from the overbrimming leaves. The hollow echo of its fall reminded the wagoner painfully of the grim Leveler. Then hard by came down another drop, then two or three. Presently there was a continual tapping of these heavy drops upon the dead leaves, the road, and the travelers. The nearer boughs were beaded with the mist to the grayness of aged men, and the rusty red leaves of the beeches were hung with similar drops, like diamonds on auburn hair.

At the roadside hamlet called Roy-Town, just beyond this wood, was the old inn Buck's Head. It was about a mile and a half from Weatherbury, and in the meridian times of stagecoach traveling had been the place where many coaches changed and kept their relays of horses. All the old stabling was now pulled down, and little remained besides the habitable inn itself, which, standing a little way back from the road, signified its existence to people far up and down the highway by a sign hanging from the horizontal bough of an elm on the opposite side of the way.

Travelers—for the variety *tourist* had hardly developed into a distinct species at this date—sometimes said in passing when they cast their eyes up to the sign-bearing tree, that artists were fond of representing the signboard hanging thus, but that they themselves had never before noticed so perfect an instance in actual working order. It was near this tree that the wagon was standing into which Gabriel Oak crept on his first journey to Weatherbury; but, owing to the darkness, the sign and the inn had been unobserved.

The manners of the inn were of the old established type. Indeed, in the minds of its frequenters they existed as unalterable formulae: for example—

Rap with the bottom of your pint for more liquor. For tobacco, shout.
In calling for the girl in waiting, say, "Maid!"
Ditto for the landlady, "Old Soul!" etc., etc.

It was a relief to Joseph's heart when the friendly signboard came in view, and, stopping his horse immediately beneath it, he proceeded to fulfill an intention made a long time before. His spirits were oozing out of him quite. He turned the horse's head to the green bank, and entered the hostel for a mug of ale.

Going down into the kitchen of the inn, the floor of which was a step below the passage, which in its turn was a step below the road outside, what should Joseph see to gladden his eyes but two copper-colored disks, in the form of the countenances of Mr. Jan Coggan and Mr. Mark Clark. These owners of the two most appreciative throats in the neighborhood, within the pale of respectability, were now sitting face to face over a three-legged circular table, having an iron rim to keep cups and pots from being accidentally elbowed off; they might have been said to resemble the setting sun and the full moon shining *vis-à-vis* across the globe.

"Why, 'tis neighbor Poorgrass!" said Mark Clark. "I'm sure your face don't praise your mistress's table, Joseph."

"I've had a very pale companion for the last four miles," said Joseph, indulging in a shudder toned down by resignation. "And to speak the truth, 'twas beginning to tell upon me. I assure ye, I ha'n't seed the color of victuals or drink since breakfast time this morning, and that was no more than a dew-bit afield."

"Then drink, Joseph, and don't restrain yourself!" said Coggan, handing him a hooped mug three-quarters full.

Joseph drank for a moderately long time, then for a longer time, saying, as he lowered the jug, " 'Tis pretty drinking—very pretty drinking, and is more than cheerful on my melancholy errand, so to speak it."

"True, drink is a pleasant delight," said Jan, as one who repeated a truism so familiar to his brain that he hardly noticed its passage over his tongue; and, lifting the cup, Coggan tilted his head gradually backward, with closed eyes, that his expectant soul might not be diverted for one instant from its bliss by irrelevant surroundings.

"Well, I must be on again," said Poorgrass. "Not but that I should like another nip with ye; but the parish might lose confidence in me if I was seed here."

"Where be ye trading o't to today, then, Joseph?"

"Back to Weatherbury. I've got poor little Fanny Robin in my wagon outside, and I must be at the churchyard gates at a quarter to five with her."

"Aye—I've heard of it. And so she's nailed up in parish boards after all, and nobody to pay the bell shilling and the grave half crown."

"The parish pays the grave half crown, but not the bell shilling, because the bell's a luxury: but 'a can hardly do without the grave, poor body. However, I expect our mistress will pay all."

"A pretty maid as ever I see! But what's yer hurry, Joseph? The poor woman's dead, and you can't bring her to life, and you may as well sit down comfortable, and finish another with us."

"I don't mind taking just the least thimbleful ye can dream of more with ye, sonnies. But only a few minutes, because 'tis as 'tis."

"Of course, you'll have another drop. A man's twice the man afterward. You feel so warm and glorious, and you whop and slap at your work without any trouble, and everything goes on like sticks abreaking. Too much liquor is bad, and leads us to that horned man in the smoky house; but after all, many people haven't the gift of enjoying a wet, and since we be highly favored with a power that way, we should make the most o't."

"True," said Mark Clark. " 'Tis a talent the Lord has mercifully bestowed upon us, and we ought not to neglect it. But, what with the parsons and clerks and school people and serious tea parties, the merry old ways of good life have gone to the dogs—upon my carcass, they have!"

"Well, really, I must be onward again now," said Joseph.

"Now, now, Joseph; nonsense! The poor woman is dead, isn't she, and what's your hurry?"

"Well, I hope Providence won't be in a way with me for my doings," said Joseph, again sitting down. "I've been troubled with weak moments lately, 'tis true. I've been drinky once this month already, and I did not go to church a-Sunday, and I dropped a curse or two yesterday; so I don't want to go too far for my safety. Your next world is your next world, and not to be squandered offhand."

"I believe ye to be a chapel member, Joseph. That I do."

"Oh, no, no! I don't go so far as that."

"For my part," said Coggan, "I'm staunch Church of England."

"Aye, and faith, so be I," said Mark Clark.

"I won't say much for myself; I don't wish to," Coggan continued, with that tendency to talk on principles which is characteristic of the barleycorn. "But I've never changed a single doctrine: I've stuck like a plaster to the old faith I was born in. Yes; there's this to be said for the Church, a man can belong to the Church and bide in his cheerful old inn, and never trouble or worry his mind about doctrines at all. But to be a meetinger, you must go to chapel in all winds and weathers, and make yerself as frantic as a skit. Not but that chapel members be clever chaps enough in their way. They can lift up beautiful prayers out of their own heads, all about their families and shipwrecks in the newspaper."

"They can—they can," said Mark Clark, with corroborative feeling; "but we Churchmen, you see, must have it all printed aforehand, or, dang it

all, we should no more know what to say to a great
gaffer like the Lord than babes unborn."

"Chapelfolk be more hand-in-glove with them
above than we," said Joseph thoughtfully.

"Yes," said Coggan. "We know very well that if
anybody do go to heaven, they will. They've
worked hard for it, and they deserve to have it,
such as 'tis. I bain't such a fool as to pretend that
we who stick to the Church have the same chance
as they, because we know we have not. But I hate
a feller who'll change his old ancient doctrines for
the sake of getting to heaven. I'd as soon turn
king's-evidence for the few pounds you get. Why,
neighbors, when every one of my taties were
frosted, our Pa'son Thirdly were the man who gave
me a sack for seed, though he hardly had one for
his own use, and no money to buy 'em. If it hadn't
been for him, I shouldn't hae had a tatie to put in
my garden. D'ye think I'd turn after that? No, I'll
stick to my side; and if we be in the wrong, so be it:
I'll fall with the fallen!"

"Well said—very well said," observed Joseph.
"However, folks, I must be moving now: upon my
life I must. Pa'son Thirdly will be waiting at the
church gates, and there's the woman a-biding outside in the wagon."

"Joseph Poorgrass, don't be so miserable! Pa'son
Thirdly won't mind. He's a generous man; he's
found me in tracts for years, and I've consumed
a good many in the course of a long and shady
life; but he's never been the man to cry out at the
expense. Sit down."

The longer Joseph Poorgrass remained, the less
his spirit was troubled by the duties which
devolved upon him this afternoon. The minutes
glided by uncounted, until the evening shades began perceptibly to deepen, and the eyes of the three
were but sparkling points on the surface of dark-

ness. Coggan's repeater struck six from his pocket in the usual still small tones.

At that moment hasty steps were heard in the entry, and the door opened to admit the figure of Gabriel Oak, followed by the maid of the inn bearing a candle. He stared sternly at the one lengthy and two round faces of the sitters, which confronted him with the expressions of a fiddle and a couple of warming pans. Joseph Poorgrass blinked, and shrank several inches into the background.

"Upon my soul, I'm ashamed of you; 'tis disgraceful, Joseph, disgraceful!" said Gabriel indignantly. "Coggan, you call yourself a man, and don't know better than this."

Coggan looked up indefinitely at Oak, one or other of his eyes occasionally opening and closing of its own accord, as if it were not a member, but a dozy individual with a distinct personality.

"Don't take on so, shepherd!" said Mark Clark, looking reproachfully at the candle, which appeared to possess special features of interest for his eyes.

"Nobody can hurt a dead woman," at length said Coggan, with the precision of a machine. "All that could be done for her is done—she's beyond us: and why should a man put himself in a tearing hurry for lifeless clay that can neither feel nor see, and don't know what you do with her at all? If she'd been alive, I would have been the first to help her. If she now wanted victuals and drink, I'd pay for it, money down. But she's dead, and no speed of ours will bring her to life. The woman's past us —time spent upon her is throwed away: why should we hurry to do what's not required? Drink, shepherd, and be friends, for tomorrow we may be like her."

"We may," added Mark Clark emphatically, at

once drinking himself, to run no further risk of losing his chance by the event alluded to, Jan meanwhile merging his additional thoughts of tomorrow in a song:

        To-mor-row, to-mor-row!
And while peace and plen-ty I find at my board,
    With a heart free from sick-ness and sor-row,
With my friends will I share what to-day may af-
        ford,
    And let them spread the ta-ble to-mor-row.
        To-mor-row, to-mor——

"Do hold thy horning, Jan!" said Oak; and turning upon Poorgrass, "as for you, Joseph, who do
your wicked deeds in such confoundedly holy ways,
you are as drunk as you can stand."

"No, Shepherd Oak, no! Listen to reason, shepherd. All that's the matter with me is the affliction
called a multiplying eye, and that's how it is I look
double to you—I mean, you look double to me."

"A multiplying eye is a very bad thing," said
Mark Clark.

"It always comes on when I have been in a public house a little time," said Joseph Poorgrass
meekly. "Yes; I see two of every sort, as if I were
some holy man living in the times of King Noah
and entering into the ark. . . . Y-y-y-yes," he
added, becoming much affected by the picture of
himself as a person thrown away, and shedding
tears; "I feel too good for England: I ought to have
lived in Genesis by rights, like the other men of
sacrifice, and then I shouldn't have b-b-been called
a d-d-drunkard in such a way!"

"I wish you'd show yourself a man of spirit, and
not sit whining there!"

"Show myself a man of spirit? . . . Ah, well! let
me take the name of drunkard humbly—let me be
a man of contrite knees—let it be! I know that I

always do say 'Please God' afore I do anything,
from my getting up to my going down of the same,
and I be willing to take as much disgrace as there
is in that holy act. Hah, yes! . . . But not a man of
spirit? Have I ever allowed the toe of pride to be
lifted against my hinder parts without groan-
ing manfully that I question the right to do
so? I inquire that query boldly?"

"We can't say that you have, Hero Poorgrass,"
admitted Jan.

"Never have I allowed such treatment to pass
unquestioned! Yet the shepherd says in the face of
that rich testimony that I be not a man of spirit!
Well, let it pass by, and death is a kind friend!"

Gabriel, seeing that neither of the three was in a
fit state to take charge of the wagon for the remainder of the journey, made no reply, but, closing the door again upon them, went across to where
the vehicle stood, now getting indistinct in the fog
and gloom of this mildewy time. He pulled the
horse's head from the large patch of turf it had
eaten bare, readjusted the boughs over the coffin,
and drove along through the unwholesome night.

It had gradually become rumored in the village
that the body to be brought and buried that day
was all that was left of the unfortunate Fanny
Robin who had followed the Eleventh from Casterbridge through Melchester and onward. But,
thanks to Boldwood's reticence and Oak's generosity, the lover she had followed had never been
individualized as Troy. Gabriel hoped that the
whole truth of the matter might not be published
till at any rate the girl had been in her grave for a
few days, when the interposing barriers of earth
and time, and a sense that the events had been
somewhat shut into oblivion, would deaden the
sting that revelation and invidious remark would
have for Bathsheba just now.

By the time that Gabriel reached the old

manor house, her residence, which lay in his way to the church, it was quite dark. A man came from the gate and said through the fog, which hung between them like blown flour—

"Is that Poorgrass with the corpse?"

Gabriel recognized the voice as that of the parson.

"The corpse is here, sir," said Gabriel.

"I have just been to inquire of Mrs. Troy if she could tell me the reason of the delay. I am afraid it is too late now for the funeral to be performed with proper decency. Have you the registrar's certificate?"

"No," said Gabriel. "I expect Poorgrass has that; and he's at the Buck's Head. I forgot to ask him for it."

"Then that settles the matter. We'll put off the funeral till tomorrow morning. The body may be brought on to the church, or it may be left here at the farm and fetched by the bearers in the morning. They waited more than an hour, and have now gone home."

Gabriel had his reasons for thinking the latter a most objectionable plan, notwithstanding that Fanny had been an inmate of the farmhouse for several years in the lifetime of Bathsheba's uncle. Visions of several unhappy contingencies which might arise from this delay flitted before him. But his will was not law, and he went indoors to inquire of his mistress what were her wishes on the subject. He found her in an unusual mood: her eyes as she looked up to him were suspicious and perplexed as with some antecedent thought. Troy had not yet returned. At first Bathsheba assented with a mien of indifference to his proposition that they should go on to the church at once with their burden; but immediately afterward, following Gabriel to the gate, she swerved to the extreme of solicitousness on Fanny's account, and desired that the girl might be brought into the house. Oak argued upon the convenience of leaving her in the wagon, just as she lay now, with her flowers and green leaves about her, merely wheeling the vehicle into the coachhouse till the morning, but to no purpose. "It is unkind and unchristian," she said, "to leave the poor thing in a coachhouse all night."

"Very well, then," said the parson. "And I will arrange that the funeral shall take place early to-morrow. Perhaps Mrs. Troy is right in feeling that we cannot treat a dead fellow creature too thoughtfully. We must remember that though she may have erred grievously in leaving her home, she is still our sister; and it is to be believed that God's uncovenanted mercies are extending toward her, and that she is a member of the flock of Christ."

The parson's words spread into the heavy air with a sad yet unperturbed cadence, and Gabriel shed an honest tear. Bathsheba seemed unmoved. Mr. Thirdly then left them, and Gabriel lighted a lantern. Fetching three other men to assist him, they bore the unconscious truant indoors, placing the coffin on two benches in the middle of a little sitting room next the hall, as Bathsheba directed.

Every one except Gabriel Oak then left the room. He still indecisively lingered beside the body. He was deeply troubled at the wretchedly ironical aspect that circumstances were putting on with regard to Troy's wife, and at his own powerlessness to counteract them. In spite of his careful maneuvering here all this day, the very worst event that could in any way have happened in connection with the burial had happened now. Oak imagined a terrible discovery resulting from this afternoon's work that might cast over Bathsheba's life a shade which the interposition of many lapsing years might but indifferently lighten, and which nothing at all might altogether remove.

Suddenly, as in a last attempt to save Bathsheba from, at any rate, immediate anguish, he looked again, as he had looked before, at the chalk writing upon the coffin lid. The scrawl was this simple one, *"Fanny Robin and child."* Gabriel took his handkerchief and carefully rubbed out the two latter words, leaving visible the inscription *"Fanny Robin"* only. He then left the room, and went out quietly by the front door.

43. Fanny's Revenge

"Do you want me any longer, ma'am?" inquired Liddy, at a later hour the same evening, standing by the door with a chamber candlestick in her hand, and addressing Bathsheba, who sat cheerless and alone in the large parlor beside the first fire of the season.

"No more tonight, Liddy."

"I'll sit up for master if you like, ma'am. I am not at all afraid of Fanny, if I may sit in my own room and have a candle. She was such a childlike, nesh young thing that her spirit couldn't appear to anybody if it tried, I'm quite sure."

"Oh, no, no! You go to bed. I'll sit up for him myself till twelve o'clock, and if he has not arrived by that time, I shall give him up and go to bed too."

"It is half-past ten now."

"Oh: is it?"

"Why don't you sit upstairs, ma'am?"

"Why don't I?" said Bathsheba desultorily. "It isn't worth while—there's a fire here, Liddy." She suddenly exclaimed in an impulsive and excited whisper, "Have you heard anything strange said of Fanny?" The words had no sooner escaped her than an expression of unutterable regret crossed her face, and she burst into tears.

"No—not a word!" said Liddy, looking at the weeping woman with astonishment. "What is it makes you cry so, ma'am; has anything hurt you?" She came to Bathsheba's side with a face full of sympathy.

"No, Liddy—I don't want you any more. I can hardly say why I have taken so to crying lately: I never used to cry. Goodnight."

Liddy then left the parlor and closed the door.

Bathsheba was lonely and miserable now; not lonelier actually than she had been before her marriage; but her loneliness then was to that of the present time as the solitude of a mountain is to the solitude of a cave. And within the last day or two had come these disquieting thoughts about her husband's past. Her wayward sentiment that evening concerning Fanny's temporary resting place had been the result of a strange complication of impulses in Bathsheba's bosom. Perhaps it would be more accurately described as a determined rebellion against her prejudices, a revulsion from a lower instinct of uncharitableness, which would have withheld all sympathy from the dead woman, because in life she had preceded Bathsheba in the attentions of a man whom Bathsheba had by no means ceased from loving, though her love was sick to death just now with the gravity of a further misgiving.

In five or ten minutes there was another tap at

the door. Liddy reappeared, and coming in a little way stood hesitating, until at length she said, "Maryann has just heard something very strange, but I know it isn't true. And we shall be sure to know the rights of it in a day or two."

"What is it?"

"Oh, nothing connected with you or us, ma'am. It is about Fanny. That same thing you have heard."

"I have heard nothing."

"I mean that a wicked story is got to Weatherbury within this last hour—that—" Liddy came close to her mistress and whispered the remainder of the sentence slowly into her ear, inclining her head as she spoke in the direction of the room where Fanny lay.

Bathsheba trembled from head to foot.

"I don't believe it!" she said excitedly. "And there's only one name written on the coffin cover."

"Nor I ma'am. And a good many others don't; for we should surely have been told more about it if it had been true—don't you think so ma'am?"

"We might or we might not."

Bathsheba turned and looked into the fire, that Liddy might not see her face. Finding that her mistress was going to say no more, Liddy glided out, closed the door softly, and went to bed.

Bathsheba's face, as she continued looking into the fire that evening, might have excited solicitousness on her account even among those who loved her least. The sadness of Fanny Robin's fate did not make Bathsheba's glorious, although she was the Esther to this poor Vashti, and their fates might be supposed to stand in some respects as contrasts to each other. When Liddy came into the room a second time the beautiful eyes which met hers had worn a listless, weary look. When she went out after telling the story they had expressed wretchedness

in full activity. Her simple country nature, fed on
old-fashioned principles, was troubled by that
which would have troubled a woman of the world
very little, both Fanny and her child, if she had one,
being dead.

Bathsheba had grounds for conjecturing a connection between her own history and the dimly
suspected tragedy of Fanny's end which Oak and
Boldwood never for a moment credited her with
possessing. The meeting with the lonely woman on
the previous Saturday night had been unwitnessed
and unspoken of. Oak may have had the best of intentions in withholding for as many days as possible
the details of what had happened to Fanny;
but had he known that Bathsheba's perceptions
had already been exercised in the matter, he would
have done nothing to lengthen the minutes of suspense she was now undergoing, when the certainty
which must terminate it would be the worst fact
suspected after all.

She suddenly felt a longing desire to speak to
someone stronger than herself, and so get strength
to sustain her surmised position with dignity and
her carking doubts with stoicism. Where could she
find such a friend? Nowhere in the house. She was
by far the coolest of the women under her roof.
Patience and suspension of judgment for a few
hours were what she wanted to learn, and there
was nobody to teach her. Might she but go to Gabriel Oak!—but that could not be. What a way Oak
had, she thought, of enduring things. Boldwood,
who seemed so much deeper and higher and
stronger in feeling than Gabriel, had not yet learnt,
any more than she herself, the simple lesson which
Oak showed a mastery of by every turn and look
he gave—that among the multitude of interests
by which he was surrounded, those which affected
his personal well-being were not the most absorb-

ing and important in his eyes. Oak meditatively
looked upon the horizon of circumstances without
any special regard to his own standpoint in the
midst. That was how she would wish to be. But
then Oak was not racked by incertitude upon the
inmost matter of his bosom, as she was at this moment. Oak knew all about Fanny that she wished
to know—she felt convinced of that. If she were to
go to him now at once and say no more than these
few words, "What is the truth of the story?" he
would feel bound in honor to tell her. It would be
an inexpressible relief. No further speech would
need to be uttered. He knew her so well that no
eccentricity of behavior in her would alarm him.

She flung a cloak round her, went to the door
and opened it. Every blade, every twig was still.
The air was yet thick with moisture, though somewhat less dense than during the afternoon, and a
steady smack of drops upon the fallen leaves under
the boughs was almost musical in its soothing regularity. It seemed better to be out of the house
than within it, and Bathsheba closed the door, and
walked slowly down the lane till she came opposite
to Gabriel's cottage, where he now lived alone,
having left Coggan's house through being pinched
for room. There was a light in one window only,
and that was downstairs. The shutters were not
closed, nor was any blind or curtain drawn over
the window, neither robbery nor observation being
a contingency which could do much injury to the
occupant of the domicile. Yes, it was Gabriel himself who was sitting up: he was reading. From her
standing place in the road she could see him
plainly, sitting quite still, his light curly head upon
his hand, and only occasionally looking up to snuff
the candle which stood beside him. At length he
looked at the clock, seemed surprised at the lateness
of the hour, closed his book, and arose. He was go-

ing to bed, she knew, and if she tapped it must be done at once.

Alas for her resolve! She felt she could not do it. Not for worlds now could she give a hint about her misery to him, much less ask him plainly for information on the cause of Fanny's death. She must suspect, and guess, and chafe, and bear it all alone.

Like a homeless wanderer she lingered by the bank, as if lulled and fascinated by the atmosphere of content which seemed to spread from that little dwelling, and was so sadly lacking in her own. Gabriel appeared in an upper room, placed his light in the window bench, and then—knelt down to pray. The contrast of the picture with her rebellious and agitated existence at this same time was too much for her to bear to look upon longer. It was not for her to make a truce with trouble by any such means. She must tread her giddy distracting measure to its last note, as she had begun it. With a swollen heart she went again up the lane, and entered her own door.

More fevered now by a reaction from the first feelings which Oak's example had raised in her, she paused in the hall, looking at the door of the room wherein Fanny lay. She locked her fingers, threw back her head, and strained her hot hands rigidly across her forehead, saying, with a hysterical sob, "Would to God you would speak and tell me your secret, Fanny! . . . Oh, I hope, hope it is not true that there are two of you! . . . If I could only look in upon you for one little minute, I should know all!"

A few moments passed, and she added, slowly, "*And I will.*"

Bathsheba in after times could never gauge the mood which carried her through the actions following this murmured resolution on this memorable evening of her life. She went to the lumber closet for a screwdriver. At the end of a short though undefined time she found herself in the small room, quivering with emotion, a mist before her eyes, and an excruciating pulsation in her brain, standing beside the uncovered coffin of the girl whose conjectured end had so entirely engrossed her, and saying to herself in a husky voice as she gazed within—

"It was best to know the worst, and I know it now!"

She was conscious of having brought about this situation by a series of actions done as by one in an extravagant dream; of following that idea as to method, which had burst upon her in the hall with glaring obviousness, by gliding to the top of the stairs, assuring herself by listening to the heavy breathing of her maids that they were asleep, gliding down again, turning the handle of the door within which the young girl lay, and deliberately setting herself to do what, if she had anticipated any such undertaking at night and alone, would have horrified her, but which, when done, was not so dreadful as was the conclusive proof of her husband's conduct which came with knowing beyond doubt the last chapter of Fanny's story.

Bathsheba's head sank upon her bosom, and the breath which had been bated in suspense, curiosity, and interest, was exhaled now in the form of a whispered wail: "Oh-h-h!" she said, and the silent room added length to her moan.

Her tears fell fast beside the unconscious pair in the coffin: tears of a complicated origin, of a nature indescribable, almost indefinable except as other than those of simple sorrow. Assuredly their wonted fires must have lived in Fanny's ashes when events were so shaped as to chariot her hither in this natural, unobtrusive, yet effectual manner. The one feat alone—that of dying—by which a mean condition could be resolved into a grand one, Fanny had achieved. And to that destiny subjoined this reencounter tonight, which had, in Bathsheba's wild imagining, turned her companion's failure to success, her humiliation to triumph, her lucklessness to ascendency; it had thrown over herself a garish light of mockery, and set upon all things about her an ironical smile.

Fanny's face was framed in by that yellow hair of hers; and there was no longer much room for doubt as to the origin of the curl owned by Troy. In Bathsheba's heated fancy the innocent white countenance expressed a dim triumphant consciousness of the pain she was retaliating for her pain with all the merciless rigor of the Mosaic law: "Burning for burning; wound for wound; strife for strife."

Bathsheba indulged in contemplations of escape from her position by immediate death, which, thought she, though it was an inconvenient and awful way, had limits to its inconvenience and awfulness that could not be overpassed; whilst the shames of life were measureless. Yet even this scheme of extinction by death was but tamely copying her rival's method without the reasons which had glorified it in her rival's case. She glided rapidly up and down the room, as was mostly her habit when excited, her hands hanging clasped in front of her, as she thought and in part expressed in broken words: "Oh, I hate her, yet I don't mean that I hate her, for it is grievous and wicked; and yet I hate her a little! Yes, my flesh insists upon hating her, whether my spirit is willing or no! . . . If she had only lived, I could have been angry and cruel toward her with some justification; but to be vindictive toward a poor dead woman recoils upon myself. O God, have mercy! I am miserable at all this!"

Bathsheba became at this moment so terrified at

her own state of mind that she looked around for some sort of refuge from herself. The vision of Oak kneeling down that night recurred to her, and with the imitative instinct which animates women she seized upon the idea, resolved to kneel, and, if possible, pray. Gabriel had prayed; so would she.

She knelt beside the coffin, covered her face with her hands, and for a time the room was silent as a tomb. Whether from a purely mechanical, or from any other cause, when Bathsheba arose it was with a quieted spirit, and a regret for the antagonistic instincts which had seized upon her just before.

In her desire to make atonement she took flowers from a vase by the window, and began laying them around the dead girl's head. Bathsheba knew no other way of showing kindness to persons departed than by giving them flowers. She knew not how long she remained engaged thus. She forgot time, life, where she was, what she was doing. A slamming together of the coachhouse doors in the yard brought her to herself again. An instant after, the front door opened and closed, steps crossed the hall, and her husband appeared at the entrance to the room, looking in upon her.

He beheld it all by degrees, stared in stupefaction at the scene, as if he thought it an illusion raised by some fiendish incantation. Bathsheba, pallid as a corpse on end, gazed back at him in the same wild way.

So little are instinctive guesses the fruit of a legitimate induction that, at this moment, as he stood with the door in his hand, Troy never once thought of Fanny in connection with what he saw. His first confused idea was that somebody in the house had died.

"Well—what?" said Troy blankly.

"I must go! I must go!" said Bathsheba, to herself more than to him. She came with a dilated eye toward the door, to push past him.

"What's the matter, in God's name? Who's dead?" said Troy.

"I cannot say; let me go out. I want air!" she continued.

"But no; stay, I insist!" He seized her hand, and then volition seemed to leave her, and she went off into a state of passivity. He, still holding her came up the room, and thus, hand in hand, Troy and Bathsheba approached the coffin's side.

The candle was standing on a bureau close by them, and the light slanted down, distinctly enkindling the cold features of mother and babe. Troy looked in, dropped his wife's hand, knowledge of it all came over him in a lurid sheen, and he stood still.

So still he remained that he could be imagined to have left in him no motive power whatever. The clashes of feeling in all directions confounded one another, produced a neutrality, and there was motion in none.

"Do you know her?" said Bathsheba, in a small enclosed echo, as from the interior of a cell.

"I do," said Troy.

"Is it she?"

"It is."

He had originally stood perfectly erect. And now, in the well-nigh congealed immobility of his frame could be discerned an incipient movement, as in the darkest night may be discerned light after a while. He was gradually sinking forward. The lines of his features softened, and dismay modulated to illimitable sadness. Bathsheba was regarding him from the other side, still with parted lips and distracted eyes. Capacity for intense feeling is proportionate to the general intensity of nature, and perhaps in all Fanny's sufferings, much greater relatively to her strength, there never was a time when she suffered in an absolute sense what Bathsheba suffered now.

What Troy did was to sink upon his knees with an indefinable union of remorse and reverence upon his face, and, bending over Fanny Robin, gently kissed her, as one would kiss an infant asleep to avoid awakening it.

At the sight and sound of that, to her, unendurable act, Bathsheba sprang toward him. All the strong feelings which had been scattered over her existence since she knew what feeling was, seemed gathered together into one pulsation now. The revulsion from her indignant mood a little earlier, when she had meditated upon compromised honor, forestallment, eclipse in maternity by another, was violent and entire. All that was forgotten in the simple and still strong attachment of wife to husband. She had sighed for her self-completeness then, and now she cried aloud against the severance of the union she had deplored. She flung her arms round Troy's neck, exclaiming wildly from the deepest deep of her heart—

"Don't—don't kiss them! Oh, Frank, I can't bear it—I can't! I love you better than she did: kiss me too, Frank—kiss me! *You will, Frank, kiss me too!*"

There was something so abnormal and startling in the childlike pain and simplicity of this appeal from a woman of Bathsheba's caliber and independence, that Troy, loosening her tightly clasped arms from his neck, looked at her in bewilderment. It was such an unexpected revelation of all women being alike at heart, even those so different in their accessories as Fanny and this one beside him, that Troy could hardly seem to believe her to be his proud wife Bathsheba. Fanny's own spirit seemed to be animating her frame. But this was the mood of a few instants only. When the momentary surprise had passed, his expression changed to a silencing imperious gaze.

"I will not kiss you!" he said, pushing her away.

Had the wife now but gone no further. Yet, perhaps, under the harrowing circumstances, to speak out was the one wrong act which can be better understood, if not forgiven in her, than the right and politic one, her rival being now but a corpse. All the feeling she had been betrayed into showing she drew back to herself again by a strenuous effort of self-command.

"What have you to say as your reason?" she asked, her bitter voice being strangely low—quite that of another woman now.

"I have to say that I have been a bad, black-hearted man," he answered.

"And that this woman is your victim; and I not less than she."

"Ah! don't taunt me, madam. This woman is more to me, dead as she is, than ever you were, or are, or can be. If Satan had not tempted me with that face of yours, and those cursed coquetries, I should have married her. I never had another thought till you came in my way. Would to God that I had; but it is all too late! I deserve to live in torment for this!" He turned to Fanny then. "But never mind, darling," he said, "in the sight of Heaven you are my very, very wife!"

At these words there arose from Bathsheba's lips a long, low cry of measureless despair and indignation, such a wail of anguish as had never before been heard within those old inhabited walls. It was the Τετέλεσται of her union with Troy.

"If she's—that,—what—am I?" she added, as a continuation of the same cry, and sobbing pitifully: and the rarity with her of such abandonment only made the condition more dire.

"You are nothing to me—nothing," said Troy heartlessly. "A ceremony before a priest doesn't make a marriage. I am not morally yours."

A vehement impulse to flee from him, to run

from this place, hide, and escape his words at any price, not stopping short of death itself, mastered Bathsheba now. She waited not an instant, but turned to the door and ran out.

44. *Under a Tree — Reaction*

BATHSHEBA WENT ALONG the dark road, neither knowing nor caring about the direction or issue of her flight. The first time that she definitely noticed her position was when she reached a gate leading into a thicket overhung by some large oak and beech trees. On looking into the place, it occurred to her that she had seen it by daylight on some previous occasion, and that what appeared like an impassable thicket was in reality a brake of fern now withering fast. She could think of nothing better to do with her palpitating self than to go in here and hide; and entering, she lighted on a spot sheltered from the damp fog by a reclining trunk, where she sank down upon a tangled couch of fronds and stems. She mechanically pulled some armfuls round her to keep off the breezes, and closed her eyes.

Whether she slept or not that night Bathsheba was not clearly aware. But it was with a freshened existence and a cooler brain that, a long time afterward, she became conscious of some interesting proceedings which were going on in the trees above her head and around.

A coarse-throated chatter was the first sound.

It was a sparrow just waking.

Next: "Chee-weeze-weeze-weeze!" from another retreat.

It was a finch.

Third: "Tink-tink-tink-tink-a-chink!" from the hedge.

It was a robin.

"Chuck-chuck-chuck!" overhead.

A squirrel.

Then, from the road, "With my ra-ta-ta, and my rum-tum-tum!"

It was a ploughboy. Presently he came opposite, and she believed from his voice that he was one of the boys on her own farm. He was followed by a shambling tramp of heavy feet, and looking through the ferns Bathsheba could just discern in the wan light of daybreak a team of her own horses. They stopped to drink at a pond on the other side of the way. She watched them flouncing into the pool, drinking, tossing up their heads, drinking again, the water dribbling from their lips in silver threads. There was another flounce, and they came out of the pond, and turned back again toward the farm.

She looked further around. Day was just dawning, and beside its cool air and colors her heated actions and resolves of the night stood out in lurid contrast. She perceived that in her lap, and clinging to her hair, were red and yellow leaves which had come down from the tree and settled silently upon her during her partial sleep. Bathsheba shook her dress to get rid of them, when multitudes of the same family lying round about her rose and fluttered away in the breeze thus created, "like ghosts from an enchanter fleeing."

There was an opening toward the east, and the glow from the as yet unrisen sun attracted her eyes thither. From her feet, and between the beautiful yellowing ferns with their feathery arms, the ground sloped downward to a hollow, in which was a species of swamp, dotted with fungi. A morning mist hung over it now—a fulsome yet magnificent silvery veil, full of light from the sun, yet semi-opaque—the hedge behind it being in some measure hidden by its hazy luminousness. Up the sides of this depression grew sheaves of the common rush, and here and there a peculiar species of flag, the blades of which glistened in the emerging sun, like scythes. But the general aspect of the swamp was malignant. From its moist and poisonous coat seemed to be exhaled the essences of evil things in the earth, and in the waters under the earth. The fungi grew in all manner of positions from rotting leaves and tree stumps, some exhibiting to her listless gaze their clammy tops, others their oozing gills. Some were marked with great splotches, red as arterial blood, others were saffron yellow, and others tall and attenuated, with stems like macaroni. Some were leathery and of richest browns. The hollow seemed a nursery of pestilences small and great, in the immediate neighborhood of comfort and health, and Bathsheba arose with a tremor at the thought of having passed the night on the brink of so dismal a place.

There were now other footsteps to be heard along the road. Bathsheba's nerves were still unstrung: she crouched down out of sight again, and the pedestrian came into view. He was a schoolboy, with a bag slung over his shoulder containing his dinner, and a book in his hand. He paused by the gate, and, without looking up, continued murmuring words in tones quite loud enough to reach her ears.

" 'O Lord, O Lord, O Lord, O Lord, O Lord'— that I know out o' book. 'Give us, give us, give us, give us, give us'—that I know. 'Grace that, grace that, grace that, grace that'—that I know." Other words followed to the same effect. The boy was of the dunce class apparently; the book was a psalter, and this was his way of learning the collect. In the worst attacks of trouble there appears to be always a superficial film of consciousness which is left disengaged and open to the notice of trifles, and Bathsheba was faintly amused at the boy's method, till he too passed on.

By this time stupor had given place to anxiety, and anxiety began to make room for hunger and thirst. A form now appeared upon the rise on the other side of the swamp, half-hidden by the mist, and came toward Bathsheba. The woman—for it was a woman—approached with her face askance, as if looking earnestly on all sides of her. When she got a little further round to the left, and drew nearer, Bathsheba could see the newcomer's profile against the sunny sky, and knew the wavy sweep from forehead to chin, with neither angle nor decisive line anywhere about it, to be the familiar contour of Liddy Smallbury.

Bathsheba's heart bounded with gratitude in the thought that she was not altogether deserted, and she jumped up. "Oh, Liddy!" she said, or attempted to say; but the words had only been framed by her lips; there came no sound. She had lost her voice by exposure to the clogged atmosphere all these hours of night.

"Oh, ma'am! I am so glad I have found you," said the girl, as soon as she saw Bathsheba.

"You can't come across," Bathsheba said in a whisper, which she vainly endeavored to make loud enough to reach Liddy's ears. Liddy, not knowing this, stepped down upon the swamp, saying, as she did so, "It will bear me up, I think."

Bathsheba never forgot that transient little picture of Liddy crossing the swamp to her there in the morning light. Iridescent bubbles of dank subterranean breath rose from the sweating sod beside the waiting maid's feet as she trod, hissing as they burst and expanded away to join the vapory firmament above. Liddy did not sink, as Bathsheba had anticipated.

She landed safely on the other side, and looked up at the beautiful though pale and weary face of her young mistress.

"Poor thing!" said Liddy, with tears in her eyes. "Do hearten yourself up a little, ma'am. However did—"

"I can't speak above a whisper—my voice is gone for the present," said Bathsheba hurriedly. "I suppose the damp air from that hollow has taken it away. Liddy, don't question me, mind. Who sent you—anybody?"

"Nobody. I thought, when I found you were not at home, that something cruel had happened. I fancy I heard his voice late last night; and so, knowing something was wrong—"

"Is he at home?"

"No; he left just before I came out."

"Is Fanny taken away?"

"Not yet. She will soon be—at nine o'clock."

"We won't go home at present, then. Suppose we walk about in this wood?"

Liddy, without exactly understanding everything, or anything, in this episode, assented, and they walked together further among the trees.

"But you had better come in, ma'am, and have something to eat. You will die of a chill!"

"I shall not come indoors yet—perhaps never."

"Shall I get you something to eat, and something else to put over your head besides that little shawl?"

"If you will, Liddy."

Liddy vanished, and at the end of twenty minutes returned with a cloak, hat, some slices of bread and butter, a teacup, and some hot tea in a little china jug.

"Is Fanny gone?" said Bathsheba.

"No," said her companion, pouring out the tea. Bathsheba wrapped herself up and ate and drank sparingly. Her voice was then a little clearer, and a trifling color returned to her face. "Now we'll walk about again," she said.

They wandered about the wood for nearly two hours, Bathsheba replying in monosyllables to Liddy's prattle, for her mind ran on one subject, and one only. She interrupted with—

"I wonder if Fanny is gone by this time?"

"I will go and see."

She came back with the information that the men were just taking away the corpse; that Bathsheba had been inquired for; that she had replied to the effect that her mistress was unwell and could not be seen.

"Then they think I am in my bedroom?"

"Yes." Liddy then ventured to add: "You said when I first found you that you might never go home again—you didn't mean it, ma'am?"

"No; I've altered my mind. It is only women with no pride in them who run away from their husbands. There is one position worse than that of being found dead in your husband's house from his ill-usage, and that is, to be found alive through having gone away to the house of somebody else. I've thought of it all this morning, and I've chosen my course. A runaway wife is an encumbrance to everybody, a burden to herself and a byword—all of which make up a heap of misery greater than any that comes by staying at home—though this may include the trifling items of insult, beating, and starvation. Liddy, if ever you marry—

God forbid that you ever should!—you'll find yourself in a fearful situation; but mind this, don't you
flinch. Stand your ground, and be cut to pieces.
That's what I'm going to do."

"Oh, mistress, don't talk so!" said Liddy, taking
her hand, "but I knew you had too much sense to
bide away. May I ask what dreadful thing it is that
has happened between you and him?"

"You may ask; but I may not tell."

In about ten minutes they returned to the house
by a circuitous route, entering at the rear. Bathsheba glided up the back stairs to a disused attic,
and her companion followed.

"Liddy," she said, with a lighter heart, for youth
and hope had begun to reassert themselves; "you
are to be my confidante for the present—somebody
must be—and I choose you. Well, I shall take up
my abode here for a while. Will you get a fire
lighted, put down a piece of carpet, and help me
to make the place comfortable? Afterward, I want
you and Maryann to bring up that little stump bedstead in the small room, and the bed belonging to
it, and a table, and some other things. . . . What
shall I do to pass the heavy time away?"

"Hemming handkerchiefs is a very good thing,"
said Liddy.

"Oh, no, no! I hate needlework—I always did."

"Knitting?"

"And that, too."

"You might finish your sampler. Only the carnations and peacocks want filling in; and then it
could be framed and glazed, and hung beside your
aunt's, ma'am."

"Samplers are out of date—horribly countrified.
No, Liddy, I'll read. Bring up some books—not
new ones. I haven't heart to read anything new."

"Some of your uncle's old ones, ma'am?"

"Yes. Some of those we stowed away in boxes."

A faint gleam of humor passed over her face as she said: "Bring Beaumont and Fletcher's *Maid's Tragedy*; and the *Mourning Bride*; and—let me see— *Night Thoughts,* and the *Vanity of Human Wishes.*"

"And that story of the black man, who murdered his wife Desdemona? It is a nice dismal one that would suit you excellent just now."

"Now, Liddy, you've been looking into my books, without telling me; and I said you were not to! How do you know it would suit me? It wouldn't suit me at all."

"But if the others do—"

"No, they don't; and I won't read dismal books. Why should I read dismal books, indeed? Bring me *Love in a Village,* and the *Maid of the Mill,* and *Doctor Syntax,* and some volumes of the *Spectator.*"

All that day Bathsheba and Liddy lived in the attic in a state of barricade; a precaution which proved to be needless as against Troy, for he did not appear in the neighborhood or trouble them at all. Bathsheba sat at the window till sunset, sometimes attempting to read, at other times watching every movement outside without much purpose, and listening without much interest to every sound.

The sun went down almost blood-red that night, and a livid cloud received its rays in the east. Up against this dark background the west front of the church tower—the only part of the edifice visible from the farmhouse windows—rose distinct and lustrous, the vane upon the summit bristling with rays. Hereabouts, at six o'clock, the young men of the village gathered, as was their custom, for a game of Prisoners' base. The spot had been consecrated to this ancient diversion from time immemorial, the old stocks conveniently forming a base facing the boundary of the churchyard, in front of which the ground was trodden hard and bare as a pavement by the players. She could see the brown and black heads of the young lads darting about right and left, their white shirtsleeves gleaming in the sun; whilst occasionally a shout and a peal of hearty laughter varied the stillness of the evening air. They continued playing for a quarter of an hour or so, when the game concluded abruptly, and the players leapt over the wall and vanished round to the other side behind a yew tree, which was also half behind a beech, now spreading in one mass of golden foliage, on which the branches traced black lines.

"Why did the base players finish their game so suddenly?" Bathsheba inquired, the next time that Liddy entered the room.

"I think 'twas because two men came just then from Casterbridge and began putting up a grand carved tombstone," said Liddy. "The lads went to see whose it was."

"Do you know?" Bathsheba asked.

"I don't," said Liddy.

45. Troy's Romanticism

WHEN TROY'S WIFE had left the house at the previous midnight his first act was to cover the dead from sight. This done he ascended the stairs, and throwing himself down upon the bed dressed as he was, he waited miserably for the morning.

Fate had dealt grimly with him through the last

four-and-twenty hours. His day had been spent in a way which varied very materially from his intentions regarding it. There is always an inertia to be overcome in striking out a new line of conduct— not more in ourselves, it seems, than in circumscribing events, which appear as if leagued together to allow no novelties in the way of amelioration.

Twenty pounds having been secured from Bathsheba, he had managed to add to the sum every farthing he could muster on his own account, which had been seven pounds ten. With this money, twenty-seven pounds ten in all, he had hastily driven from the gate that morning to keep his appointment with Fanny Robin.

On reaching Casterbridge he left the horse and trap at an inn, and at five minutes before ten came back to the bridge at the lower end of the town, and sat himself upon the parapet. The clocks struck the hour, and no Fanny appeared. In fact, at that moment she was being robed in her graveclothes by two attendants at the Union poorhouse—the first and last tiring women the gentle creature had ever been honored with. The quarter went, the half hour. A rush of recollection came upon Troy as he waited: this was the second time she had broken a serious engagement with him. In anger he vowed it should be the last, and at eleven o'clock, when he had lingered and watched the stones of the bridge till he knew every lichen upon their faces, and heard the chink of the ripples underneath till they oppressed him, he jumped from his seat, went to the inn for his gig, and in a bitter mood of indifference concerning the past, and recklessness about the future, drove on to Budmouth races.

He reached the racecourse at two o'clock, and remained either there or in the town till nine. But Fanny's image, as it had appeared to him in the somber shadows of that Saturday evening, returned to his mind, backed up by Bathsheba's reproaches.

He vowed he would not bet, and he kept his vow, for on leaving the town at nine o'clock in the evening he had diminished his cash only to the extent of a few shillings.

He trotted slowly homeward, and it was now that he was struck for the first time with a thought that Fanny had been really prevented by illness from keeping her promise. This time she could have made no mistake. He regretted that he had not remained in Casterbridge and made inquiries. Reaching home he quietly unharnessed the horse and came indoors, as we have seen, to the fearful shock that awaited him.

As soon as it grew light enough to distinguish objects, Troy arose from the coverlet of the bed, and in a mood of absolute indifference to Bathsheba's whereabouts, and almost oblivious of her existence, he stalked downstairs and left the house by the back door. His walk was toward the churchyard, entering which he searched around till he found a newly dug unoccupied grave—the grave dug the day before for Fanny. The position of this having been marked, he hastened on to Casterbridge, only pausing and musing for a while at the hill whereon he had last seen Fanny alive.

Reaching the town, Troy descended into a side street and entered a pair of gates surmounted by a board bearing the words, "Lester, stone and marble mason." Within were lying about stones of all sizes and designs, inscribed as being sacred to the memory of unnamed persons who had not yet died.

Troy was so unlike himself now in look, word, and deed, that the want of likeness was perceptible even to his own consciousness. His method of engaging himself in this business of purchasing a tomb was that of an absolutely unpracticed man. He could not bring himself to consider, calculate, or economize. He waywardly wished for something, and he set about obtaining it like a child in a nursery. "I want a good tomb," he said to the man who stood in a little office within the yard. "I want as good a one as you can give me for twenty-seven pounds."

It was all the money he possessed.

"That sum to include everything?"

"Everything. Cutting the name, carriage to Weatherbury, and erection. And I want it now, at once."

"We could not get anything special worked this week."

"I must have it now."

"If you would like one of these in stock it could be got ready immediately."

"Very well," said Troy, impatiently. "Let's see what you have."

"The best I have in stock is this one," said the stonecutter, going into a shed. "Here's a marble headstone beautifully crocketed, with medallions beneath of typical subjects; here's the footstone after the same pattern, and here's the coping to enclose the grave. The polishing alone of the set cost me eleven pounds—the slabs are the best of their kind, and I can warrant them to resist rain and frost for a hundred years without flying."

"And how much?"

"Well, I could add the name, and put it up at Weatherbury for the sum you mention."

"Get it done today, and I'll pay the money now."

The man agreed, and wondered at such a mood in a visitor who wore not a shred of mourning. Troy then wrote the words which were to form the inscription, settled the account and went away. In the afternoon he came back again, and found that the lettering was almost done. He waited in the yard till the tomb was packed, and saw it placed in the cart and starting on its way to Weatherbury, giving directions to the two men who were to accompany it to inquire of the sexton for the grave of the person named in the inscription.

It was quite dark when Troy came out of Casterbridge. He carried rather a heavy basket upon his arm, with which he strode moodily along the road, resting occasionally at bridges and gates, whereon he deposited his burden for a time. Midway on his journey he met, returning in the darkness, the men and the wagon which had conveyed the tomb. He merely inquired if the work was done, and, on being assured that it was, passed on again.

Troy entered Weatherbury churchyard about ten o'clock, and went immediately to the corner where he had marked the vacant grave early in the morning. It was on the obscure side of the tower, screened to a great extent from the view of passers along the road—a spot which until lately had been abandoned to heaps of stones and bushes of alder, but now it was cleared and made orderly for interments, by reason of the rapid filling of the ground elsewhere.

Here now stood the tomb as the men had stated, snow white and shapely in the gloom, consisting of head and foot stone, and enclosing border of marble work uniting them. In the midst was mold, suitable for plants.

Troy deposited his basket beside the tomb, and vanished for a few minutes. When he returned he carried a spade and a lantern, the light of which he directed for a few moments upon the marble, whilst he read the inscription. He hung his lantern on the lowest bough of the yew tree, and took from his basket flower roots of several varieties. There were bundles of snowdrop, hyacinth and crocus bulbs, violets and double daisies, which were to bloom in early spring, and of carnations, pinks, picotees, lilies of the valley, forget-me-not, summer's farewell, meadow-saffron and others, for the later seasons of the year.

Troy laid these out upon the grass, and with an impassive face set to work to plant them. The snowdrops were arranged in a line on the outside of the coping, the remainder within the enclosure of the grave. The crocuses and hyacinths were to grow in rows; some of the summer flowers he placed over her head and feet, the lilies and forget-me-nots over her heart. The remainder were dispersed in the spaces between these.

Troy, in his prostration at this time, had no perception that in the futility of these romantic doings, dictated by a remorseful reaction from previous indifference, there was any element of absurdity. Deriving his idiosyncrasies from both sides of the Channel, he showed at such junctures as the present the inelasticity of the Englishman, together with that blindness to the line where sentiment verges on mawkishness, characteristic of the French.

It was a cloudy, muggy, and very dark night, and the rays from Troy's lantern spread into the two old yews with a strange illuminating power, flickering, as it seemed, up to the black ceiling of cloud above. He felt a large drop of rain upon the back of his hand, and presently one came and entered one of the holes of the lantern, whereupon the candle sputtered and went out. Troy was weary, and it being now not far from midnight, and the rain threatening to increase, he resolved to leave the finishing touches of his labor until the day should break. He groped along the wall and over the graves in the dark till he found himself round at the north side. Here he entered the porch, and, reclining upon the bench within, fell asleep.

46. *The Gargoyle: Its Doings*

THE TOWER of Weatherbury Church was a square
erection of fourteenth-century date, having two
stone gargoyles on each of the four faces of its parapet. Of these eight carved protuberances only two
at this time continued to serve the purpose of their
erection—that of spouting the water from the lead
roof within. One mouth in each front had been
closed by bygone churchwardens as superfluous,
and two others were broken away and choked—a
matter not of much consequence to the well-being of the tower, for the two mouths which still
remained open and active were gaping enough to
do all the work.

It has been sometimes argued that there is no
truer criterion of the vitality of any given art period
than the power of the master spirits of that time in
grotesque; and certainly in the instance of Gothic
art there is no disputing the proposition. Weatherbury tower was a somewhat early instance of the
use of an ornamental parapet in parish as distinct
from cathedral churches, and the gargoyles, which
are the necessary correlatives of a parapet, were
exceptionally prominent—of the boldest cut that
the hand could shape, and of the most original design that a human brain could conceive. There was,
so to speak, that symmetry in their distortion which
is less the characteristic of British than of Con-

tinental grotesques of the period. All the eight were different from each other. A beholder was convinced that nothing on earth could be more hideous than those he saw on the north side until he went round to the south. Of the two on this latter face, only that at the southeastern corner concerns the story. It was too human to be called like a dragon, too impish to be like a man, too animal to be like a fiend, and not enough like a bird to be called a griffin. This horrible stone entity was fashioned as if covered with a wrinkled hide; it had short, erect ears, eyes starting from their sockets, and its fingers and hands were seizing the corners of its mouth, which they thus seemed to pull open to give free passage to the water it vomited. The lower row of teeth was quite washed away, though the upper still remained. Here and thus, jutting a couple of feet from the wall against which its feet rested as a support, the creature had for four hundred years laughed at the surrounding landscape, voicelessly in dry weather, and in wet with a gurgling and snorting sound.

Troy slept on in the porch, and the rain increased outside. Presently the gargoyle spat. In due time a small stream began to trickle through the seventy feet of aerial space between its mouth and the ground, which the water drops smote like duckshot in their accelerated velocity. The stream thickened in substance, and increased in power, gradually spouting farther and yet farther from the side of the tower. When the rain fell in a steady and ceaseless torrent the stream dashed downward in volumes.

We follow its course to the ground at this point of time. The end of the liquid parabola has come forward from the wall, has advanced over the plinth moldings, over a heap of stones, over the marble border, into the midst of Fanny Robin's grave.

The force of the stream had, until very lately, been received upon some loose stones spread thereabout which had acted as a shield to the soil under the onset. These during the summer had been cleared from the ground, and there was now nothing to resist the downfall but the bare earth. For several years the stream had not spouted so far from the tower as it was doing on this night, and such a contingency had been overlooked. Sometimes this obscure corner received no inhabitant for the space of two or three years, and then it was usually but a pauper, a poacher, or other sinner of undignified sins.

The persistent torrent from the gargoyle's jaws directed all its vengeance into the grave. The rich tawny mold was stirred into motion, and boiled like chocolate. The water accumulated and washed deeper down, and the roar of the pool thus formed spread into the night as the head and chief among other noises of the kind created by the deluging rain. The flowers so carefully planted by Fanny's repentant lover began to move and writhe in their bed. The winter-violets turned slowly upside down, and became a mere mat of mud. Soon the snowdrop and other bulbs danced in the boiling mass like ingredients in a cauldron. Plants of the tufted species were loosened, rose to the surface, and floated off.

Troy did not awake from his comfortless sleep till it was broad day. Not having been in bed for two nights his shoulders felt stiff, his feet tender, and his head heavy. He remembered his position, arose, shivered, took the spade, and again went out.

The rain had quite ceased, and the sun was shining through the green, brown, and yellow leaves, now sparkling and varnished by the raindrops to the brightness of similar effects in the landscapes of Ruysdael and Hobbema, and full of all those infinite beauties that arise from the union of water and color with high lights. The air was rendered so transparent by the heavy fall of rain that the autumn hues of the middle distance were as rich as those near at hand, and the remote fields intercepted by the angle of the tower appeared in the same plane as the tower itself.

He entered the gravel path which would take him behind the tower. The path, instead of being stony as it had been the night before, was browned over with a thin coating of mud. At one place in the path he saw a tuft of stringy roots washed white and clean as a bundle of tendons. He picked it up—surely it could not be one of the primroses he had planted? He saw a bulb, another, and another as he advanced. Beyond doubt they were the crocuses. With a face of perplexed dismay Troy turned the corner and then beheld the wreck the stream had made.

The pool upon the grave had soaked away into the ground, and in its place was a hollow. The disturbed earth was washed over the grass and pathway in the guise of the brown mud he had already seen, and it spotted the marble tombstone with the same stains. Nearly all the flowers were washed clean out of the ground, and they lay, roots upward, on the spots whither they had been splashed by the stream.

Troy's brow became heavily contracted. He set his teeth closely, and his compressed lips moved as those of one in great pain. This singular accident, by a strange confluence of emotions in him, was felt as the sharpest sting of all. Troy's face was very expressive, and any observer who had seen him now would hardly have believed him to be a man who had laughed, and sung, and poured love trifles into a woman's ear. To curse his miserable lot was at first his impulse, but even that lowest stage of rebellion needed an activity whose absence was necessarily antecedent to the existence of the morbid misery which wrung him. The sight, coming as it did, superimposed upon the other dark scenery of the previous days, formed a sort of climax to the whole panorama, and it was more than he could endure. Sanguine by nature, Troy had a power of eluding grief by simply adjourning it. He could put off the consideration of any particular specter till the matter had become old and softened by time. The planting of flowers on Fanny's grave had been perhaps but a species of elusion of the primary grief, and now it was as if his intention had been known and circumvented.

Almost for the first time in his life Troy, as he stood by this dismantled grave, wished himself another man. It is seldom that a person with much animal spirit does not feel that the fact of his life being his own is the one qualification which singles it out as a more hopeful life than that of others who may actually resemble him in every particular. Troy had felt, in his transient way, hundreds of times, that he could not envy other people their condition, because the possession of that condition would have necessitated a different personality, when he desired no other than his own. He had not minded the peculiarities of his birth, the vicissitudes of his life, the meteorlike uncertainty of all that related to him, because these appertained to the hero of his story, without whom there would have been no story at all for him; and it seemed to be only in the nature of things matters would right themselves at some proper date and wind up well. This very morning the illusion completed its disappearance, and, as it were, all of a sudden, Troy hated himself. The suddenness was probably more apparent than real. A coral reef which just comes short of the ocean surface is no more to the horizon

than if it had never been begun, and the mere
finishing stroke is what often appears to create an
event which has long been potentially an accom-
plished thing.

He stood and meditated—a miserable man.
Whither should he go? "He that is accursed, let
him be accursed still," was the pitiless anathema
written in this spoliated effort of his newborn solicitousness. A man who has spent his primal
strength in journeying in one direction has not
much spirit left for reversing his course. Troy had,
since yesterday, faintly reversed his; but the
merest opposition had disheartened him. To turn
about would have been hard enough under the
greatest providential encouragement; but to find
that Providence, far from helping him into a new
course, or showing any wish that he might adopt
one, actually jeered his first trembling and critical
attempt in that kind, was more than nature could
bear.

He slowly withdrew from the grave. He did not
attempt to fill up the hole, replace the flowers, or
do anything at all. He simply threw up his cards
and forswore his game for that time and always.
Going out of the churchyard silently and unobserved—none of the villagers having yet risen—he
passed down some fields at the back, and emerged
just as secretly upon the high road. Shortly afterward he had gone from the village.

Meanwhile, Bathsheba remained a voluntary
prisoner in the attic. The door was kept locked,
except during the entries and exits of Liddy, for
whom a bed had been arranged in a small adjoining room. The light of Troy's lantern in the
churchyard was noticed about ten o'clock by the
maid-servant, who casually glanced from the window in that direction whilst taking her supper,
and she called Bathsheba's attention to it. They

looked curiously at the phenomenon for a time, until Liddy was sent to bed.

Bathsheba did not sleep very heavily that night. When her attendant was unconscious and softly breathing in the next room, the mistress of the house was still looking out of the window at the faint gleam spreading from among the trees—not in a steady shine, but blinking like a revolving coastlight, though this appearance failed to suggest to her that a person was passing and repassing in front of it. Bathsheba sat here till it began to rain, and the light vanished, when she withdrew to lie restlessly in her bed and reenact in a worn mind the lurid scene of yesternight.

Almost before the first faint sign of dawn appeared she arose again, and opened the window to obtain a full breathing of the new morning air, the panes being now wet with trembling tears left by the night rain, each one rounded with a pale luster caught from primrose hued slashes through a cloud low down in the awakening sky. From the trees came the sound of steady dripping upon the drifted leaves under them, and from the direction of the church she could hear another noise—peculiar, and not intermittent like the rest, the purl of water falling into a pool.

Liddy knocked at eight o'clock, and Bathsheba unlocked the door.

"What a heavy rain we've had in the night, ma'am!" said Liddy, when her inquiries about breakfast had been made.

"Yes; very heavy."

"Did you hear the strange noise from the church-yard?"

"I heard one strange noise. I've been thinking it must have been the water from the tower spouts."

"Well, that's what the shepherd was saying, ma'am. He's now gone on to see."

"Oh! Gabriel has been here this morning?"

"Only just looked in in passing—quite in his old way, which I thought he had left off lately. But the tower spouts used to spatter on the stones, and we are puzzled, for this was like the boiling of a pot."

Not being able to read, think, or work, Bathsheba asked Liddy to stay and breakfast with her. The tongue of the more childish woman still ran upon recent events. "Are you going across to the church, ma'am?" she asked.

"Not that I know of," said Bathsheba.

"I thought you might like to go and see where they have put Fanny. The trees hide the place from your window."

Bathsheba had all sorts of dreads about meeting her husband. "Has Mr. Troy been in tonight?" she said.

"No, ma'am; I think he's gone to Budmouth."

Budmouth! The sound of the word carried with it a much diminished perspective of him and his deeds; there were thirteen miles interval betwixt them now. She hated questioning Liddy about her husband's movements, and indeed had hitherto sedulously avoided doing so; but now all the house knew that there had been some dreadful disagreement between them, and it was futile to attempt disguise. Bathsheba had reached a stage at which people cease to have any appreciative regard for public opinion.

"What makes you think he has gone there?" she said.

"Laban Tall saw him on the Budmouth road this morning before breakfast."

Bathsheba was momentarily relieved of that wayward heaviness of the past twenty-four hours which had quenched the vitality of youth in her without substituting the philosophy of maturer years, and she resolved to go out and walk a little way.

So when breakfast was over she put on her bonnet, and took a direction toward the church. It was nine o'clock, and the men having returned to work again from their first meal, she was not likely to meet many of them in the road. Knowing that Fanny had been laid in the reprobates' quarter of the graveyard, called in the parish "behind church," which was invisible from the road, it was impossible to resist the impulse to enter and look upon a spot which, from nameless feelings, she at the same time dreaded to see. She had been unable to overcome an impression that some connection existed between her rival and the light through the trees.

Bathsheba skirted the buttress, and beheld the hole and the tomb, its delicately veined surface splashed and stained just as Troy had seen it and left it two hours earlier. On the other side of the scene stood Gabriel. His eyes, too, were fixed on the tomb, and her arrival having been noiseless, she had not as yet attracted his attention. Bathsheba did not at once perceive that the grand tomb and the disturbed grave were Fanny's, and she looked on both sides and around for some humbler mound, earthed up and clodded in the usual way. Then her eye followed Oak's, and she read the words with which the inscription opened:

Erected by Francis Troy in Beloved Memory of Fanny Robin.

Oak saw her, and his first act was to gaze inquiringly and learn how she received this knowledge of the authorship of the work, which to himself had caused considerable astonishment. But such discoveries did not much affect her now. Emotional convulsions seemed to have become the commonplaces of her history, and she bade him good morning, and asked him to fill in the hole with the spade which was standing by. Whilst Oak was doing as she desired, Bathsheba collected the flowers, and began planting them with that sympathetic manipulation of roots and leaves which is so conspicuous in a woman's gardening, and which flowers seem to understand and thrive upon. She requested Oak to get the churchwardens to turn the leadwork at the mouth of the gargoyle that hung gaping down upon them, that by this means the stream might be directed sideways, and a repetition of the accident prevented. Finally, with the superfluous magnanimity of a woman whose narrower instincts have brought down bitterness upon her instead of love, she wiped the mud spots from the tomb as if she rather liked its words than otherwise, and went home again.[1]

47. *Adventures by the Shore*

TROY WANDERED ALONG toward the south. A composite feeling, made up of disgust with the, to him, humdrum tediousness of a farmer's life, gloomy images of her who lay in the churchyard, remorse, and a general averseness to his wife's society, impelled him to seek a home in any place on earth save Weatherbury. The sad accessories of Fanny's end confronted him as vivid pictures which threatened to be indelible, and made life in Bathsheba's house intolerable. At three in the afternoon he found himself at the foot of a slope more than a

---

[1] The local tower and churchyard do not answer precisely to the foregoing description.

mile in length, which ran to the ridge of a range of
hills lying parallel with the shore, and formed a
monotonous barrier between the basin of cultivated
country inland and the wilder scenery of the coast.
Up the hill stretched a road nearly straight and
perfectly white, the two sides approaching each
other in a gradual taper till they met the sky at the
top about two miles off. Throughout the length of
this narrow and irksome inclined plane not a sign
of life was visible on this garish afternoon. Troy
toiled up the road with a languor and depression
greater than any he had experienced for many a
day and year before. The air was warm and muggy,
and the top seemed to recede as he approached.

At last he reached the summit, and a wide and
novel prospect burst upon him with an effect almost like that of the Pacific upon Balboa's gaze.
The broad steely sea, marked only by faint lines,
which had a semblance of being etched thereon to
a degree not deep enough to disturb its general
evenness, stretched the whole width of his front
and round to the right, where, near the town and
port of Budmouth, the sun bristled down upon it,
and banished all color, to substitute in its place a
clear oily polish. Nothing moved in sky, land, or
sea, except a frill of milkwhite foam along the
nearer angles of the shore, shreds of which licked
the contiguous stones like tongues.

He descended and came to a small basin of sea
enclosed by the cliffs. Troy's nature freshened
within him; he thought he would rest and bathe
here before going further. He undressed and
plunged in. Inside the cove the water was uninteresting to a swimmer, being smooth as a pond,
and to get a little of the ocean swell Troy presently
swam between the two projecting spurs of rock
which formed the pillars of Hercules to this min-
iature Mediterranean. Unfortunately for Troy a

current unknown to him existed outside, which, unimportant to craft of any burden, was awkward for
a swimmer who might be taken in it unawares.
Troy found himself carried to the left and then
round in a swoop out to sea.

He now recollected the place and its sinister
character. Many bathers had there prayed for a dry
death from time to time, and, like Gonzalo also,
had been unanswered; and Troy began to deem it
possible that he might be added to their number.
Not a boat of any kind was at present within sight,
but far in the distance Budmouth lay upon the sea,
as if it were quietly regarding his efforts, and beside
the town the harbor showed its position by a dim
meshwork of ropes and spars. After well-nigh ex-
hausting himself in attempts to get back to the
mouth of the cove, in his weakness swimming several inches deeper than was his wont, keeping up
his breathing entirely by his nostrils, turning upon
his back a dozen times over, swimming *en papillon,*
and so on, Troy resolved as a last resource to tread
water at a slight incline, and so endeavor to reach
the shore at any point, merely giving himself a gentle impetus inward whilst carried on in the general
direction of the tide. This, necessarily a slow process, he found to be not altogether so difficult, and
though there was no choice of a landing place—the
objects on shore passing by him in a sad and slow
procession—he perceptibly approached the extremity of a spit of land yet farther to the right, now
well defined against the sunny portion of the horizon. While the swimmer's eyes were fixed upon the
spit as his only means of salvation on this side of
the Unknown, a moving object broke the outline of
the extremity, and immediately a ship's boat appeared, manned with several sailor lads, her bows
toward the sea.

All Troy's vigor spasmodically revived to prolong the struggle yet a little further. Swimming with his right arm, he held up his left to hail them, splashing upon the waves, and shouting with all his might. From the position of the setting sun his white form was distinctly visible upon the now deep-hued bosom of the sea to the east of the boat, and the men saw him at once. Backing their oars and putting the boat about, they pulled toward him with a will, and in five or six minutes from the time of his first halloo, two of the sailors hauled him in over the stern.

They formed part of a brig's crew, and had come ashore for sand. Lending him what little clothing they could spare among them as a slight protection against the rapidly cooling air, they agreed to land him in the morning; and without further delay, for it was growing late, they made again toward the roadstead where their vessel lay.

And now night drooped slowly upon the wide watery levels in front; and at no great distance from them, where the shoreline curved round, and formed a long riband of shade upon the horizon, a series of points of yellow light began to start into existence, denoting the spot to be the site of Budmouth, where the lamps were being lighted along the parade. The cluck of their oars was the only sound of any distinctness upon the sea, and as they labored amid the thickening shades the lamplights grew larger, each appearing to send a flaming sword deep down into the waves before it, until there arose, among other dim shapes of the kind, the form of the vessel for which they were bound.

48. *Doubts Arise — Doubts Linger*

BATHSHEBA UNDERWENT the enlargement of her
husband's absence from hours to days with a slight
feeling of surprise, and a slight feeling of relief;
yet neither sensation rose at any time far above the
level commonly designated as indifference. She belonged to him: the certainties of that position were
so well defined, and the reasonable probabilities of
its issue so bounded, that she could not speculate
on contingencies. Taking no further interest in
herself as a splendid woman, she acquired the indifferent feelings of an outsider in contemplating
her probable fate as a singular wretch; for Bathsheba drew herself and her future in colors that no
reality could exceed for darkness. Her original vigorous pride of youth had sickened, and with it had
declined all her anxieties about coming years, since
anxiety recognizes a better and a worse alternative,
and Bathsheba had made up her mind that alter-
natives on any noteworthy scale had ceased for
her. Soon, or later—and that not very late—her
husband would be home again. And then the days
of her tenancy of the Upper Farm would be num-
bered. There had originally been shown by the
agent to the estate some distrust of Bathsheba's
tenure as James Everdene's successor, on the score
of her sex, and her youth, and her beauty; but the
peculiar nature of her uncle's will, his own

frequent testimony before his death to her cleverness in such a pursuit, and her vigorous marshaling of the numerous flocks and herds which came suddenly into her hands before negotiations were concluded, had won confidence in her powers, and no further objections had been raised. She had latterly been in great doubt as to what the legal effects of her marriage would be upon her position; but no notice had been taken as yet of her change of name, and only one point was clear—that in the event of her own or her husband's inability to meet the agent at the forthcoming January rentday, very little consideration would be shown, and, for that matter, very little would be deserved. Once out of the farm the approach of poverty would be sure.

Hence Bathsheba lived in a perception that her purposes were broken off. She was not a woman who could hope on without good materials for the process, differing thus from the less farsighted and energetic, though more petted ones of the sex, with whom hope goes on as a sort of clockwork which the merest food and shelter are sufficient to wind up; and perceiving clearly that her mistake had been a fatal one, she accepted her position, and waited coldly for the end.

The first Saturday after Troy's departure she went to Casterbridge alone, a journey she had not before taken since her marriage. On this Saturday Bathsheba was passing slowly on foot through the crowd of rural businessmen gathered as usual in front of the markethouse, who were as usual gazed upon by the burghers with feelings that those healthy lives were dearly paid for by exclusion from possible aldermanship, when a man, who had apparently been following her, said some words to another on her left hand. Bathsheba's ears were keen as those of any wild animal, and she distinctly heard what the speaker said, though her back was toward him.

"I am looking for Mrs. Troy. Is that she there?"

"Yes; that's the young lady, I believe," said the person addressed.

"I have some awkward news to break to her. Her husband is drowned."

As if endowed with the spirit of prophecy, Bathsheba gasped out, "No, it is not true; it cannot be true!" Then she said and heard no more. The ice of self-command which had latterly gathered over her was broken, and the currents burst forth again, and overwhelmed her. A darkness came into her eyes, and she fell.

But not to the ground. A gloomy man, who had been observing her from under the portico of the old corn exchange when she passed through the group without, stepped quickly to her side at the moment of her exclamation, and caught her in his arms as she sank down.

"What is it?" said Boldwood, looking up at the bringer of the big news, as he supported her.

"Her husband was drowned this week while bathing in Lulwind Cove. A coastguardsman found his clothes, and brought them into Budmouth yesterday."

Thereupon a strange fire lighted up Boldwood's eye, and his face flushed with the suppressed excitement of an unutterable thought. Everybody's glance was now centered upon him and the unconscious Bathsheba. He lifted her bodily off the ground, and smoothed down the folds of her dress as a child might have taken a stormbeaten bird and arranged its ruffled plumes, and bore her along the pavement to the King's Arms Inn. Here he passed with her under the archway into a private room; and by the time he had deposited—so lothly—the precious burden upon a sofa, Bathsheba had opened her eyes. Remembering all that had occurred, she murmured, "I want to go home!"

Boldwood left the room. He stood for a moment in the passage to recover his senses. The experience had been too much for his consciousness to keep up with, and now that he had grasped it it had gone again. For those few heavenly, golden moments she had been in his arms. What did it matter about her not knowing it? She had been close to his breast; he had been close to hers.

He started onward again, and sending a woman to her, went out to ascertain all the facts of the case. These appeared to be limited to what he had already heard. He then ordered her horse to be put into the gig, and when all was ready returned to inform her. He found that, though still pale and unwell, she had in the meantime sent for the Budmouth man who brought the tidings, and learnt from him all there was to know.

Being hardly in a condition to drive home as she had driven to town, Boldwood, with every delicacy of manner and feeling, offered to get her a driver, or to give her a seat in his phaeton, which was more comfortable than her own conveyance. These proposals Bathsheba gently declined, and the farmer at once departed.

About half-an-hour later she invigorated herself by an effort, and took her seat and the reins as usual—in external appearance much as if nothing had happened. She went out of the town by a tortuous back street, and drove slowly along, unconscious of the road and the scene. The first shades of evening were showing themselves when Bathsheba reached home, where, silently alighting and leaving the horse in the hands of the boy, she proceeded at once upstairs. Liddy met her on the landing. The news had preceded Bathsheba to Weatherbury by half-an-hour, and Liddy looked inquiringly into her mistress's face. Bathsheba had nothing to say.

She entered her bedroom and sat by the window, and thought and thought till night enveloped her, and the extreme lines only of her shape were visible. Somebody came to the door, knocked, and opened it.

"Well, what is it, Liddy?" she said.

"I was thinking there must be something got for you to wear," said Liddy, with hesitation.

"What do you mean?"

"Mourning."

"No, no, no," said Bathsheba hurriedly.

"But I suppose there must be something done for poor—"

"Not at present, I think. It is not necessary."

"Why not, ma'am?"

"Because he's still alive."

"How do you know that?" said Liddy, amazed.

"I don't know it. But wouldn't it have been different, or shouldn't I have heard more, or wouldn't they have found him, Liddy?—or—I don't know how it is, but death would have been different from how this is. I am perfectly convinced that he is still alive!"

Bathsheba remained firm in this opinion till Monday, when two circumstances conjoined to shake it. The first was a short paragraph in the local newspaper, which, beyond making by a methodizing pen formidable presumptive evidence of Troy's death by drowning, contained the important testimony of a young Mr. Barker, M.D., of Budmouth, who spoke to being an eyewitness of the accident, in a letter to the editor. In this he stated that he was passing over the cliff on the remoter side of the cove just as the sun was setting. At that time he saw a bather carried along in the current outside the mouth of the cove, and guessed in an instant that there was but a poor chance for him unless he should be possessed of unusual muscular powers. He drifted behind a projection of the coast, and Mr. Barker followed along the shore in the same direction. But by the time that he could reach an elevation sufficiently great to command a view of the sea beyond, dusk had set in, and nothing further was to be seen.

The other circumstance was the arrival of his clothes, when it became necessary for her to examine and identify them—though this had virtually been done long before by those who inspected the letters in his pockets. It was so evident to her in the midst of her agitation that Troy had undressed in the full conviction of dressing again almost immediately, that the notion that anything but death could have prevented him was a perverse one to entertain.

Then Bathsheba said to herself that others were assured in their opinion; strange that she should not be. A strange reflection occurred to her, causing her face to flush. Suppose that Troy had followed Fanny into another world. Had he done this intentionally, yet contrived to make his death appear like an accident? Nevertheless, this thought of how the apparent might differ from the real—made vivid by her bygone jealousy of Fanny, and the remorse he had shown that night—did not blind her to the perception of a likelier difference, less tragic, but to herself far more disastrous.

When alone late that evening beside a small fire, and much calmed down, Bathsheba took Troy's watch into her hand, which had been restored to her with the rest of the articles belonging to him. She opened the case as he had opened it before her a week ago. There was the little coil of pale hair which had been as the fuse to this great explosion.

"He was hers and she was his; they should be gone together," she said. "I am nothing to either of them, and why should I keep her hair?" She took it in her hand, and held it over the fire. "No—I'll not burn it—I'll keep it in memory of her, poor thing!" she added, snatching back her hand.

49. Oak's Advancement — A Great Hope

THE LATER AUTUMN and the winter drew on apace, and the leaves lay thick upon the turf of the glades and the mosses of the woods. Bathsheba, having previously been living in a state of suspended feeling which was not suspense, now lived in a mood of quietude which was not precisely peacefulness. While she had known him to be alive she could have thought of his death with equanimity; but now that it might be she had lost him, she regretted that he was not hers still. She kept the farm going, raked in her profits without caring keenly about them, and expended money on ventures because she had done so in bygone days, which, though not long gone by, seemed infinitely removed from her present. She looked back upon that past over a great gulf, as if she were now a dead person, having the faculty of meditation still left in her, by means of which, like the moldering gentlefolk of the poet's story, she could sit and ponder what a gift life used to be.

However, one excellent result of her general

apathy was the long-delayed installation of Oak as bailiff; but he having virtually exercised that function for a long time already, the change, beyond the substantial increase of wages it brought, was little more than a nominal one addressed to the outside world.

Boldwood lived secluded and inactive. Much of his wheat and all his barley of that season had been spoilt by the rain. It sprouted, grew into intricate mats, and was ultimately thrown to the pigs in armfuls. The strange neglect which had produced this ruin and waste became the subject of whispered talk among all the people round; and it was elicited from one of Boldwood's men that forgetfulness had nothing to do with it, for he had been reminded of the danger to his corn as many times and as persistently as inferiors dared to do. The sight of the pigs turning in disgust from the rotten ears seemed to arouse Boldwood, and he one evening sent for Oak. Whether it was suggested by Bathsheba's recent act of promotion or not, the farmer proposed at the interview that Gabriel should undertake the superintendence of the Lower Farm as well as of Bathsheba's, because of the necessity Boldwood felt for such aid, and the impossibility of discovering a more trustworthy man. Gabriel's malignant star was assuredly setting fast.

Bathsheba, when she learnt of this proposal—for Oak was obliged to consult her—at first languidly objected. She considered that the two farms together were too extensive for the observation of one man. Boldwood, who was apparently determined by personal rather than commercial reasons, suggested that Oak should be furnished with a horse for his sole use, when the plan would present no difficulty, the two farms lying side by side. Boldwood did not directly communicate with her during these negotiations, only speaking to Oak, who

was the go-between throughout. All was harmoni-
ously arranged at last, and we now see Oak
mounted on a strong cob, and daily trotting the
length and breadth of about two thousand acres in
a cheerful spirit of surveillance, as if the crops all
belonged to him—the actual mistress of the one-
half, and the master of the other, sitting in their
respective homes in gloomy and sad seclusion.

Out of this there arose, during the spring suc-
ceeding, a talk in the parish that Gabriel Oak was
feathering his nest fast.

"Whatever d'ye think?" said Susan Tall, "Gable
Oak is coming it quite the dand. He now wears
shining boots with hardly a hob in 'em, two or three
times a week, and a tall hat a-Sundays, and 'a hardly
knows the name of smock-frock. When I see people
strut enough to be cut up into bantam cocks, I
stand dormant with wonder, and says no more!"

It was eventually known that Gabriel, though
paid a fixed wage by Bathsheba independent of
the fluctuations of agricultural profits, had made an
engagement with Boldwood by which Oak was to
receive a share of the receipts—a small share certainly, yet it was money of a higher quality than
mere wages, and capable of expansion in a way that
wages were not. Some were beginning to consider
Oak a "near" man, for though his condition had
thus far improved, he lived in no better style than
before, occupying the same cottage, paring his own
potatoes, mending his stockings, and sometimes
even making his bed with his own hands. But as
Oak was not only provokingly indifferent to public
opinion, but a man who clung persistently to old
habits and usages, simply because they were old,
there was room for doubt as to his motives.

A great hope had latterly germinated in Boldwood, whose unreasoning devotion to Bathsheba
could only be characterized as a fond madness which

neither time nor circumstance, evil nor good report, could weaken or destroy. This fevered hope had grown up again like a grain of mustard seed during the quiet which followed the hasty conjecture that Troy was drowned. He nourished it fearfully, and almost shunned the contemplation of it in earnest, lest facts should reveal the wildness of the dream. Bathsheba having at last been persuaded to wear mourning, her appearance as she entered the church in that guise was in itself a weekly addition to his faith that a time was coming—very far off perhaps, yet surely nearing—when his waiting on events should have its reward. How long he might have to wait he had not yet closely considered. What he would try to recognize was that the severe schooling she had been subjected to had made Bathsheba much more considerate than she had formerly been of the feelings of others, and he trusted that, should she be willing at any time in the future to marry any man at all, that man would be himself. There was a substratum of good feeling in her: her self-reproach for the injury she had thoughtlessly done him might be depended upon now to a much greater extent than before her infatuation and disappointment. It would be possible to approach her by the channel of her good nature, and to suggest a friendly businesslike compact between them for fulfillment at some future day, keeping the passionate side of his desire entirely out of her sight. Such was Boldwood's hope.

To the eyes of the middle-aged, Bathsheba was perhaps additionally charming just now. Her exuberance of spirit was pruned down; the original phantom of delight had shown herself to be not too bright for human nature's daily food, and she had been able to enter this second poetical phase without losing much of the first in the process.

Bathsheba's return from a two months' visit to

her old aunt at Norcombe afforded the impassioned and yearning farmer a pretext for inquiring directly after her—now possible in the ninth month of her widowhood—and endeavoring to get a notion of her state of mind regarding him. This occurred in the middle of the haymaking, and Boldwood contrived to be near Liddy, who was assisting in the fields.

"I am glad to see you out of doors, Lydia," he said pleasantly.

She simpered, and wondered in her heart why he should speak so frankly to her.

"I hope Mrs. Troy is quite well after her long absence," he continued, in a manner expressing that the coldest-hearted neighbor could scarcely say less about her.

"She is quite well, sir."

"And cheerful, I suppose."

"Yes, cheerful."

"Fearful, did you say?"

"Oh, no. I merely said she was cheerful."

"Tells you all her affairs?"

"No, sir."

"Some of them?"

"Yes, sir."

"Mrs. Troy puts much confidence in you, Lydia; and very wisely, perhaps."

"She do, sir. I've been with her all through her troubles, and was with her at the time of Mr. Troy's going and all. And if she were to marry again I expect I should bide with her."

"She promises that you shall—quite natural," said the strategic lover, throbbing throughout him at the presumption which Liddy's words appeared to warrant—that his darling had thought of remarriage.

"No—she doesn't promise it exactly. I merely judge on my own account."

"Yes, yes, I understand. When she alludes to the possibility of marrying again, you conclude—"

"She never do allude to it, sir," said Liddy, thinking how very stupid Mr. Boldwood was getting.

"Of course not," he returned hastily, his hope falling again. "You needn't take quite such long reaches with your rake, Lydia—short and quick ones are best. Well, perhaps, as she is absolute mistress again now, it is wise of her to resolve never to give up her freedom."

"My mistress did certainly once say, though not seriously, that she supposed she might marry again at the end of seven years from last year, if she cared to risk Mr. Troy's coming back and claiming her."

"Ah, six years from the present time. Said that she might. She might marry at once in every reasonable person's opinion, whatever the lawyers may say to the contrary."

"Have you been to ask them?" said Liddy innocently.

"Not I," said Boldwood, growing red. "Liddy, you needn't stay here a minute later than you wish, so Mr. Oak says. I am now going on a little further. Good afternoon."

He went away vexed with himself, and ashamed of having for this one time in his life done anything which could be called underhand. Poor Boldwood had no more skill in finesse than a battering ram, and he was uneasy with a sense of having made himself to appear stupid and, what was worse, mean. But he had, after all, lighted upon one fact by way of repayment. It was a singularly fresh and fascinating fact, and though not without its sadness it was pertinent and real. In little more than six years from this time Bathsheba might certainly marry him. There was something definite in that hope, for admitting that there might have been no deep thought in her words to Liddy about marriage, they showed at least her creed on the matter.

This pleasant notion was now continually in his mind. Six years were a long time, but how much shorter than never, the idea he had for so long been obliged to endure! Jacob had served twice seven years for Rachel: what were six for such a woman as this? He tried to like the notion of waiting for her better than that of winning her at once. Boldwood felt his love to be so deep and strong and eternal, that it was possible she had never yet known its full volume, and this patience in delay would afford him an opportunity of giving sweet proof on the point. He would annihilate the six years of his life as if they were minutes—so little did he value his time on earth beside her love. He would let her see, all those six years of intangible ethereal courtship, how little care he had for anything but as it bore upon the consummation.

Meanwhile the early and the late summer brought round the week in which Greenhill Fair was held. This fair was frequently attended by the folk of Weatherbury.

50. The Sheep Fair
— Troy Touches His Wife's Hand

GREENHILL WAS THE NIJNI NOVGOROD of South Wessex; and the busiest, merriest, noisiest day of the whole statute number was the day of the sheep fair. This yearly gathering was upon the summit of a hill which retained in good preservation the remains of an ancient earthwork, consisting of a huge rampart and entrenchment of an oval form encircling the top of the hill, though somewhat broken

down here and there. To each of the two chief openings on opposite sides a winding road ascended,
and the level green space of ten or fifteen acres enclosed by the bank was the site of the fair. A few
permanent erections dotted the spot, but the
majority of visitors patronized canvas alone for resting and feeding under during the time of their so-
journ here.

Shepherds who attended with their flocks from
long distances started from home two or three days,
or even a week, before the fair, driving their charges
a few miles each day—not more than ten or twelve
—and resting them at night in hired fields by the
wayside at previously chosen points, where they
fed, having fasted since morning. The shepherd of
each flock marched behind, a bundle containing his
kit for the week strapped upon his shoulders, and in
his hand his crook, which he used as the staff of his
pilgrimage. Several of the sheep would get worn
and lame, and occasionally a lambing occurred on
the road. To meet these contingencies, there was
frequently provided, to accompany the flocks from
the remoter points, a pony and wagon into which
the weakly ones were taken for the remainder of the
journey.

The Weatherbury Farms, however, were no such
long distance from the hill, and those arrangements
were not necessary in their case. But the large
united flocks of Bathsheba and Farmer Boldwood
formed a valuable and imposing multitude which
demanded much attention, and on this account Gabriel, in addition to Boldwood's shepherd and Cain
Ball, accompanied them along the way, through the
decayed old town in Kingsbere, and upward to the
plateau—old George the dog of course behind them.

When the autumn sun slanted over Greenhill
this morning and lighted the dewy flat upon its
crest, nebulous clouds of dust were to be seen float-

ing between the pairs of hedges which streaked the wide prospect around in all directions. These gradually converged upon the base of the hill, and the flocks became individually visible, climbing the serpentine ways which led to the top. Thus, in a slow procession, they entered the opening to which the roads tended, multitude after multitude, horned and hornless—blue flocks and red flocks, buff flocks and brown flocks, even green and salmon-tinted flocks, according to the fancy of the colorist and custom of the farm. Men were shouting, dogs were barking, with greatest animation, but the thronging travelers in so long a journey had grown nearly indifferent to such terrors, though they still bleated piteously at the unwontedness of their experiences, a tall shepherd rising here and there in the midst of them, like a gigantic idol amid a crowd of prostrate devotees.

The great mass of sheep in the fair consisted of South Downs and the old Wessex horned breeds; to the latter class Bathsheba's and Farmer Boldwood's mainly belonged. These filled in about nine o'clock, their vermiculated horns loping gracefully on each side of their cheeks in geometrically perfect spirals, a small pink and white ear nestling under each horn. Before and behind came other varieties, perfect leopards as to the full rich substance of their coats, and only lacking the spots. There were also a few of the Oxfordshire breed, whose wool was beginning to curl like a child's flaxen hair, though surpassed in this respect by the effeminate Leicesters, which were in turn less curly than the Cotswolds. But the most picturesque by far was a small flock of Exmoors, which chanced to be there this year. Their pied faces and legs, dark and heavy horns, tresses of wool hanging round their swarthy foreheads, quite relieved the monotony of the flocks in that quarter.

All these bleating, panting, and weary thousands had entered and were penned before the morning had far advanced, the dog belonging to each flock being tied to the corner of the pen containing it. Alleys for pedestrians intersected the pens, which soon became crowded with buyers and sellers from far and near.

In another part of the hill an altogether different scene began to force itself upon the eye toward mid-day. A circular tent, of exceptional newness and size, was in course of erection here. As the day drew on, the flocks began to change hands, lightening the shepherds' responsibilities; and they turned their attention to this tent and inquired of a man at work there, whose soul seemed concentrated on tying a bothering knot in no time, what was going on.

"The Royal Hippodrome Performance of Turpin's Ride to York and the Death of Black Bess," replied the man promptly, without turning his eyes or leaving off tying.

As soon as the tent was completed the band struck up highly stimulating harmonies, and the announcement was publicly made, Black Bess standing in a conspicuous position on the outside, as a living proof, if proof were wanted, of the truth of the oracular utterances from the stage over which the people were to enter. These were so convinced by such genuine appeals to heart and understanding both that they soon began to crowd in abundantly, among the foremost being visible Jan Coggan and Joseph Poorgrass, who were holiday keeping here today.

"That's the great ruffen pushing me!" screamed a woman in front of Jan over her shoulder at him when the rush was at its fiercest.

"How can I help pushing ye when the folk behind push me?" said Coggan, in a deprecating tone, turning his head toward the aforesaid folk as far as he could without turning his body, which was jammed as in a vice.

There was a silence; then the drums and trumpets again sent forth their echoing notes. The crowd was again ecstasied, and gave another lurch in which Coggan and Poorgrass were again thrust by those behind upon the women in front.

"Oh, that helpless feymels should be at the mercy of such ruffens!" exclaimed one of these ladies again, as she swayed like a reed shaken by the wind.

"Now," said Coggan, appealing in an earnest voice to the public at large as it stood clustered about his shoulder blades, "did ye ever hear such a onreasonable woman as that? Upon my carcass, neighbors, if I could only get out of this cheese wring, the damn women might eat the show for me!"

"Don't ye lose yer temper, Jan!" implored Joseph Poorgrass, in a whisper. "They might get their men to murder us, for I think by the shine of their eyes that they be a sinful form of womankind."

Jan held his tongue, as if he had no objection to be pacified to please a friend, and they gradually reached the foot of the ladder, Poorgrass being flattened like a jumping jack, and the sixpence, for admission, which he had got ready half-an-hour earlier, having become so reeking hot in the tight squeeze of his excited hand that the woman in spangles, brazen rings set with glass diamonds, and with chalked face and shoulders, who took the money of him, hastily dropped it again from a fear that some trick had been played to burn her fingers. So they all entered, and the cloth of the tent, to the eyes of an observer on the outside, became bulged into innumerable pimples such as we observe on a sack of potatoes, caused by the various human heads, backs, and elbows at high pressure within.

At the rear of the large tent there were two small dressing tents. One of these, allotted to the male performers, was partitioned into halves by a cloth; and in one of the divisions there was sitting on the grass, pulling on a pair of jackboots, a young man whom we instantly recognize as Sergeant Troy.

Troy's appearance in this position may be briefly accounted for. The brig aboard which he was taken in Budmouth Roads was about to start on a voyage, though somewhat short of hands. Troy read the articles and joined, but before they sailed a boat was despatched across the bay to Lulwind Cove; as he had half expected, his clothes were gone. He ultimately worked his passage to the United States, where he made a precarious living in various towns as Professor of Gymnastics, Sword Exercise, Fencing, and Pugilism. A few months were sufficient to give him a distaste for this kind of life. There was a certain animal form of refinement in his nature; and however pleasant a strange condition might be whilst privations were easily warded off, it was disadvantageously coarse when money was short. There was ever present, too, the idea that he could claim a home and its comforts did he but choose to return to England and Weatherbury Farm. Whether Bathsheba thought him dead was a frequent subject of curious conjecture. To England he did return at last; but the fact of drawing nearer to Weatherbury abstracted its fascinations, and his intention to enter his old groove at that place became modified. It was with gloom he considered on landing at Liverpool that if he were to go home his reception would be of a kind very unpleasant to contemplate; for what Troy had in the way of emotion was an occasional fitful sentiment which sometimes caused him as much inconvenience as emotion of a strong and healthy kind. Bathsheba was not a woman to be made a fool of, or a woman to suffer in silence; and how could he endure existence with a spirited wife to whom at first entering he would be beholden for food and lodging? Moreover, it was not at all unlikely that his wife would fail at her farming, if she had not already done so; and he would then become liable for her maintenance: and what a life such a future of poverty with her would be, the specter of Fanny constantly between them, harrowing his temper and embittering her words! Thus, for reasons touching on distaste, regret, and shame commingled, he put off his return from day to day, and would have decided to put it off altogether if he could have found anywhere else the ready-made establishment which existed for him there.

At this time—the July preceding the September in which we find him at Greenhill Fair—he fell in with a traveling circus which was performing in the outskirts of a northern town. Troy introduced himself to the manager by taming a restive horse of the troupe, hitting a suspended apple with a pistol bullet fired from the animal's back when in full gallop, and other feats. For his merits in these—all more or less based upon his experiences as a dragoon guardsman—Troy was taken into the company, and the play of Turpin was prepared with a view of his personation of the chief character. Troy was not greatly elated by the appreciative spirit in which he was undoubtedly treated, but he thought the engagement might afford him a few weeks for consideration. It was thus carelessly, and without having formed any definite plan for the future, that Troy found himself at Greenhill Fair with the rest of the company on this day.

And now the mild autumn sun got lower, and in front of the pavilion the following incident had taken place. Bathsheba—who was driven to the fair that day by her odd man Poorgrass—had, like everyone else, read or heard the announcement that Mr. Francis, the Great Cosmopolitan Equestrian and Roughrider, would enact the part of Turpin, and she was not yet too old and careworn to be without a little curiosity to see him. This particular show was by far the largest and grandest in the fair, a horde of little shows grouping themselves under its shade like chickens around a hen. The crowd has passed in, and Boldwood, who had been watching all the day for an opportunity of speaking to her, seeing her comparatively isolated, came up to her side.

"I hope the sheep have done well today, Mrs. Troy?" he said nervously.

"Oh, yes, thank you," said Bathsheba, color springing up in the center of her cheeks. "I was fortunate enough to sell them all just as we got upon the hill, so we hadn't to pen at all."

"And now you are entirely at leisure?"

"Yes, except that I have to see one more dealer in two hours' time: otherwise I should be going home. I was looking at this large tent and the announcement. Have you ever seen the play of 'Turpin's Ride to York'? Turpin was a real man, was he not?"

"Oh, yes, perfectly true—all of it. Indeed, I think I've heard Jan Coggan say that a relation of his knew Tom King, Turpin's friend, quite well."

"Coggan is rather given to strange stories connected with his relations, we must remember. I hope they can all be believed."

"Yes, yes; we know Coggan. But Turpin is true enough. You have never seen it played, I suppose?"

"Never. I was not allowed to go into these places when I was young. Hark! What's that prancing? How they shout!"

"Black Bess just started off, I suppose. Am I right in supposing you would like to see the performance,

Mrs. Troy? Please excuse my mistake, if it is one; but if you would like to, I'll get a seat for you with pleasure." Perceiving that she hesitated, he added, "I myself shall not stay to see it: I've seen it before."

Now Bathsheba did care a little to see the show, and had only withheld her feet from the ladder because she feared to go in alone. She had been hoping that Oak might appear, whose assistance in such cases was always accepted as an inalienable right, but Oak was nowhere to be seen; and hence it was that she said, "Then if you will just look in first, to see if there's room, I think I will go in for a minute or two."

And so a short time after this Bathsheba appeared in the tent with Boldwood at her elbow, who, taking her to a "reserved" seat, again withdrew.

This feature consisted of one raised bench in a very conspicuous part of the circle, covered with red cloth, and floored with a piece of carpet, and Bathsheba immediately found, to her confusion, that she was the single reserved individual in the tent, the rest of the crowded spectators, one and all, standing on their legs on the borders of the arena, where they got twice as good a view of the performance for half the money. Hence as many eyes were turned upon her, enthroned alone in this place of honor, against a scarlet background, as upon the ponies and clown who were engaged in preliminary exploits in the center, Turpin not having yet appeared. Once there, Bathsheba was forced to make the best of it and remain: she sat down, spreading her skirts with some dignity over the unoccupied space on each side of her, and giving a new and feminine aspect to the pavilion. In a few minutes she noticed the fat red nape of Coggan's neck among those standing just below her, and Joseph Poorgrass' saintly profile a little further on.

The interior was shadowy with a peculiar shade. The strange luminous semiopacities of fine autumn afternoons and eves intensified into Rembrandt effects the few yellow sunbeams which came through holes and divisions in the canvas, and spirited like jets of gold dust across the dusky blue atmosphere of haze pervading the tent, until they alighted on inner surfaces of cloth opposite, and shone like little lamps suspended there.

Troy, on peeping from his dressing tent through a slit for a reconnoiter before entering, saw his unconscious wife on high before him as described, sitting as queen of the tournament. He started back in utter confusion, for although his disguise effectually concealed his personality, he instantly felt that she would be sure to recognize his voice. He had several times during the day thought of the possibility of some Weatherbury person or other appearing and recognizing him; but he had taken the risk carelessly. If they see me, let them, he had said. But here was Bathsheba in her own person; and the reality of the scene was so much intenser than any of his prefigurings that he felt he had not half enough considered the point.

She looked so charming and fair that his cool mood about Weatherbury people was changed. He had not expected her to exercise this power over him in the twinkling of an eye. Should he go on and care nothing? He could not bring himself to do that. Beyond a politic wish to remain unknown, there suddenly arose in him now a sense of shame at the possibility that his attractive young wife, who already despised him, should despise him more by discovering him in so mean a condition after so long a time. He actually blushed at the thought, and was vexed beyond measure that his sentiments of dislike toward Weatherbury should have led him to dally about the country in this way.

But Troy was never more clever than when absolutely at his wits' end. He hastily thrust aside the curtain dividing his own little dressing space from that of the manager and proprietor, who now appeared as the individual called Tom King as far down as his waist, and as the aforesaid respectable manager thence to his toes.

"Here's the devil to pay!" said Troy.

"How's that?"

"Why, there's a blackguard creditor in the tent I don't want to see, who'll discover me and nab me as sure as Satan if I open my mouth. What's to be done?"

"You must appear now, I think."

"I can't."

"But the play must proceed."

"Do you give out that Turpin has got a bad cold, and can't speak his part, but that he'll perform it just the same without speaking."

The proprietor shook his head.

"Anyhow, play or no play, I won't open my mouth," said Troy firmly.

"Very well, then let me see. I tell you how we'll manage," said the other, who perhaps felt it would be extremely awkward to offend his leading man just at this time. "I won't tell 'em anything about your keeping silence; go on with the piece and say nothing, doing what you can by a judicious wink now and then, and a few indomitable nods in the heroic places, you know. They'll never find out that the speeches are omitted."

This seemed feasible enough, for Turpin's speeches were not many or long, the fascination of the piece lying entirely in the action; and accordingly the play began, and at the appointed time Black Bess leapt into the grassy circle amid the plaudits of the spectators. At the turnpike scene, where Bess and Turpin are hotly pursued at midnight by the officers, and the half-awake gatekeeper in his tasseled nightcap denies that any horseman has passed, Coggan uttered a broadchested "Well done!" which could be heard all over the fair above the bleating, and Poorgrass smiled delightedly with a nice sense of dramatic contrast between our hero, who coolly leaps the gate, and halting justice in the form of his enemies, who must needs pull up cumbersomely and wait to be let through. At the death of Tom King, he could not refrain from seizing Coggan by the hand, and whispering, with tears in his eyes, "Of course he's not really shot, Jan—only seemingly!" And when the last sad scene came on, and the body of the gallant and faithful Bess had to be carried out on a shutter by twelve volunteers from among the spectators, nothing could restrain Poorgrass from lending a hand, exclaiming, as he asked Jan to join him, " 'Twill be something to tell of at Warren's in future years, Jan, and hand down to our children." For many a year in Weatherbury, Joseph told, with the air of a man who had had experiences in his time, that he touched with his own hand the hoof of Bess as she lay upon the board upon his shoulder. If, as some thinkers hold, immortality consists in being enshrined in others' memories, then did Black Bess become immortal that day if she never had done so before.

Meanwhile Troy had added a few touches to his ordinary makeup for the character, the more effectually to disguise himself, and though he had felt faint qualms on first entering, the metamorphosis effected by judiciously "lining" his face with a wire rendered him safe from the eyes of Bathsheba and her men. Nevertheless, he was relieved when it was got through.

There was a second performance in the evening, and the tent was lighted up. Troy had taken his part very quietly this time, venturing to introduce a few speeches on occasion; and was just concluding it when, whilst standing at the edge of the circle contiguous to the first row of spectators, he observed within a yard of him the eye of a man darted keenly into his side features. Troy hastily shifted his position, after having recognized in the scrutineer the knavish bailiff Pennyways, his wife's sworn enemy, who still hung about the outskirts of Weatherbury.

At first Troy resolved to take no notice and abide by circumstances. That he had been recognized by this man was highly probable; yet there was room for a doubt. Then the great objection he had felt to allowing news of his proximity to precede him to Weatherbury in the event of his return, based on a feeling that knowledge of his present occupation would discredit him still further in his wife's eyes, returned in full force. Moreover, should he resolve not to return at all, a tale of his being alive and being in the neighborhood would be awkward; and he was anxious to acquire a knowledge of his wife's temporal affairs before deciding which to do.

In this dilemma Troy at once went out to reconnoiter. It occurred to him that to find Pennyways, and make a friend of him if possible, would be a very wise act. He had put on a thick beard borrowed from the establishment, and in this he wandered about the fair field. It was now almost dark, and respectable people were getting their carts and gigs ready to go home.

The largest refreshment booth in the fair was provided by an innkeeper from a neighboring town. This was considered an unexceptionable place for obtaining the necessary food and rest: Host Trencher (as he was jauntily called by the local newspaper) being a substantial man of high repute for catering through all the country round. The tent was divided into first- and second-class compart-

ments, and at the end of the first-class division was a
yet further enclosure for the most exclusive, fenced
off from the body of the tent by a luncheon bar, behind which the host himself stood, bustling about
in white apron and shirtsleeves, and looking as if
he had never lived anywhere but under canvas all
his life. In these penetralia were chairs and a table,
which, on candles being lighted, made quite a cosy
and luxurious show, with an urn, plated tea and
coffee pots, china teacups, and plum cakes.

Troy stood at the entrance to the booth, where a
Gypsy woman was frying pancakes over a little fire
of sticks and selling them at a penny a piece, and
looked over the heads of the people within. He
could see nothing of Pennyways, but he soon discerned Bathsheba through an opening into the reserved space at the further end. Troy thereupon retreated, went round the tent into the darkness, and
listened. He could hear Bathsheba's voice immediately inside the canvas; she was conversing with
a man. A warmth overspread his face: surely she was
not so unprincipled as to flirt in a fair! He wondered
if, then, she reckoned upon his death as an absolute certainty. To get at the root of the matter,
Troy took a penknife from his pocket and softly
made two little cuts crosswise in the cloth, which,
by folding back the corners, left a hole the size of
a wafer. Close to this he placed his face, withdrawing it again in a movement of surprise; for his eye
had been within twelve inches of the top of Bathsheba's head. It was too near to be convenient. He
made another hole a little to one side and lower
down, in a shaded place beside her chair, from which
it was easy and safe to survey her by looking horizontally.

Troy took in the scene completely now. She was
leaning back, sipping a cup of tea that she held in
her hand, and the owner of the male voice was

Boldwood, who had apparently just brought the cup to her. Bathsheba, being in a negligent mood, leant so idly against the canvas that it was pressed to the shape of her shoulder, and she was, in fact, as good as in Troy's arms; and he was obliged to keep his breast carefully backward that she might not feel its warmth through the cloth as he gazed in.

Troy found unexpected chords of feeling to be stirred again within him as they had been stirred earlier in the day. She was handsome as ever, and she was his. It was some minutes before he could counteract his sudden wish to go in, and claim her. Then he thought how the proud girl who had always looked down upon him even whilst it was to love him, would hate him on discovering him to be a strolling player. Were he to make himself known, that chapter of his life must at all risks be kept forever from her and from the Weatherbury people, or his name would be a byword throughout the parish. He would be nicknamed "Turpin" as long as he lived. Assuredly before he could claim her these few past months of his existence must be entirely blotted out.

"Shall I get you another cup before you start, ma'am?" said Farmer Boldwood.

"Thank you," said Bathsheba. "But I must be going at once. It was great neglect in that man to keep me waiting here till so late. I should have gone two hours ago, if it had not been for him. I had no idea of coming in here; but there's nothing so refreshing as a cup of tea, though I should never have got one if you hadn't helped me."

Troy scrutinized her cheek as lit by the candles, and watched each varying shade thereon, and the white shell-like sinuosities of her little ear. She took out her purse and was insisting to Boldwood on paying for her tea for herself, when at this moment

Pennyways entered the tent. Troy trembled: here was his scheme for respectability endangered at once. He was about to leave his hole of espial, attempt to follow Pennyways, and find out if the ex-bailiff had recognized him, when he was arrested by the conversation, and found he was too late.

"Excuse me, ma'am," said Pennyways; "I've some private information for your ear alone."

"I cannot hear it now," she said coldly. That Bathsheba could not endure this man was evident; in fact, he was continually coming to her with some tale or other, by which he might creep into favor at the expense of persons maligned.

"I'll write it down," said Pennyways confidently. He stooped over the table, pulled a leaf from a warped pocketbook, and wrote upon the paper, in a round hand—

"Your husband is here. I've seen him. Who's the fool now?"

This he folded small, and handed toward her. Bathsheba would not read it; she would not even put out her hand to take it. Pennyways, then, with a laugh of derision, tossed it into her lap, and, turning away, left her.

From the words and action of Pennyways, Troy, though he had not been able to see what the ex-bailiff wrote, had not a moment's doubt that the note referred to him. Nothing that he could think of could be done to check the exposure. "Curse my luck!" he whispered, and added imprecations which rustled in the gloom like a pestilent wind. Meanwhile Boldwood said, taking up the note from her lap—

"Don't you wish to read it, Mrs. Troy? If not, I'll destroy it."

"Oh, well," said Bathsheba carelessly, "perhaps it is unjust not to read it; but I can guess what it is about. He wants me to recommend him, or it is to tell me of some little scandal or another connected with my work people. He's always doing that."

Bathsheba held the note in her right hand. Boldwood handed toward her a plate of cut bread-and-butter; when, in order to take a slice, she put the note into her left hand, where she was still holding the purse, and then allowed her hand to drop beside her close to the canvas. The moment had come for saving his game, and Troy impulsively felt that he would play the card. For yet another time he looked at the fair hand, and saw the pink fingertips, and the blue veins of the wrist, encircled by a bracelet of coral chippings which she wore: how familiar it all was to him! Then, with the lightning action in which he was such an adept, he noiselessly slipped his hand under the bottom of the tentcloth, which was far from being pinned tightly down, lifted it a little way keeping his eye to the hole, snatched the note from her fingers, dropped the canvas, and ran away in the gloom toward the bank and ditch, smiling at the scream of astonishment which burst from her. Troy then slid down on the outside of the rampart, hastened round in the bottom of the entrenchment to a distance of a hundred yards, ascended again, and crossed boldly in a slow walk toward the front entrance of the tent. His object was now to get to Pennyways, and prevent a repetition of the announcement until such time as he should choose.

Troy reached the tent door, and standing among the groups there gathered, looked anxiously for Pennyways, evidently not wishing to make himself prominent by inquiring for him. One or two men were speaking of a daring attempt that had just been made to rob a young lady by lifting the canvas of the tent beside her. It was supposed that the rogue had imagined a slip of paper which she held in her hand to be a bank note, for he had seized it, and made off with it, leaving her purse behind. His

chagrin and disappointment at discovering its
worthlessness would be a good joke, it was said.
However, the occurrence seemed to have become
known to few, for it had not interrupted a fiddler,
who had lately begun playing by the door of the
tent, nor the four bowed old men with grim countenances and walking sticks in hand, who were dancing "Major Malley's Reel" to the tune. Behind
these stood Pennyways. Troy glided up to him,
beckoned, and whispered a few words; and with a
mutual glance of concurrence the two men went
into the night together.

51. *Bathsheba Talks with Her Outrider*

THE ARRANGEMENT for getting back again to Weatherbury had been that Oak should take the place
of Poorgrass in Bathsheba's conveyance and drive
her home, it being discovered late in the afternoon
that Joseph was suffering from his old complaint, a
multiplying eye, and was, therefore, hardly trustworthy as coachman and protector to a woman. But
Oak had found himself so occupied, and was full
of so many cares relative to those portions of Boldwood's flocks that were not disposed of, that Bathsheba, without telling Oak or anybody, resolved to
drive home herself, as she had many times done
from Casterbridge Market, and trust to her good
angel for performing the journey unmolested. But

having fallen in with Farmer Boldwood accidentally
(on her part at least) at the refreshment tent, she
found it impossible to refuse his offer to ride on
horseback beside her as escort. It had grown twilight
before she was aware, but Boldwood assured her
that there was no cause for uneasiness, as the moon
would be up in half-an-hour.

Immediately after the incident in the tent she
had risen to go—now absolutely alarmed and really
grateful for her old lover's protection—though regretting Gabriel's absence, whose company she
would have much preferred, as being more proper
as well as more pleasant, since he was her own man-
aging man and servant. This, however, could not be
helped; she would not, on any consideration, treat
Boldwood harshly, having once already ill-used him,
and the moon having risen, and the gig being ready,
she drove across the hilltop in the wending ways
which led downward—to oblivious obscurity, as it
seemed, for the moon and the hill it flooded with
light were in appearance on a level, the rest of the
world lying as a vast shady concave between them.
Boldwood mounted his horse, and followed in close
attendance behind. Thus they descended into the
lowlands, and the sounds of those left on the hill
came like voices from the sky, and the lights were
as those of a camp in heaven. They soon passed the
merry stragglers in the immediate vicinity of the
hill, traversed Kingsbere, and got upon the high
road.

The keen instincts of Bathsheba had perceived
that the farmer's staunch devotion to herself was
still undiminished, and she sympathized deeply. The
sight had quite depressed her this evening; had reminded her of her folly; she wished anew, as she had
wished many months ago, for some means of making reparation for her fault. Hence her pity for
the man who so persistently loved on to his own in-

jury and permanent gloom had betrayed Bathsheba into an injudicious considerateness of manner, which appeared almost like tenderness, and gave new vigor to the exquisite dream of a Jacob's seven years' service in poor Boldwood's mind.

He soon found an excuse for advancing from his position in the rear, and rode close by her side. They had gone two or three miles in the moonlight, speaking desultorily across the wheel of her gig concerning the fair, farming, Oak's usefulness to them both, and other indifferent subjects, when Boldwood said suddenly and simply—

"Mrs. Troy, you will marry again some day?"

This point-blank query unmistakably confused her, and it was not till a minute or more had elapsed that she said, "I have not seriously thought of any such subject."

"I quite understand that. Yet your late husband has been dead nearly one year, and—"

"You forget that his death was never absolutely proved, and may not have taken place; so that I may not be really a widow," she said, catching at the straw of escape that the fact afforded.

"Not absolutely proved, perhaps, but it was proved circumstantially. A man saw him drowning, too. No reasonable person has any doubt of his death; nor have you, ma'am, I should imagine."

"Oh, yes I have, or I should have acted differently," she said, gently. "From the first I have had a strange unaccountable feeling that he could not have perished. But I have been able to explain that in several ways since. Even were I half persuaded that I shall see him no more, I am far from thinking of marriage with another. I should be very contemptible to indulge in such a thought."

They were silent now awhile, and having struck into an unfrequented track across a common, the creaks of Boldwood's saddle and her gig springs were all the sounds to be heard. Boldwood ended the pause.

"Do you remember when I carried you fainting in my arms into the King's Arms, in Casterbridge? Every dog has his day: that was mine."

"I know—I know it all," she said, hurriedly.

"I, for one, shall never cease regretting that events so fell out as to deny you to me."

"I, too, am very sorry," she said, and then checked herself. "I mean, you know, I am sorry you thought I—"

"I have always this dreary pleasure in thinking over those past times with you—that I was something to you before *he* was anything, and that you belonged *almost* to me. But, of course, that's nothing. You never liked me."

"I did; and respected you, too."

"Do you now?"

"Yes."

"Which?"

"How do you mean which?"

"Do you like me, or do you respect me?"

"I don't know—at least, I cannot tell you. It is difficult for a woman to define her feelings in language which is chiefly made by men to express theirs. My treatment of you was thoughtless, inexcusable, wicked! I shall eternally regret it. If there had been anything I could have done to make amends I would most gladly have done it—there was nothing on earth I so longed to do as to repair the error. But that was not possible."

"Don't blame yourself—you were not so far in the wrong as you suppose. Bathsheba, suppose you had real complete proof that you are what, in fact, you are—a widow—would you repair the old wrong to me by marrying me?"

"I cannot say. I shouldn't yet, at any rate."

"But you might at some future time of your life?"

"Oh, yes, I might at some time."

"Well, then, do you know that without further proof of any kind you may marry again in about six years from the present—subject to nobody's objection or blame?"

"Oh, yes," she said, quickly. "I know all that. But don't talk of it—seven or six years—where may we all be by that time?"

"They will soon glide by, and it will seem an astonishingly short time to look back upon when they are past—much less than to look forward to now."

"Yes, yes; I have found that in my own experience."

"Now, listen once more," Boldwood pleaded. "If I wait that time, will you marry me? You own that you owe me amends—let that be your way of making them."

"But, Mr. Boldwood—six years—"

"Do you want to be the wife of any other man?"

"No indeed! I mean, that I don't like to talk about this matter now. Perhaps it is not proper, and I ought not to allow it. Let us drop it. My husband may be living, as I said."

"Of course, I'll drop the subject if you wish. But propriety has nothing to do with reasons. I am a middle-aged man, willing to protect you for the remainder of our lives. On your side, at least, there is no passion or blamable haste—on mine, perhaps, there is. But I can't help seeing that if you choose from a feeling of pity, and, as you say, a wish to make amends, to make a bargain with me for a far ahead time—an agreement which will set all things right and make me happy, late though it may be— there is no fault to be found with you as a woman. Hadn't I the first place beside you? Haven't you been almost mine once already? Surely you can say to me as much as this, you will have me back again should circumstances permit? Now, pray speak! O Bathsheba, promise—it is only a little promise —that if you marry again, you will marry me!"

His tone was so excited that she almost feared him at this moment, even whilst she sympathized. It was a simple physical fear—the weak of the strong; there was no emotional aversion or inner repugnance. She said, with some distress in her voice, for she remembered vividly his outburst on the Yalbury Road, and shrank from a repetition of his anger:

"I will never marry another man whilst you wish me to be your wife, whatever comes—but to say more—you have taken me so by surprise—"

"But let it stand in these simple words—that in six years' time you will be my wife? Unexpected accidents we'll not mention, because those, of course, must be given way to. Now, this time I know you will keep your word."

"That's why I hesitate to give it."

"But do give it! Remember the past, and be kind."

She breathed; and then said mournfully: "Oh, what shall I do? I don't love you, and I much fear that I never shall love you as much as a woman ought to love a husband. If you, sir, know that, and I can yet give you happiness by a mere promise to marry at the end of six years, if my husband should not come back, it is a great honor to me. And if you value such an act of friendship from a woman who doesn't esteem herself as she did, and has little love left, why I—I will—"

"Promise!"

"—Consider, if I cannot promise soon."

"But soon is perhaps never?"

"Oh, no, it is not! I mean soon. Christmas, we'll say."

"Christmas!" He said nothing further till he added: "Well, I'll say no more to you about it till that time."

Bathsheba was in a very peculiar state of mind, which showed how entirely the soul is the slave of the body, the ethereal spirit dependent for its quality upon the tangible flesh and blood. It is hardly too much to say that she felt coerced by a force stronger than her own will, not only into the act of promising upon this singularly remote and vague matter, but into the emotion of fancying that she ought to promise. When the weeks intervening between the night of this conversation and Christmas day began perceptibly to diminish, her anxiety and perplexity increased.

One day she was led by an accident into an oddly confidential dialogue with Gabriel about her difficulty. It afforded her a little relief—of a dull and cheerless kind. They were auditing accounts, and something occurred in the course of their labors, which led Oak to say, speaking of Boldwood, "He'll never forget you, ma'am, never."

Then out came her trouble before she was aware; and she told him how she had again got into the toils; what Boldwood had asked her, and how he was expecting her assent. "The most mournful reason of all for my agreeing to it," she said sadly, "and the true reason why I think to do so for good or for evil, is this—it is a thing I have not breathed to a living soul as yet—I believe that if I don't give my word, he'll go out of his mind."

"Really, do ye?" said Gabriel, gravely.

"I believe this," she continued, with reckless frankness, "and Heaven knows I say it in a spirit the very reverse of vain, for I am grieved and troubled to my soul about it—I believe I hold that man's future in my hand. His career depends entirely upon my treatment of him. Oh, Gabriel, I tremble at my responsibility, for it is terrible!"

"Well, I think this much, ma'am, as I told you years ago," said Oak, "that his life is a total blank

whenever he isn't hoping for 'ee; but I can't suppose—I hope that nothing so dreadful hangs on to
it as you fancy. His natural manner has always
been dark and strange, you know. But since the
case is so sad and oddlike, why don't ye give the
conditional promise? I think I would."

"But is it right? Some rash acts of my past life
have taught me that a watched woman must have
very much circumspection to retain only a very little credit, and I do want and long to be discreet in
this! And six years—why we may all be in our
graves by that time, even if Mr. Troy does not come
back again, which he may not impossibly do! Such
thoughts give a sort of absurdity to the scheme.
Now, isn't it preposterous, Gabriel? However he
came to dream of it, I cannot think. But is it
wrong? You know—you are older than I."

"Eight years older, ma'am."

"Yes, eight years—and is it wrong?"

"Perhaps it would be an uncommon agreement
for a man and woman to make: I don't see anything really wrong about it," said Oak, slowly. "In
fact the very thing that makes it doubtful if you
ought to marry en under any condition, that is,
your not caring about him—for I may suppose—"

"Yes, you may suppose that love is wanting," she
said shortly. "Love is an utterly bygone, sorry,
wornout, miserable thing with me—for him or any-
one else."

"Well, your want of love seems to me the one
thing that takes away harm from such an agreement with him. If wild heat had to do wi' it, making ye long to overcome the awkwardness about
your husband's vanishing, it mid be wrong; but a
cold-hearted agreement to oblige a man seems different, somehow. The real sin, ma'am, in my
mind, lies in thinking of ever wedding wi' a man
you don't love honest and true."

"That I'm willing to pay the penalty of," said Bathsheba, firmly. "You know, Gabriel, that is what I cannot get off my conscience—that I once seriously injured him in sheer idleness. If I had never played a trick upon him, he would never have wanted to marry me. Oh, if I could only pay some heavy damages in money to him for the harm I did, and so get the sin off my soul that way! . . . Well, there's the debt, which can only be discharged in one way, and I believe I am bound to do it if it honestly lies in my power, without any consideration of my own future at all. When a rake gambles away his expectations, the fact that it is an inconvenient debt doesn't make him the less liable. I've been a rake, and the single point I ask you is, considering that my own scruples, and the fact that in the eye of the law my husband is only missing, will keep any man from marrying me until seven years have passed—am I free to entertain such an idea, even though 'tis a sort of penance—for it will be that? I *hate* the act of marriage under such circumstances, and the class of women I should seem to belong to by doing it!"

"It seems to me that all depends upon whe'r you think, as everybody else do, that your husband is dead."

"I shall get to, I suppose, because I cannot help feeling what would have brought him back long before this time if he had lived."

"Well, then, in a religious sense you will be as free to *think* o' marrying again as any real widow of one year's standing. But why don't ye ask Mr. Thirdly's advice on how to treat Mr. Boldwood?"

"No. When I want a broad-minded opinion for general enlightenment, distinct from special advice, I never go to a man who deals in the subject professionally. So I like the parson's opinion on law, the lawyer's on doctoring, the doctor's on busi ness, and my businessman's—that is, yours—on morals."

"And on love—"

"My own."

"I'm afraid there's a hitch in that argument," said Oak, with a grave smile.

She did not reply at once, and then saying, "Good evening, Mr. Oak," went away.

She had spoken frankly, and neither asked nor expected any reply from Gabriel more satisfactory than that she had obtained. Yet in the centermost parts of her complicated heart there existed at this minute a little pang of disappointment, for a reason she would not allow herself to recognize. Oak had not once wished her free that he might marry her himself—had not once said, "I could wait for you as well as he." That was the insect sting. Not that she would have listened to any such hypothesis. Oh, no—for wasn't she saying all the time that such thoughts of the future were improper, and wasn't Gabriel far too poor a man to speak sentiment to her? Yet he might have just hinted about that old love of his, and asked, in a playful offhand way, if he might speak of it. It would have seemed pretty and sweet, if no more; and then she would have shown how kind and inoffensive a woman's "No" can sometimes be. But to give such cool advice—the very advice she had asked for—it ruffled our heroine all the afternoon.

52. *Converging Courses*

CHRISTMAS EVE CAME, and a party that Boldwood was to give in the evening was the great subject of talk in Weatherbury. It was not that the rarity of Christmas parties in the parish made this one a wonder, but that Boldwood should be the giver. The announcement had had an abnormal and incongruous sound, as if one should hear of croquet playing in a cathedral aisle, or that some much-respected judge was going upon the stage. That the party was intended to be a truly jovial one there was no room for doubt. A large bough of mistletoe had been brought from the woods that day and suspended in the hall of the bachelor's home. Holly and ivy had followed in armfuls. From six that morning till past noon the huge woodfire in the kitchen roared and sparkled at its highest, the kettle, the saucepan, and the three-legged pot appearing in the midst of the flames like Shadrach, Meshach, and Abednego; moreover, roasting and basting operations were continually carried on in front of the genial blaze.

As it grew later the fire was made up in the large long hall into which the staircase descended, and all encumbrances were cleared out for dancing. The log which was to form the back-brand of the evening fire was the uncleft trunk of a tree, so unwieldy that it could be neither brought nor rolled to its place; and accordingly two men were to be observed dragging and heaving it in by chains and levers as the hour of assembly drew near.

In spite of all this, the spirit of revelry was wanting in the atmosphere of the house. Such a thing had never been attempted before by its owner, and it was now done as by a wrench. Intended gaieties would insist upon appearing like solemn grandeurs, the organization of the whole effort was carried out coldly by hirelings, and a shadow seemed to move about the rooms, saying that the proceedings were unnatural to the place and the lone man who lived therein, and hence not good.

II

Bathsheba was at this time in her room, dressing for the event. She had called for candles, and Liddy entered and placed one on each side of her mistress' glass.

"Don't go away, Liddy," said Bathsheba, almost timidly. "I am foolishly agitated—I cannot tell why. I wish I had not been obliged to go to this dance; but there's no escaping now. I have not spoken to Mr. Boldwood since the autumn, when I promised to see him at Christmas on business, but I had no idea there was to be anything of this kind."

"But I would go now," said Liddy, who was going with her; for Boldwood had been indiscriminate in his invitations.

"Yes, I shall make my appearance, of course," said Bathsheba. "But I am *the cause* of the party, and that upsets me!—Don't tell, Liddy."

"Oh, no, ma'am. You the cause of it, ma'am?"

"Yes. I am the reason of the party—I. If it had not been for me, there would never have been one. I can't explain any more—there's no more to be explained. I wish I had never seen Weatherbury."

"That's wicked of you—to wish to be worse off than you are."

"No, Liddy. I have never been free from trouble since I have lived here, and this party is likely to bring me more. Now, fetch my black silk dress, and see how it sits upon me."

"But you will leave off that, surely, ma'am? You have been a widow lady fourteen months, and ought to brighten up a little on such a night as this."

"Is it necessary? No; I will appear as usual, for if I were to wear any light dress people would say things about me, and I should seem to be rejoicing when I am solemn all the time. The party doesn't suit me a bit; but never mind, stay and help to finish me off."

III

Boldwood was dressing also at this hour. A tailor from Casterbridge was with him, assisting him in the operation of trying on a new coat that had just been brought home.

Never had Boldwood been so fastidious, unreasonable about the fit, and generally difficult to please. The tailor walked round and round him, tugged at the waist, pulled the sleeve, pressed out the collar, and for the first time in his experience Boldwood was not bored. Times had been when the farmer had exclaimed against all such niceties as childish, but now no philosophic or hasty rebuke whatever was provoked by this man for attaching as much importance to a crease in the coat as to an earthquake in South America. Boldwood at last expressed himself nearly satisfied, and paid the bill, the tailor passing out of the door just as Oak came in to report progress for the day.

"Oh, Oak," said Boldwood. "I shall of course see you here tonight. Make yourself merry. I am determined that neither expense nor trouble shall be spared."

"I'll try to be here, sir, though perhaps it may not be very early," said Gabriel, quietly. "I am glad indeed to see such a change in 'ee from what it used to be."

"Yes—I must own it—I am bright tonight: cheerful and more than cheerful—so much so that I am almost sad again with the sense that all of it is passing away. And sometimes, when I am excessively hopeful and blithe, a trouble is looming in the distance: so that I often get to look upon gloom in me with content, and to fear a happy mood. Still this may be absurd—I feel that it is absurd. Perhaps my day is dawning at last.

"I hope it 'ill be a long and fair one."

"Thank you—thank you. Yet perhaps my cheerfulness rests on a slender hope. And yet I trust my hope. It is faith, not hope. I think this time I reckon with my host. Oak, my hands are a little shaky, or something: I can't tie this neckerchief properly. Perhaps you will tie it for me. The fact is, I have not been well lately, you know."

"I am sorry to hear that, sir."

"Oh, it's nothing. I want it done as well as you can, please. Is there any late knot in fashion, Oak?"

"I don't know, sir," said Oak. His tone had sunk to sadness.

Boldwood approached Gabriel, and as Oak tied the neckerchief the farmer went on feverishly—

"Does a woman keep her promise, Gabriel?"

"If it is not inconvenient to her she may."

"—Or rather an implied promise."

"I won't answer for her implying," said Oak, with faint bitterness. "That's a word as full o' holes as a sieve with them."

"Oak, don't talk like that. You have got quite cynical lately—how is it? We seem to have shifted our positions: I have become the young and hopeful man, and you the old and unbelieving one. However, does a woman keep a promise, not to marry, but to enter on an engagement to marry at some time? Now you know women better than I— tell me."

"I am afeard you honor my understanding too much. However, she may keep such a promise, if it is made with an honest meaning to repair a wrong."

"It has not gone far yet, but I think it will soon —yes, I know it will," he said, in an impulsive whisper. "I have pressed her upon the subject, and she inclines to be kind to me, and to think of me as a husband at a long future time, and that's enough for me. How can I expect more? She has a notion that a woman should not marry within seven years of her husband's disappearance—that her own self shouldn't, I mean—because his body was not found. It may be merely this legal reason which influences her, or it may be a religious one, but she is reluctant to talk on the point. Yet she has promised—implied—that she will ratify an engagement tonight."

"Seven years," murmured Oak.

"No, no—it's no such thing!" he said, with impatience. "Five years, nine months, and a few days. Fifteen months nearly have passed since he vanished, and is there anything so wonderful in an engagement of little more than five years?"

"It seems long in a forward view. Don't build too much upon such promises, sir. Remember, you have once be'n deceived. Her meaning may be good; but there—she's young yet."

"Deceived? Never!" said Boldwood, vehemently. "She never promised me at that first time, and hence she did not break her promise! If she promises me, she'll marry me. Bathsheba is a woman to her word."

IV

Troy was sitting in a corner of The White Hart tavern at Casterbridge, smoking and drinking a steaming mixture from a glass. A knock was given at the door, and Pennyways entered.

"Well, have you seen him?" Troy inquired, pointing to a chair.

"Boldwood?"

"No—Lawyer Long."

"He wadn' at home. I went there first, too."

"That's a nuisance."

" 'Tis rather, I suppose."

"Yet I don't see that, because a man appears to be drowned and was not, he should be liable for anything. I shan't ask any lawyer—not I."

"But that's not it, exactly. If a man changes his name and so forth, and takes steps to deceive the world and his own wife, he's a cheat, and that in the eye of the law is ayless a rogue, and that is ayless a lammocken vagabond; and that's a punishable situation."

"Ha-ha! Well done, Pennyways." Troy had laughed, but it was with some anxiety that he said, "Now, what I want to know is this, do you think there's really anything going on between her and Boldwood? Upon my soul, I should never have believed it! How she must detest me! Have you found out whether she has encouraged him?"

"I haen't been able to learn. There's a deal of feeling on his side seemingly, but I don't answer for her. I didn't know a word about any such thing till yesterday, and all I heard then was that she was gwine to the party at his house tonight. This is the first time she has ever gone there, they say. And they say that she've not so much as spoke to him since they were at Greenhill Fair: but what can folk believe o't? However, she's not fond of him—quite offish and quite careless, I know."

"I'm not so sure of that. . . . She's a handsome woman, Pennyways, is she not? Own that you never saw a finer or more splendid creature in your life. Upon my honor, when I set eyes upon her that day I wondered what I could have been made of to be able to leave her by herself so long. And then I was hampered with that bothering show, which I'm free of at last, thank the stars." He smoked on awhile, and then added, "How did she look when you passed by yesterday?"

"Oh, she took no great heed of me, ye may well fancy; but she looked well enough, far's I know. Just flashed her haughty eyes upon my poor scram body, and then let them go past me to what was yond, much as if I'd been no more than a leafless tree. She had just got off her mare to look at the last wring-down of cider for the year; she had been riding, and so her colors were up and her breath rather quick, so that her bosom plimmed and fell —plimmed and fell—every time plain to my eye. Aye, and there were the fellers round her wringing down the cheese and bustling about and saying, 'Ware o' the pommy, ma'am: 'twill spoil yer gown.' 'Never mind me,' says she. Then Gabe brought some of the new cider, and she must needs go drinking it through a strawmote, and not in a nateral way at all. 'Liddy,' says she, 'bring indoors a few gallons, and I'll make some cider wine.' Sergeant, I was no more to her than a morsel of scroff in the fuelhouse!"

"I must go and find her out at once—Oh, yes, I see that—I must go. Oak is head man still, isn't he?"

"Yes, 'a b'lieve. And at Little Weatherbury Farm too. He manages everything."

" 'Twill puzzle him to manage her, or any other man of his compass!"

"I don't know about that. She can't do without him, and knowing it well he's pretty independent. And she've a few soft corners to her mind, though I've never been able to get into one, the devil's in't!"

"Ah, baily, she's a notch above you, and you must own it: a higher class of animal—a finer tissue. However, stick to me, and neither this haughty goddess, dashing piece of womanhood, Juno-wife of mine (Juno was a goddess, you know), nor anybody else shall hurt you. But all this wants looking into, I perceive. What with one thing and another, I see that my work is well cut out for me."

V

"How do I look tonight, Liddy?" said Bathsheba, giving a final adjustment to her dress before leaving the glass.

"I never saw you look so well before. Yes—I'll tell you when you looked like it—that night, a year and a half ago, when you came in so wildlike, and scolded us for making remarks about you and Mr. Troy."

"Everybody will think that I am setting myself to captivate Mr. Boldwood, I suppose," she murmured. "At least they'll say so. Can't my hair be brushed down a little flatter? I dread going—yet I dread the risk of wounding him by staying away."

"Anyhow, ma'am, you can't well be dressed plainer than you are, unless you go in sackcloth at once. 'Tis your excitement is what makes you look so noticeable tonight."

"I don't know what's the matter, I feel wretched at one time, and buoyant at another. I wish I could have continued quite alone as I have been for the last year or so, with no hopes and no fears, and no pleasure and no grief."

"Now just suppose Mr. Boldwood should ask you —only just suppose it—to run away with him, what would you do, ma'am?"

"Liddy—none of that," said Bathsheba, gravely. "Mind, I won't hear joking on any such matter. Do you hear?"

"I beg pardon, ma'am. But knowing what rum things we women be, I just said—however, I won't speak of it again."

"No marrying for me yet for many a year; if ever, 'twill be for reasons very, very different from those you think, or others will believe! Now get my cloak, for it is time to go."

VI

"Oak," said Boldwood, "before you go I want to mention what has been passing in my mind lately —that little arrangement we made about your share in the farm I mean. That share is small, too small, considering how little I attend to business now, and how much time and thought you give to it. Well, since the world is brightening for me, I want to show my sense of it by increasing your proportion in the partnership. I'll make a memorandum of the arrangement which struck me as likely to be convenient, for I haven't time to talk about it now; and then we'll discuss it at our leisure. My intention is ultimately to retire from the management altogether, and until you can take all the expenditure upon your shoulders, I'll be a sleeping partner in the stock. Then, if I marry her—and I hope—I feel I shall, why—"

"Pray don't speak of it, sir," said Oak, hastily. "We don't know what may happen. So many upsets may befall 'ee. There's many a slip, as they say— and I would advise you—I know you'll pardon me this once—not to be *too sure*."

"I know, I know. But the feeling I have about increasing your share is on account of what I know of you. Oak, I have learnt a little about your secret: your interest in 'her is more than that of bailiff for an employer. But you have behaved like a man, and I, as a sort of successful rival—successful partly through your goodness of heart—should like definitely to show my sense of your friendship under what must have been a great pain to you."

"Oh, that's not necessary, thank 'ee," said Oak, hurriedly. "I must get used to such as that; other men have, and so shall I."

Oak then left him. He was uneasy on Boldwood's account, for he saw anew that this constant passion of the farmer made him not the man he once had been.

As Boldwood continued awhile in his room alone —ready and dressed to receive his company—the mood of anxiety about his appearance seemed to pass away, and to be succeeded by a deep solemnity. He looked out of the window, and regarded the dim outline of the trees upon the sky, and the twilight deepening to darkness.

Then he went to a locked closet, and took from a locked drawer therein a small circular case the size of a pillbox, and was about to put it into his pocket. But he lingered to open the cover and take a momentary glance inside. It contained a woman's finger-ring, set all the way round with small diamonds, and from its appearance had evidently been recently purchased. Boldwood's eyes dwelt upon its many sparkles a long time, though that its material aspect concerned him little was plain from his manner and mien, which were those of a mind following out the presumed thread of that jewel's future history.

The noise of wheels at the front of the house became audible. Boldwood closed the box, stowed it away carefully in his pocket, and went out upon the landing. The old man who was his indoor factotum came at the same moment to the foot of the stairs.

"They be coming, sir—lots of 'em—a-foot and a-driving!"

"I was coming down this moment. Those wheels I heard—is it Mrs. Troy?"

"No, sir—'tis not she yet."

A reserved and somber expression had returned to Boldwood's face again, but it poorly cloaked his feelings when he pronounced Bathsheba's name; and his feverish anxiety continued to show its existence by a galloping motion of his fingers upon the side of his thigh as he went down the stairs.

VII

"How does this cover me?" said Troy to Pennyways. "Nobody would recognize me now, I'm sure."

He was buttoning on a heavy gray overcoat of Noachian cut, with cape and high collar, the latter being erect and rigid, like a girdling wall, and nearly reaching to the verge of a traveling cap which was pulled down over his ears.

Pennyways snuffed the candle, and then looked up and deliberately inspected Troy.

"You've made up your mind to go then?" he said.

"Made up my mind? Yes; of course I have."

"Why not write to her? 'Tis a very queer corner that you have got into, sergeant. You see, all these things will come to light if you go back, and they won't sound well at all. Faith, if I was you I'd even bide as you be—a single man of the name of Francis. A good wife is good, but the best wife is not so good as no wife at all. Now that's my outspoke mind, and I've been called a long-headed feller here and there."

"All nonsense!" said Troy, angrily. "There she is with plenty of money, and a house and farm, and horses, and comfort, and here am I living from hand to mouth—a needy adventurer. Besides, it is no use talking now; it is too late, and I am glad of it; I've been seen and recognized here this very afternoon. I should have gone back to her the day after the fair, if it hadn't been for you talking about the law, and rubbish about getting a separation; and I don't put it off any longer. What the deuce put it into my head to run away at all, I can't think! Humbugging sentiment—that's what it was. But what man on earth was to know that his wife would be in such a hurry to get rid of his name!"

"I should have known it. She's bad enough for anything."

"Pennyways, mind who you are talking to."

"Well, sergeant, all I say is this, that if I were you I'd go abroad again where I came from—'tisn't too late to do it now. I wouldn't stir up the business and get a bad name for the sake of living with her —for all that about your playacting is sure to come out, you know, although you think otherwise. My eyes and limbs, there'll be a racket if you go back just now—in the middle of Boldwood's Christmasing!"

"H'm, yes. I expect I shall not be a very welcome guest if he has her there," said the sergeant, with a slight laugh. "A sort of Alonzo the Brave; and when I go in the guests will sit in silence and fear, and all laughter and pleasure will be hushed, and the lights in the chamber burn blue, and the worms—Ugh, horrible!—Ring for some more brandy, Pennyways, I felt an awful shudder just then! Well, what is there besides? A stick—I must have a walking stick."

Pennyways now felt himself to be in something of a difficulty, for should Bathsheba and Troy become reconciled it would be necessary to regain her good opinion if he would secure the patronage of her husband. "I sometimes think she likes you yet, and is a good woman at bottom," he said, as a saving sentence. "But there's no telling to a certainty from a body's outside. Well, you'll do as you like about going, of course, sergeant, and as for me, I'll do as you tell me."

"Now, let me see what the time is," said Troy, after emptying his glass in one draught as he stood. "Half-past six o'clock. I shall not hurry along the road, and shall be there then before nine."

53.　Concurritur — Horae Momento

OUTSIDE THE FRONT of Boldwood's house a group of men stood in the dark, with their faces toward the door, which occasionally opened and closed for the passage of some guest or servant, when a golden rod of light would stripe the ground for the moment and vanish again, leaving nothing outside but the glowworm shine of the pale lamp amid the evergreens over the door.

"He was seen in Casterbridge this afternoon—so the boy said," one of them remarked in a whisper. "And I for one believe it. His body was never found, you know."

" 'Tis a strange story," said the next. "You may depend upon't that she knows nothing about it."

"Not a word."

"Perhaps he don't mean that she shall," said another man.

"If he's alive and here in the neighborhood, he means mischief," said the first. "Poor young thing: I do pity her, if 'tis true. He'll drag her to the dogs."

"Oh, no; he'll settle down quiet enough," said one disposed to take a more hopeful view of the case.

"What a fool she must have been ever to have had anything to do with the man! She is so self-willed and independent too, that one is more minded to say it serves her right than pity her."

"No, no! I don't hold with 'ee there. She was no otherwise than a girl mind, and how could she tell what the man was made of? If 'tis really true, 'tis too hard a punishment, and more than she ought to hae. Hullo, who's that?" This was to some footsteps that were heard approaching.

"William Smallbury," said a dim figure in the shades, coming up and joining them. "Dark as a hedge, tonight, isn't it? I all but missed the plank over the river ath'art there in the bottom—never did such a thing before in my life. Be ye any of Boldwood's workfolk?" He peered into their faces.

"Yes—all o' us. We met here a few minutes ago."

"Oh, I hear now—that's Sam Samway: thought I knowed the voice, too. Going in?'

"Presently. But I say, William," Samway whispered, "have ye heard this strange tale?"

"What—that about Sergeant Troy being seen, d'ye mean, souls?" said Smallbury, also lowering his voice.

"Aye, in Casterbridge."

"Yes, I have. Laban Tall named a hint of it to me but now—but I don't think it. Hark, here Laban comes himself, 'a b'lieve." A footstep drew near.

"Laban?"

"Yes, 'tis I," said Tall.

"Have ye heard any more about that?"

"No," said Tall, joining the group. "And I'm inclined to think we'd better be quiet. If so be 'tis not true, 'twill flurry her, and do her much harm to repeat it; and if so be 'tis true, 'twill do no good to forestall her time o' trouble. God send that it mid be a lie, for though Henery Fray and some of 'em do speak against her, she's never been anything but fair to me. She's hot and hasty, but she's a brave girl who'll never tell a lie however much the truth may harm her, and I've no cause to wish her evil."

"She never do tell women's little lies, that's true; and 'tis a thing that can be said of very few. Aye, all the harm she thinks she says to yer face: there's nothing underhand wi' her."

They stood silent then, every man busied with his own thoughts, during which interval sounds of merriment could be heard within. Then the front door again opened, the rays streamed out, the well-known form of Boldwood was seen in the rectangular area of light, the door closed, and Boldwood walked slowly down the path.

" 'Tis master," one of the men whispered, as he neared them. "We'd better stand quiet—he'll go in again directly. He would think it unseemly o' us to be loitering here."

Boldwood came on, and passed by the men without seeing them, they being under the bushes on the grass. He paused, leant over the gate, and breathed a long breath. They heard low words come from him.

"I hope to God she'll come, or this night will be nothing but misery to me! O my darling, my darling, why do you keep me in suspense like this?"

He said this to himself, and they all distinctly heard it. Boldwood remained silent after that, and the noise from indoors was again just audible, until, a few minutes later, light wheels could be distinguished coming down the hill. They drew nearer, and ceased at the gate. Boldwood hastened back to the door, and opened it; and the light shone upon Bathsheba coming up the path.

Boldwood compressed his emotion to mere welcome: the men marked her light laugh and apology as she met him: he took her into the house; and the door closed again.

"Gracious heaven, I didn't know it was like that with him!" said one of the men. "I thought that fancy of his was over long ago."

"You don't know much of master, if you thought that," said Samway.

"I wouldn't he should know we heard what 'a said for the world," remarked a third.

"I wish we had told of the report at once," the first uneasily continued. "More harm may come of this than we know of. Poor Mr. Boldwood, it will be hard upon en. I wish Troy was in—Well, God forgive me for such a wish! A scoundrel to play a poor wife such tricks. Nothing has prospered in Weatherbury since he came here. And now I've no heart to go in. Let's look into Warren's for a few minutes first, shall us, neighbors?"

Samway, Tall, and Smallbury agreed to go to Warren's, and went out at the gate, the remaining ones entering the house. The three soon drew near the malthouse, approaching it from the adjoining orchard, and not by way of the street. The pane of glass was illuminated as usual. Smallbury was a little in advance of the rest, when, pausing, he turned suddenly to his companions and said, "Hist! See there."

The light from the pane was now perceived to be shining not upon the ivied wall as usual, but upon some object close to the glass. It was a human face.

"Let's come closer," whispered Samway; and they approached on tiptoe. There was no disbelieving the report any longer. Troy's face was almost close to the pane, and he was looking in. Not only was he looking in, but he appeared to have been arrested by a conversation which was in progress in the malthouse, the voices of the interlocutors being those of Oak and the maltster.

"The spree is all in her honor, isn't it—hey?" said the old man. "Although he made believe 'tis only keeping up o' Christmas?"

"I cannot say," replied Oak.

"Oh, 'tis true enough, faith. I cannot understand Farmer Boldwood being such a fool at his time of life as to ho and hanker after thik woman in the way 'a do, and she not care a bit about en."

The men, after recognizing Troy's features, withdrew across the orchard as quietly as they had come. The air was big with Bathsheba's fortunes tonight: every word everywhere concerned her. When they were quite out of earshot all by one instinct paused.

"It gave me quite a turn—his face," said Tall, breathing.

"And so it did me," said Samway. "What's to be done?"

"I don't see that 'tis any business of ours," Smallbury murmured dubiously.

"But it is! 'Tis a thing which is everybody's business," said Samway. "We know very well that master's on a wrong tack, and that she's quite in the dark, and we should let 'em know at once. Laban, you know her best—you'd better go and ask to speak to her."

"I bain't fit for any such thing," said Laban, nervously. "I should think William ought to do it if anybody. He's oldest."

"I shall have nothing to do with it," said Smallbury. "'Tis a ticklish business altogether. Why, he'll go on to her himself in a few minutes, ye'll see."

"We don't know that he will. Come, Laban."

"Very well, if I must I must, I suppose," Tall reluctantly answered. "What must I say?"

"Just ask to see master."

"Oh, no; I shan't speak to Mr. Boldwood. If I tell anybody, 'twill be mistress."

"Very well," said Samway.

Laban then went to the door. When he opened it the hum of bustle rolled out as a wave upon a still strand—the assemblage being immediately inside the hall—and was deadened to a murmur as he closed it again. Each man waited intently, and looked around at the dark tree tops gently rocking against the sky and occasionally shivering in a slight wind, as if he took interest in the scene, which neither did. One of them began walking up and down, and then came to where he started from and stopped again, with a sense that walking was a thing not worth doing now.

"I should think Laban must have seen mistress by this time," said Smallbury, breaking the silence. "Perhaps she won't come and speak to him."

The door opened. Tall appeared, and joined them.

"Well?" said both.

"I didn't like to ask for her after all," Laban faltered out. "They were all in such a stir, trying to put a little spirit into the party. Somehow the fun seems to hang fire, though everything's there that a heart can desire, and I couldn't for my soul interfere and throw damp upon it—if 'twas to save my life, I couldn't!"

"I suppose we had better all go in together," said Samway, gloomily. "Perhaps I may have a chance of saying a word to master."

So the men entered the hall, which was the room selected and arranged for the gathering because of its size. The younger men and maids were at last just beginning a dance. Bathsheba had been perplexed how to act, for she was not much more than a slim young maid herself, and the weight of stateliness sat heavy upon her. Sometimes she thought she ought not to have come under any circumstances; then she considered what cold unkindness that would have been, and finally resolved upon the middle course of staying for about an hour only, and gliding off unobserved, having from the first made up her mind that she could on no account dance, sing, or take any active part in the proceedings.

Her allotted hour having been passed in chatting and looking on, Bathsheba told Liddy not to hurry herself, and went to the small parlor to prepare for departure, which, like the hall, was decorated with holly and ivy, and well lighted up.

Nobody was in the room, but she had hardly been there a moment when the master of the house entered.

"Mrs. Troy—you are not going?" he said. "We've hardly begun!"

"If you'll excuse me, I should like to go now." Her manner was restive, for she remembered her promise, and imagined what he was about to say. "But as it is not late," she added, "I can walk home, and leave my man and Liddy to come when they choose."

"I've been trying to get an opportunity of speaking to you," said Boldwood. "You know perhaps what I long to say?"

Bathsheba silently looked on the floor.

"You do give it?" he said, eagerly.

"What?" she whispered.

"Now, that's evasion! Why, the promise. I don't

want to intrude upon you at all, or to let it become known to anybody. But do give your word! A mere business compact, you know, between two people who are beyond the influence of passion." Boldwood knew how false this picture was as regarded himself; but he had proved that it was the only tone in which she would allow him to approach her. "A promise to marry me at the end of five years and three-quarters. You owe it to me!"

"I feel that I do," said Bathsheba, "that is, if you demand it. But I am a changed woman—an unhappy woman—and not—not—"

"You are still a very beautiful woman," said Boldwood. Honesty and pure conviction suggested the remark, unaccompanied by any perception that it might have been adopted by blunt flattery to soothe and win her.

However, it had not much effect now, for she said, in a passionless murmur which was in itself a proof of her words: "I have no feeling in the matter at all. And I don't at all know what is right to do in my difficult position, and I have nobody to advise me. But I give my promise, if I must. I give it as the rendering of a debt, conditionally, of course, on my being a widow."

"You'll marry me between five and six years hence?"

"Don't press me too hard. I'll marry nobody else."

"But surely you will name the time, or there's nothing in the promise at all?"

"Oh, I don't know, pray let me go!" she said, her bosom beginning to rise. "I am afraid what to do! I want to be just to you, and to be that seems to be wronging myself, and perhaps it is breaking the commandments. There is considerable doubt of his death, and then it is dreadful; let me ask a solicitor, Mr. Boldwood, if I ought or no!"

"Say the words, dear one, and the subject shall be dismissed; a blissful loving intimacy of six years, and then marriage—Oh, Bathsheba, say them!" he begged in a husky voice, unable to sustain the forms of mere friendship any longer. "Promise yourself to me; I deserve it, indeed I do, for I have loved you more than anybody in the world! And if I said hasty words and showed uncalled-for heat of manner toward you, believe me, dear, I did not mean to distress you; I was in agony, Bathsheba, and I did not know what I said. You wouldn't let a dog suffer what I have suffered, could you but know it! Sometimes I shrink from your knowing what I have felt for you, and sometimes I am distressed that all of it you never will know. Be gracious, and give up a little to me, when I would give up my life for you!"

The trimmings of her dress, as they quivered against the light, showed how agitated she was, and at last she burst out crying. "And you'll not—press me—about anything more—if I say in five or six years?" she sobbed, when she had power to frame the words.

"Yes, then I'll leave it to time."

"Very well. If he does not return, I'll marry you in six years from this day, if we both live," she said solemnly.

"And you'll take this as a token from me."

Boldwood had come close to her side, and now he clasped one of her hands in both his own, and lifted it to his breast.

"What is it? Oh I cannot wear a ring!" she exclaimed, on seeing what he held; "besides, I wouldn't have a soul know that it's an engagement! Perhaps it is improper? Besides, we are not engaged in the usual sense, are we? Don't insist, Mr. Boldwood—don't!" In her trouble at not being able to get her hand away from him at once, she stamped passionately on the floor with one foot, and tears crowded to her eyes again.

"It means simply a pledge—no sentiment—the seal of a practical compact," he said more quietly, but still retaining her hand in his firm grasp. "Come, now!" And Boldwood slipped the ring on her finger.

"I cannot wear it," she said, weeping as if her heart would break. "You frighten me, almost. So wild a scheme! Please let me go home!"

"Only tonight: wear it just tonight, to please me!"

Bathsheba sat down in a chair, and buried her face in her handkerchief, though Boldwood kept her hand yet. At length she said, in a sort of hopeless whisper—

"Very well, then, I will tonight, if you wish it so earnestly. Now loosen my hand; I will, indeed I will wear it tonight."

"And it shall be the beginning of a pleasant secret courtship of six years, with a wedding at the end?"

"It must be, I suppose, since you will have it so!" she said, fairly beaten into nonresistance.

Boldwood pressed her hand, and allowed it to drop in her lap. "I am happy now," he said. "God bless you!"

He left the room, and when he thought she might be sufficiently composed sent one of the maids to her. Bathsheba cloaked the effects of the late scene as she best could, followed the girl, and in a few moments came downstairs with her hat and cloak on, ready to go. To get to the door it was necessary to pass through the hall, and before doing so she paused on the bottom of the staircase which descended into one corner, to take a last look at the gathering.

There was no music or dancing in progress just

now. At the lower end, which had been arranged for the workfolk specially, a group conversed in whispers, and with clouded looks. Boldwood was standing by the fireplace, and he, too, though so absorbed in visions arising from her promise that he scarcely saw anything, seemed at that moment to have observed their peculiar manner, and their looks askance.

"What is it you are in doubt about, men?" he said.

One of them turned and replied uneasily: "It was something Laban heard of, that's all, sir."

"News? Anybody married or engaged, born or dead?" inquired the farmer, gaily. "Tell it to us, Tall. One would think from your looks and mysterious ways that it was something very dreadful indeed."

"Oh, no, sir, nobody is dead," said Tall.

"I wish somebody was," said Samway, in a whisper.

"What do you say, Samway?" asked Boldwood, somewhat sharply. "If you have anything to say, speak out; if not, get up another dance."

"Mrs. Troy has come downstairs," said Samway to Tall. "If you want to tell her, you had better do it now."

"Do you know what they mean?" the farmer asked Bathsheba, across the room.

"I don't in the least," said Bathsheba.

There was a smart rapping at the door. One of the men opened it instantly, and went outside.

"Mrs. Troy is wanted," he said, on returning.

"Quite ready," said Bathsheba. "Though I didn't tell them to send."

"It is a stranger, ma'am," said the man by the door.

"A stranger?" she said.

"Ask him to come in," said Boldwood.

The message was given, and Troy, wrapped up

to his eyes as we have seen him, stood in the doorway.

There was an unearthly silence, all looking toward the newcomer. Those who had just learnt that he was in the neighborhood recognized him instantly; those who did not were perplexed. Nobody noted Bathsheba. She was leaning on the stairs. Her brow had heavily contracted; her whole face was pallid, her lips apart, her eyes rigidly staring at their visitor.

Boldwood was among those who did not notice that he was Troy. "Come in, come in!" he repeated, cheerfully, "and drain a Christmas beaker with us, stranger!"

Troy next advanced into the middle of the room, took off his cap, turned down his coat collar, and looked Boldwood in the face. Even then Boldwood did not recognize that the impersonator of Heaven's persistent irony toward him, who had once before broken in upon his bliss, scourged him, and snatched his delight away, had come to do these things a second time. Troy began to laugh a mechanical laugh: Boldwood recognized him now.

Troy turned to Bathsheba. The poor girl's wretchedness at this time was beyond all fancy or narration. She had sunk down on the lowest stair; and there she sat, her mouth blue and dry, and her dark eyes fixed vacantly upon him, as if she wondered whether it were not all a terrible illusion.

Then Troy spoke. "Bathsheba, I come here for you!"

She made no reply.

"Come home with me: come!"

Bathsheba moved her feet a little, but did not rise.

Troy went across to her.

"Come, madam, do you hear what I say?" he said, peremptorily.

A strange voice came from the fireplace—a voice

sounding far off and confined, as if from a
dungeon. Hardly a soul in the assembly recognized
the thin tones to be those of Boldwood. Sudden
despair had transformed him.

"Bathsheba, go with your husband!"

Nevertheless, she did not move. The truth was
that Bathsheba was beyond the pale of activity—
and yet not in a swoon. She was in a state of mental
gutta serena; her mind was for the minute totally
deprived of light at the same time that no obscura-
tion was apparent from without.

Troy stretched out his hand to pull her toward
him, when she quickly shrank back. This visible
dread of him seemed to irritate Troy, and he seized
her arm and pulled it sharply. Whether his grasp
pinched her, or whether his mere touch was the
cause, was never known, but at the moment of his
seizure she writhed, and gave a quick, low scream.

The scream had been heard but a few seconds
when it was followed by a sudden deafening report
that echoed through the room and stupefied them
all. The oak partition shook with the concussion,
and the place was filled with gray smoke.

In bewilderment they turned their eyes to Boldwood. At his back, as he stood before the fireplace,
was a gun rack, as is usual in farmhouses, constructed to hold two guns. When Bathsheba had
cried out in her husband's grasp, Boldwood's face
of gnashing despair had changed. The veins had
swollen, and a frenzied look had gleamed in his
eye. He had turned quickly, taken one of the guns,
cocked it, and at once discharged it at Troy.

Troy fell. The distance apart of the two men was
so small that the charge of shot did not spread in
the least, but passed like a bullet into his body. He
uttered a long guttural sigh—there was a contraction—an extension—then his muscles relaxed, and
he lay still.

Boldwood was seen through the smoke to be now again engaged with the gun. It was double-barreled, and he had, meanwhile, in some way fastened his handkerchief to the trigger, and with his foot on the other end was in the act of turning the second barrel upon himself. Samway his man was the first to see this, and in the midst of the general horror darted up to him. Boldwood had already twitched the handkerchief, and the gun exploded a second time, sending its contents, by a timely blow from Samway, into the beam which crossed the ceiling.

"Well, it makes no difference!" Boldwood gasped. "There is another way for me to die."

Then he broke from Samway, crossed the room to Bathsheba, and kissed her hand. He put on his hat, opened the door, and went into the darkness, nobody thinking of preventing him.

54. *After the Shock*

BOLDWOOD PASSED INTO THE HIGH ROAD, and turned in the direction of Casterbridge. Here he walked at an even, steady pace over Yalbury Hill, along the dead level beyond, mounted Mellstock Hill, and between eleven and twelve o'clock crossed the Moor into the town. The streets were nearly deserted now, and the waving lamp flames only lighted up rows of gray shop shutters, and strips of white paving upon which his step echoed as he passed along. He turned to the right, and halted before an archway of heavy stonework, which was closed by an iron-studded pair of doors. This was the entrance to the jail, and over it a lamp was fixed, the light enabling the wretched traveler to find a bellpull.

The small wicket at last opened, and a porter appeared. Boldwood stepped forward, and said something in a low tone, when, after a delay, another man came. Boldwood entered, and the door was closed behind him, and he walked the world no more.

Long before this time Weatherbury had been thoroughly aroused, and the wild deed which had terminated Boldwood's merrymaking became known to all. Of those out of the house Oak was one of the first to hear of the catastrophe, and when he entered the room, which was about five minutes after Boldwood's exit, the scene was terrible. All the female guests were huddled aghast against the walls like sheep in a storm, and the men were bewildered as to what to do. As for Bathsheba, she had changed. She was sitting on the floor beside the body of Troy, his head pillowed in her lap, where she had herself lifted it. With one hand she held her handkerchief to his breast and covered the wound, though scarcely a single drop of blood had flowed, and with the other she tightly clasped one of his. The household convulsion had made her herself again. The temporary coma had ceased, and activity had come with the necessity for it. Deeds of endurance which seem ordinary in philosophy are rare in conduct, and Bathsheba was astonishing all around her now, for her philosophy was her conduct, and she seldom thought practicable what she did not practice. She was of the stuff of which great men's mothers are made. She was indispensable to high generation, hated at tea parties, feared in shops, and loved at crises. Troy recumbent in his wife's lap formed now the sole spectacle in the middle of the spacious room.

"Gabriel," she said, automatically, when he entered, turning up a face of which only the well-known lines remained to tell him it was hers, all else in the picture having faded quite. "Ride to Casterbridge instantly for a surgeon. It is, I believe, useless, but go. Mr. Boldwood has shot my husband."

Her statement of the fact in such quiet and simple words came with more force than a tragic declamation, and had somewhat the effect of setting the distorted images in each mind present into proper focus. Oak, almost before he had comprehended anything beyond the briefest abstract of the event, hurried out of the room, saddled a horse and rode away. Not till he had ridden more than a mile did it occur to him that he would have done better by sending some other man on this errand, remaining himself in the house. What had become of Boldwood? He should have been looked after. Was he mad—had there been a quarrel? Then how had Troy got there? Where had he come from? How did this remarkable reappearance effect itself when he was supposed by many to be at the bottom of the sea? Oak had in some measure been prepared for the presence of Troy by hearing a rumor of his return just before entering Boldwood's house; but before he had weighed that information, this fatal event had been superimposed. However, it was too late now to think of sending another messenger, and he rode on, in the excitement of these self-inquiries not discerning, when about three miles from Casterbridge, a square-figured pedestrian passing along under the dark hedge in the same direction as his own.

The miles necessary to be traversed, and other hindrances incidental to the lateness of the hour and the darkness of the night, delayed the arrival of Mr. Aldritch, the surgeon; and more than three hours passed between the time at which the shot was fired and that of his entering the house. Oak was additionally detained in Casterbridge through having to give notice to the authorities of what had happened; and he then found that Boldwood had also entered the town, and delivered himself up.

In the meantime the surgeon, having hastened into the hall at Boldwood's, found it in darkness and quite deserted. He went on to the back of the house, where he discovered in the kitchen an old man, of whom he made inquiries.

"She's had him took away to her own house, sir," said his informant.

"Who has?" said the doctor.

"Mrs. Troy. 'A was quite dead, sir."

This was astonishing information. "She had no right to do that," said the doctor. "There will have to be an inquest, and she should have waited to know what to do."

"Yes, sir; it was hinted to her that she had better wait till the law was known. But she said law was nothing to her, and she wouldn't let her dear husband's corpse bide neglected for folks to stare at for all the crowners in England."

Mr. Aldritch drove at once back again up the hill to Bathsheba's. The first person he met was poor Liddy, who seemed literally to have dwindled smaller in these few latter hours. "What has been done?" he said.

"I don't know, sir," said Liddy, with suspended breath. "My mistress has done it all."

"Where is she?"

"Upstairs with him, sir. When he was brought home and taken upstairs, she said she wanted no further help from the men. And then she called me, and made me fill the bath, and after that told me I had better go and lie down because I looked so ill. Then she locked herself into the room alone with him, and would not let a nurse come in, or anybody at all. But I thought I'd wait in the next room in case she should want me. I heard her moving about inside for more than an hour, but she only came out once, and that was for more candles, because hers had burnt down into the socket. She said we were to let her know when you or Mr. Thirdly came, sir."

Oak entered with the parson at this moment, and they all went upstairs together, preceded by Liddy Smallbury. Everything was silent as the grave when they paused on the landing. Liddy knocked, and Bathsheba's dress was heard rustling across the room: the key turned in the lock, and she opened the door. Her looks were calm and nearly rigid, like a slightly animated bust of Melpomene.

"Oh, Mr. Aldritch, you have come at last," she murmured from her lips merely, and threw back the door. "Ah, and Mr. Thirdly. Well, all is done, and anybody in the world may see him now." She then passed by him, crossed the landing, and entered another room.

Looking into the chamber of death she had vacated they saw by the light of the candles which were on the drawers a tall straight shape lying at the further end of the bedroom, wrapped in white. Everything around was quite orderly. The doctor went in, and after a few minutes returned to the landing again, where Oak and the parson still waited.

"It is all done, indeed, as she says," remarked Mr. Aldritch, in a subdued voice. "The body has been undressed and properly laid out in grave clothes. Gracious Heaven—this mere girl! She must have the nerve of a stoic!"

"The heart of a wife merely," floated in a

whisper about the ears of the three, and turning they saw Bathsheba in the midst of them. Then, as if at that instant to prove that her fortitude had been more of will than of spontaneity, she silently sank down between them and was a shapeless heap of drapery on the floor. The simple consciousness that superhuman strain was no longer required had at once put a period to her power to continue it.

They took her away into a further room, and the medical attendance which had been useless in Troy's case was invaluable in Bathsheba's, who fell into a series of fainting fits that had a serious aspect for a time. The sufferer was got to bed, and Oak, finding from the bulletins that nothing really dreadful was to be apprehended on her score, left the house. Liddy kept watch in Bathsheba's chamber, where she heard her mistress moaning in whispers through the dull slow hours of that wretched night: "Oh, it is my fault—how can I live! O Heaven, how can I live!"

55. The March Following — "Bathsheba Boldwood"

WE PASS RAPIDLY on into the month of March, to a breezy day without sunshine, frost, or dew. On Yalbury Hill, about midway between Weatherbury and Casterbridge, where the turnpike road passes over the crest, a numerous concourse of people had gathered, the eyes of the greater number being frequently stretched afar in a northerly direction. The groups consisted of a throng of idlers, a party of javelin men, and two trumpeters, and in the midst were carriages, one of which contained the high sheriff. With the idlers, many of whom had mounted to the top of a cutting formed for the road, were several Weatherbury men and boys— among others Poorgrass Coggan and Cain Ball.

At the end of half-an-hour a faint dust was seen in the expected quarter, and shortly after a traveling carriage, bringing one of the two judges on the Western Circuit, came up the hill and halted on the top. The judge changed carriages whilst a flourish was blown by the big-cheeked trumpeters, and a procession being formed of the vehicles and javelin men, they all proceeded toward the town, excepting the Weatherbury men, who as soon as they had seen the judge move off returned home again to their work.

"Joseph, I zeed you squeezing close to the carriage," said Coggan, as they walked. "Did ye notice my lord judge's face?"

"I did," said Poorgrass, "I looked hard at en, as if I would read his very soul; and there was mercy in his eyes—or to speak with the exact truth required of us at this solemn time, in the eye that was toward me."

"Well, I hope for the best," said Coggan, "though bad that must be. However, I shan't go to the trial, and I'd advise the rest of ye that bain't wanted to bide away. 'Twill disturb his mind more than anything to see us there staring at him as if he were a show."

"The very thing I said this morning," observed Joseph. " 'Justice is come to weigh him in the balances,' I said in my reflectious way, 'and if he's found wanting, so be it unto him,' and a bystander said, 'Hear, hear! A man who can talk like that ought to be heard.' But I don't like dwelling upon it, for my few words are my few words, and not much; though the speech of some men is rumored abroad as though by nature formed for such."

"So 'tis, Joseph. And now, neighbors, as I said, every man bide at home."

The resolution was adhered to; and all waited anxiously for the news next day. Their suspense was diverted, however, by a discovery which was made in the afternoon, throwing more light on Boldwood's conduct and condition than any details which had preceded it.

That he had been from the time of Greenhill Fair until the fatal Christmas Eve in excited and unusual moods was known to those who had been intimate with him; but nobody imagined that there had shown in him unequivocal symptoms of the mental derangement which Bathsheba and Oak, alone of all others and at different times, had momentarily suspected. In a locked closet was now discovered an extraordinary collection of articles. There were several sets of ladies' dresses in the piece, of sundry expensive materials; silks and satins, poplins and velvets, all of colors which from Bathsheba's style of dress might have been judged to be her favorites. There were two muffs, sable and ermine. Above all there was a case of jewelry, containing four heavy gold bracelets and several lockets and rings, all of fine quality and manufacture. These things had been bought in Bath and other towns from time to time, and brought home by stealth. They were all carefully packed in paper, and each package was labeled "Bathsheba Boldwood," a date being subjoined six years in advance in every instance.

These somewhat pathetic evidences of a mind crazed with care and love were the subject of discourse in Warren's malthouse when Oak entered from Casterbridge with tidings of the sentence. He came in the afternoon, and his face, as the kiln glow shone upon it, told the tale sufficiently well. Boldwood, as every one supposed he would do, had pleaded guilty, and had been sentenced to death.

The conviction that Boldwood had not been morally responsible for his later acts now became general. Facts elicited previous to the trial had pointed strongly in the same direction, but they had not been of sufficient weight to lead to an order for an examination into the state of Boldwood's mind. It was astonishing, now that a presumption of insanity was raised, how many collateral circumstances were remembered to which a condition of mental disease seemed to afford the only explanation—among others, the unprecedented neglect of his cornstacks in the previous summer.

A petition was addressed to the Home Secretary, advancing the circumstances which appeared to justify a request for a reconsideration of the sentence. It was not "numerously signed" by the inhabitants of Casterbridge, as is usual in such cases, for Boldwood had never made many friends over the counter. The shops thought it very natural that a man who, by importing direct from the producer, had daringly set aside the first great principle of provincial existence, namely, that God made country villages to supply customers to country towns, should have confused ideas about the Decalogue. The prompters were a few merciful men who had perhaps too feelingly considered the facts latterly unearthed, and the result was that evidence was taken which it was hoped might remove the crime, in a moral point of view, out of the category of willful murder, and lead it to be regarded as a sheer outcome of madness.

The upshot of the petition was waited for in Weatherbury with solicitous interest. The execution had been fixed for eight o'clock on a Saturday morning about a fortnight after the sentence was passed, and up to Friday afternoon no answer had been received. At that time Gabriel came from Casterbridge jail, whither he had been to wish Boldwood good-bye, and turned down a bystreet to avoid the town. When past the last house he heard a hammering, and lifting his bowed head he looked back for a moment. Over the chimneys he could see the upper part of the jail entrance, rich and glowing in the afternoon sun, and some moving figures were there. They were carpenters lifting a post into vertical position within the parapet. He withdrew his eyes quickly and hastened on.

It was dark when he reached home, and half the village was out to meet him.

"No tidings," Gabriel said, wearily. "And I'm afraid there's no hope. I've been with him more than two hours."

"Do ye think he *really* was out of his mind when he did it?" said Smallbury.

"I can't honestly say that I do," Oak replied. "However, that we can talk of another time. Has there been any change in mistress this afternoon?"

"None at all."

"Is she downstairs?"

"No. And getting on so nicely as she was too. She's but very little better now again than she was at Christmas. She keeps on asking if you be come, and if there's news, till one's wearied out wi' answering her. Shall I go and say you've come?"

"No," said Oak. "There's a chance yet; but I couldn't stay in town any longer—after seeing him too. So Laban—Laban is here, isn't he?"

"Yes," said Tall.

"What I've arranged is, that you shall ride to town the last thing tonight; leave here about nine, and wait a while there, getting home about twelve.

If nothing has been received by eleven tonight, they say there's no chance at all."

"I do so hope his life will be spared," said Liddy. "If it is not, she'll go out of her mind too. Poor thing; her sufferings have been dreadful; she deserves anybody's pity."

"Is she altered much?" said Coggan.

"If you haven't seen poor mistress since Christmas, you wouldn't know her," said Liddy. "Her eyes are so miserable that she's not the same woman. Only two years ago she was a romping girl, and now she's this!"

Laban departed as directed, and at eleven o'clock that night several of the villagers strolled along the road to Casterbridge and awaited his arrival— among them Oak, and nearly all the rest of Bathsheba's men. Gabriel's anxiety was great that Boldwood might be saved, even though in his conscience he felt that he ought to die; for there had been qualities in the farmer which Oak loved. At last, when they all were weary the tramp of a horse was heard in the distance—

> First dead, as if on turf it trode,
> Then, clattering, on the village road
> In other pace than forth he yode.

"We shall soon know now, one way or other," said Coggan, and they all stepped down from the bank on which they had been standing into the road, and the rider pranced into the midst of them.

"Is that you, Laban?" said Gabriel.

"Yes—'tis come. He's not to die. 'Tis confinement during Her Majesty's pleasure."

"Hurrah!" said Coggan, with a swelling heart. "God's above the devil yet!"

56. *Beauty in Loneliness — After All*

BATHSHEBA REVIVED with the spring. The utter prostration that had followed the low fever from which she had suffered diminished perceptibly when all uncertainty upon every subject had come to an end.

But she remained alone now for the greater part of her time, and stayed in the house, or at furthest went into the garden. She shunned every one, even Liddy, and could be brought to make no confidences, and to ask for no sympathy.

As the summer drew on she passed more of her time in the open air, and began to examine into farming matters from sheer necessity, though she never rode out or personally superintended as at former times. One Friday evening in August she walked a little way along the road and entered the village for the first time since the somber event of the preceding Christmas. None of the old color had as yet come to her cheek, and its absolute paleness was heightened by the jet black of her gown, till it appeared preternatural. When she reached a little shop at the other end of the place, which stood nearly opposite to the churchyard, Bathsheba heard singing inside the church, and she knew that the singers were practicing. She crossed the road, opened the gate, and entered the graveyard, the high sills of the church windows effectually screening her from the eyes of those gathered within. Her stealthy walk was to the nook wherein Troy had worked at planting flowers upon Fanny Robin's grave, and she came to the marble tombstone.

A motion of satisfaction enlivened her face as she read the complete inscription. First came the words of Troy himself:

ERECTED BY FRANCIS TROY
IN BELOVED MEMORY OF
FANNY ROBIN,
WHO DIED OCTOBER 9, 18—,
AGED 20 YEARS.

Underneath this was now inscribed in new letters:

IN THE SAME GRAVE LIE
THE REMAINS OF THE AFORESAID
FRANCIS TROY,
WHO DIED DECEMBER 24TH, 18—,
AGED 26 YEARS.

Whilst she stood and read and meditated the tones of the organ began again in the church, and she went with the same light step round to the porch and listened. The door was closed, and the choir was learning a new hymn. Bathsheba was stirred by emotions which latterly she had assumed to be altogether dead within her. The little attenuated voices of the children brought to her ear in distinct utterance the words they sang without thought or comprehension—

Lead, kindly Light, amid the encircling gloom,
    Lead Thou me on.

Bathsheba's feeling was always to some extent dependent upon her whim, as is the case with many other women. Something big came into her throat and an uprising to her eyes—and she thought that she would allow the imminent tears to flow if they wished. They did flow and plenteously, and one fell upon the stone bench beside her. Once that she had begun to cry for she hardly knew what, she could not leave off for crowding thoughts she knew too well. She would have given anything in the world to be, as those children were, unconcerned at the meaning of their words, because too innocent to feel the necessity for any such expression. All the impassioned scenes of her brief experience seemed to revive with added emotion at that moment, and those scenes which had been without emotion during enactment had emotion then. Yet grief came to her rather as a luxury than as the scourge of former times.

Owing to Bathsheba's face being buried in her hands she did not notice a form which came quietly into the porch, and on seeing her, first moved as if to retreat, then paused and regarded her. Bathsheba did not raise her head for some time, and when she looked round her face was wet, and her eyes drowned and dim. "Mr. Oak," exclaimed she, disconcerted, "how long have you been here?"

"A few minutes, ma'am," said Oak, respectfully.

"Are you going in?" said Bathsheba; and there came from within the church as from a prompter—

I loved the garish day, and, spite of fears,
Pride ruled my will: remember not past years.

"I was," said Gabriel. "I am one of the bass singers, you know. I have sung bass for several months."

"Indeed: I wasn't aware of that. I'll leave you, then."

Which I have loved long since, and lost awhile,

sang the children.

"Don't let me drive you away, mistress. I think I won't go in tonight."

"Oh, no—you don't drive me away."

Then they stood in a state of some embarrassment, Bathsheba trying to wipe her dreadfully drenched and inflamed face without his noticing her. At length Oak said, "I've not seen you—I mean spoken to you—since ever so long, have I?" But he feared to bring distressing memories back, and interrupted himself with: "Were you going into church?"

"No," she said. "I came to see the tombstone privately—to see if they had cut the inscription as I wished. Mr. Oak, you needn't mind speaking to me, if you wish to, on the matter which is in both our minds at this moment."

"And have they done it as you wished?" said Oak.

"Yes. Come and see it, if you have not already."

So together they went and read the tomb. "Eight months ago!" Gabriel murmured when he saw the date. "It seems like yesterday to me."

"And to me as if it were years ago—long years, and I had been dead between. And now I am going home, Mr. Oak."

Oak walked after her. "I wanted to name a small matter to you as soon as I could," he said with hesitation. "Merely about business, and I think I may just mention it now, if you'll allow me."

"Oh, yes, certainly."

"It is that I may soon have to give up the management of your farm, Mrs. Troy. The fact is, I am thinking of leaving England—not yet, you know—next spring."

"Leaving England!" she said, in surprise, and genuine disappointment. "Why, Gabriel, what are you going to do that for?"

"Well, I've thought it best," Oak stammered out. "California is the spot I've had in my mind to try."

"But it is understood everywhere that you are going to take poor Mr. Boldwood's farm on your own account?"

"I've had the refusal o' it 'tis true; but nothing is settled yet, and I have reasons for gieing up. I shall finish out my year there as manager for the trustees, but no more."

"And what shall I do without you? Oh, Gabriel, I don't think you ought to go away. You've been with me so long—through bright times and dark times—such old friends as we are—that it seems unkind almost. I had fancied that if you leased the other farm as master, you might still give a helping look across at mine. And now going away!"

"I would have willingly."

"Yet now that I am more helpless than ever you go away!"

"Yes, that's the ill fortune o' it," said Gabriel, in a distressed tone. "And it is because of that very helplessness that I feel bound to go. Good afternoon, ma'am," he concluded, in evident anxiety to get away, and at once went out of the churchyard by a path she could follow on no pretense whatever.

Bathsheba went home, her mind occupied with a new trouble, which being rather harassing than deadly was calculated to do good by diverting her from the chronic gloom of her life. She was set thinking a great deal about Oak and of his wish to shun her; and there occurred to Bathsheba several incidents of her latter intercourse with him, which, trivial when singly viewed, amounted together to a perceptible disinclination for her society. It broke upon her at length as a great pain that her last old disciple was about to forsake her and flee. He who had believed in her and argued on her side when all the rest of the world was against her, had at last like the others become weary and neglectful of the old cause, and was leaving her to fight her battles alone.

Three weeks went on, and more evidence of his

want of interest in her was forthcoming. She
noticed that instead of entering the small parlor or
office where the farm accounts were kept, and waiting, or leaving a memorandum as he had hitherto
done during her seclusion, Oak never came at all
when she was likely to be there, only entering at
unseasonable hours when her presence in that part
of the house was least to be expected. Whenever he
wanted directions he sent a message, or note with
neither heading nor signature, to which she was
obliged to reply in the same offhand style. Poor
Bathsheba began to suffer now from the most torturing sting of all—a sensation that she was despised.

The autumn wore away gloomily enough amid
these melancholy conjectures, and Christmas Day
came, completing a year of her legal widowhood,
and two years and a quarter of her life alone. On
examining her heart it appeared beyond measure
strange that the subject of which the season might
have been supposed suggestive—the event in the
hall at Boldwood's—was not agitating her at all;
but instead, an agonizing conviction that everybody abjured her—for what she could not tell—
and that Oak was the ringleader of the recusants.
Coming out of church that day she looked round
in hope that Oak, whose bass voice she had heard
rolling out from the gallery overhead in a most unconcerned manner, might chance to linger in her
path in the old way. There he was, as usual, coming
down the path behind her. But on seeing Bathsheba
turn, he looked aside, and as soon as he got beyond
the gate, and there was the barest excuse for a
divergence, he made one, and vanished.

The next morning brought the culminating
stroke; she had been expecting it long. It was a
formal notice by letter from him that he should not
renew his engagement with her for the following
Lady-day.

Bathsheba actually sat and cried over this letter most bitterly. She was aggrieved and wounded that the possession of hopeless love from Gabriel, which she had grown to regard as her inalienable right for life, should have been withdrawn just at his own pleasure in this way. She was bewildered too by the prospect of having to rely on her own resources again: it seemed to herself that she never could again acquire energy sufficient to go to market, barter, and sell. Since Troy's death Oak had attended all sales and fairs for her, transacting her business at the same time with his own. What should she do now? Her life was becoming a desolation.

So desolate was Bathsheba this evening, that in an absolute hunger for pity and sympathy, and miserable in that she appeared to have outlived the only true friendship she had ever owned, she put on her bonnet and cloak and went down to Oak's house just after sunset, guided on her way by the pale primrose rays of a crescent moon a few days old.

A lively firelight shone from the window, but nobody was visible in the room. She tapped nervously, and then thought it doubtful if it were right for a single woman to call upon a bachelor who lived alone, although he was her manager, and she might be supposed to call on business without any real impropriety. Gabriel opened the door, and the moon shone upon his forehead.

"Mr. Oak," said Bathsheba faintly.

"Yes; I am Mr. Oak," said Gabriel. "Who have I the honor—Oh, how stupid of me, not to know you, mistress!"

"I shall not be your mistress much longer, shall I, Gabriel?" she said in pathetic tones.

"Well, no. I suppose—But come in, ma'am. Oh —and I'll get a light," Oak replied, with some awkwardness.

"No; not on my account."

"It is so seldom that I get a lady visitor that I'm afraid I haven't proper accommodation. Will you sit down, please? Here's a chair, and there's one, too. I am sorry that my chairs all have wood seats, and are rather hard, but I—was thinking of getting some new ones." Oak placed two or three for her.

"They are quite easy enough for me."

So down she sat, and down sat he, the fire dancing in their faces, and upon the old furniture,

> all a-sheenen
> Wi' long years o' handlen.[1]

that formed Oak's array of household possessions, which sent back a dancing reflection in reply. It was very odd to these two persons, who knew each other passing well, that the mere circumstance of their meeting in a new place and in a new way should make them so awkward and constrained. In the fields, or at her house, there had never been any embarrassment; but now that Oak had become the entertainer their lives seemed to be moved back again to the days when they were strangers.

"You'll think it strange that I have come, but—"

"Oh, no; not at all."

"But I thought—Gabriel, I have been uneasy in the belief that I have offended you, and that you are going away on that account. It grieved me very much, and I couldn't help coming."

"Offended me! As if you could do that, Bath-sheba!"

"Haven't I?" she asked, gladly. "But, what are you going away for else?"

"I am not going to emigrate, you know; I wasn't aware that you would wish me not to when I told

---

[1] W. Barnes.

'ee, or I shouldn't have thought of doing it," he said, simply. "I have arranged for Little Weatherbury Farm, and shall have it in my own hands at Lady-day. You know I've had a share in it for some time. Still that wouldn't prevent my attending to your business as before, hadn't it been that things have been said about us."

"What?" said Bathsheba in surprise. "Things said about you and me! What are they?"

"I cannot tell you."

"It would be wiser if you were to, I think. You have played the part of mentor to me many times, and I don't see why you should fear to do it now."

"It is nothing that you have done, this time. The top and tail o't this—that I'm sniffing about here, and waiting for poor Boldwood's farm, with a thought of getting you some day."

"Getting me! What does that mean?"

"Marrying of 'ee, in plain British. You asked me to tell, so you mustn't blame me."

Bathsheba did not look quite so alarmed as if a cannon had been discharged by her ear, which was what Oak had expected. "Marrying me! I didn't know it was that you meant," she said, quietly. "Such a thing as that is too absurd—too soon—to think of, by far!"

"Yes; of course, it is too absurd. I don't desire any such thing; I should think that was plain enough by this time. Surely, surely you be the last person in the world I think of marrying. It is too absurd, as you say."

" 'Too—s-s-soon' were the words I used."

"I must beg your pardon for correcting you, but you said, 'too absurd,' and so do I."

"I beg your pardon too!" she returned, with tears in her eyes. " 'Too soon' was what I said. But it doesn't matter a bit—not at all—but I only meant, 'too soon.' Indeed, I didn't, Mr. Oak, and you must believe me!"

Gabriel looked her long in the face, but the fire-light being faint there was not much to be seen. "Bathsheba," he said, tenderly and in surprise, and coming closer: "If I only knew one thing—whether you would allow me to love you and win you, and marry you after all—If I only knew that!"

"But you never will know," she murmured.

"Why?"

"Because you never ask."

"Oh—Oh!" said Gabriel, with a low laugh of joyousness. "My own dear—"

"You ought not to have sent me that harsh letter this morning," she interrupted. "It shows you didn't care a bit about me, and were ready to desert me like all the rest of them! It was very cruel of you, considering I was the first sweetheart that you ever had, and you were the first I ever had; and I shall not forget it!"

"Now, Bathsheba, was ever anybody so provoking?" he said, laughing. "You know it was purely that I, as an unmarried man, carrying on a business for you as a very taking young woman, had a proper hard part to play—more particular that people knew I had a sort of feeling for 'ee; and I fancied, from the way we were mentioned together, that it might injure your good name. Nobody knows the heat and fret I have been caused by it."

"And was that all?"

"All."

"Oh, how glad I am I came!" she exclaimed, thankfully, as she rose from her seat. "I have thought so much more of you since I fancied you did not want even to see me again. But I must be going now, or I shall be missed. Why, Gabriel," she said, with a slight laugh, as they went to the door, "it seems exactly as if I had come courting you—how dreadful!"

"And quite right, too," said Oak. "I've danced

at your skittish heels, my beautiful Bathsheba, for many a long mile, and many a long day; and it is hard to begrudge me this one visit."

He accompanied her up the hill, explaining to her the details of his forthcoming tenure of the other farm. They spoke very little of their mutual feelings; pretty phrases and warm expressions being probably unnecessary between such tried friends. Theirs was that substantial affection which arises (if any arises at all) when the two who are thrown together begin first by knowing the rougher sides of each other's character, and not the best till further on, the romance growing up in the interstices of a mass of hard prosaic reality. This good-fellowship—*camaraderie*—usually occurring through similarity of pursuits, is unfortunately seldom superadded to love between the sexes, because men and women associate, not in their labors, but in their pleasures merely. Where, however, happy circumstance permits its development, the compounded feeling proves itself to be the only love which is strong as death—that love which many waters cannot quench, nor the floods drown, beside which the passion usually called by the name is evanescent as steam.

57. A Foggy Night and Morning — Conclusion

"THE MOST PRIVATE, secret, plainest wedding that it is possible to have."

Those had been Bathsheba's words to Oak one evening, some time after the event of the preceding chapter, and he meditated a full hour by the clock upon how to carry out her wishes to the letter.

"A license—oh, yes, it must be a license," he said to himself at last. "Very well, then; first, a license."

On a dark night, a few days later, Oak came with mysterious steps from the surrogate's door in Casterbridge. On the way home he heard a heavy tread in front of him, and, overtaking the man, found him to be Coggan. They walked together into the village until they came to a little lane behind the church, leading down to the cottage of Laban Tall, who had lately been installed as clerk of the parish, and was yet in mortal terror at church on Sundays when he heard his lone voice among certain hard words of the Psalms, whither no man ventured to follow him.

"Well, goodnight, Coggan," said Oak, "I'm going down this way."

"Oh!" said Coggan, surprised; "what's going on tonight, then, make so bold, Mr. Oak?"

It seemed rather ungenerous not to tell Coggan, under the circumstances, for Coggan had been true as steel all through the time of Gabriel's unhappiness about Bathsheba, and Gabriel said, "You can keep a secret, Coggan?"

"You've proved me, and you know."

"Yes, I have, and I do know. Well, then, mistress and I mean to get married tomorrow morning."

"Heaven's high tower! And yet I've thought of such a thing from time to time; true, I have. But keeping it so close! Well, there, 'tis no consarn of mine, and I wish 'ee joy o' her."

"Thank you, Coggan. But I assure 'ee that this great hush is not what I wished for at all, or what either of us would have wished if it hadn't been for certain things that would make a gay wedding seem hardly the thing. Bathsheba has a great wish that all the parish shall not be in church, looking at her —she's shylike and nervous about it, in fact—so I be doing this to humor her."

"Aye, I see: quite right, too, I suppose I must say. And you be now going down to the clerk."

"Yes; you may as well come with me."

"I am afeard your labor in keeping it close will be throwed away," said Coggan, as they walked along. "Labe Tall's old woman will horn it all over parish in half-an-hour."

"So she will, upon my life; I never thought of that," said Oak, pausing. "Yet I must tell him tonight, I suppose, for he's working so far off, and leaves early."

"I'll tell 'ee how we could tackle her," said Coggan. "I'll knock and ask to speak to Laban outside the door, you standing in the background. Then he'll come out, and you can tell yer tale. She'll never guess what I want en for; and I'll make up a few words about the farmwork, as a blind."

This scheme was considered feasible; and Coggan advanced boldly, and rapped at Mrs. Tall's door. Mrs. Tall herself opened it.

"I wanted to have a word with Laban."

"He's not at home and won't be this side of eleven o'clock. He've been forced to go over to Yalbury since shutting out work. I shall do quite as well."

"I hardly think you will. Stop a moment," and Coggan stepped round the corner of the porch to consult Oak.

"Who's t'other man, then?" said Mrs. Tall.

"Only a friend," said Coggan.

"Say he's wanted to meet mistress near church hatch tomorrow morning at ten," said Oak, in a whisper. "That he must come without fail, and wear his best clothes."

"The clothes will floor us as safe as houses!" said Coggan.

"It can't be helped," said Oak. "Tell her."

So Coggan delivered the message. "Mind, het or wet, blow or snow, he must come," added Jan. "'Tis very particular, indeed. The fact is, 'tis to witness her sign some law work about taking shares wi' another farmer for a long span o' years. There, that's what 'tis, and now I've told 'ee, Mother Tall, in a way I shouldn't ha' done if I hadn't loved 'ee so hopeless well."

Coggan retired before she could ask any further; and next they called at the vicar's in a manner which excited no curiosity at all. Then Gabriel went home, and prepared for the morrow.

"Liddy," said Bathsheba, on going to bed that night, "I want you to call me at seven o'clock tomorrow, in case I shouldn't wake."

"But you always do wake afore then, ma'am."

"Yes, but I have something important to do, which I'll tell you of when the time comes, and it's best to make sure."

Bathsheba, however, awoke voluntarily at four, nor could she by any contrivance get to sleep again.

About six, being quite positive that her watch had stopped during the night, she could wait no longer. She went and tapped at Liddy's door, and after some labor awoke her.

"But I thought it was I who had to call you?" said the bewildered Liddy. "And it isn't six yet."

"Indeed it is; how can you tell such a story, Liddy! I know it must be ever so much past seven. Come to my room as soon as you can; I want you to give my hair a good brushing."

When Liddy came to Bathsheba's room her mistress was already waiting. Liddy could not understand this extraordinary promptness. "Whatever *is* going on, ma'am?" she said.

"Well, I'll tell you," said Bathsheba, with a mischievous smile in her bright eyes. "Farmer Oak is coming here to dine with me today!"

"Farmer Oak—and nobody else?—you two alone?"

"Yes."

"But is it safe, ma'am, after what's been said?" asked her companion, dubiously. "A woman's good name is such a perishable article that—"

Bathsheba laughed with a flushed cheek, and whispered in Liddy's ear, although there was nobody present. Then Liddy stared and exclaimed, "Souls alive, what news! It makes my heart go quite bumpity-bump!"

"It makes mine rather furious, too," said Bathsheba. "However, there's no getting out of it now!"

It was a damp disagreeable morning. Nevertheless, at twenty minutes to ten o'clock, Oak came out of his house, and

> Went up the hillside
> With that sort of stride
A man puts out when walking in search of a bride,

and knocked at Bathsheba's door. Ten minutes later a large and smaller umbrella might have been seen moving from the same door, and through the mist along the road to the church. The distance was not more than a quarter of a mile, and these two sensible persons deemed it unnecessary to drive. An observer must have been very close indeed to discover that the forms under the umbrellas were those of Oak and Bathsheba, arm-in-arm for the first time in their lives, Oak in a greatcoat extending to his knees, and Bathsheba in a cloak that reached her clogs. Yet, though so plainly dressed, there was a certain rejuvenated appearance about her:

As though a rose should shut and be a bud again.

Repose had again incarnadined her cheeks; and having, at Gabriel's request, arranged her hair this morning as she had worn it years ago on Norcombe Hill, she seemed in his eyes remarkably like the girl of that fascinating dream, which, considering that she was now only three or four-and-twenty, was perhaps not very wonderful. In the church were Tall, Liddy, and the parson, and in a remarkably short space of time the deed was done.

The two sat down very quietly to tea in Bathsheba's parlor in the evening of the same day, for it had been arranged that Farmer Oak should go there to live, since he had as yet neither money, house, nor furniture worthy of the name, though he was on a sure way toward them, whilst Bathsheba was, comparatively, in a plethora of all three.

Just as Bathsheba was pouring out a cup of tea, their ears were greeted by the firing of a cannon, followed by what seemed like a tremendous blowing of trumpets, in the front of the house.

"There!" said Oak, laughing. "I knew those fellows were up to something, by the look on their faces."

Oak took up the light and went into the porch, followed by Bathsheba with a shawl over her head. The rays fell upon a group of male figures gathered upon the gravel in front, who, when they saw the newly married couple in the porch, set up a loud "Hurrah!" and at the same moment bang again went the cannon in the background, followed by a hideous clang of music from a drum, tambourine, clarionet, serpent, hautboy, tenor viol, and double bass—the only remaining relics of the true and original Weatherbury band—venerable worm-eaten instruments, which had celebrated in their own persons the victories of Marlborough, under the fingers of the forefathers of those who played them now. The performers came forward, and marched up to the front.

"Those bright boys, Mark Clark and Jan, are at the bottom of all this," said Oak. "Come in, souls, and have something to eat and drink wi' me and my wife."

"Not tonight," said Mr. Clark, with evident self-denial. "Thank ye all the same; but we'll call at a more seemly time. However, we couldn't think of letting the day pass without a note of admiration of some sort. If ye could send a drop of som'at down to Warren's, why so it is. Here's long life and happiness to neighbor Oak and his comely bride!"

"Thank ye; thank ye all," said Gabriel. "A bit and a drop shall be sent to Warren's for ye at once. I had a thought that we might very likely get a salute of some sort from our old friends, and I was saying so to my wife but now."

"Faith," said Coggan, in a critical tone, turning to his companions, "the man hev learnt to say 'my wife' in a wonderful naterel way, considering how very youthful he is in wedlock as yet—hey, neighbors all?"

"I never heerd a skillful old married feller of

twenty years' standing pipe 'my wife' in a more used note than 'a did," said Jacob Smallbury. "It might have been a little more true to nater if't had been spoke a little chillier, but that wasn't to be expected just now."

"That improvement will come wi' time," said Jan, twirling his eye.

Then Oak laughed, and Bathsheba smiled (for she never laughed readily now) , and their friends turned to go.

"Yes; I suppose that's the size o't," said Joseph Poorgrass with a cheerful sigh as they moved away; "and I wish him joy o' her; though I were once or twice upon saying today with holy Hosea, in my scripture manner, which is my second nature, 'Ephraim is joined to idols: let him alone.' But since 'tis as 'tis, why, it might have been worse, and I feel my thanks accordingly."